REBUILD THE WORLD: MAINE

POST-APOCALYPTIC
CITY-BUILDING GAMELIT BOOK 2

JUSTIN MARKS

Rebuild the World: Maine
Post-Apocalyptic City-Building GameLit Book 2

Copyright © 2026 by Justin Marks
Cover created by Markee Books
Editing and Formatting by Wickedly Deviant LLC

All rights reserved.
ISBN: 978-1-968858-15-5

Dedication

Thanks for waiting for book two in this series. The medical issues threw a wrench into my plans and delayed this book by six months. Thanks to the great medical providers who helped me, I came through everything okay. All of you who reached out and offered support made the process easier. I hope you all enjoy the story.

What Came Before

While Devin worked in his home office on the Alaskan island he had moved to a few months before, the world went dark. He was searching the web to figure out what was going on when it happened again. Then an AI hologram appeared and explained the situation. Alien ships were chasing criminals through Earth's solar system, and their engines caused disruptions in the sun. The long-term impact of their trip through our solar system was to toss Earth into an ice age.

Vlad, the AI, explained that Devin was one of the people selected to use nanotechnology to help a portion of humanity survive until the aliens could return far in the future. Devin also needed to lead the effort to clear out pockets of alien criminals who had landed on Earth. With his friend Alex, who was local to the area, Devin began creating an oasis for humanity on Prince of Wales Island and the surrounding islands.

The process was made far more difficult by repeated solar flares caused by the alien engines' effects on the sun. The flares were contaminated by the faster-than-light drives that had passed through our solar system, making their impact far worse than normal solar flares. In addition to disrupting and destroying much of humanity's technology, the flares disrupted the atmosphere. That inhibited communication on the surviving equipment in the world. People were on their own as the world froze.

Figuring out how to utilize the nanotechnology resources and keep people alive was challenging. The new technology enabled the creation of a settlement that could survive, and even thrive, more than 200 degrees below zero. Unfortunately, creating the structures, building the infrastructure, and researching improvements were not quick processes, and the cold worsened daily. Keeping people safe and motivated was a challenge in itself. All available resources had to be used to keep people alive.

After learning that the alien criminal threat was worse than initially thought, Devin helped create a group of enforcers to eliminate the aliens on their island. After addressing the threat and stabilizing his starting town, Devin led teams to rescue and rebuild surrounding communities on his home island. He focused on growing Klawock to a point where it could survive on its own. Still, he had time to rescue the nearby island communities of Ketchikan and Wrangell while doing so.

Despite some setbacks and challenges, 77 days after everything started, Klawock and the rest of the Prince of Wales Island were deemed safe from the criminals and on a path to surviving the ice age. As expected, Devin was sent to help another community after completing his first major mission. He was sent to a new location, not knowing if he could ever contact everyone he had worked with since the cold arrived. He had no idea where he was going, but he was able to take some supplies, personal items, and Vlad with him. The supply crates held weapons, ammunition, camping supplies, some books, and other useful items. All he knew was that more people needed his help and time was running out worldwide.

1

The wave of sparkling blue light that transported me from my home in Alaska left me disoriented as it faded away. I tried to keep my footing as the light vanished from my vision. The sensation of movement while standing still during transport was intense. To make it worse, I could not see anything as my eyes fought the aftereffect of the transport lights. I could hear people moving around and some muffled speech, so I knew I was not alone. I frantically blinked my eyes and rotated to face the sounds I could hear.

"Hey buddy, I don't know what's going on here, but put your hands up, or we'll shoot you," someone said to me as I moved.

I froze and raised my hands slowly. The accent made me think I had ended up in the northeastern part of the United States. Whoever was talking spoke English with a New England accent. Unfortunately, I did not have enough experience to pinpoint their location beyond that. There were blinking notification icons I could see despite the aftereffects of the transport. I did not want to be distracted by reading them, so I left them minimized for the moment. Vlad kept quiet and blended into the supplies I had brought so that no one could see him. We had decided that having him seen too early would likely get me shot.

I spoke carefully, "Look, I'm not a threat. The transport was bright enough to impair my vision, so I can't really see anything at the moment, but I'm happy to wait for that to clear up while keeping my hands up. Can you tell me where I ended up?"

Someone spoke up, but was quickly cut off. A muffled conversation ensued, and then someone spoke up again.

"You're in Augusta, Maine," the same person from before said. "It's not like that's a secret, but we want to know how you got here. You don't look like those aliens that have been attacking us, but teleportation isn't something that humans can do. Right now, we have almost no working technology."

"It's a long story, but I can give you the short version," I said.

"That's a good start," the same voice answered.

"This whole mess with an ice age was caused by alien cops

who were chasing the criminal aliens who are probably attacking you. After accidentally messing up our sun, they left technology for some people like me to protect against the cold and face the aliens. I'm 100% human here, but, yeah, I have access to some alien technology to help with survival," I said, blinking a few times as I started to see shapes around me. "Is there going to be a way for me to head inside and talk to whoever is in charge soon? I'm bundled up, but it's still cold out here."

"I'm sure the bigwigs are talking inside," the same person said. I could see his outline now, and I could see that he was one of four people aiming weapons at me from the porch of a large building. "We're just the guards, and no one told us what to do with weird teleporting people. It's barely five in the morning, and the people in charge were all asleep when you got here. We sent a runner to wake them up as soon as the blue lights started."

"No problem, I'll keep my hands up as I said, but I'm going to be reviewing some informational messages only I can see. Don't worry if I look a little distracted, I'm still paying attention, but they cover some of my vision."

Before I could pull up the first screen, another guard asked if it was like a game interface, and I said it was like a digital heads-up display. The one asking the question was excited about the interface. At the same time, another guard was dismissive of the whole idea that I had access to futuristic tech. He did not seem to believe that there were screens visible only to me. Either way, I told them I would explain everything in more detail when I met with everyone, but I needed to check things out now.

The first information box I expanded was my mission box for Klawock.

Klawock Settlement Mission: Rewards

The community of Klawock and the surrounding communities have been secured and should survive until Earth's sun is repaired. While the power and housing situation is rated marginal, that score reflects your decision to expand the mission's scope and successfully protect other communities. Rewards have been increased to reflect the boost in planetary nano production from your successful mission expansion.

- 2,027 work units
- 2,027 material units

- 1,013 settlement tokens
- 4 personal tokens
- Processing Portal Upgrade

The oddly specific bonus numbers caught my attention. I quickly figured out what they were based on after pulling up Klawock's status when I left. "So, the work and material unit bonuses are half of the population in Klawock when I left. The settlement tokens are a quarter of the population, and the personal tokens are one for every 1,000 people," I muttered as I worked through the numbers, ignoring the looks I was getting as I talked aloud. Knowing how the mission rewards worked would allow me to plan for the future. "Those bonuses are going to help me get this settlement started quickly."

I ignored the conversation the guards were having based on what I was saying. Instead, I was reading another message that had popped up and expanded on its own. Vlad could now send me messages, which was a useful improvement when he was hiding from view, and we did not want people to hear him talking.

I have been upgraded as well. We can now message each other directly, regardless of where I am or what I'm doing. That is my only enhancement, as the nano rewards distributed to my upgrades have been limited. The focus is on your rewards that will help you succeed here, not my upgrades. The planetary situation grows more precarious by the day, and every architect worldwide receives nano support based on their contributions to saving people. Check the mission message waiting for you and then decide what to do.

I mentally composed my response to Vlad, watching it type itself out before being sent to him. Then I pulled up the next message waiting for me. One of the guards had headed back inside to see what to do with me, so I took advantage of the delay. I needed to check all the messages before I talked to people anyway. As soon as I saw what the next message was about, I kept my comments to myself.

Augusta Settlement Mission

Earth's rapid cooling is progressing at the 77-day post-solar incursion mark. Secure this community to survive for up to 200 years in this altered environment, while defending against assaults by off-world criminals. Beware: Global temperature is expected to continue decreasing for an extended period before stabilizing. Effects are moderated while heat sinks are depleted, and then will accelerate. The larger population at this location will require prompt, decisive action to address their issues. You may migrate to the next mission at any time. The success of the prior mission will determine the starting resources for the next mission. You have limited time to save outposts of humanity and put them on a path to survival as a species until remediation of your star is possible.

I was still reviewing the mission when another message from Vlad popped up over it. As soon as I read it, I had to stop myself from reaching for a gun.

"Guys, the alien criminal forces you've been fighting can sense my arrival, and they're on their way," I called out. "They want to make sure you don't get any help from me. I wanted to do this the slow way, but there must have been a scouting party close by, so there's no time to waste. I have a holographic assistant who looks like an alien, but he's a good guy. He's got better scouting abilities than all of us, so he's popping out. Please don't shoot at him. It will go right through him and hit other stuff."

"Whatever, keep your hands up," the guy who seemed to have a problem with me called out. He started to say something else when Vlad stepped out of the supplies. He shot at Vlad, despite what I had just said. Since Vlad was in front of my supplies, I hoped the bullets wouldn't damage any of them.

"Four golems are coming from the north, and they contain two different criminals' signatures, so there may be multiple criminals in the area with them," Vlad yelled as he moved in that direction.

"I'm drawing my gun now. I'll keep it facing away from you all and toward the golems," I said. "If you shoot me, I'm going to be really pissed, and you all don't want me leaving you to survive the ice age on your own."

As I grabbed the gun and made sure it was ready to fire, I was tense, hoping I would not be shot in the back. The other group was behind me, so I hoped they did not see me as a threat. I was facing away from them, so it was not like I was going to shoot them. Still, that meant I couldn't see them as I focused on the direction Vlad had indicated. Without the second chance perk, I doubted I would have turned my back on armed people like that.

"I can incapacitate targets when they come into view," I told the others after Vlad confirmed one syndicate member was with the golems. "I'll lock down the alien. If I get him early, I'll lock down a golem too, but I don't want to tip my hand before I can lock the alien down. They are the larger threat. I'm saving the other charges in case this is a feint. Take out the three golems still moving before we focus back on the targets I lock down with my perks."

There was no time to discuss anything more before the golems all came into view, followed by the syndicate member. It got off two shots before I could incapacitate it. The one aimed at me missed me, but I heard a wet thunk behind me as it hit someone, followed by some swearing. Seeing the aliens using guns here was an unwelcome surprise. I set that aside to focus on locking down my targets with the incapacitate criminal perk and opening fire. I was using a bolt-action rifle as those handled the cold better. My shots were slower and more methodical than the guards', but with the help of the people behind me, the targets all died quickly.

"I'm scouting," Vlad announced. "Nothing else is in range at the moment, though. This looks like the result of our bad luck to have one of their patrols nearby when we arrived, not an all-out assault."

I checked my status sheet, and three spheres and one nano matrix were added to my totals, confirming the alien was dead. The golems did not play dead, so a gunshot must have destroyed the fourth sphere that had not shown up in my inventory. This group did not yet know they needed to avoid hitting those.

The same jerk who had a problem with me raised his rifle and pointed it at me as I turned around and moved toward the injured guard. I could see he was lying on the ground with a dark patch that had to be blood in the snow near him.

"I just want to help. I have a perk that speeds healing, and I heard someone get hit. I needed to make sure I was targeting the right person," I said. While I was talking, I got a good look at the injured guard and targeted him with my medical effect perk. "Hey, you, guy who was hit. How are you feeling now?"

"Damn, that almost doesn't hurt anymore," the guy who had been hit said as he sat up and poked at his injury. "There's still some bleeding, but the big hole in my side is mostly gone."

I told him I was using another charge, then going back to review my messages while we waited for the people in charge to decide what to do. The injured guard was sent inside to tell them to expedite the process after my second healing charge was used on him. The injury and the hole in his clothes gave him an excuse to escape the cold. He also seemed to be firmly on my side now.

I started reviewing the status sheet for the town I was in, but got cut off when people came out and summoned Vlad and me inside.

"Can someone bring my supplies in?" I asked, reaching into one of the crates I had brought. "I'm just grabbing this nano heater to prove what I'll be telling you about the technology I can access, and so I can warm up inside."

I did not wait for the okay and grabbed the heater before walking back to my guards. I still had my rifle, but the safety was on, and it was slung over my back while I carried the nano heater. I was led inside the building and down a hallway to a room that had clearly been repurposed from a game room into a meeting room.

The room had ten people already seated around three tables shoved together, and I was led to a seat on the far side of the tables by myself, facing everyone. The setup gave off interrogation vibes, but I had not expected to be welcomed with open arms. I was still counting it as a win that no one had shot at me yet. I sat down and placed the heater on the table in front of them. Everyone was bundled up, and it felt like it was in the low 50s inside, even with a large fire burning in the fireplace in the corner.

I took the time to look at everyone while I waited for someone else to speak. Every member of the group looked tired and appeared as if they had dressed in a rush.

"Okay, it looks like everyone is here and mostly awake. I'm Erin. Nominally in charge as the mayor when all this happened," the woman across from me said. "The man to my right is Steve, but everyone calls him O'Donnell. He's the former chief of police and the current person in charge of our defenses."

From there, I was introduced to the other people at the tables. I hoped Vlad would keep track of everyone. I knew I would forget some names. He was getting strange looks as he hovered behind me, but no one had commented on him yet, so the guards must have given some brief information on both of us. The one thing I noted was that it was a college town, as one of the people in charge was the former student body president, Daryl, who represented the students trapped in town. I nodded to each person as they were introduced and tried to gauge their reaction to my presence. People seemed cautious and a bit hostile. Some of them clearly hoped I was here to make things better, though, which made me think I had a shot at keeping things positive.

"I'm Devin, and my holographic alien sidekick is Vlad," I said when it was my turn to talk. "I was at home in Klawock, Alaska, when the world changed, and I got this nanotechnology downloaded into me. I stayed there until I finished securing that town and some surrounding ones to survive the cold. After that, I was teleported here to help all of you out."

That raised a firestorm of questions and shouts, which I let run for a few minutes before speaking up again. "Look, I'll tell you everything I know, but can you save your questions for after I'm done? Also, if there's a projector here, I can display stuff off my tablet to save time."

That earned me a pained laugh, and I was told that there was no more electricity. All the town's power-generation systems had failed or run out of fuel, so they could not project anything. My comment about saving some of the detailed information until after I had set up a power grid got everyone's attention. The focus on me was compounded when I began by explaining that I had a nano heater that ran on stored power, which I would use to warm the room while we talked. The heater resembled a metal box, so when I activated it and the room began to warm, another round of questions ensued.

After a few more minutes of trying to get us back on track, Erin got everyone to shut up so I could keep talking. I explained what I knew about the aliens who caused all this when they chased criminals through our solar system. Vlad interjected with details about the criminals being chased and what happened to our sun. Daryl, the youngest person I faced, snickered when I shared the criminal group's name.

"I laughed too when Vlad told me they were called the Scaled Syndicate," I said when I saw him chuckle. "Part of it is the translation, but it's still a funny name for reptilian aliens. Unfortunately, it looks like most of the criminals landed on Earth instead of staying on their ship, as Vlad's people thought. They can also sense the technology I'm using to help people. Now that they know I'm here, they know you might survive instead of freezing to death. They will probably get more aggressive now that time is not on their side. At the last settlement, we ended up killing most of them after they realized they could not wait for everyone to die. The rest teleported away when they knew they could not win."

"They were not expecting humans' level of resistance," Vlad said. "For a primitive species, you have considerable firepower and resources. Those criminals can be a danger to your people, but Devin can capture their technology. That will enhance your region's chances of survival. Their supplies mean their presence isn't entirely harmful. Working to clear them out fully ensures they are not a long-term threat to this region."

After a few reminders to let me finish the story before the questions started, I dove into the crucial information they needed. I provided an overview of the nanostructures I could build, how resource generation worked, and even covered the research functionality. As I kept talking, everyone else took notes and scribbled questions using the firelight and candlelight.

I wrapped up my overview by reading the Augusta Mission to them, word-for-word. "My goal is to set you all up to survive as quickly as I can, so that I can move on to wherever the nano controller sends me next. It's only going to keep getting colder, and supplies are running out worldwide. I need to keep moving to new missions so I can save as many people as possible. The longer it takes to save you all, the more people die elsewhere," I said. "I will be in charge of planning the town and building the nanostructures while I'm here, but I'm not looking forward to taking on any other responsibilities."

"Really?" O'Donnell asked when I said I did not want more power than that.

"It's your town, and you all know how to keep it running. I was in Klawock for about two-and-a-half months. I want to wrap things up here faster than that, if possible. To do that, I need to focus on building stuff and fighting aliens."

When I finished talking and sat back, that was the signal for people to start asking me questions in earnest. From the number of shouted questions, there were more of those than I had expected. It was quickly clear that people wanted to know what was happening in the rest of the world, and I had to admit that I really only knew about my part of Alaska and a little about the Pacific Northwest. Both places had little contact with anything outside their immediate area. To make it worse, it sounded like this area had received even more solar flares from the start.

"The Earth's rotation meant some places got more flares or more intense flares," Vlad said. "It looks like the technology failed even faster and more thoroughly here."

There were also many questions about the status of our sun. I could tell people had been holding out hope that things would get better, but they were not surprised to hear it would not change before the aliens came back to fix it. The sun's output dropping that much was not something anyone honestly expected to turn around on its own, but there had been some hope.

The discussion about the medical clinics sparked a conversation about the medical challenges they faced. The council representative for health was the one to bring the questioning to an end when he heard how the clinics worked.

"We need to let Devin start building these medical structures right now. There are a lot of sick people, and we don't have time to waste hours on questions. We need to get started," Joey said. "Half of you don't even believe he can do what he says he can. Let him prove it so we can move on to making plans. If he's lying, we'll learn that soon enough. If he's not, then we can get to making real decisions instead of arguing if he's telling the truth."

"I have to build stuff out in the order that makes the most sense, but we'll get the medical pods up as soon as we can," I said. "Pods with no power or water would be pointless, but the sooner we have medical pods, the sooner we can save people and conserve your remaining stock of medical supplies. I'm ready to get started, and it looks like I showed up in a space with plenty of open area to build stuff."

"You appeared in the park in front of the capital, and we're in the Department of Transportation Offices," Erin said. "All the trees in the area were cut down to dry so we could burn them. There's nothing else of note in the park if you want to build your supposed nanostructures there."

I had dropped hints that buildings had to be built in a specific order to ensure room for pods indoors and to supply the resources they needed, so they had some idea that I had a plan to follow. The first thing to place was the settlement portal. I liked the idea of putting it at the center of everything, where it could be well defended.

As everyone followed me outside, I pulled up the interface for the settlement portal. The template was the same as the one I saw when founding Klawock's nano system.

Settlement Processing Portal
This portal serves as the basis for the architect's class. Feed materials into this portal to add to the settlement materials inventory to build other structures. All materials for blueprint construction will be pulled from the settlement inventory. Settlement Processing Portal efficiency is set to _____%. Daily capacity is limited to _____ processing units. Portal has _____ work pods.

With the mission rewards and what I had saved up before I left Klawock, I had 1,943 settlement tokens to spend. Unfortunately, that did not go far in upgrading the portal, given the rapid rise in the cost of increasing daily capacity. It took just 10 tokens to raise the daily capacity from 50 to 60. The next ten capacity units cost two tokens each, and the next ten cost three each. The cost just kept increasing following that pattern. For 1,710 settlement tokens, I increased the daily capacity to 230 units. I knew material units would be the bottleneck again, so I was willing to spend most of my tokens on improving that from the start. With that done, I spent 60 tokens to raise efficiency to

80%, and 30 more to buy four work pods.

As soon as everything was set up, I warned people not to freak out, then placed the portal in the park's largest open space. As I already had some supplies from the mission completion, I could build the portal in the open. After that, I would immediately build a structure around it to protect both the portal and the work pods. I did not want a repeat of having the portal in a legacy building that was hard to heat. There were gasps from the people as the portal formed, complete with its four work pods. I ignored everyone and quickly selected the large crafting bay, a new structure to me, and placed the building's wire frame around the portal before starting construction.

Large Crafting Bay Blueprint

- Unlock 50 tokens, purchase 1 token
- 150 material units, 150 work units
- Supports 0 work pods / 10 pod slots
- Size up to 30' x 30'
- Power required: 150-250 power units
- Water required 10 water units
- Safe to -50 degrees base, -125 degrees at full power

"Hey, I know this is all cool to watch, but you need to back up," I said to the three people who had moved up to look at the portal. "I'm building the structure around the portal, and you can't be in the way."

As soon as people moved back, the building began to take shape. It was about the size of a three-car garage. With the portal on one side, there was room for a vehicle or two on the other side, along with some storage. The building was a single-story structure with 12-foot ceilings. Despite its simplicity, it would take 10 minutes to form, given its size. There were even two basic restrooms inside the space.

The commotion had woken more people up, and there were shouts behind us as the building formed around the portal. While everyone was focused on the building taking shape in a wave of blue light and nanomachines, I quickly placed blueprints for a windmill and a water tower and fed resources into their construction. There were still six free work pod slots in the crafting bay after using four slots for the portal's pods, so I could assign the four new work pods there, where it would be warm.

Since the crafting bay was a new structure, I completed the usual hidden mission that appeared the first time I built something new. That earned me a personal token and four settlement tokens. I looked the notice over quickly before getting back to talking to the mass of people, who were now crowding around me. More people streamed out of nearby structures as time passed.

Hidden Mission Completed
Garner the resources and support to complete your first large crafting structure. You receive four settlement tokens and a personal token.

"Everyone, let's grab my supplies and take them inside where it's warm and there's running water," I said. My earlier request to move my supplies inside had been ignored, which turned out to be for the best. Now they were easy to move into the new building. "If my math is right, it's around 5 in the morning here, and I have more to explain and build before I nap."

"Holy crap, it's warm in here. Like, it's actually warm," I heard someone say once the entire group had forced their way inside the new building. It had been a single trip to collect all my belongings, thanks to the number of helpers. Inside, it was warm enough that people shed all their outerwear as they looked around at the portal and the work pods.

People streamed in from the surrounding buildings as word of the new structure spread. O'Donnell tried to maintain control over who came in, but he could not stop those who wanted access to the working bathrooms and the warmth. Many of them ignored me and enjoyed the heat while waiting in line for the bathroom. Even the lights were a hit. When people discovered the power outlets, a rush to retrieve the few surviving electronics was triggered. Some people had saved stuff, even after the power went out.

"Give me a little space and let me grab this projector. Now that I have a display screen on the processing portal, I can pull up information and then take a picture to share with everyone." As I was talking, I dug through my supplies, pulled out my projector, and plugged it in. Then I snapped a photo of the portal information on my tablet to share with everyone.

Settlement Processing Portal
This portal serves as the basis for the architect's class. Feed materials into this portal to add to the settlement materials inventory to build other structures. All materials for blueprint construction will be pulled from the settlement inventory. Settlement Processing Portal efficiency is set to 80%. Daily capacity is limited to 230 processing units. The portal has four work pods. Up to 50% of the processing limit can be utilized remotely.

"Hey, Vlad, what's this remote utilization? Is that the extra reward from the first mission?" I asked. As he floated over, everyone's eyes followed him, and conversation died off.

"Yes, it's part of the reward, and it will allow you to absorb materials within the settlement's range directly into the processing portal. Keeping the portal fed remotely will make everything easier as the cold worsens. There are also options to automate collection bins so citizens can place refuse in designated locations. It will then be fed into the portal when there is spare processing capacity or using the capacity you have allocated for that," Vlad said. "For now, you should consider clearing the stumps and benches in the park to make room for more structures."

"I'm going to do that now. You all can get back to your conversation. I'll be ready to start planning in a few more minutes," I said.

With Vlad's help, I figured out how to access a new interface that let me see everything in range that the portal could target. I cleared out the park space near the portal and then switched my focus to looking at the settlement sheet for Augusta. I reviewed it silently while others explored the bay and the portal. Seeing the small numbers for the nanostructures and infrastructure after the numbers we had built up in Klawock was sobering. Their food situation was not too bad in the short term, but it would plummet in eight or nine months. It looked like heat was the bigger issue, though, since they had less than one month of fuel left according to the projections.

I reviewed all the details and planned my next steps. I had spent most of the settlement tokens I had brought and earned from the mission, so I needed to make the best use of the remaining 78 tokens I had. Before I went any further, I pulled up the settlement information on the screen and projected it for everyone to see. This should put to rest questions about the authenticity of my nanotechnology and show everyone the challenges they faced without my help. With any luck, the information would look correct to anyone who knew the area. It would also show that they needed my help if they did not want to die.

Augusta Settlement		**Population**	16,217
Food Supply	213 days	**Heat Supply**	31 days
Housing	21,856 people	**Survivable Housing**	0 people
Food Production	17%	**Secure Food Production**	0%
Power Production	25- 245 units	**Power Draw**	175- 275 units
Power Storage	3/ 110 units	**Indoor Pod Slots**	8/ 10
Water Production	275 units	**Water Draw**	10 units
Work Units	1,727 units	**Material Units**	1,732 units
Research Units	0 units		
Production Structures	Processing Portal	Work Pods x 8	Large Windmill x 1
Large Water Tower x 1			
Enhanced Structures	Large Crafting Bay x 1		
Deferred Maintenance	0 units	**Material Maintenance**	0 units

2

There were gasps and shouts of panic as people began reading the projected information about the town. Some of the council members I had been talking to were clearly unhappy that everyone could see the projected remaining food and heating capacity. I got the feeling they had been keeping just how bad it was from most of the population, but the cat was now out of the bag. At the same time, a decent percentage of the crowd seemed more resigned than shocked. The general public may have had a clearer sense of where things stood than the council assumed. It would not be the first time the rumor mill was more accurate than leaders thought.

"Before everyone freaks out, the status you're seeing is not horrible. Those numbers are worst case, as I'm sure people are finding more food and fuel every day," I said loudly enough for everyone to hear. "It just shows how important it is for us to work as a team to get you set up, so I can head to the next location I need to help. If it had taken me another month to get Klawock set up before I transferred here, things would be a lot worse. The same holds for wherever I'm sent next."

"Not that bad?" someone in the crowd called out. "You do see that we'll all freeze in 31 days, right?"

"That report shows when your heat sources will no longer be able to maintain standard warmth if nothing else changes. I'm going to start changing that today. As we form new buildings, not only will those buildings have a self-sustaining heat supply, but they will buy us time because there will be less drain on the legacy heat reserves," I said. "As Vlad will remind us, there are rules about what nanostructures can be used for housing. This one can't be used for people to live in, but even having people working here during the day will lower fuel usage elsewhere. And if you notice, the windmill and water tower are already providing sustainable water and power. We have time to do this before things get too bad."

"And those estimates of remaining time are for optimal nutrition and heat," Vlad pointed out, repeating my earlier point.

"I have seen that humans can survive on less-than-optimal resources for extended periods of time. In reality, there is some extra time than what is shown before the majority of you die."

Since we now had such a large group watching me, I pivoted to discussing the work pods and the need to get people inside them as soon as possible. The proof that I could actually create a working building from thin air was giving me a window to push things forward. I let Erin know her council could organize it all, but if people were not in the pods, we would run out of resources to build new structures quickly.

"So, we have to get into these strange pods and let them use us for resources?" someone called out.

"This building was created with nanotechnology. To build more, we need resources from the pods to use the materials we process in the portal. I can make a few structures with the resources I brought, but you all can see the city's information sheet. It's going to take a lot of buildings to keep you all alive, and this is how we build them," I said.

A few brave people began entering the pods, prompting the leaders to focus on the next steps.

"Four-hour shifts mean we need six people per pod, right?" O'Donnell asked. "That's 48 people for these eight pods, and the number will go up quickly. I'll send someone to get the first two shifts organized, but people assigned to the pods need to camp here while waiting."

"It's actually a little less than four hours, but that's to allow you to sync the pods up and account for people getting in and out," I said.

"Don't forget this is one of the buildings that can't be used for housing. People can work and hang out here, but they can't live or sleep here," Vlad said. "Devin will probably create housing near here quickly, though. Until then, they can use this space to wait for their shift to start, but afterward, they will need a place to sleep. Four hours in the pod will require 16 hours of sleep to recover, and they will be unable to stay awake long after exiting. That's why each person can only do one shift per day."

"Technically, you can do a shift every 20 hours, but that leaves no time for anything other than sleep and gulping down meals. There's no reason to have that sort of cycle with all the people we have available. As for this building's limitations, I know it's arbitrary, but the way it's been explained to me is that structures like this are built at a discount because of those limitations. Supposedly, this forces us to create a mix of buildings that maintain the ambient nanoconcentration required for long-term survival. Regardless, I plan on adding pods quickly. Plan for 20 pods and 120 people to start. Select a few people who can manage a greenhouse as well," I said. "We want to get food production going as quickly as possible."

People rushed off to organize the pod workers after O'Donnell gave a nod. Before I could start talking about the rest of my plans, O'Donnell pulled me to the side of the room where we could speak slightly more privately. I was curious, so I let him lead me to the side. There were still people around, but his glares kept people from getting too close while we talked.

"There was some information about people like you before we lost all communication," he whispered. "There were few details, but it seems you architects are genuinely helping. Let's be honest, we don't have many options, so I have to trust you. As you can imagine, though, factions within what's left of the government would like to control your power. Reading between the lines, I think there was an attempt to gain control of an architect early on, and it didn't go well," he said.

"That makes sense, and I have ways to get around attempts like that if anyone gets any ideas," I said. "Not that I plan on sharing details about my contingency plans."

"The last communication I saw was an order to support architects and to collect information about them for later use. I'm not going to be an obstacle to you here. At the same time, I want to be clear that I'll be collecting any information you share. I want to work with you, but I've got to think about the big picture. Being upfront about that seemed to be the way to go."

I paused for a second before I answered. This was a dynamic I did not expect, but I appreciated the candor. O'Donnell seemed like someone I would rather work with than have cause problems for me.

"Good to know," I finally said. "I'm sure the government could be a problem for me in the future if it survives or even still exists. For now, I want to avoid politics. The goal here is to keep people from dying. Worrying about government intrigue is a problem we can deal with after people are saved. You back me up, I'll listen to the leaders here, and we'll save everyone. Just keep in mind, I'm in charge of what I build and how things are laid out in the settlement. I'm also thinking about how this will affect what happens when I leave. Augusta is not my only focus."

"You'll need me to keep people moving in the right direction, so they need to see that we're still in charge," he said. While we were talking, he was reading the letter of recommendation from the Coast Guard commander in Ketchikan that I had pulled out to show him. As I had hoped, it seemed to have an impact. At least he should know I had the right goals, whatever else we ended up disagreeing on.

There were a few more rounds of back-and-forth posturing, which cemented our respective positions. He would support me enough to save his people, but he wanted to keep his authority so he could make sure people were safe.

When it was clear we were generally aligned, I led us back to the group to start rolling out the first stages of my building plan. Thanks to Vlad's scouting, I had confirmed there was no immediate threat from the syndicate, so we had some time. Plus, O'Donnell told me he had people on guard duty. He had even beefed up the patrols after the last attack. With that in mind, I decided to focus on the syndicate once the town's basic infrastructure was in place. The key to winning over the people here was to show them what I could do to improve their chances of survival. This building was impressive, but it was just the start.

"Okay, here's what I'm thinking. We should start with a quad block of three dorms and a barn. That gives us housing for 90 people, 180 if we double people up. Since all the buildings have greenhouses in the attics, there will also be four second-floor greenhouses to train people to grow food for the future. That's in addition to the lower floor of the barn for livestock." As I talked to the group, I pulled up information about the buildings on the portal display for people to see.

"If those barns can keep the animals alive and breeding, we need more of them," someone from the back said. "There are still enough dairy cows to maintain breeding stock if we can feed them and keep them from freezing."

"The cows are the most important, but after that, we need room for the chickens, rabbits, fish, and goats," someone else called out. "Those have been easier to keep alive for our future food needs because they are small, but it's getting tough as supplies and heat run low."

I was surprised to learn there were a good number of animals in the area, along with food for them. It turned out that people who were more used to the cold were better at this than I expected. I revised the plan to start with three barns and one dorm. There was some grumbling from people who wanted housing, but we had to secure the food source first. If the animals died, we could not easily replace them. Based on the animals we needed to house, all three barns would have chicken runs. Two would have rabbit warrens, and one would have a space for random animals and pets. I knew some people would keep their pets with them or sneak them back into housing when there was room, but this would handle the issue for now.

All that would take up the spaces in the barns designed for the smaller animals. The spaces for large animals would be for fish, goats, and cows across the three barns.

By this point, word had spread, and it seemed like much of the city was trying to squeeze into the crafting bay to follow along with my plans. I shared the barn blueprint with everyone while I focused on what came next.

Large Barn Blueprint

- Unlock 25 tokens, purchase 1 token
- 150 material units, 150 work units
- Supports 0-4 work pods / 2 pod slots
- Top-floor greenhouse
- Power required 100-250 power units based on the weather
- Water required 50 water units
- Safe to -50 degrees base, -125 degrees at full power
- Produces food for 125 people

"We need a fourth barn if we want room for all the cows,"

Jon, one of the people planning to work the barns, said. "We've still got 32 cows and two bulls. Swap things around so the spot for various animals is in a barn without cows. That's where we will keep the bulls. We can use this space to store feed in addition to the barns, right?"

"Can people live in the barns if we focus on building them, or is it like this crafting space?" O'Donnell asked. "We need to keep our animals alive, but we also need to stop using our fuel to keep people warm."

"The barns are not set up for people to live there, but they can. Any buildings where animals or humans normally live count as valid places for humans to sleep. Once we build medical clinics, people can live in those, too," I said. "Remember, the windmills will supply surplus power to heat legacy buildings while we get stuff built, so that will help stretch your heating supplies. Speaking of building, let's bundle up and get these four barns built so you can start planning the livestock moves and get people settled."

Most of the group wanted to come outside to see the construction. I was among the first out and spent a few minutes surveying the open space and planning the placement of buildings. Once I placed the blueprints exactly as I wanted, I fed the resources into them, and all four buildings rose simultaneously. The nano construction was enough to light the area with its blue glow. The slowly brightening horizon could not compete with the light cast by the nanomachines forming the buildings. The light shows also kept people distracted for a few more minutes.

Once the buildings were complete, the settlement was short on power. We needed at least three windmills, even though the weather was not too extreme. From the comments people were making, I had learned we were in a relatively warm spell, so I knew there would be a power usage spike as soon as it got colder. Before I built those, though, I wanted to get a dorm and at least one medical clinic up and running. I was tempted to wait for more resources to build an apartment block instead of a dorm, but I decided that smaller buildings with more pods and pod slots were the way to go. With a population well over the 5,000-person cap limiting pods in Klawock, we would not be limited to 100 work pods here, and I wanted to get pods up and running as soon as possible.

"I have not hooked them up to power or water yet," I told people before they started moving toward the new buildings. "I'm building a dorm, and then I'll build out more power so everything can be hooked up."

The dorm had to come first, as we were almost out of spots for work pods, and I did not want any of them created outside to be moved later. As soon as the dorm was placed, I confirmed the direction toward the largest concentration of people in legacy buildings. I moved in that direction to place two more windmills to expand the reach of our power infrastructure. Initially, there would be little free power, but I wanted to plan and get the grid near where people lived. When I placed both windmills, I had only one settlement token left, so I had to wait until more resources were generated before continuing construction. The clinic had to wait to be built, much to Joey's displeasure.

"That's not really enough power for everything, but it's enough to keep things somewhat warm for now," I said as I connected the buildings to the power grid. "The construction bottleneck is settlement tokens right now, so I'll set most pods to focus on producing those. We'll use that to get more power generation in place by this evening."

From there, I went to the new pods with the group and set them up as people entered them. There were now 22 pods, and I assigned 18 to generate settlement tokens and the rest to generate work units. By the time all the discussion and construction were complete, it was just after seven in the morning, so I asked for help to move my supplies into the two-person room in the dorm I had just created. I was claiming that for myself. I did not know anyone well enough to share a room, and I did not want to deal with a random roommate. That got a few grumbles as everyone else was doubling up, and I had a two-person room to myself. O'Donnell and other leaders silenced the grumbles. I would share my space if the situation became dire, but we had time to build stuff out without a rush.

"You all can decide who moves into the buildings. I recommend that the people working the pods live as close to them as possible. The same goes for the barns," I told Erin and

O'Donnell when people started asking me if they could have a bunk in the dorm. "You know the situation better than I do, so I won't be involved in deciding who goes where. Let's plan a noon meeting in the crafting bay. There's much more to go over, but I need a break. I prioritized this first part to get pods running so we have the resources for the next phase. Now we have time to think before we make more plans, and I want to get some input from you before we build more."

I made sure I wouldn't just be talking to the council at the next meeting. I wanted to hear from anyone who could provide a more detailed overview of the town. That meant people who would manage construction and representatives of the town's other factions needed to be at the meeting. I also wanted any information on the syndicate members in the area.

For his part, Vlad asked for maps to review. The last thing I did before heading to my room was to hand out the perishable supplies I brought and the ration bars I could generate. Generating those spawned more questions for me to answer, but made me even more popular when people knew I could create food out of thin air. I kept a few of the ration bars for myself and told everyone I would meet them by the portal at noon to start planning what was next.

"I don't know what I was expecting, but it was not that," I said to Vlad as soon as I closed the door to my room in the dorm. I would need a mattress and other stuff later, but I could use my camping mat and blankets to nap. I needed a moment of privacy to regroup before meeting with the larger group again.

Vlad popped in and out of the room while I talked to myself and unpacked. After confirming that the soundproofing in this building was the same as in Klawock, he returned so we could talk without fear of being overheard.

"There's no way to know for sure, but I agree most of O'Donnell's knowledge about the architects comes from one that your government tried to control early on," Vlad said. "I have not heard anything about that, so it must have been a non-issue for the architect and they just moved on."

"That had to hurt if they had to give up mission rewards. At least it seems the government learned that trying to control us won't work, but I'm not sure I totally trust that O'Donnell guy.

He wants to help people, but he has an agenda that might not align with mine. He's already said he'll report everything back to some central authority if he gets a chance," I said.

"I doubt there is much government, if any, left to report to, and your perks make it a non-issue," Vlad said.

"Yeah, I'm sure he'd control my technology if he could, but he can't. I knew abstractly how much easier the situation was in Alaska, with people who knew me. I hadn't internalized the difference until I arrived, though. I'm going to have to watch what I say and do more carefully here."

"This is what you can expect moving forward with people who don't know you. At least you know that very little knowledge about architects has spread even in less rural places. For now, a few people know a little, but that could help. It doesn't seem they even know you can create enforcers. If they had known about that, someone would have asked about it. That means knowledge is limited and from right after architects were created."

"I'll keep that in mind. If the syndicate is not a significant threat right now, I may hold off on mentioning the enforcers until I get a better feel for the area," I said. "I don't want to deal with empowering the wrong people on top of everything else."

"Waiting on the enforcers is a good idea if you can. It sounds like they haven't had many issues with the syndicate yet, but that could change now. They will sense both you and the portal, and it sounds like the one you killed is the first death for this syndicate group. They know you're a threat now. It's almost confirmed they have a processing portal you can steal from them, and that will definitely require enforcers."

"It seems like things are on track. I'm going to rest for a bit now. You know how annoying I get when I'm tired. It's worse than when I'm hungry. I should be focused on being polite if this next meeting ends up half as challenging as I expect." I finished setting up the room while I talked, then checked that the door was locked before getting into bed and setting my alarm.

I wanted to be up at 11 to shower and get ready for the meeting, so I had only three hours of sleep, but it was enough. I had gotten good at falling asleep quickly, and I slept for almost the entire time before my alarm went off.

“Is everything good out there, Vlad?” I asked as I grabbed a clean set of clothes and shower supplies. Bundling up and repeatedly shifting from cold to hot made showering more necessary than before. For some reason, I initially thought the ice age would mean less showering. In reality, the temperature changes made me sweat more than I had expected.

“There seem to be ongoing disagreements about the housing and whether beds should be in the halls. I now see that you were correct. The situation in Alaska was more of an outlier than I had expected. You are closer to us as a race than I realized,” Vlad said after checking what was going on in the dorm. “You should be fine to get a shower, though. Just don’t let them pull you into arguments.”

Vlad was not making up the conflict outside. I could hear the yelling as soon as I opened the door. The bathroom was right around the corner, and I got in there before I could be waylaid. One person tried to talk to me while I was showering, but I cut that off quickly.

After a quick shower, a few more minutes getting ready in my room, and another check of the status sheets, I headed to the portal building early with people following behind me. I had moved all three of my rifles into my room and had one cleaned and ready to take with me. Hopefully, it would fire if I needed it. I also had two more incapacitate criminal charges for the day, but I was unsure if they would work on any of the humans here if they turned on me. The target had to be generally seen as a criminal by the community. They probably saw me as the criminal if anything.

The midday heat had made a difference, and the outside temperature had risen to nearly 20 degrees below zero. It made for a nice walk over to the portal and explained why a few power units had been saved in the windmill’s batteries while I slept. I watched a pickup unloading hay into one of the barns as I walked over. I was glad to see that not everyone was sitting around and arguing. When I got to the bay, I saw another truck unloading materials in the open space to the side, which had to be for the portal.

“It’s good to see you still have some vehicles running,” I said as I went over to help unload the truck. “I know we were running out of ones that could survive the cold back home."

"There was not a lot left that survived the pulses, and they are failing quickly. At least the cold has helped extend the life of gas, but it's getting sketchy, too. The last time I checked, 32 vehicles were still running in the entire city, and over half of those are cars that can't be used because of the snow. We're using them as long as we can until they die. So, for now, it's bringing stuff here for the portal and getting the feed over here for the surviving animals," one of the guys helping unload said.

"The good news is that they just have to hold out until we can afford the new vehicles that the nano power grid can support. You'll like those a lot better," I said as the last items on the truck were unloaded. "I'm glad you have not started feeding the portal yet, as I want to use up the rest of the remote absorption before we dump all this in."

It looked like someone had moved tables into the open space and set them up for the meeting. A new group of aides was already putting out notepads and water. It looked like these tables were set up for 20 people. That many people arguing about the next steps seemed like a recipe for disaster, but I had asked for it. The people I had been helping unload the vehicles saw where I was looking and promised to leave the room before the meeting started.

"Nope, that's not how I do things. Your leadership can run their meetings however they want, but anyone who wants to can listen to most of the meetings I am in. You should let us talk unless we are doing something really dumb, but you can listen and give me advice afterwards," I said before adding. "Well, people who can fit in the room. Let's not make it too crowded in here, but people who are inside can pass on what was discussed to those who are busy or can't fit."

That was a popular answer among the people unloading supplies, and they were spreading the word. This place was going to be filled with random people and probably cause problems for the council and me in the short term, but it would help in the long run. The council had agreed there could be an audience, but I assumed they had planned to handpick it. If they did not like a random group watching, they could get over it. Ensuring that my ideas and reasoning are heard without the council filtering them would prevent me from being sidelined before I even started my work.

I sat in the seat with my name on it and started making notes for the meeting. The aides asked if I wanted them to get people here early to start the meeting, but I said no. I wanted to ensure my thoughts were in order before we started. It also gave me time to scan the area around the portal for materials I could absorb for material units. The settlement's extended range, thanks to the windmills, meant I had an extended range for the material absorption power, too. I noted down the closest building for possible absorption, then adjusted the settings so that trash collection in the new buildings automatically fed the portal. We had learned in Klawock that processing trash was not the best use of processing power. The advantage was that it provided an easy source of materials, with the added benefit of reducing disease risk.

I wrote down which resource collection I wanted to automate, and more people had already wandered in for the meeting by then. In addition to the original group, representatives from the various factions in the cities were present. After the cold had begun, people reorganized into groups that reflected their desires. It was all just as political as I feared.

The last group to arrive was O'Donnell and two of his aides. After a round of greetings and introductions, we all sat down. Food was in front of us, and we all ate and got to know each other. The conversation over lunch was light, and I was talking with the surrounding audience. The meal was basic and plain, and I was glad that, at least in public, the leaders were eating like everyone else. I let the casual conversations last long enough to ease the tension, but I kicked the meeting off when it looked like people were ready to dive in.

"Thanks to everyone who came here. I've got some ideas on what we need to do next, so let's run through those and I can get your feedback as we go," I said. That earned a few glares from council members who obviously had other ideas about how the meeting should be run, but I ignored them as I began talking about custom houses, my first agenda item.

3

“Enough! Look, I don’t want to be rude, but there’s a ton of stuff to get through,” I said loudly after yet another interruption as I tried to explain how the custom house construction would work. “I want you all to hear what’s going on and ask questions, but you’ve got to let me finish explaining this. Once I’m done, I’ll answer questions. This is all interrelated, and you have to understand how the research boosts work to see why we need to follow a single blueprint whenever we can.”

That got people quiet for a minute, and I was about to continue when a few people started throwing out ideas again.

“Okay,” I said loudly enough to cut off the comments that were starting. I could tell some were genuine, but some seemed coordinated. I had a feeling that some leaders had tried to organize opposition to my plans to show they were in charge. For the moment, I planned to bulldoze over their efforts to control the meeting.

Before I showed up, people had little hope for their long-term survival, and now it was clear they had hope but were also angling for power. I planned to leverage that to get what I needed while avoiding the politics swirling around me. With a real gap in the conversation, I laid out why the custom houses were a great use of resources, enabling many nanostructures to be built quickly.

“This all seems like a lot of work based just on your word,” Daryl, the college’s student president, said after I described the process for building custom houses to match the ones in Klawock so they could be converted into nano homes. “Even if it all works like you say it does, it will take a long time to create enough housing and resources for everyone. Who decides who gets what while you’re making us all follow your plan?”

I was tempted to ignore the comment and keep going, but there were enough nods around the table that I could not let it pass. “Seriously? You realize that without my help, everyone here will die, right? It will be centuries before it gets warm again, and that depends on the aliens returning. Resources will not last until humanity can figure things out on its own. When I got here, there were 31 days before you all ran out of heat and froze. Even if you can extend that on your own, your remaining time is measured in months. Stop fighting for an advantage over the other leaders here and focus on saving everyone. If we get stuff built quickly, it won't matter who got a bed first. Plus, integrating buildings into the nano system fixes and completes many aspects of the construction process. These buildings should be going up in a week or less with enough workers and organization."

That outburst elicited our audience's first genuine reaction and validated my decision to let locals listen in. Despite the leaders' infighting, none of them wanted to be the reason I left. I could see that the people at the table with me also realized their options were limited by the audience. I let my words sink in for a few minutes before I continued, laying out what needed to happen. I was willing to paper over the conflicts, using their fear to succeed in my mission. Solving their political problems was not my mission.

"So, I need a team assigned to collect materials to feed the portal and guide me to what structures I can start remotely disassembling. We can use the portal to eliminate trash and hazardous materials, but that's secondary to focusing on generating material units. There also needs to be enough people to operate all the work pods. Housing around the park will be tight at first, so people should plan on a few weeks of moving back and forth between work and sleep. I want the people living in the housing here to be the ones working in the pods, the food production, and the custom house production."

"Do you care who they are?" O'Donnell asked.

"As long as they're willing to work or old enough for the pods to accept them, it doesn't matter to me. You should spread the effort among all the factions here. I can see that a bunch of groups are represented here, but I won't get into that. I'm also planning to build some clinics soon. We need power, water, and infrastructure for them, but I know we need to start addressing medical issues. Start planning who will be treated in them. My only requirement relating to the medical pods is to keep one of them accessible for emergencies. That means cycling people, so a pod will always be available within 30 minutes in the event of an emergency. I'll also heal people toward the end of each day with my perk, so set up a process to tell me who to help."

Daryl opened his mouth to ask a question, but Erin elbowed him to shut him up. "We'll get the housing and medical plans organized on our own and let you know if we have any questions," she said.

I figured they wanted to meet in private to make their plans, without airing more dirty laundry in front of an audience. A small part of me wanted to keep the conversations in public, but a larger part just wanted them out of my hair. If letting them make deals secretly kept me out of the drama, I was okay with that, as long as it did not make my job harder.

"Great, get me the maps of the area and people who can help with my projects, and we're good. I also want to have a team I can work with to coordinate the defense against the syndicate. Make sure everyone stays on alert, not just any assigned guards. Vlad thinks the syndicate is likely to react to my presence and the fact that I killed one of them," I said.

"So, we're in danger because you're here now?" Daryl asked before anyone could stop him.

"Sort of," I said. "You know the aliens have been watching you, and they wanted you dead. Now they know they can't just wait for everyone here to freeze to death. The danger's the same, just sped up."

"They want to take over the planet, and their goal has been your death since they got here," Vlad said. "There's a reason they were being hunted down by my people to be arrested. They have a habit of exploiting primitive worlds like yours. Now they know they can't do this the easy way and have to try to stop Devin from helping you. If we hadn't come, they would have waited until you were dead or close to dead to attack. Stop trying to make Devin the bad guy and help him save you."

"Donna will organize the guard team you want," O'Donnell said, breaking the sudden silence. He pointed to the woman in the group who had confronted me when I teleported in. She had been the only one easy to deal with, so I was happy with the choice.

I spoke briefly with Donna, then started bundling up while the council kept talking. There seemed to be a game of chicken going on as they waited for someone to make the call to move the meeting. I had said what I needed to and was taking Donna and two of her guards to explore the immediate area with a local who could guide us. We were going to examine the building they designated for initial destruction through the portal. I wanted to see it first to ensure it was the right choice to remove. I also wanted to see the before-and-after of remote processing on a building. I could not process an entire building at once, so it was essential to figure out how to dismantle it without causing it to collapse on anything important.

The trip out to see the building was cold, but not unbearable. I had not yet told people here that I could handle the cold better because of my class, so I mirrored their reactions to the temperature. When I was at the building slated for processing, I learned I could control the portal's absorption anywhere within the town's range. I had assumed I needed to be at the portal to consume materials remotely, but Vlad confirmed I could use that ability out here.

After half an hour spent checking the building from the inside, we moved outside, and I began processing it. Everyone watched as I carefully started dissolving the building from the roof down. Even demolishing a two-story building was enough to stress me out. I was glad to start with a smaller building before I worked on some of the larger buildings around the small park where I had set up shop. Even combining what I could see and a virtual schematic from the portal to target and remove portions of the building made me wish I had taken some architecture classes. I hoped I could do it without causing a collapse.

"It looks like this is consuming more material than I expected, but we are getting a good return," I said after using up the 115 points of processing power that could be used remotely. That 50% remote usage does not apply to the 50 bonus points of processing power we get from my perk. Still, I can see this building lasting another ten days or more before I've depleted it. Make sure no one enters the building or gets too close. It's not stable anymore."

"We'll make sure people know to avoid it," Donna said. "This whole area was deserted quickly. These old commercial buildings were not as well-suited to the cold as residential buildings."

"Great, and Jason, could your team pick the next building and double-check that there's nothing inside you want to save?" I told the guy the council sent out to organize scavenging for me. "We didn't have time to do a detailed search with the first one, but we should do that before I start clearing the next one. There's plenty of time to do it right for the next building."

After that, everyone but Jason returned to the warmth of the crafting bay. I wanted to check all the pods and make sure those were all organized. I needed to build more housing as soon as I had the tokens, so staying on top of pod production was essential. After checking all the pods, I returned to the portal space to review area maps. While I waited for the resources to build more, I could use the time to plan what to do if the aliens attacked.

We started by reviewing where the locals had encountered golems and the few reported sightings of syndicate members before I arrived. Almost every encounter was to the southwest, on the way to Portland, Maine's largest city. O'Donnell kept meticulous records of the encounters and had his theories about what they were doing.

"The consensus is that they are preventing us from helping each other. Portland is only 50 miles away, and we could have worked with them to survive. There were a few trips right after everything went to hell, but those trips died off quickly. Amid possible alien and golem ambushes, the snow, and technological troubles, contact with Portland quickly died out. We had more contact with Bangor before it got too cold, but that ended within a month. It's closer to us, just 30 miles to the northeast, but it was still too dangerous," Donna said. "They have a lot fewer people than Portland, though. There were around 30,000 people there, a fraction of the 200,000 or more that were in Portland when this all started."

Other small towns and cities in the area were highlighted as places they wanted to contact when they had reliable transportation.

Looking at the map, it was clear that Augusta was ideally located to help this entire region. The number of people who could be saved here was staggering compared to those on Prince of Wales Island and in the surrounding communities. I would have to balance finishing the mission in Augusta with giving them a path to support the people in the surrounding cities, assuming they were all still alive.

In addition to planning for a future encounter with the aliens, I began planning where to place windmills and houses to recharge vehicles and sustain a long-term connection to Portland and Bangor. I held off on discussing those plans yet, though.

We were close enough to other cities that people might head this way once they knew we had food and heat. I thought it was unlikely, but you never knew if things were desperate. There might even be people trying to make their way here before the syndicate was driven out. That had not been an issue back home.

People arriving from other towns would add to the politics I would be dealing with. It made sense to put in enough effort to build a power base among the people here so they could handle newcomers on my behalf. Ignoring politics too much now would lead to problems later, and I was already changing my plans. We needed to help people before they learned about us and braved the cold to get here.

Space would be the other issue. Even with the portal processing buildings and materials, I would soon run out of space for buildings in the park. It would take too long to demolish the buildings in the area. Based on that, I planned to use windmills and water towers to reach nearby green spaces and athletic fields, then head southwest through the suburbs to more green spaces.

People rotated in and out of the building, advising me as I pored over the maps. Everyone had their opinions, but conversations stayed polite. After the earlier press of questions, I was glad people were now focused on being helpful. It was clear that a few of them had agendas, but overall, they had shifted to focusing on survival rather than the town's politics. I managed to wrap up this planning pass before four, so I could do a circuit of the pods and build the two structures I had planned.

While doing that, I used my three remaining personal tokens to increase the boosted mind perk to the fifth level. I had seen that settlement tokens would be the bottleneck for a while. Not only did I need them for buildings, but also for vehicles and building integration. The three new levels would increase my daily bonus settlement tokens to five. Because I got the three bonus tokens immediately, it also meant I had enough tokens to build another dorm and windmill.

"That's left us with just enough power and short on water," I said after the two structures had formed in the next quad block and toward the next park. "I built the dorm first so there would be spots for the pods that come with the windmill I just built and the water tower that would be up next. Balancing pod slots with construction is its own puzzle when there are few open slots. Even when there are resources to build another structure, we have to wait for indoor pod spaces to be available. We don't want pods outdoors, and we don't want to waste tokens moving them later. That's why I built the dorm first. That will change once custom houses start coming online. They add pod spots without generating new pods, so building them will solve the pod space problem."

Two teams were already unloading supplies for the first two custom houses. They were using the portal building to stay warm between moving supplies and starting construction. To speed things up, I took my portable nano heater over there for them to use.

"You can use this to heat a tent between the building sites. That will save time as you work," I said, showing them how to work it. "Once the first building's walls are up, you can use it to take the edge off for the team working inside."

"When we get all the teams going, we plan on building five of these houses at a time," the foreman, Bryan, said. "We'll need four more of these heaters to keep people safe and warm."

"It costs 200 settlement tokens to buy one of these. We can't afford more of them for a while. There are a ton of things we need that cost settlement tokens. It takes almost 70 days for a single pod to generate 200 tokens, and we only have 26 pods right now," I said. "Do your best with the one heater. I'll be working on getting enough windmills to generate surplus electricity so you can use the legacy heaters that are still working. They are not as efficient, but they'll do for now."

"I figured it would not be that easy to get a bunch of your fancy heaters, but it was worth asking," Bryan said. "If you can get us all housing out here, that will be enough for now. I'll start collecting old heaters that run, and we'll use whatever heat we can to speed things up. The plan is to have teams working 12-hour shifts if they can live here. That lets there be two workers taking turns in each bed."

"Talk to O'Donnell and the others. They'll do what they can, but we need space for the pod workers, too. It will be tight until we get a few of your houses built. I'd recommend using the first two houses you build for your workers. They can also serve as warming stations for houses under construction. Now that there is space to keep the animals alive, the focus will be on housing for everyone. Still, with 10 teams of 40 people each working on these houses, when everything's going, that's 200 beds needed for them. That's a lot of space," I said as I made some notes. I was getting more involved in housing allocation than planned. "I'll advocate for you to get some spots allocated, though."

With all the buildings that had sprung up, the surrounding area was bustling as people moved supplies, animals, and people into the buildings. It was also noisy as people dug holes in the frozen soil for the pier-and-beam foundations of the custom houses. At least the water towers were already clearing the snow, making construction much easier.

I claimed a mattress and some basic supplies for my room before I toured the barns and greenhouses. Although I had limited experience in either area, I spoke with people back home about them and made copies of their notes. I used that experience to answer the questions about the spaces that I could.

I spent a few hours talking to everyone working on food production about how quickly the plants grew, and how the animals raised in the barns grew faster and were more fertile. Most of the teams assigned to the building were glad to have my notes and promised to add their comments as they worked, so I could take them on my next mission.

"No," I said, trying not to laugh as I repeated my spiel in the last of the barns and got a new question. "We had people living in the barns for a while, and there were no signs of increased fertility in the humans, just the animals. Normal precautions should be fine, right, Vlad?"

"Yes, the nanostructures do not cause changes in sapient beings, so it will not change anything about your workers' fertility," Vlad said as I fought not to laugh.

Most of the people working in the barns were surprised at the question, too. No one else had thought of it, but as soon as it was raised, I could see the panic in some people's eyes. Some animal enclosures were still pretty light on animals, so cots had been set up in those areas for people to sleep on with temporary walls for privacy. The question made me wonder what had already gone on in the new buildings.

The upside was that someone had raided an office building for cubicle walls that gave at least some privacy. I told them to save more of those cubical walls. We had not had any significant amount to use back in Klawock, but they would come in handy as people crowded into spaces in a cold snap. The conversations with people and one more scouting trip around the area kept me busy until the pod collection at eight in the evening.

I had just enough tokens to build another water tower, and then I shifted most of the pods to work unit production. By the time morning rolled around, I wanted to buy an apartment block, which needed 1,000 work units.

The dinner meeting with the leadership group from earlier went smoothly this time. From their actions at this meeting, it was clear they had either worked through their issues or found a way to ignore them enough to present a unified front when meeting with me. There were still plenty of hints that they were at odds and that most local leaders were unhappy with me. Still, I was willing to play along if they could stay civil. Their geniality was tested when I discussed the need to house the construction workers in the apartment I was building in the morning. Thankfully, the veneer of politeness held while I explained the reasoning. We needed those custom houses to get people housed quickly, so we needed the teams ready to work. We did not need them waiting for rides back and forth to the worksite. It was a short-term hit to their plans in return for a long-term boost.

"I'll be ready to build the apartment complex and another windmill tomorrow morning. The first medical clinics are on the list after those structures are built. I know they're taking longer than expected, but my plans change on a dime as stuff comes up. Right now, one of our main issues is the lack of settlement tokens, but once we catch up on those, we'll need the material units or work units. With three main resources, we will always be short on one. There are some alien devices I can use to speed up construction or for other purposes, if you all have any. The spheres in the golems that the aliens had used to attack can create more tokens and for other things."

"We have collected them, but they don't seem to do anything," O'Donnell said. "We even sent two off to other cities at the start of all this, and they could not find anything special about them."

"Well, they're something only architects can use. The other reason I brought them up is that they automatically move to my status sheet if I get close enough to them. It's automatic, so if people have some stored somewhere and I get too close, they will seem to vanish. Once I absorb them that way, they stay with me until I use them. Same as the nano matrix items, the syndicate members drop."

My statement started an entire conversation that ended with everyone gathering around the processing portal screen, so I could share my status screen and show them what I was talking about.

"I need to set up a monitor here so I can project the copies I keep on my tablet," I said. While talking, I ensured the basic information screen appeared without the skill descriptions. I did not need to give them too many details about my perks. The subclass unlock would spark conversation, and I planned to use it to test the waters about telling them about classes in general.

Devin Martin		**Age**	32
Class	Architect	**Sub-Class**	N/A
Perks	AI Assistant	Second Chance L3	Boosted Materials L14
Boosted Vigor L10	Boosted Stamina L10	System Integration L1	Boosted Mind L5
Medical Effect L3	Commanding Presence L5	Extended Range L8	Incapacitate Criminal L4
Debuffs			

Physical Score	8 (+20)	**Mental Score**	11(+5)
Leadership Score	7 (+5)		
Settlement Tokens	0	**Personal Tokens**	0
Spheres	53	**Nano Matrix**	1
Sub-Class Unlocks	Soldier		

"As I encounter certain things, they get stored somewhere only I can access and appear on this sheet," I said as I pointed out the tokens, spheres, and the matrix.

"It's because the items are converted to a nano signature stored in your personal nano matrix. The item itself is gone. That's why you can't return them to people," Vlad said. "It's an upgrade to make your missions easier by always having key components at hand."

"And it made a tremendous difference here. Almost half the settlement tokens I used to improve the processing portal were collected in Klawock, and the rest came from completing the mission. The people there let me focus their work pods on settlement tokens to bring here because upgrading the portal at the start will make a huge difference for this mission," I said. "I also get personal tokens to spend on perks from completing missions or absorbing nano matrices. Those are a big boost as well. That's over 100 bonus material units daily and five bonus settlement tokens I am generating from perks to build the infrastructure here. Not to mention the bonus healing perk and the food rations I generate. It's a great boost while I'm here, but when I'm gone, your ability to build will drop off, and things will get more expensive. We'll get into that when it's close to time for me to leave."

"What's that sub-class of soldier?" O'Donnell asked. "And why is your sub-class listed as N/A if you have the soldier class?"

"I got that sub-class option for killing a syndicate member in a one-on-one fight to the death," I said. "I almost died too, but in the end I made it, and they didn't."

"While it's a strong class, it would not improve Devin's ability to save people from the cold. He also does not need it.

His perks already boost his abilities far beyond those of other humans, and he does not plan to assault syndicate bases alone," Vlad said. "His current skills were enough for him to help take out a syndicate member and four golems when he arrived here after all."

Vlad and I had debated whether I should let them underestimate me or make it clear I was a badass that they needed to be careful around. Both choices had their risks, but I figured there would be less crap to deal with if they remembered I was stronger than they were. I was reticent to reveal the details of my other skills, but the names gave some hints of what they could do.

"When I activate a sub-class and take it, I will have a way to grant that class to other eligible people," I added. "Right now, I can only have one, and I want to find a better match. Granting classes to people is something we will talk about when things are more stable. When I leave, you need at least one person with a class, so that building new nanostructures will only be twice as expensive instead of four times as expensive."

I used the overload of information to cut off the flow of questions and made plans to tour more of the local area after I built the dorm in the morning. Even though we were low on settlement tokens, I wanted to see if any existing buildings could be integrated. I also wanted to scout out the routes to various open spaces. Looking at it on the map was great, but I needed to see them in person.

With that taken care of, I removed myself from the meeting and headed to the new dorm, where people were waiting for my healing charges. After that, I found Bryan and told him there would be an entire apartment block for his crew the next morning, thanks to the council's decision. If they doubled the bed count and took turns in the beds, it would just hold his planned team of 400 people. I asked Vlad to remind me to watch the maintenance backlog closely, given the crowding.

As I returned to the dorm, the cold was rolling in. The mattress and curtains for my room were resting outside the door. I appreciated that it looked like no one had tried to break in. One of the people in the hall helped me get the mattress into my room and onto the top bunk. The bottom bunk was full of the supplies

I had brought with me. I needed to organize them again and repack everything when I had time. Well, when I had time and was motivated. As soon as I was alone in my room, I got ready for bed and read for a few hours before calling it a night. I could have spent more time talking to people, but I needed a break after dealing with politics all day. On top of that, I was already missing my friends back in Klawock. It was sinking in that there would be a lot of bouncing around, and meeting people I would never see or talk to again as I completed missions around the world.

"Not a bad start," I said to Vlad before drifting off to sleep. "There's a lot to do, but if we get them set up right, this could save a lot more people than the work back home."

"And dealing with this group will get you ready for larger, more desperate groups in the future," Vlad said.

I managed not to think about how much harder things were likely to get based on that comment and focused on getting a good night's sleep.

4

The next morning, I was up in time for breakfast before the next round of building. Meals today for the people living in the barns and the dorm were brought in from the surrounding area, but after I got the apartments built, the plan was to use the kitchens there to feed the residents of the other buildings I was putting up. The apartments had ample kitchen space for all that cooking.

Either way, I was bundled up and ready to collect resources when the pods turned over at eight. A small crowd had formed to see the next round of construction, and I double-checked that I had enough resources for what I had planned. I had just enough settlement tokens with my daily bonus and a whole seven spare work units, but it was enough.

"Okay, everyone who has free time is welcome to watch, but before I build anything, Jason is going to feed the portal, and I am going to step out to work on absorbing the building I started working on yesterday," I said. "I need some more material units to build stuff, and we may as well get that done now."

That was enough to thin the crowd. Between people who did not have time to wait, and those who did not want to be outside in the cold, it came down to a crowd of about 25 following the guards and me as I carefully demolished more of the building I had begun yesterday.

Everything started well, but as I was getting close to the end of the remote processing for the day, a chunk of the building's side collapsed outward, kicking up a huge cloud of snow. Even with the water towers, it was taking some time to convert all the snow to water, so there was still a lot of snow around the edges of the park. I was placing the water towers so they would clear the park itself. No one was hurt, but we were all covered in snow and had to wait a few moments before we could see again. I did not have enough remote processing points to clear the rubble, but the guards said it would be fine to leave it there for a day or two.

With the excitement over, we made our way to the western end of Capital Park. I had started construction in the middle of the park. The current plan was to place two apartment blocks at the west and east ends, then fill the rest of the space with custom houses and smaller support structures. I had to get people to move back again before I could place the blueprint for the apartment block. It needed to finish forming before I placed the next windmill, or I would not have slots for its pods.

"Okay, you can start moving people into the housing and get people into the pods," I exclaimed as soon as the nano construction was finished. I was not sure who in the group was responsible for getting the apartments furnished and occupied. I just knew the council must have assigned someone to it. "If you want to watch the construction of the new windmill, follow me. This will get some spare power supply for heaters and recharging more devices."

The windmill was technically outside the park and in the front area of the deserted state capital. It was a massive stone structure, destined to be reclaimed for future use. I had heard people talk about its symbolism and how it needed saving. I had not yet mentioned that it could be converted using settlement tokens. It was a massive undertaking, requiring 5,000 settlement tokens, while custom houses needed only 25. I imagined reclaiming it would be a project for the future, when the settlement was far more established, and I was long gone.

With the windmill built, I was totally out of settlement tokens and down to seven work units. That meant I had eight hours to explore before I could build the first medical center. I was trying to avoid Joey as I had pushed off building the medical clinic a few times, and he was getting annoyed with me. Most of the people watching the construction peeled off, and it was just Donna and the two guards she had brought that continued on to explore with me.

"So, Donna, what were you doing before the end of the world?" I asked as she began leading me north to a smaller park and some green space. As we traveled, I could see stumps everywhere. It looked like there had been a lot more trees around here that had already been cut down for wood.

"I was working at a bar, and my husband worked construction. That ended pretty quickly when everything changed. I've always been a good shot and needed something to do, so I volunteered to be a guard when those plant creatures started attacking," she said. "Other than dealing with the people in charge, the job is not half bad."

"Yeah, I'd like to skip the politics and get things done, but it never works that way. At least the politics do not seem to be stopping my work here," I said. I monitored the other guards to make sure I was not causing too many problems with my comments.

"They're not bad people for the most part. It's just that they don't trust each other and can see what is coming. I think before you showed up, they all knew it was just a matter of time before we fell," she said. "I think a lot of us knew that deep down. I hope that with you creating a future where we can survive, they can focus on the big picture and not their tribes."

"Expecting every place to be as community-minded as an island where everyone knew each other wasn't reasonable, but I was hoping I'd get lucky again," I said. Donna seemed independent of the factions and made a good choice as the first enforcer in town. If I were lucky, she would qualify when I started scanning. I had some time to watch how she interacted with people before I could get the class pod built, but I was glad to have someone who might stay out of politics and focus on what needed to be done.

Our conversation wrapped up as we arrived at the next park. Macomber Park was a fraction of the size of the park I had started building in, but Donna pointed out all the open land around it. I would need to clear out stumps and some rubble, but then there was a lot of space. All the houses and buildings we passed on the way were deserted, and none could be converted into nanostructures.

As we walked back, Donna led us to the east to mirror the railroad tracks and the frozen-over river. Having the river there would limit our construction in that direction. Even with it frozen over, I did not want to build on it. I was asking how quickly the river froze when Vlad interrupted.

"Do these tracks go to the nearest large cities? It's clear the snow started heavier here, and it is staying heavier than where you started, Devin. There are purpose-built rail vehicles powered by nanotechnology that you can purchase with tokens.

You can also convert the rails to nano rails to keep them in good shape."

"I think the cargo rails go up to Bangor and down to Portland," Donna said when we both looked at her. "I can check with the team when we get back."

"The tracks do go both places," one of the other guards with us said. "My dad worked for the railroad before all this happened, so I know the rails were still working before the aliens messed everything up."

While they were talking, I made my way over to where I thought the tracks were and started clearing snow so I could focus on them.

Custom Railway Integration

- Integration 1 token per 100 feet
- Power required 1-2 power units based on weather
- Safe for travel to -60 degrees base, -200 degrees at full power

"Cheaper than I thought. Just 53 tokens per mile is a lot better than I was expecting," I said as I did the math. It would not be cheap, but it was a real possibility.

"It does not extend the settlement range," Vlad warned. "That's the main reason it's so cheap. It will only carry the power it needs, but just the tracks alone will not let you create a link between the main settlement and locations further away. It will also be more expensive if the tracks are damaged and will potentially cause a larger-than-expected maintenance backlog."

I nodded, but I was already plotting to use the tracks as the path for nano vehicle-type transports to travel. I could start with windmills for power and even houses along the way for long stretches. The tracks and the train might come after I left, but the tracks had the potential to rebuild societal connections.

I slotted that idea into my list of things to plan for as we passed home base and kept heading south along the river. There was a lot of open space along the riverfront and around the YMCA fields and buildings. The police station was still in good shape, but was not flagged as something I could integrate. We had just passed the police station when Daryl approached us at a quick walk.

"There you are. I was hoping to run into you and have time to talk to you one-on-one," he said as soon as he got close. "It was tough figuring out your route without making it look like I was hunting for you."

"I don't care if you're one of the decent council members," Donna said. I could clearly hear an accusation in her voice. "I made it clear I was not selling the route, so people could ambush Devin to talk. I don't play favorites between you. Still, since you did figure it out, I'm willing to drop back a little to give you all some privacy, if Devin wants me to."

I appreciated that she was deferring to me and making it clear she was not doing whatever Daryl wanted. I was also curious what Daryl thought was so important, so I nodded to Donna. There was an awkward silence as we waited for some privacy, and I let the silence linger while Daryl decided what to say now that he had his chance.

"Look, man, I'm not going to wander in the snow in silence," I finally said when he had not spoken after a few minutes. "You did all this cloak-and-dagger business to talk to me without the other council members, so you'd best get on with it."

"Fine, I'm not sure what I'm doing. I ended up on the council because I was student body president, and lots of students are trapped here. I won student body president because I was popular, not because I knew how to navigate all these politics. Just don't trust everyone from the start, as I did. Erin can be cool, but everyone has their agendas."

"And you don't have an agenda?" I asked.

"Not really, I just wanted you to be careful and tell you that we have a lot of students here from in-state. The other people on the council might not want to lose a bunch of healthy college students, but if you make places like Portland and Bangor safe. There are about 1,000 of us who will want to leave once things are stable. Just keep that in mind," he said in a rush. "If you help us get in touch with our families and help them, you'll get a lot of loyalty from the students, and there are like 4,000 of us left."

That was useful information. I had not realized that the student body made up nearly a quarter of the population, but it made sense. They were young and healthy. They probably had the highest survival rate in town. That also meant they were the largest faction despite their lack of political power. They would be an ally I could leverage.

"I'll keep that in mind. I'm not that much older than all of you, so I get it. My family is not around anymore, so there's no rush to get to them, but you all have family close, and that's got to be rough," I said. "I'll keep your warning in mind and think about Portland and Bangor. If we take out the aliens and capture their base, I will probably have a way to get Portland started on nanotechnology construction independent of Augusta, which will be important given their size. Without another portal to anchor a nano based settlement, many people will have to try to migrate here in the long run. If they last that long."

"I'll let the people who matter know, quietly," Daryl said. "If that's the way to save people around here, we'll do what we need to. If it weren't for the aliens in the way, we would have already made a run for Portland, but no one is that dumb with the aliens and those plant monsters waiting."

"Is that all?" I asked after a minute of silence. When he nodded yes, I waved Donna and the guards up. I was sure one of the guards would report back to the other council members about the meeting, but what I had learned would make up for that future drama.

Daryl headed back toward the main park as we continued exploring, looping west through more residential areas. Seeing everything in person was better than just looking at maps, and I knew Vlad was getting even more out of it than I was. With the cold and the snow, we were not moving quickly, but it was enough to keep us warm. I was in better shape than I had been when all this started.

"Well, that's a pleasant surprise," I said as we started to curve back to the base. "Those two houses can be converted into nano houses. They are a little more expensive than usual. When they are not built exactly to the blueprint, it takes more tokens and maintenance work to standardize them, but that's a nice boost to housing if I build some infrastructure this way. There's even open yard space for two or three more custom houses. It could be a little enclave to set up in the future."

"I'll make sure they are noted for future occupation," Donna said. “We won’t loot them or damage them. We’ll even stuff useful stuff inside from surrounding houses if we get the chance.”

While we were talking, a message from Vlad popped up.

That’s not the only surprise. Someone has used one of these houses as a cache for spheres. Your count just went up by 18. Donna took us on a specific route that didn’t make sense. I think she knew where it was and guided us there. She’s playing her own game, but it helps us.

I nodded in acknowledgment, but said nothing. I would wait to bring it up and see what council members reacted. They knew the spheres were useful to me, so it looked like someone had tried to hide them.

By the time we made it back to base, it had been almost six hours of walking and was well past lunch. I created my daily allotment of ration bars and distributed them to the group to eat or pass on. I just kept three of them for myself so I could eat in my room. I did not want to be taking food from the communal pot.

Before I could escape to my room to recover from the trek and rest, Joey and two other medical staff members cornered me to make sure the medical clinic was next. Once I confirmed I would build it after my break, when I had the resources, they began asking me questions about how the clinics would work. They wanted to rank people on a triage list and needed more information. The first question confirmed that anything could be cured with enough time. Then they shifted to asking about timelines for curing different conditions. I shared what I knew, but I acknowledged there were gaps in my knowledge.

“As far as I know, it can cure anything other than old age, but some stuff takes way longer to cure,” I finally repeated. “If you all can make a list of timelines for me to take to the next mission, I’d be grateful. I only know what I heard, and the documentation I brought this time was focused on what to cure, not timelines.”

After a few less-than-subtle hints, they left me alone for a few hours but made it clear they would be waiting for me at four. I took the chance to hide in my room. No one had confronted me about my talk with Daryl or the spheres I collected, and I wanted to put that off as long as possible.

After a few hours of resting and discussing plans with Vlad, I left my room just before four. They had left me alone in my room, but there was a group waiting for me with Erin and O'Donnell in addition to Joey and his staff.

"I've got to collect from the pods before I can build anything," I said instead of greeting them. "If you don't want to follow me around, you can meet me at the portal building, as I'm going to build the first clinic near there."

Everyone other than O'Donnell split off to wait for me. He followed me to the barns and the apartment building to collect tokens and work units.

"It seems you've collected some materials that are not yours," O'Donnell said as soon as we were away from the others. "Did you think we wouldn't find out?"

"I was clear with you all that spheres in my range are automatically collected. I'm not even sure when I got them. I noticed them on my information sheet when I was back in my room. I don't know what you want me to do about it, and I'm sure that you couldn't use them without me anyway."

"The only reason I'm not making a bigger deal about this is that I got a complete report on your activities, and it does not seem that you made any effort to find the spheres or react to them. Your choice of walking companions was questionable, though. Do you want to share what that was about?"

"Man, you need to chill out. I'm not here to cause problems. You know my statistics on your survivability were accurate, even if they were conservative, and that the government isn't coming to save you. I'm not going to be part of helping or hurting any of your machinations. I'm also not disclosing the contents of my private conversations to you or anyone else. You need me. I don't need you."

With that, I sped into the apartment complex, knowing he would have to shut up or risk being overheard. I spoke with a few people, then collected from the pods, kept a quick pace to the other pod locations, and returned to the group waiting for me.

I explained that I had sufficient resources for one clinic with two medical pods, and the second clinic was planned for the morning, once they had a sense of how the pods worked. The clinic formed quickly, and I recommended they use the office for housing.

"It's even got a bathroom, and you can use the dorms when you need a shower. Use the clinic space for the people I will heal each day and those waiting their turn in the pods," I said as I showed Joey and his team how to use the pods and run the diagnostics.

We used one of his staff members to check the diagnostic function. It correctly flagged his vision loss but also flagged pancreatic cancer.

"We're going to have to think about how to message that," Joey said as they went over the results. "With how detailed these scans are, we are going to find a lot of things about people that they didn't know. Even though we can cure it, some people are going to have problems dealing with learning they have cancer or other diseases."

"That was the key problem before the research upgrade that allowed the doctors to decide what to cure," I said. "We would put someone in to cure diabetes, and they would have six other issues and monopolize a pod for days. At the beginning, you will need to prioritize emergent conditions, or ones that are draining resources. You can select what to cure and what to leave for now. Cancer that can be treated in six months is not a good use of the pod time yet."

"Keep people alive until we get caught up," Joey said. "It sucks, but I get it. It even flagged the missing appendix, so it looks like organs can be regrown. In the long term, every issue can be treated, but with the number of people we have, that's a long time based on these time estimates to repair things."

"And you'll keep getting new clinics for a while. It's just that I need to balance them with everything else. Healing everyone so they can freeze or starve because I put too many resources in clinics does no good. Be ready for more medical issues to show up as we take in people from surrounding communities as well."

"Do we really have time to build more of these clinics instead of food and housing? We've got bigger problems, and we've been getting along okay so far," O'Donnell asked.

"We've been surviving because of the stored medicine and the fact that it takes a while for a lot of medical issues to become fatal. We're on a time limit here, too," Erin said. "You'd know that if you came to more of the planning meetings and not just the defense-focused ones."

"She's right. Based on our data back home, the average person needs two days in a pod to resolve all issues. That means each pod can fully treat fewer than 200 people per year. Even if no one joined your community, that's 40 years to cycle everyone through a pod with just two running," I said. It was clear no one had done the math. "And it's not all big things, too. People with severe vision impairment have no way to get new glasses. No matter how careful you are, they will eventually break. Medical issues like that need to be fixed sooner than 40 years from now."

Joey gave me a grateful look but did not interject as he and his team transferred the first two patients into the pods. I reminded him that they needed to time the pods after I built the next clinic, so there would be one available in short order for any emergencies.

"One more clinic in the morning, then focusing back on other structures," I said as we walked out. "We only officially have housing for 170 people. Even if we triple the number of people per building, those buildings would still be enough to house only a fraction of the 16,000 here. Food is not much better. When the current buildings are up to speed, they can feed 516 people at full rations."

"We need more power and water, too," Erin pointed out. "Now that people know they are available, all the excess is getting used as soon as it's created."

I checked and saw that she was right. Even the battery storage was at zero. I took the time to recheck the numbers as we stepped into the crafting bay. A large portion of it had been converted into a daycare for children with nowhere else to go, but there was still room to meet.

"Okay, new plan. After the next clinic, I'll build windmills and water towers in a two-to-one ratio as long as there is pod space. As soon as the pod space fills up, I'll build more apartment blocks and greenhouses. Probably at a two-to-one ratio as well. Each of those buildings provides ten pod slots, and eight of them are excess. We need more pods to pay for more stuff. It will be a boring few days while I get that built out, but we can take that time to make plans for the aliens and our train to Bangor."

Both of those suggestions generated excitement and kept the conversation going until I headed back to my room for some much-needed sleep.

In the morning, I built the clinic and another windmill. This one started extending our range toward the two houses I could integrate. After that, I assisted with house construction in the park for the first half of the day, then helped Jason's crew collect materials to feed into the portal. Being in a larger city meant there were almost limitless supplies of debris to feed into the portal. Not only could I disassemble stuff, but there were also numerous buildings full of junk. The main issue was transporting it. I hoped the weather and vehicles would hold out until we could afford nano vehicles.

Jason must have felt the same way. When they were not transporting construction supplies, they were stacking debris piles around the portal building. Talking to the people working on the projects was a relief. They felt like the people I had left behind. Most of them just wanted to make things work and were far less interested in politics than the council. The exceptions were the college students. Most of them wanted to return to their families, and they were overrepresented on the work crews, so I heard about that frequently. It was also clear that word had spread that we needed to clear the aliens to reach Portland, and there were numerous questions about my plans for that.

I left at four to do the next round of construction, but things were wrapping up anyway. With the light fading at four, all work other than building the custom houses shut down. Those used pre-apocalyptic lights to keep working as long as it was not too cold.

I had sufficient resources to add another windmill and water tower. That maxed out my pod slots, so now I needed the next build to be my second apartment block. I also set aside a portion of the power generation to charge the batteries, making their power storage off-limits for use without my approval. I remembered the cold snaps that spiked our power usage back home and wanted to have the windmill batteries charged while it was not too cold. Saving up 770 power units would take a few days, and it was best to do it while we could.

While I was getting that all set up, I received a notification about completed research. Klawock and Ketchikan had completed their first research since I left, and I pulled up all the research for review. I had not looked at it because conducting research here was low on my priority list. Now that there had been an upgrade, I needed to track the research track's current status.

Purchased Research

- Improved resource generation. The selected blueprint will produce 1% more of the selected resource (1% more than the maximum amount for variable resource generation)
  - Large Windmill Blueprint Level 10. First added effect: each windmill has a battery with half its production capacity.
  - Large Water Tower Blueprint. Level 10. First added effect: each water tower has a small hydropower effect, adding 25 units of power production.
- Improved resource utilization. The selected blueprint will require 1% fewer material units to build. Cost 50 research tokens for Level 1
  - Apartment Block Blueprint Level 10. First added effect: each apartment block has a two-unit basement level, expanding its capacity by ten people
- Medical Pod Improvement. Medical pods will be 1% more effective. Level 10. First added effect: treatment options will be shown, and any number can be selected.
- Improved insulation: The selected blueprint will require 1% less electricity due to superior insulation. Cost 50 research tokens for Level 1
  - Greenhouse Complex. Level 10. First added effect: each greenhouse includes a basement that houses ten workers.
  - Large Custom House. Level 10. First added effect: each large custom house's base and maximum supported temperature is increased by ten degrees.

The large custom house insulation was new and had been upgraded to Level 10. In addition to the minor power savings, it could now withstand colder temperatures. We knew the custom houses were not as cold-resistant as pure nanostructures, so it was good to see they were improving. It also meant the houses would operate at baseline temperatures longer before increasing the power load. Even better, it meant that the people back home had to be doing well. If there were issues, they would not be focused on research. With proof that my friends were doing okay, I was in a good mood the rest of the night.

I was still smiling in the morning, to the point that people asked me about it over breakfast. I was happy to explain why I was in a good mood. Talking about home and the benefits of research was always a good thing. From there, I headed out to gather resources and continue the portal's remote processing.

By the time I was done, I had enough to build a second apartment and free up more pod slots. Unfortunately, my large stock of material units had been depleted, and I was down to just 52. It reverted to being the bottleneck, just as it was back in Klawock. The few days of having more than I could use had been nice, though.

5

"We're hitting a wall on nano construction," I said to the group around me. "We're low on material units, and there's only one way I know to address that quickly. How soon can we meet with everyone so I can tell them the plan?"

Since the portal room was nearby when I announced this, Donna felt safe splitting off to start hunting for people while I made my way inside. She did make me promise to stay inside while she set everything up. She warned me it could take a few hours to gather everyone, and I let her know I would stay inside working on my plan. She could let me know when everyone was available to meet after she had found them all.

Once inside, at a table in the corner, I pulled out my tablet. Before I did anything, I pulled up my personal information to check my status, then used the nano matrix I had looted from the aliens we killed right after I teleported in. It gave me five personal tokens, and I used four of them on the boosted materials perk. With two more ranks, ten more material units were generated per day. That alone would not make a huge difference. It was a start, though, and if I could get 27 more personal tokens, I could raise the boosted materials and boosted stamina perks to level 20.

"That's another 60 material units daily if I can do that," I muttered to myself. "An extra apartment every week would make a difference, and maybe I could even push that higher."

I switched to running numbers to figure out the best way to speed things up by focusing on converting buildings, since they only needed settlement tokens. There was a lot of mumbling coming from me, but no one bothered me until Donna returned and let me know the council would meet in an hour.

"Perfect, and you'll be here too, right?" I asked. "This is going to affect you, in a good way, if you want it to. It's just that I want to tell you all at once, if that's alright?"

"As long as you keep me out of the politics," she answered. When I shrugged at that, she sighed but did not say anything else.

I knew her husband was working on building the two houses for conversion, and her kid was waiting for his turn in the medical pod. Having her whole family involved seemed to make her more agreeable to supporting whatever I was trying to do. I would try to keep her out of politics, but I had a feeling she would be key to the future, and politics would follow.

After the council arrived, I laid out the issue with the material units. "Even at this speed, I can probably save you all," I said as I wrapped up my presentation. "It's just too slow when I think about all the other places that need me. The easiest way I know to speed things up is to increase my perks, and to do that, I need to take out more of the aliens to collect their nano matrices."

"That's easier said than done," O'Donnell said. "We don't want to throw away people fighting them and their golems. We don't even know how many of them there are or what powers they have."

"Vlad and I know a lot about them, and as to fighting them, I have the solution for that. The primary use of the spheres I brought and the ones I collected here is to infuse people with nanoparticles and grant them a class," I said. I let the uproar die down before I continued. "Right now, the only class I can grant is the enforcer class. It's more focused on police activity, but it can also make fighting the aliens a lot easier. I have enough spheres to create three enforcers, which would be a good strike force when you include Vlad and me."

"What 'powers' does this class get, and how dangerous is getting the class?" O'Donnell asked.

"It's not dangerous at all. I have to scan people to see if they are compatible, and not very many are. It seems that around 3% of those tested even qualify. If someone is a match and we have the spheres, they can be infused. That can be a painful one-hour process depending on how good a match they are," I said.

"They all get a skill that will point them toward criminals based on community beliefs. It also works to find aliens in range," Vlad added. "The other skill allows them to incapacitate a criminal once per day. As they defend the settlement, they can grow their perk points as well. Devin has to complete quests for perk points, but they need to eliminate threats. The other route to go is that any person with a class can use a nano matrix to absorb perk points."

It took an hour to hash out the plan for creating enforcers. The fact that I was the only one who could run the tests and could test only six people per hour made things complicated. I had to repeatedly tell them I would be the only one able to test people or grant classes until I left and passed control over to someone else.

The additional information that one of the people granted a class would be in charge of the portal, nano construction, and granting classes when I left made the debate over whom to test worse. They understood the need for a class holder, so buying nanostructures after I left just cost double what I paid instead of four times as much. At the same time, that meant none of the council members could have that power unless they qualified for a class and were willing to fight the aliens.

That led to an argument over who got the class. The council members wanted their respective people to be the only options to take over when I left. I had to push back on their plans on who to assign to the enforcer class. We needed to see who was interested and qualified first. Since the testing also involved a power draw, we agreed to three days of testing with 35 tests per day. That would be about seven hours of my time per day and 350 power units.

Tempers were still raw, but we had a plan, so Erin spoke up in the first lull. "You said this was the easier way. What are the other options?"

"You could have more people working on custom houses. They don't take material units, just settlement tokens, and those are easier to scale up production on," I said. "The other option is more research to reduce building costs. The apartment blocks are just 450 material units instead of 500, thanks to research back home in Alaska. Research tokens take pod time, though, so we need to depend on Klawock and Ketchikan to help with that. They just upgraded the custom houses to handle cold even better for less power, but I'm not sure what they will work on next."

I answered a few more questions about the research process and got their commitment to start three more houses today. They had wanted to wait to see how the integration process worked, but I had convinced them we could not wait to throw more people at construction. While they started planning who to have me test, I moved to a corner of the room that would be good for testing.

I used the last of our material units to build the class testing pod and asked Donna to get inside. Of the 105 tests I agreed to run over the next three days, the council would select 100 people to take the test, and I would select five. My slots were being used for Donna and her two guards, who had been protecting me, and two more slots I had not yet picked.

"You're sure this is safe," she asked as she got in the pod.

"I've tested hundreds of people back home. There were no issues at all," I answered. "I'm really hoping all three of you are a match, as we work well together."

When she nodded, I triggered the pod cycle, and most of the people in the building crowded to watch. Over the ten minutes it took, they wandered off because there was nothing to see during the testing.

"Congratulations," I told Donna as the lid opened, and she got out. "It shows that you have a 93% match. That's enough to get the class."

After the two other guards congratulated her, the next one got in. The council members left after that to start getting the rest of the people I would be testing. As they left, I messaged Vlad privately. I had figured out how to make our private conversations look more like a text chain than pop-up messages.

That seems a little too convenient, right? I wanted someone I trusted to qualify, and she does. I'm not complaining, but what are the odds?

The odds are horrible, he responded. *Your nano density is likely increasing, and Donna has already been around you for an extended period of time. You can't change the rules, but you can nudge things. I don't know for sure, but it's likely you influenced her chances of becoming an enforcer. I can't confirm that, though.*

Great, so that means I can warp reality now. Let's keep that to ourselves, I messaged back while keeping my expression neutral.

You may have a minor influence on probability in your vicinity when the conditions are right, Vlad responded. *But close enough. I agree we should not discuss it aloud until we know more.*

While I was talking to Vlad and getting the guard into the pod, Donna collected herself and started asking questions about the class, what it would mean to get it, and what it would be like to travel with me to face the aliens.

"I have to talk to my family," she finally said. "It's not a decision I can make by myself."

"Of course. And we won't even start discussing who gets the three slots until the three days of testing are done, so you have time. I want someone I know and trust in the group, but it's your call. There is real danger in taking the class and fighting the aliens. You'll also be away for some extended periods hunting aliens until this group of them gets cleared out."

Neither of the other guards proved a match for the class, and the council was still arguing over who would be on the list. That meant I had a few hours free to check in on the construction of the custom houses. Bryan was already busy getting the next three houses started, but he promised the first two would be ready in two days. I made a note to have the 50 settlement tokens ready to integrate both houses as soon as both crews completed them. I hoped that after they saw the houses ready for occupancy, they would increase the number of work crews. They were really slacking compared to back home, after accounting for population size. The good news was that they were following the plans well, and the two houses nearing completion matched what I remembered back home.

Two hours of checking on progress while staying out of the way was enough time spent that I could head to the apartment block for an early communal lunch. The meals were not particularly healthy, but there were enough calories in what they were scrounging together from supplies to keep people up and moving. It would be at least another week before any of the food-producing buildings started supplementing meals. Even then, the current buildings would only supply enough food for one meal per person every week and a half, and that was after a full ramp-up.

"We might have to figure out how to build a custom greenhouse," I muttered to Vlad as I finished eating.

Before Vlad or anyone else could answer, a runner showed up at my table to let me know the council had picked the first 30 people and was forming them up for testing in the portal building. I turned in my dirty dishes and headed back to start the testing. With 30 people to test, it would take more than five hours, and I wanted to get them done before it got too late.

"Is this everyone?" I asked Erin when I got to the testing pod. When she said it was, I asked Vlad to keep track of people, as I would not remember all the faces. "Who's first?"

When no one answered, I picked a person at random and told them to get in. "If you can organize yourselves, I'll follow that order. If not, I'll pick people at random," I said. "This is a long, boring process, and I want to get through it as soon as possible."

The factions within the group were clear to see. People were clumped together, and it looked like each council member had picked three to five people for this round of testing. When the first guy was done, I let him know he was not a match and selected another person at random, as they still had not agreed on the order.

I made small talk with Erin as I cycled through the scans. Toward the end of the scanning, Eric, a 22-year-old senior at the local college, was the second person after Donna to qualify for the class. He was one of the people whose family were down in Portland. He was ready to become an enforcer and start fighting aliens immediately.

"We told you that decisions on who will be selected to get the first three slots will come at the end," Erin said as he asked to get his class right away. "There are six more people to get scanned today. Seven, if you count me, plus the next two days. We'll figure it out after that."

"Whatever, you know I'll be a good choice," Eric said before heading over to his friends, who were congratulating him.

"Sorry about that," I told Erin. "I thought you were here to oversee the process and chat, not to get scanned. I wouldn't have made you wait so long if I had known that's why you were here."

"Getting details on how this all works and your thoughts on the settlement was a good use of time, and got me out of a stack of paperwork," she said. "I don't mind going last. Your arrival has given us hope, but it's also given me a lot more work to handle."

The rest of the scanning was uneventful, and no one else qualified for the class. As we were wrapping up, I pulled Donna aside and asked her to pick people for my other two slots. I wanted to test people she would want to work with if she took the class. We both knew that the odds were against either of the people she picked being a match, but I wanted to give her a chance to have input.

With almost no material units left, I did not bother to collect resources that evening. I planned to do that in the morning when I would have the resources to build something. I also told people I would test 20 more candidates in the morning and 20 in the afternoon. With the candidates Donna was selecting, we would get through 75 people total by the end of day two. That left only 30 for the last day. I planned to have time available to test a few more people if we did not have three options identified by the end of the planned testing.

The following morning, when I collected resources, I decided to use them to buy three more windmills. We had two more days of testing, and then the 50 power units per enforcer we created to cover. We also had some custom houses coming online that would increase the grid's power draw. With the slower building going on, we were getting plenty of work units from the pods, so all the new ones were set to generate settlement tokens, and I switched two of the work-unit generating pods back to tokens, too.

The windmills I had added stretched my range to the two houses I could integrate, and even though that left them isolated, I converted the cheaper one. Not only was it more expensive to convert these houses than to integrate houses built to the blueprints, but it also added to the maintenance backlog. I still had a few days before I needed to switch some pods over to addressing that backlog, but it was growing.

"There is a large nano signature on the south side of town toward the syndicate," Vlad said to the group that had followed to watch me integrate the house. "I know people have pulled away from this side of town because of the alien presence, and people here should be more careful. You should also ensure that the residents of this house can defend themselves. Once enforcers are created, one of them should live here."

"Vlad's right. It's hopefully not a huge risk in the few days before we take the fight to them, but it's good to be ready for anything. I'll integrate the neighboring house before the end of the day. If you are doubling up, that's space for 72 people, that's warm with bathrooms and kitchens. They don't all need to be armed guards, but some should be. Everyone here should be keeping an eye out."

With my work done there until I collected more tokens, I headed back to set up testing the morning group of candidates. None of them qualified, not even the two friends Donna had brought to get tested. The afternoon round of testing went just as poorly, but a group was gathering in the bay with me as I wrapped up. These were some of the people moving into the second house I was going to integrate next. A lot of the new residents were already staged at the house I converted in the morning, but the rest were going down with my guards and me.

"Give me 15 minutes to circle the area and collect the tokens I need to convert your house, and then we can all head down," I called out.

I converted two more pods to tokens as I looked ahead to the next day and the additional houses to be integrated in the park. Then we headed out as a group in the fading light.

Despite my warnings about the dangers, some families with younger children were in this group. There were plenty of people to guard the building, but I was still surprised to see any children. Their excitement as they all watched the blue light of the nanomachines pass over their new house while I converted it was refreshing, though.

As soon as I said it was complete, people started rushing inside to stake out their living space and get things set up. The rest of us made our way back through the snow. I needed to add some water towers to clear the snow in this area as well.

The excitement from adding the new house lasted until I got back to the portal bay, where Joey was waiting to demand another clinic.

"I didn't want to bother you so soon," he said, almost apologetically. "It's just that the pods are finding way more issues to fix than we thought. The four pods are not even enough to make a dent in the number of patients we need to treat. Even when we prioritize critical issues, it feels like we get further behind as we scan each person. We heard you are going to start fighting the aliens. If that causes injuries, we need more medical pods to stay on top of emergencies, let alone get ahead."

When I did not answer right away, he pulled out a stack of papers to prove what he was saying. I let him flip through some of the information because I was curious what they were finding. It looked like the delay in starting treatment compared to Klawock had been long enough to really stack on issues without being so long that the sick population started to succumb to the illnesses.

"This is worse than I had expected. You know everything I need to do is an emergency, but I agree we need to give you more resources," I said. "I can squeeze in two more clinics tomorrow. That will double your pods and clinic space, but that will have to do for a while as I focus on other priorities."

Getting a promise of two more clinics the next day was more than he had hoped for, which made him happy. He left after promising to prepare a more detailed write-up on medical issues and solutions I could take with me on my next mission.

I also checked with the teams working on the houses and confirmed they were on track for a noon integration into the settlement the next day. These houses were safer because of their location. They would take in families of workers who were currently in marginal housing. The council followed my advice and shifted people around to shutter the marginal housing as quickly as possible. We needed to get people out of the buildings using more resources to keep them warm.

I made a point of spending some time that day hanging out with people while avoiding the local politics. Although I initially hoped to do my job and leave, I realized I needed local roots and to get to know people. Even if I were going to move on soon, seeing people as more than numbers in the town information screen was important. There were also many questions for me, and some people had good ideas to consider.

The big news I learned was that there was one group on the east side of the river with a working greenhouse. If someone had found a way to make a greenhouse work with legacy technology, they could probably design a greenhouse for integration. Since that was high on my priority list, I made a note to ask Donna about a trip over there as soon as possible.

There was also a lot of excitement about the idea of getting a train to Bangor running. Several people had worked on the railroad in some fashion or another. I took down all their names to contact again when we were ready for that effort.

Even with my desire to mingle more, the long day had me worn out before it got too late, and I headed back to bed. I also wanted to give my guards a chance to get a good night's sleep. While I was inside my room, they could take a break.

My building spree in the morning, with two new clinics and a water tower positioned on the way to the houses from the prior day, used up all but 2 of the material units and left me with 47 settlement tokens. That was three shy of what I needed for the two new houses, but I'd be able to collect plenty at noon before I integrated them.

The morning's scans once again turned up no one qualified for the enforcer class. O'Donnell was in this group and took it as a personal affront that he was not qualified for the class when 'some college punk' had qualified. I was glad no one else was around to hear his comment, as it could have caused problems with the other college students waiting their turn to be scanned. I was surprised to see that he and Erin were the only council members willing to risk fighting aliens to get a class.

"We don't even have the three candidates we need yet," I pointed out after he complained about his results. "You all should start thinking about another list of people to scan. I don't want to take on the aliens until I have three enforcers to back me up. Even with three enforcers, we're not attacking the alien base. We can fight their scouts and collect enough spheres to create more enforcers and hopefully get a nano matrix or two for my perks."

"We'll start on the next list. It sounds like we'll need it later, even if you get lucky today," O'Donnell said. "We'll send ten extra people today as well."

Over lunch, I collected the next round of settlement tokens, then headed out to the two completed houses when I got word they were ready. This time, I decided to make it more of a production and boost the morale of the people building these in the cold.

"This first integration is a big deal," I said, straining to make myself heard. As I started talking, people quieted down. "These teams building houses get us around one of the main bottlenecks with the nanotechnology I brought. Without people building houses for integration, you would run out of legacy fuel before there was nano housing for everyone. I know doubling up is going to be crowded, but every person in one of these houses is one more person you don't need to burn your dwindling fuel supply to keep warm. Do what you can to support these teams as they keep building houses as quickly as they can."

That drew an enthusiastic cheer from the crowd for the construction team, and they all looked proud to receive the recognition. I seized the moment and integrated both houses while the cheering continued. The conversion and rush to check out the upgraded houses kept the excitement going as I turned to Bryan.

"Good work. I know that's a tight timeline, even with so many people and the simplification of electric and plumbing thanks to the nano connections."

"It was rough, but I think we can sustain the pace," he said. "I've been talking to the council, and they are giving me all the people and resources I need to get the supplies and build more houses. Our new plan is to grow this group and build three houses instead of two over the next six days. The general plan is to increase the number of houses we build each cycle until we reach our maximum. The other group that is being formed will be doing the same."

"That's perfect. It lets me focus more on food and connecting to other communities to help them," I said. "The more you can build, the better. It's not only planning housing for everyone here but also for the people who will begin migrating in from other areas as word gets out when we contact others."

"I've done the math," Bryan said. "I'm already planning for two hundred houses like this in the first wave, but I think we'll be building them until we run out of supplies."

"That sounds like a plan. I may find someone with a greenhouse blueprint for your teams to build, in addition to the houses. I want to find examples of greenhouse designs that use different materials from those used in current houses. The major concern is finding enough glass," I said.

After dropping that nugget for him to think about, I headed back to start scanning more people. Another college student, Wendy, was a match and scored a 97% compatibility rank, our highest yet. I went ahead and tested the other ten that had been sent across, but none were compatible either. Like Eric, Wendy was all in as soon as she learned she was a match. Once the candidates had cleared out, I found Donna.

"I don't mean to push, but I need to know if you want the role. There are three of you identified. If you want it, I'll push the council to agree to upgrading all three of you tomorrow. If not, I'll keep scanning people until we find a third," I said.

"My family agreed that I should take the chance if no one who was a better match came up," she answered. "In a way, this makes it easier. I don't need to worry about whether someone else will do a better job than I do."

"As long as you're sure. I don't mind testing more people if you're feeling pressured," I said. When she nodded she was sure, I chuckled. "Now for the hardest part. Getting the council to agree to this team. There are going to be a lot of factions less than happy about who got picked this round. Honestly, though, one of the goals is to set up a settlement in Portland. That's where Eric and Wendy want to end up, so it works well to have people ready to take over managing the portal there."

"Have fun with that meeting," Donna said. "I am having dinner with my family. You'll be safe meeting with the council. Well, safe from anything I can protect you from, and I'll be back in the morning to play bodyguard. Don't give my guys trouble in the meantime."

6

There had already been a meeting set to discuss the new enforcer selection after the testing was completed, and this one was being held in the council's old meeting room. It went against my desire to be open about stuff, but it made sense this time. We were likely to discuss the candidates in more detail, and I didn't want anyone to feel attacked by what was said during the meeting.

"Well, the good news is we found three people who can be enforcers," I said as I sat down. "I was worried for a while today, but it looks like the 3% average compatibility continues to be a good estimate."

"Do we really want something this important to be left to chance like that, with no choice?" O'Donnell asked. "I'm sure they are fine people, but we're effectively just taking people at random with only three choices."

Most of the heads were nodding, except Daryl, who knew that two of the three were college students, so his group was overrepresented. Erin was neutral, which gave me hope that this could be resolved without dragging on for hours.

"They all seem competent, and I don't want to drag this process on. We still need to spend tomorrow giving them the class, then time to train together. Each day we waste looking for more people, with no promise that we find any that are a better choice, is another day without the bonus material units," I said before targeting my argument. "A two-day delay potentially costs us more than enough resources for another clinic. Seven and a half days is enough time for another apartment block. Every day we delay is also another day where they can mount an attack against us or one of the other communities around here."

The comment about the medical team was enough to get Joey nodding, and Erin started nodding too when the apartment block was mentioned. I knew she was getting a lot of complaints about housing. Everyone wanted to live in the fancy new places that were warm and had running water.

"And the selections are not entirely random. They are listed as viable candidates because of nano compatibility, which means they have the potential to be good enforcers," Vlad added.

"Would one more day really hurt?" O'Donnell asked. "While I'm sure these people are fine. A little more variety and a wider age range would help. We are making these people de facto police, and two of them don't even really live here. I think it should be the council's choice, not Devin's. Unless he's trying to take control of the community."

"It can be my choice and have nothing to do with taking over the community. It's not like these are the last of the enforcers. I'll keep testing twenty or so people a day as long as I'm not out on a mission. With any luck, this first group will begin collecting more spheres and be ready to add more enforcers. We need at least eight to mount an attack safely, or as safe as we can be. If I keep testing people, you all can use those results to make a list of whom to activate once we collect enough spheres. With three slots right now, someone is going to feel left out no matter how many days I spend scanning people," I said.

The argument dragged on for another 15 minutes, but my openness to continuing the scanning and creating five more enforcers, when we had the spheres, was enough to tame much of the opposition.

"I'd agree with you if these were the only three enforcers that were being created, but as Devin said, this is just the start of the process. I will feel much safer as soon as we get more enforcers created," Erin said to O'Donnell as their discussion continued.

People kept talking for a few more minutes, but as soon as it was clear O'Donnell's side had lost the majority, he quickly gave in. It was clear he did not want to be on the losing side of an argument, so he quickly claimed credit for the compromise. As long as I got what I wanted, I let him claim his credit.

"So, we're agreed," I said. "I'll grant Donna, Eric, and Wendy the enforcer class tomorrow. That's three hours and a lot of power, so I'll only do 15 scans after lunch. Then I'll do 20 scans each day I'm here, starting the day after, as long as we don't need power due to a cold snap. I will let you know each day when to have the people there for testing the next day."

It was a close thing, but I managed not to roll my eyes when O'Donnell thanked me for agreeing to their terms and being so agreeable. I had to wonder if his grandstanding fooled anyone on the council or if he just did it out of habit. Either way, I would not delay the meeting's end by pointing out that they were the ones agreeing with me. I said goodbye and headed out after ensuring Daryl would let Eric and Wendy know to meet me at the pod the next day.

As I headed back to my room, I pondered the next steps. I had not decided if it was worth spending 400 settlement tokens to buy two communication devices. Having them when we headed south to face the aliens would make me feel better, but it would be a huge drain on our build-out. I needed to get more pods and more buildings. Any equipment I buy now would slow down our long-term buildup. Still, dying because we could not ask for help would slow things down as well.

I would ask the team once we started training, but I was leaning towards waiting for any equipment. I added it to my list of things to pack when I was done here and heading to the next mission, though. I wanted to start with them next time.

In the morning, I collected resources as usual, but I just built one more windmill. I placed it on the edge of the river so I could potentially extend the settlement to the greenhouse I wanted to look at. I decided to save up material units for a greenhouse or an apartment block, which is why I limited my build. I needed to assess whether manually constructed greenhouses were a viable option before deciding what to build next.

By the time all that was done and I had eaten, my three enforcer candidates were waiting for me near the class pod. They all looked somewhat nervous, but also excited.

"Have you decided who's going first?" I asked after exchanging greetings and a bit of small talk. "It's an hour per person, so we'll be here all morning."

"I'm pulling rank and going first," Donna said as she moved toward the pod.

I was not sure what rank she had to pull, but the other two did not protest, although Eric looked annoyed. Most of the council was present to watch the process. At least they were standing back and not crowding too closely, except for Daryl, who was talking to Wendy and Eric. I could not decide if he was oblivious to the politics of clarifying to everyone that his faction had come out on top in the enforcer selection, or if he was making a point. I decided not to worry about it and focused on making sure Donna was ready.

"As I warned you, it will be somewhat painful. Everyone back home felt some level of pain, even though they were asleep during the process. You can plan on eating a lot and sleeping a lot the rest of today, and we'll start training tomorrow."

"It's all taken care of. My husband is home with extra food for me and took the day off. I'll be heading back there as soon as this is over. He's keeping Alex at home because we didn't want him to witness the process in case I react badly to it. You'll have to stay out of trouble today with me at home and not guarding you," Donna said as she got into the pod.

I waited until she was settled, then triggered the class infusion cycle. I checked my sphere count, then monitored the process closely for a few minutes. Everything looked normal, so I pulled out my tablet to get some work done.

"You all are welcome to stick around, but that's the extent of the excitement," I said loudly enough for everyone to hear.

"The nano infusion is at a subatomic level that humans couldn't see even with a microscope," Vlad added. People had grown more comfortable with him, and he was happy to share knowledge.

Donna and Eric both got the enforcer class without issue and headed off to recover. Wendy's process was going fine, but halfway through, I got a message from Vlad, who was back out scouting. We were worried that the aliens had been so quiet since that first fight.

We've got a problem here, he said. *If I'm reading the signs right, a storm is moving in, and it's a big one that will plunge temperatures far below the current normal. We've got about 12 hours before it really picks up, but people should start preparing now.*

How sure are you? I asked as I looked around. All the council members had realized how boring this was and left, except Daryl. I would need to use him to trigger the settlement's reaction to the incoming storm.

As sure as I can be for an alien hologram who has only been monitoring the weather here for six days. So, pretty sure, Vlad

said.

Even through the text message, I could hear the snark. He was clearly developing a stronger personality over time.

"Daryl," I called. "Vlad's been monitoring the weather, and he thinks there's a big storm coming. We've got about 12 hours until it hits, so people need to start preparing. I'd recommend increasing the number of people in the completed nanostructures to three times the normal number. Also, let Jason know we need to use the processing portal's capacity at midnight when it refreshes, not in the morning. I'll use that to make another apartment block, so you should have people ready to move in. The storm should not be too bad at that point, and that will protect over 300 more people if they triple up while the storm is here."

As soon as he hurried off, I turned to one of my guards and instructed him to go talk to Donna and Eric. With the storm coming, I planned to open up my room to the three new enforcers and Donna's husband, and son. I knew none of them had nano housing yet, and this would ensure they were protected and that we could plan and train if we were all stuck indoors due to the storm.

Everyone in the portal bay had heard me talking, and I spent the rest of the time giving advice while I was waiting for Wendy's process to end. I was telling her the plan after she got out of the pod when the entire council showed up, following Daryl. Wendy took one look at them and hurried off to get her essentials and move them to my room.

"How accurate is this forecast?" Erin said as soon as she was close enough to talk without yelling. "We have not had a really bad cold snap compared to our normal winter yet, but from what Daryl said, we need to get ready."

"There's always some guesswork in a forecast, but he's got the best senses for detecting changes in the atmosphere, and he's our only supercomputer that can crunch all the data. Like I told Daryl, you should plan to fill all the nanostructures to triple capacity. It will be tight, and tempers will fray, but if I add an apartment block at midnight, we can get almost 1,600 people into housing that can handle the cold with no issues."

"Any other advice?" O'Donnell asked. I was glad to see he

was focused on the issue at hand and not the posturing from the day before. "It sounds like you've been through this before."

"Stockpile at least three days of food where everyone will be staying. Places without kitchens need ready-to-heat-and-eat meals. Plan to limit medical travel, so have the next few rounds of patients in the clinics to rotate into the pods as needed. If the weather allows, you can schedule people to spend up to eight hours at a time here in the portal room to stay warm, but make sure they are not living here. Oh, and use the nano heater that the construction workers have been using after they finish work today. They will not be working if the storm is as bad as Vlad thinks it will be," I said as people nodded along.

"We'll get people moving around and clear out the most problematic housing still in use," Erin said. With the return of power, she had a tablet instead of a notebook and was taking notes on it. "I'm thinking we have this be a permanent move for people. They'll stay crowded until new housing opens. They would have been next up for new housing anyway."

"Don't forget there will be no more class testing until this is over," I added. "We've been running near baseline power with the current temperature, which draws about 1,100 power units daily. With production running at 2,000 units per day, there was not enough excess power to charge the batteries, power legacy devices, and run the tests. Power usage spikes as the temperature drops. We could easily reach 2,500 power units per day. Worst case is a maximum power draw of 4,000 units, and we're nowhere near producing that."

I outlined the plan to charge the batteries and then live off the power they produced for as long as possible. Once demand exceeded production, the nanostructures would start lowering the temperature to 55 degrees or even lower before tapping into the batteries. There were also the 500 power units I was setting aside for legacy heating systems.

"If it's really cold and stays that way, I'll be building more windmills every day to supplement our power. After a certain level of cold, it's a safer way to save people than building new structures that people have to go outside to move into," I wrapped up by saying. "We've got some warning, and you have dramatically more resources than last week. Take the time to get everything done without panicking. This is survivable with minimal losses if we do it right."

I held Jason back to let him know I planned to use my remote portal absorption right at midnight, if the cold was not too bad. If it were too cold, we might just be processing his stack of materials for a few days. By the time I was done talking, the bay had pretty much cleared out as people headed out to prepare for the cold.

When I got back to my room, it was a mess. The guard who had gone to talk to Donna had taken one of my keys, so a crowd was setting up the room. Everyone was there, except Donna's husband. They were all trying to arrange people's stuff. I grabbed some of my supplies and took them upstairs to stash out of the way in a corner of the greenhouse so everyone's essentials could fit in the room. It was still tight, and I was worried people would complain. Thankfully, when I returned, people were in high spirits.

"Thank you for this. Having somewhere warm for Alex while this is going on makes it all easier," Donna said as she tucked him into a sleeping bag on the lower bunk. "Larry went back to work. They want to get as much done on the houses as possible before it gets too cold."

"We'll make it work. I'll be up and around a lot, but I'll try to work around whatever bed rotation schedule you all set up," I said. "Managing power and heat during a storm takes a lot of time and monitoring, but we have time to make some plans. The other thing I had not brought up is that taking a class improves your resistance to cold. The four of us will be the emergency squad if something happens during the storm and it's too cold for other people to go out."

"I wondered about that," Wendy said. "I felt warmer on my way over, but thought it was all in my head. How much colder can we handle?"

"It's not on the information we can see, and it was never quantified back home. As far as we can tell, it's at least 10 degrees of protection and will increase as you level up your perks. I can handle some real cold now. It still doesn't feel good, but won't harm you as fast," I said.

I let them keep talking as I reviewed the settlement

information. I had been ignoring maintenance, but it was creeping up quickly, and I knew it would spike as we overloaded all the buildings. I had a few minutes until noon and switched six pods from producing work units to addressing the maintenance that did not require material units to fix. The plan was to defer the 37 points of material maintenance until we could spare the material units. For now, I could get ahead of the 92 units of regular maintenance before it grew too high.

As I traveled around updating the pods, it was refreshing to see people crowding into buildings. There were beds in the greenhouse area, in the halls, and elsewhere. There were already some frayed tempers and shouting, but that calmed down when people noticed me. I tried to bolster morale, but it seemed more like people feared me than were motivated by me.

I spent the rest of the afternoon and evening checking the legacy structures connected to the power grid and setting rules for how much power each building could draw for heating. There was not enough power for any of the legacy buildings to rely on it as their only heat source, but it would augment their other heating systems. The roughest moments were when people asked about families in other towns and whether I could help them handle the cold. I had to tell them it would be awhile before I could do anything for them. Not everyone had let themselves acknowledge what a cold snap meant, but enough realized that if it were a really rough cold snap, it would mean many deaths in places without nanotechnology.

Just before midnight, I made my way to the building I was slowly disassembling via the processing portal. I had worked my way through a lot of it. I figured there were just three or four days left, and then it would be cleared out to make room for new buildings. After this one was done, I was switching to smaller buildings that could improve access to other open spaces. It was already noticeably colder, and the snow had been falling softly for a couple of hours. Combined with the wind, it looked like Vlad's prediction was accurate.

I collected all the resources from the pods and headed to the park's east side to place the third apartment block. That did not leave me enough material units to build anything else, but if needed, I could build three or four more windmills the next day.

That gave us some buffer if the cold got worse too quickly.

As soon as the apartment was built, I helped people move in. There were a lot of mattresses and supplies to carry over. It had all been staged in the portal bay, and there were cars packed with stuff outside waiting for the word that the building was ready. Moving 330 people into a new home with their supplies to live for at least a few days, along with food and other necessities, was no small task in the best of times. At midnight, in the snow and wind, with temperatures dipping below negative 40 degrees, it was nowhere near the best of times.

By the time the move was completed, it was three in the morning, and I had used two of my three healing perk charges already to deal with extreme cases of frostbite. I was worn out and hoped I had a place to sleep. There had been a lot of drama moving people in, and that wore me out faster than all the work it took to move them.

"You're back," Donna said quietly outside the door to my room. She and Eric were leaning against the wall, looking bored. "We both woke up around midnight and are mostly recovered from getting the class. Larry worked until they shut down the site, so he's got the lower bunk with Alex. Wendy has been asleep, but she should have recovered by now. Kick her out of the top bunk and get some rest. You're looking pretty rough."

I did not argue and headed into my room. Wendy was awake and climbed out of her sleeping bag before pushing it to the side of the bed. "These are your sheets, and we have been using sleeping bags, so they're clean," she whispered before heading out into the hallway.

I nodded. Seeing my bed, exhaustion kicked in, and I barely remembered to set an alarm before crawling into bed and passing out.

It was not my alarm that woke me up, but the first audible notification I had ever received from the nano interface. As soon as I woke up, Vlad was there as well. I forgot other people were in the room and cursed loudly enough to wake Larry and Alex, even though it was just two hours later, at five a.m.

WARNING

The Large Crafting Bay is being utilized as living quarters. Rectify the situation before the timer expires, or the structure will be deleted, and half the construction resources will be returned to the Architect.
14:03

"Sorry, guys," I said to Larry and Alex, as I jumped down and pulled on my outer clothes. "Some people are causing problems, and I need to take care of them. I'll try to be quiet when I get back."

"Most likely, someone is sleeping in the crafting bay," Vlad said as we exited the room. "Whoever fell asleep first is triggering this."

"Throw on your jackets and follow me," I said to all three enforcers who were just outside the room, talking quietly so as not to disturb the people sleeping in the hallway. "Some idiots are sleeping in the crafting bay, and we have 13 minutes to wake them up before the whole thing disappears around them."

They followed me to the vestibule and were getting coats on, but I left without them. The timer was counting down in the corner of my vision. We could not afford to lose the crafting bay in the middle of this storm. We could not lose it at any time, actually, but losing it now would kill people.

I slammed the door to the crafting bay open and turned the lights up to their maximum brightness, ignoring the complaints that it caused.

"Wake up whoever is sleeping in here and keep them awake," I yelled. "I warned you all that this was not a place for sleeping. In ten minutes, this whole place will vanish if people keep sleeping, and I don't have the resources to rebuild it."

I was looking around as I talked, but it was pretty clear where the guilty parties were. There was a group around a table in the back, clearly trying to wake someone sleeping under it without being noticed. I made a beeline for them as soon as I saw them.

I made it there just in time to see two people trying to slide into chairs around the table without being noticed. I realized I might be in a bad mood after being woken up with less than two hours of sleep, but I figured making an example of them might keep it from happening again.

"So, you two are the reason I got woken up after two hours of sleep. I was up all night moving 300 more people into a new building, and you numbskulls tried to sleep here. I got this alert with sound and everything, waking me up with a warning that this entire building would vanish because it was being used as living quarters. You realize how bad that would be, right?" I said. At this point, everyone in the room was glaring at them, and Donna was coming up behind me with the others.

"Look, man, I didn't think it was a big deal. We were tired, and it was not our turn for a bed. We thought you were being a jerk with these rules," one of the culprits said. "We didn't know it was real. We won't do it again."

"It's not his rule," Vlad said. "The nano controller enforces the rules to maintain the nano density required to save your planet. This space allows you to spread out, get access to more bathrooms, and avoid the cold. You all need to make sure it does not vanish because some 'numbskulls' think they can ignore the rules."

Despite everything, I had to fight back a smile at Vlad's attempt to make "numbskulls" sound normal. Laughing was not the vibe I was going for here. Before I could say anything else, Donna spoke up.

"During this cold snap, Eric, Wendy, and I will take shifts here. We'll make sure no one is sleeping, and people are rotating in and out of the building on schedule," she said. "If the storm drags on, it will get harder for people to stay awake, so we'll be here to help keep things running smoothly and make sure no more alerts go out."

"Thanks, if you've got this, I am heading back to bed," I said, giving one last glare at the people who woke me up. "Is it cool if I sleep until noon, then someone else can have the bunk?"

Eric said he was next in line for a bed, and it was fine if I used some of his time, so I headed out. The comment about sharing a bed hopefully drove home how much we were all squeezed in, even the guy providing the nanotechnology.

"You know, you never explained what would happen if we misused the buildings," I told Vlad in the vestibule as I took off my outer layers. "It would have been nice to know there were alerts like that."

"I was not sure how it would work," he said. "Also, I'm sure you noticed, but the cold and wind are still getting worse. Interior temperatures have dropped to 61 degrees and will continue to fall to maintain power across the system. Based on current readings and my projections, temperatures in buildings will drop to 48 degrees before you can build more windmills at midnight. Also, the population has dropped by 14 people."

On the one hand, it seemed like people were always dying no matter what I did to save them. I knew these numbers were an improvement, but there would likely be more deaths as the cold set in. It was tough to push it aside, but there was nothing I could do right now. Plus, I needed to be alert to do anything, so I headed to bed and hoped the conditions would not worsen much while I slept.

I woke up once that morning when Larry and Donna swapped spots. I knew Alex slept a lot because of his medical issues, so he would be sleeping during both his parent's shifts. While I was awake, I checked for any glaring issues and went back to sleep.

By the time I woke up at noon and handed the bed over to Eric, it was approaching negative 60 degrees outside and 53 degrees inside. Everyone was bundled up in the hallway, and I was wishing we could use the showers instead of turning them off to save power. I also saw that another 16 people had died while I was asleep. The one piece of good news was that we had not tapped into the batteries yet. We would have enough power to maintain minimal heat until I could build more windmills.

Wendy was over in the crafting bay, so that left Larry to talk to. He had many questions about what his wife would be doing and how safe she would be. I tried to reassure him honestly, but the whole time I was hoping I was not contradicting anything she had told him. I was not sure if she had painted a rosier picture of things than I had. Once we ran out of things to talk about, I wandered the building, answering general questions and encouraging people to keep their tempers and annoyance in check. Most of the people sleeping in weird places would have been in a colder, legacy house, so reminding them how much better they had it, despite the crowding, seemed to work most of the time.

7

By early evening, the weather was still worsening, but the cooling was slowing, so I hoped that meant we were nearing the end of it. Unfortunately, the deaths kept creeping up, even with all the advances I had brought to the city. At least new windmills would help blunt the cold and slow the deaths. I knew many people had already been saved. Unfortunately, it was hard to judge the savings against a hypothetical body count.

As it approached midnight, Jason and his team arrived to start dumping debris into the portal. I talked to him briefly before bundling up to use the remote feature again. Even with our classes, it was bitterly cold for both Donna and me, but I wanted to get that building cleared as soon as possible. Since I had plenty of settlement tokens, we went right from processing to building the four windmills I could afford before heading back inside the crafting bay. Eric was the one currently on watch, ensuring no one was sleeping there.

The council was keeping a member there full-time as well, and it was O'Donnell's turn, so I passed the information on to him. "The four new windmills have stabilized our power usage, and we can get it back up to 57 degrees inside the nano structures while still slowly charging the new batteries. If the temperature stabilizes or starts warming, I'll worry less about the batteries until we get back to normal. I've also increased the energy allocated to the legacy heaters by 25%. Finally, as I warned, the crowding is also upping maintenance, but I focused more pods on that too, so it does not get out of hand."

"Are we messing up your plans by building more windmills?" he asked. "It seems like it's needed right now, but that was not what you were planning to build, was it?"

"No, but we would need them anyway, so it's not a big change in anything but sequencing. Plus, we've had several dozen people die already in this storm, and I'd like to minimize any more of that," I said.

As I talked about the deaths, I saw Donna and Eric's eyes widen. They were against the wall talking quietly, and that had sparked something. I was paying attention to them and saw that Donna was trying to get my attention.

"Sorry, my team needs to talk to me," I told O'Donnell as I walked away. Whatever it was, Donna would have just come over if she wanted him to know about it.

"When you were talking about the deaths, this popped up for me. I was able to share it with Eric, and now you. I think it's because I have been pulsing my detect criminal perk nonstop," she said. "There are a lot of criminals here, by the way, but they feel minor. It's like everyone who's ever stolen something is showing up as vaguely criminal."

I nodded, but was looking at the notification that popped up as Donna was talking.

Augusta Settlement Enforcement Mission
An entity is using the cover of the storm to eliminate residents of the settlement with impunity. Discover where the eliminations are taking place and stop them.

"Damn, from the wording, it could be an alien doing this or someone who lives here, but with the cold, I'm putting money on an alien. Vlad has been patrolling at range around my location, so it's got to be further out," I said. "Eric, go get Wendy and make sure she's bundled up for the cold. The four of us are the ones best suited for this, even if we haven't had a chance to train. Donna and I are going to talk to O'Donnell before he loses his patience and comes over here."

I explained what was going on and that we needed a census map for the southern quadrant to start our search. We would also need two people to watch the bay to ensure no one was sleeping.

"Do you want some of my people to go with you?" he asked as I finished explaining the mission.

"No, we can handle the cold better than people without a class, and we have the skills to take on aliens or their golems. With the number of deaths so far, and some of those likely from the cold, this looks like the work of a small group or one person. Your people might be helpful if it's a human doing this, but we can't count on that," I said.

It did not take long for Wendy to show up, and then we were bundling up. I wanted to start our patrol by checking in on the two custom houses I had integrated in the south. They were some of the closest spots to the aliens. If they were safe, we could use them as a base of operations to scout more of the area.

We had to wait a few more minutes before a runner showed up with a map that O'Donnell passed over to me. I let Vlad scan it, and then the four of us reviewed it before I tucked it away.

"We'll try to check in by noon even if we haven't found anything," I said. "I'll be tracking the energy usage in case I need to adjust anything, but the rules are all in place, and everyone should be fine as long as the temperature doesn't drop too much. Just keep people from despawning this building by sleeping in it. I'll be too far away to come yell at them," I warned.

With that, the four of us headed out into the cold. While we were walking, I let the team know that successful missions usually came with rewards, like perk points. That meant they had something to look forward to besides the cold and danger.

"The cold, danger, and saving people," Donna corrected me.

"You're right. I didn't mean to gloss over that. We're doing all this to make sure humanity as a whole and every person we can help survives not only the cold, but everything else going on," I said. "That's the given, underlying reason for everything we're doing."

While we made our way through the snow towards the two custom houses to the south, Donna was leading the others. She was also coordinating the three of them using their find criminal perk. I added the information I had about that perk, but my primary focus was on explaining the incapacitate criminal perk. We needed to coordinate how we would use it.

"We tested the perk back home. If all four of us use that on the same person at the same time, it still just lasts five minutes. Call it out if you're using it, so we don't waste charges. Between the four of us, that's just seven uses of the perk daily," I said.

Once we passed the range of the water towers, there were several feet of snow to push our way through. I missed the relatively lighter snow load we faced in southeastern Alaska. Not only did the snow here make moving around harder, but everywhere was an ambush point. The golems could hide anywhere, and that kept me on edge. Even with my team using their find criminal perk, I was not convinced they all knew how to use it yet.

None of the enforcers had any strong criminal pings as we made our way to the first custom house and knocked on the door. It took a minute, but the door opened, and we were welcomed inside. I knew most of the people, as I had seen them during the move-in process after I had converted the houses. They said everyone was accounted for, and they would be extra careful until we caught whoever was causing problems.

"We knew we were at risk from the aliens, so we have been careful since we moved out here," the de facto leader said. "We'll be even more careful, but I think we'll be okay."

As soon as we were sure everything was as it should be, we headed to the other custom house. Our conversation was a repeat of the first one, but this time we stayed longer to warm up and plot our next move.

"Based on everything we've heard, I say we go to the southeast and meet up with the Kennebec River. If it is the aliens, they might use the river to move up and down," Donna said. "There are a few holdouts that way we can check in on and make a large circle back to the west and then north. If I had to guess, it would be eight hours in the loop that lets us check a lot of spots and end up back here."

"That should work," I said. "If the storm is still raging, I'll need to get back to the portal at midnight to build more anyway. Hopefully, we can finish this mission quickly, but if not, it's a good starting point."

One of the men in this house was a gossip and could tell us who might be found at the houses we were planning to check. He also gave us a warning. The people further out were more independent and might not react well to being surprised by us in the middle of the storm, despite our good intentions.

When I saw Donna agree, I took the warning to heart, but it did not change what we needed to do. I checked the settlement information. Our population remained steady, and the new windmills were keeping the cold at bay, if not under control. With everyone warmed up and geared up, we headed out into the snow again. It would have been better to do this during the day, but we didn't want to wait that long if it was an attack.

The entire eight-hour loop was a bust when it came to finding any signs of aliens. We stopped at several inhabited houses along our route. There were a few threats when we knocked on their door in the middle of the night, but nothing escalated. We passed on the warning, and I passed out some of the ration bars I could generate at each place to make sure they had some additional emergency supplies.

We found one house where it appeared a family of four had frozen when their stove went out. We spent some extra time there to see if there were any signs of sabotage or tampering, but it all seemed like a tragic accident in the storm.

"I think we need a break," Eric said as we headed back to the custom house we were using as a base. "Do you think they'd let us crash for a few hours before we head back out?"

I had been thinking of heading right back out to make another loop, but from the nods from Wendy, she wanted a break, too. I wanted to keep pushing, but I also knew my perks gave me an advantage, so I agreed we could take a break for a few hours.

The people at the house gave us a hearty lunch. Even with our improved ability to handle the cold, we burned more calories than normal when we were outside. After that, we were assigned a bunk room so the others could take a three-hour nap. They fell right to sleep, but I headed back to the portal to update people there. Donna had pushed back on that, but she needed a break, and I could keep going.

I checked the information sheet as I headed back after briefing the council representative. I had been looking at it frequently, and now that I was paying attention, I saw that the citizen count had dropped by four in quick succession. I asked Vlad to review the map for locations with exactly four residents to the west. We could start our next search there. Even though I had more stamina than the rest of the team, I still needed a quick nap while the rest of the team was asleep. We had a wake-up call from the people in the house planned, so I did not worry about an alarm.

After we got back up and headed out, it only took a little over an hour to find signs of foul play. One of the houses Vlad had flagged to check, based on location, and having four residents, had its wood stove torn out of the wall, leaving a gaping hole.

Both parents had been stabbed in a way I knew was emblematic of the golems, and the two kids, one a toddler and the other a high schooler, were frozen to death. There was an immediate reaction from all of us. An icy determination to make someone pay for this followed the initial feelings of horror.

"This is recent, based on the signs," Vlad said. "It had to be within the last few hours."

That got even more of a reaction. If we had started in this direction, we might have been able to stop it. After a moment, I urged everyone to keep moving and stop speculating.

"We can come back to take care of them and give them the respect they deserve," I said. "We still have some light from the sun making its way through the storm clouds, and the golems are not that smart. I bet we can follow a trail if we start moving, right, Vlad?"

He vanished for a moment before confirming there was a faint trail he could follow. Knowing the attack had not happened all that long ago, this was our best chance to find the perpetrators, and we hurried after Vlad while remaining alert.

"I think I sense them," Donna said after 15 minutes. She pointed in the same general direction that Vlad was leading us. "We're far enough out that I can pick them out, and they are more criminal than the others, I sensed, if that makes sense.

Before I could answer, a golem popped out of a snowbank between Vlad and us.

"I've got it," I said, using one of my incapacitate criminal charges. "Let's try to take it out quietly and keep your eyes open. I can't imagine they only have one of their golems waiting for us."

Instead of guns, everyone used the clubs they were carrying. It was not fast, but it was relatively quiet. Plus, we had five minutes while the golem was incapacitated, so speed was not an issue. Vlad kept watch for any further attacks the whole time, and I backed off to watch the area as well. I did not want to accidentally get the finishing blow, as it would not help me level a perk as it would them.

I watched the area and observed the fight between scans for other attackers. It was surprising how much effort it took to kill a golem with clubs. All three of them were positioned around the golem so they could get in good swings without getting in each other's way. If they had been willing to destroy the sphere, it might have been faster to target that, but we wanted to collect it unharmed. It also seemed these plant-based bodies differed from the ones back home. These could better withstand physical damage, even though they had no real defense against gunfire. That was something to keep in mind as more and more guns failed. I might have to speed up buying nano guns.

"I think I finished it off," Wendy said after they spent a few minutes beating on the golem.

She sounded unsure of how to deal with what had just happened, but they had all done what they needed to. I was glad their first fight was against a plant monster rather than a somewhat human-looking alien. As soon as she spoke, I checked the sphere had appeared on my information sheet. That was absolute proof the target was dead.

"We need to keep moving," Vlad said. "That was not the golem who created the path, so it's likely it was a guard. Even though you were quiet, the aliens might know we're on the way, and we want to catch them before they flee or call for help."

"We didn't get much warning there, buddy," I said to Vlad before he could start scouting ahead.

"It seems I can't sense them if they are in low-power mode and motionless in the snow," Vlad admitted. "You'll have to be more careful. I will still be able to sense any that are active or any of the aliens."

"We did not sense it either," Donna said. "We're still going in the right direction, though, and it feels like we're getting close."

We moved forward, slower now. Not only was it getting darker, but we knew we could no longer depend on Vlad to sense all the golems before they attacked. This whole syndicate group seemed smarter than the aliens back home, and that was not a good thing.

At this point, we were fully out of town with no buildings in sight. That meant the snowdrifts were all over the place, and everywhere could be another ambush point. I was on edge as I tried to look in every direction at once, wondering if I had made the right choice by bringing the team out here so soon.

Then, after over an hour of boredom, everything seemed to

happen at the same time. Vlad yelled a warning about a trap and an alien ahead of us. Donna yelled about something coming up from behind, and snowbanks on either side of us exploded into clouds of snow as two more golems popped out.

My first thought was to target the alien, but it was using trees for cover. I could not see them well enough to lock them down. I swiveled to the golem on my right and was calling it out as I saw a projectile launch from another snowbank. I ignored the golem I had said I was locking down and leaped for Eric, pushing him out of the way of the projectile.

I was not in time and watched as the pole punched a four-inch hole through his upper chest. I tried to use my healing perk on him as I landed next to the body. The perk would not trigger, and it took a few tries to realize he was already dead. It took me valuable seconds to figure it out before I focused back on the fight. Donna and Wendy were shooting at the golem I had failed to lock down. They had locked down the one on the left and the one behind us, but were out of charges on their perk.

"You take care of these. I'm making sure that alien does not have any other tricks up their sleeve," I said as I locked down the other golem.

At the same time, Vlad let us know it was the only trap he had sensed power on, and it just had one shot.

"Guide me to that alien," I said. "I'm not letting anyone else die today."

With that, I started moving, using Vlad's directions to stay out of the alien's line of sight. I was not being stealthy, though. I needed it focused on me, not on what was left of my team. We played a game of cat and mouse for a few minutes while I heard the fight going on behind me. I got hit in the arm at one point and had to heal it. Unfortunately, the perk did not fix my outer gear, so I had to fight the cold seeping in after getting hit.

I think he's out of ammo, Vlad messaged after five minutes of me working my way toward the alien. *He just took off running. Either it's a trap, or he's trying to get away.*

I hesitated for a second. The incapacitate perk was wearing off any golems left, but the sounds of fighting had slowed down, so I guessed they had one left at the most.

"Do you all have it handled?" I yelled behind me. When I got a yes, I started racing after Vlad and toward the fleeing alien. I was willing to take the risk to stop it from getting away.

It just took a few moments before I burst through some trees into a clearing with a hut in the middle of the area. The alien rushed inside, and I slowed down, looking for cover to approach. I did not want to be in the open if he was reloading. I was still looking for a safe path to approach when the alien burst through the suddenly opened door on an exotic-looking snowmobile. I raised my rifle and started taking shots while also successfully using incapacitate on the aliens. The first few shots didn't seem to hit, but the third burst hit both the alien and the snowmobile.

The faint noise from the snowmobile stopped at that point, and the alien remained still. I checked with Vlad to confirm he wasn't sensing anything else and started moving forward. Part of me was hoping the alien was still alive so an enforcer could get the kill. Knowing Eric and at least a few families were dead because of the alien's actions meant I did not have any sympathy for it.

It just took a few steps forward for the nano matrix to appear on my information sheet, which proved the alien was dead. With that nano matrix proof and Vlad's reassurance, I moved toward the snowmobile and body at the same time as Donna entered the clearing and let me know they had killed all three golems, and Wendy was guarding Eric's body. I was not sure it was a good idea to split up like that, but I wanted to check the area before we did anything else, so I said nothing.

Even with the nano matrix, I wasn't sure the alien was no longer a threat. There could be more traps even if it was dead, so I started moving that way. Vlad and I were about 15 feet away when he messaged me. There was an active communication device on the alien, and someone on the other end was listening in. Other than letting me know I needed to be quiet, that changed nothing.

When I got there, I saw a damaged communication device in the alien's hand that looked similar to the ones I could buy. Vlad told me I should destroy it, but I was curious about the aliens. This was my first chance to talk to them without getting attacked, so I picked it up after confirming the alien was dead. I pressed the button to speak and started talking when Vlad yelled for me to throw it.

I reacted instantly. I had learned to follow Vlad's instructions when he yelled like that. The device was barely 20 feet away from me when it exploded and tossed me back into the snow. I went down hard enough that it hurt, but Donna was out of the blast radius and hurried toward me. I took stock of my injuries and used another of my heal charges on myself. I was still sore, but at least I could hear noise again.

"So that's new," I said, sitting up. "I did not know those had bombs in them, or I would not have passed them out to everyone back home. I also feel you could have done more than tell me I should destroy it, Vlad."

"They don't normally, and I was not sure it was trapped," Vlad answered. "That's a special modification they made to ensure their communications were not intercepted, and to take out unsuspecting people like you."

I grimaced, knowing I should have listened to him from the start. Even if part of me wanted to find a way to get along with the criminals without fighting, they kept proving that it was a bad idea.

"So is that it? Just the one alien and his golems?" Wendy asked me as she helped me up.

"It looks that way, but let's loot the hut and see what we can recover. Vlad, can we use the snowmobile, or is it rigged to blow as well?" I asked.

"It's not rigged to explode, but it's been damaged by your shots. I doubt it will move under its own power," Vlad said before leading us into the hut so he could check it out first.

Inside was spartan. It was well-built despite its appearance. It was small, though, with a bed, rations, and a portable heater. It looked like there wasn't even a bathroom, so the alien must have been using nature for that.

The place was small enough that the three of us made sure nothing was missed, and then, when Vlad said the heater and rations were safe, I grabbed them. The rations were not a big deal, but Vlad said I could convert the heater to work with my flavor of nanotechnology for just a few tokens back at base. The snowmobile could also be repaired and converted if we hauled it back into the settlement's range.

"Let's see if we can drag it back to Wendy and decide what to do from there," I said. "It's already dark, and the moon is not providing much light, but we can still somewhat see with what's filtering through the clouds."

We had flashlights, but if we used them, it would take forever for our eyes to readjust to the darkness. It took some effort to get the snowmobile upright. At least the built-in skis were already deployed, making it easy to move despite its size. We put the rations and heater on top before Donna started pulling and steering it while I pushed from behind. Once we built up speed, the hut fell behind us quickly. We had discussed destroying it, but it would make a good base location in the future. We would also know where it was if the aliens were dumb enough to reuse it.

Vlad went ahead to let Wendy know we were coming. She was standing over Eric's body, gripping her gun too tightly and scanning the woods.

"Did you get that bastard that killed Eric?" was the first thing she said as we got close.

"Yeah, we got him. He won't be picking off people in the cold anymore," Donna said before I could answer.

After that, there was an awkward silence, and then we started making plans. Wendy said we were taking Eric's body back like it was a settled fact, and I did not argue. We carefully placed him on the snowmobile and secured him in place. It felt undignified, but it was the best way to get him home. With that taken care of, we started making our way back to the custom houses.

We did not have to watch for attacks as much, although we still worried about golems left behind. Still, even taking turns on watch while the other two moved the snowmobile was tiring, and we moved much more slowly than on our way to the alien. It was past 11 p.m. when we were near the custom houses and finally in range of the settlement.

"Let's take a break here, and I'll see about getting the snowmobile fixed," I said as soon as I got the notification we were in range. It was just 173 tokens to fix it and connect it to our nano system, so I spent the tokens. Then I spent the 20 tokens to connect the heater to our grid as well. From there, it took some time to decide what to do, as there was no room for a person plus

Eric's body on the snowmobile. Finally, Donna said she would take the snowmobile and get a sled she could pull behind it before coming back for us. Now that we were in range of the network, the machines could draw power at will, so we kept the heater in case we needed it, and Donna left.

"I can't believe it all happened so fast," Wendy said as we sat there waiting for Donna to return. "I knew this was dangerous, but he was just gone all at once. It could have been me just as easily."

"It could have been any of us. It's hard to realize how dangerous it is until something like this happens," I said. "I think Eric would be glad to know that the team succeeded, though. If we hadn't gone out there, that alien would have kept picking off families. He helped save a lot of people."

Wendy's eyes were bright, but she did not say anything else as we sat there waiting for Donna. A mission completion notification interrupted the moment of contemplation. The timing made me think Donna reporting in to someone must have triggered it.

Augusta Settlement Enforcement Mission Completed The destabilizing influence has been eliminated. All surviving team members receive two personal tokens.

From the way Wendy's eyes were moving, she had gotten the same message. It did not seem to be the time to talk about rewards, though, so I stayed silent with her until Donna arrived, pulling a large sled.

There was enough room for Eric's body and Wendy and me to ride in it. Donna said people were waiting at the crafting bay even though it was nearing midnight. Even with the alien dead, the death toll was rising as the cold continued to increase slowly. It was not getting much colder now, but it had not stabilized or turned the corner. I made plans on how to deal with that and the conversations I knew were waiting after Eric's death.

Thinking of the time, though, I needed to be practical. I absorbed the nano matrix, which earned me 7 more points. I used eight points to increase the boosted materials perk to level 20.

Doing that now instead of after midnight earned us another 20 material units. I saved the other two points from the mission because no one would know they needed to feed more material into the portal if I upped the portal's processing capacity shortly before midnight. The boosted materials perk cost to level jumped to four personal tokens at level 21, so that perk would not be boosted again for a long time.

8

It was slightly after midnight when we returned to the portal building. Daryl was the first out of the building, and he went straight to where Wendy was standing, next to Eric's body. I could not hear what they were saying, but I was more focused on the rest of the council, who were waiting for me.

"Let's take this inside," I said. "It's been a long day for everyone, and I'd like to get the updates out, but for anyone who hasn't heard. The alien that was picking off families is taken care of. He won't be killing anyone else, but stopping him came with a high cost."

There were council members opposed to the public debrief, given its sensitive nature, but they gave in quickly this time. I covered everything that happened, including the alien causing casualties since the storm started, if not longer. I also describe the murdered family we found right before we chased the alien down. After that, I described the final fight.

"This group of aliens seems to be smarter than the first group I faced," I finished. "If we had not gotten a mission to find this one, I'm not sure how many of us he would have picked off during this storm. I wish there had been some way to keep Eric safe, but thanks to him and the other enforcers, who knows how many people were saved."

"I'm glad the alien was stopped, but enforcers are a rare commodity," O'Donnell said before anyone else could speak up. "You only earned back a fraction of the spheres needed to replace him."

I felt Donna tense up at the way Eric was reduced to a number, and Wendy wore a conflicted look. I tried to get a feel for the rest of the council as well before I answered.

"I feel horrible that I was unable to protect him, but being an enforcer is dangerous. The point of taking the class was to save lives, and because of him, the alien that was killing people was stopped. I'll do my best to protect everyone here, enforcer or not, but sometimes things like this happen. Once the storm's over and I start testing people again, make sure they understand what they are signing up for. I think it was pretty clear before, but death drives the risk home."

"He'd be pissed he was dead, but he was excited to be an enforcer to save people," Wendy spoke up. "Both our families are down in Portland, and if something like this were happening there, we'd want someone to protect our families. We want to protect the families here, too. If he had to die, saving people would have made him feel better about it. I will not stop helping Devin save people either."

The mood shifted after she spoke. It made people respect Eric's sacrifice for the moment rather than use it as a political weapon. It was also a clear sign of support from someone who was there and was close to Eric.

"We'll need to organize a memorial for Eric and for the people lost to the storm or the alien, but that will need to be after this storm is over. It's not safe to do it now, and we don't have the power to spare," I said, pivoting the discussion. "What's the latest on the weather, Vlad?"

"It seems like we are nearing the midpoint of this storm. The average temperature has dropped less than a degree over the last 90 minutes, but it is approaching negative 75 degrees. Even when the storm passes, it will take some time to warm back up to negative 20 or 30," Vlad said. "I would guess tonight is the coldest night we will face this storm."

"Since the power is holding, I say we delay any construction until the morning," I said. "We have the new heater that can be passed out now, but if it is warming and we are surviving, I want to use resources to focus on housing. The custom houses will be three days behind at best, thanks to this cold, and we want to get people out of the existing nano housing, so it's not stacked three-deep. That's adding too much maintenance on buildings and stress on people."

"Devin gets cranky when he's tired," Vlad added. "And he's exhausted. We should wrap this up now. If not, you'll need to excuse him."

I glared at him, but he was not wrong. It took another 15 minutes to wrap things up, but nothing important was said. Seeing we all needed sleep, Daryl said he would find a place for Wendy, and Donna said she was so tired she could crowd in with her family and leave me to my bunk.

We were all too physically and emotionally exhausted to argue. I was not sure how I managed to stumble back to my room and into bed before passing out. The only thing that woke me for a minute was seeing Eric's stuff in the room. It was a fresh reminder of what had happened, but I was tired enough to fall asleep after a moment of grief.

When I woke up to the sound of someone below me getting up and leaving the room, I took a few minutes to relax before I started reviewing the settlement's information. Three more people had died, and we were down to 16,114 inhabitants. Sensing my desire to stay quiet, Vlad messaged me to let me know the weather had turned, the temperature was slowly increasing, but the snow was now falling again. It had stopped at the height of the cold. He also let me know there was a runner in the hallway to let people know when I was up and left the room. He had spotted them without being seen, so they did not yet know I was up. I smiled at Vlad being sneaky even in the dorm.

I leaned over the side to check, and Donna and Alex were still asleep. Larry had left the room. I decided to get up and start moving. The power levels were improving as the storm calmed down, and I was going to take a shower, even though most of the showers had their power turned off. I'd let Donna and Wendy know they were cleared to shower, too, when I got back.

I was quiet enough that Donna did not move, or she was just more tired than I was. Her perk levels were a lot lower, so she was probably even more wiped out than I had been. Either way, I grabbed some clean clothes and my shower kit before heading out of the room. The runner Vlad had warned me about was straightening up from where he was leaning against the wall as soon as I stepped out.

"The council would like to meet as soon as is convenient, Sir," he said.

I was unsure how to respond to being called sir, but the message was polite. Probably from Erin, not O'Donnell, so I nodded and told him I'd meet them at the portal bay in half an hour. The messenger rushed off, and I made my way into the bathroom. I heard a few complaints when I entered one of the shower rooms and the water turned on.

"I spent a whole day trudging through the snow to kill an alien," I called out to the complainers. "I need a shower, but the good news is that the worst of the storm is over, and the showers for everyone should come online soon."

That was enough to stop most of the grumbling, and I ignored the few who were still complaining that I was abusing my position. Even though I used my control over the nano system to turn on the water, I did not take as long a shower as I would have liked. Everyone would cycle through taking fast showers for a while, and I could not justify taking a leisurely shower on top of making an exception for myself.

When I got back to the room to drop off my dirty clothes, Larry was back, and Donna was awake. I let Donna know she could take a shower whenever she wanted, and I would be staying near the portal and in meetings, so I did not need a guard for the day.

"Get some rest. One of you can use my bunk if you need to sleep more after crowding three people on that little bed," I said. When she protested, I insisted.

With that taken care of, I headed off to work on the building I was still deconstructing into the portal. Between the days of working on it and Jason's team pulling rubble from it when I accidentally made parts of it collapse, it looked like I just needed one more day to finish clearing it. I also had time to make a circuit of the work pods for the noon cycle before heading in to meet with the council again.

I was tempted to switch more pods to maintenance, since the 12 working on the backlog were not keeping up with the damage caused by the crowding, but I knew they would catch up once the crowding decreased, so I left those as they were. Work units needed to be boosted as well, but I figured that could happen as I built more structures and got more pods. As I was walking back, I used my last two personal tokens to raise the boosted stamina perk to level 11. That would be five more processing units, and that perk would boost my physical score by another point.

By the time I got to the portal area, Jason's team was already feeding material into it. I let them know about the five-point increase in processing capacity before sitting down with the council.

We started with another recounting of what had happened in the fight against the alien and where to find its victims so they could be given a proper burial. Vlad had precise information on the locations and was able to project known and suspected locations onto the map O'Donnell had. Someone just had to put a note where Vlad projected each location.

I did not let us linger on that and switched to discussing what we got out of the fight and how to utilize it. Even though I did not want to look like I was attempting to balance Eric's death, I wanted O'Donnell and his people to see we had gotten something out of the fight beyond killing the alien.

"We only earned a few spheres, so not enough to create another enforcer. I got and used a nano matrix from the alien, though. Between that and the mission rewards, I increased our daily material unit production by a flat 20 points plus five more points of processing power. That's a roughly 24-point per day boost. We also acquired that snowmobile and a second heater for far fewer settlement tokens than it would have cost to buy them.

Bryan immediately claimed the second heater once the storm had passed enough for them to get back to work on the houses. Everyone agreed with that. Anything to speed up the completion of the houses was at the top of the list. The storm had shown the value of the nano housing in a way nothing else could. Even with the extreme crowding, everyone in the nano houses had survived and was relatively comfortable. The same could not be said for the people in the older houses. The snowmobile spurred more discussion.

"What's the range on the snowmobile?" Erin asked. "Can we use it to rescue people or even contact Bangor and towns on the way there?"

"The base range is roughly 100 miles once it leaves the settlement's power grid and can no longer draw all the power it needs," Vlad said. "That is for a single rider with limited supplies, though. Pulling that sled we had attached empty will cut the range by 25 miles, and each average person in the sled will decrease it by another ten miles."

"That does not sound like a lot, but we have some options," I said. "I can create nanostructures up to 80 miles away from the settlement. That means I could ride to Bangor and build a windmill there to recharge the snowmobile. If we want to haul stuff, I can build windmills to recharge along the route. I could even build more things in Bangor to help them out, but all those resources won't help the town here. If we go there, I'll review their situation and decide whether we want to compromise the timeline of what we are building here. It's hard to make any decisions without knowing the situation. With the ability to recharge there, we could safely transport several hundred pounds of supplies or move people back and forth. It's something for all of you to consider. We won't be doing any traveling until the storm is fully dispersed, so there's plenty of time to think about that."

"We need to replace Eric, too," O'Donnell said. "We have a stash of 13 more spheres. If we pass those to you, is that enough to create another enforcer?"

No one reacted well to the replacement comment, but I let them know it would be enough. I had to bite my tongue about the fact that they had been hiding spheres from me, but I was glad to add another enforcer. The other good news I shared was an increase in the greenhouse complex resource utilization research that Klawock had purchased.

"Research is relatively cheap at the first tier, so I'm hoping they focus on that," I said. "Each level reduces the cost by five material units, so that will add up. Unfortunately, we don't have the material units to buy anything we need today. We can add an apartment block tomorrow, and we will build greenhouses at some point."

"We should also have the next batch of houses ready the day after tomorrow if Vlad is right about the storm's trajectory," Bryan said.

We were wrapping up when Donna showed up with Wendy in tow. They both looked like they had recovered from the exhaustion from the prior day, but Wendy still looked upset. It was decided that the three of us would take some rations and firewood in the snowmobile and sled and check on people outside the immediate area. Just because the death toll had mostly stabilized did not mean that everyone was in good shape.

Other than the people far on the outskirts, whom we had checked on while hunting the alien, I had not checked out how people were living in legacy structures. It was clear that, while these buildings were far better suited to the cold than those in Klawock, they were still in rough shape. It seemed like most houses were at least doubled up, with one house gutted to make the remaining one more livable. In many cases, gutting extended to tearing out the carpet in one house and putting it on the walls and ceiling in the other.

Unsurprisingly, the most common questions were about when more nano housing would be available. I had to repeatedly explain that the next round of housing would be to relieve crowding, and that more people would then be moved into nano housing. That answer was not popular, and more than a few people questioned whether we really needed to reduce crowding to prevent the buildings from wearing out faster.

"This is the best way to get everyone in housing that can survive the growing cold, and if there is another storm, the expanded housing will be stuffed full again," I started saying to people before adding the part that was most effective at quelling complaints. "And we are just taking the existing buildings from triple occupancy back down to double occupancy. That's the happy balance that does not degrade structures too quickly."

Many of the places we visited were low on firewood, so our route was repeatedly interrupted to restock houses. It was bad enough that the reserve stocks scattered around Augusta were getting low before we finally stopped for a late dinner and some sleep. As soon as we stopped using the snowmobile, Jason had people waiting to take it.

"It's much safer and more reliable. It even self-adjusts between snow and the cleared ground. It's more of a multi-surface mobile than a snowmobile," he said when I asked him about why he needed it. "The plan is to use it for moving supplies for construction and staging rubble here to process whenever you aren't using it. We're not trying to take it yet, but there's no reason to leave it sitting around when you don't need it.

I let him know I would need it again mid-morning. I planned

to look at the greenhouse on the other side of the river, and Bryan was coming with me. He did not know it yet, so I did not mention that, but I was sure he would agree to the trip.

Donna and her husband had figured out a sleeping rotation, so they were not all crammed into the lower bunk, which was one less thing I had to worry about. I let her and Wendy know I planned to get a full nine hours of sleep and would be up at seven the next morning.

I had turned all the showers back on after the temperature kept climbing, even after the sun went down. That meant there were lines for the shower rooms in the dorm, stretching down the hall. I was glad the rooms were perfectly soundproof, since the noise from people talking in the hall was pretty high, even though some people were still trying to sleep.

By the time morning rolled around and I was brushing my teeth, the lines were just as long. Listening to people talk, though, these were people who lived in nearby legacy houses. It had warmed enough that people were moving short distances again. That was a good sign, and I was in a good mood as I finished processing the building on the side of the park with Donna following me around. After that, I collected from the pods and adjusted the power settings to refill the batteries. Being able to use the windmills' built-in batteries instead of buying standalone ones was a nice savings compared to how things started in Klawock.

The maintenance backlog had jumped far more than expected, and I planned to allocate the next few pods I built to addressing it. I could not wait for the crowding to drop, given how the backlog was climbing. I popped into the portal bay to let people know I was about to build another apartment block on the east side of the park, and that they would have three hours to use the snowmobile to move people and supplies in before I would want it.

The apartment went up quickly, and people were moving in from the one next to it almost the moment it finished forming. This building increased our official housing total to support 572 people. If all the buildings were used at double occupancy, that could hold about 7% of the remaining population of Augusta. The available housing was increasing much faster than back home, but I still needed to pick up the pace if I wanted to finish this mission in a reasonable amount of time.

By the time I was back in the portal room, Wendy had joined up with us, and we talked over the plans for the day. We mostly shied away from talking about Eric, except for Wendy letting us know she planned to pick up his stuff when she grabbed her own after we were done for the day. She was permanently moving out of my spot in the dorms. That meant Donna, her family, and I would be able to use the space without as much trouble syncing times.

That still left plenty of time for me to tell Bryan I wanted him to look at the greenhouse with us to see if it could be replicated. There was grumbling about how he needed to be at the construction sites to keep people on track, but he could see the wisdom of having other buildings we could use to grow food. I think he also appreciated being recognized as the expert.

Bryan joined us for a quick lunch right before 11, and then we took the snowmobile and sled back from Jason's team for our trip. As much as I wanted to drive, Donna and Bryan knew the area best, and Donna could handle the cold better than Bryan could, so the three of us rode in the sled with some basic supplies while she drove. The ride down the banks and across the river had me on edge. Even with the river frozen solid, crossing the ice still freaked me out.

On the other side of the river, it was even less populated than where I had shown up, especially heading southeast. I called out when we left the settlement zone and started running on battery power. I was also tracking the distance in case we wanted to extend the settlement's range to the greenhouse area with power and water.

Although the trip was short, it took some time since the occupants of the few nearby buildings all wanted updates, and some of them needed some items we had brought. Things sped up as we passed the last small cluster of houses and entered the wooded area. In the middle of that was an old farmhouse with smoke rising from two chimneys and four heavily modified greenhouses in the field.

"I thought there was just one?" I yelled. The nano vehicle was not loud, but the wind was blowing. All I got back were shrugs from everyone. If they could be integrated, more greenhouses would be better, so it did not really matter.

While our nano snowmobile was mostly silent, it still made enough noise that a few guns were pointed at us from the porch as we made it up to the farmhouse. Donna knew the owners in passing and smoothed things over. It took some extra talking when they noticed Vlad, but finally, we were allowed inside to talk.

The farmhouse was decently sized, and when everything happened, the local family moved back home to consolidate. There were 21 people across four generations living there. The first thing I did was use the healing perk charges I had saved to clear up some illness and help speed the healing of a broken arm. Then we got down to business.

They knew a rough outline of what was going on, as the council's messengers had been by a few days after I showed up. There was still a lot to fill them in on. They were self-described preppers and, among all the family members, had consolidated their fuel and food stocks when everything went wrong. They even had an old tractor that still ran and two old trucks. Even with all that, the unrelenting cold was starting to overwhelm their ability to keep their greenhouses running.

"The greenhouses were supposed to supplement the food until all this blew over. It's not enough to feed us," the family's matriarch said. "Now we learn this weather's not going to blow over, and the cold is too much for our preparations. It's a hard truth to know you did not prepare enough."

"No one knew how to prepare for aliens messing up our sun. It looks like you were prepared for a lot more than most people. We want to visit your greenhouses to assess whether they can be converted using my nanotechnology and whether Bryan can replicate them. We need all the help we can get with food production, and this could be a big help. It sounds like bringing power out this way would help you all as well, right?" I asked. I was worried they would resist any connections to town, but that was unfounded. They were ready for any help that would let them stay on the farm and produce what they needed to survive.

I explained they were far enough from the settlement that I would need to place four windmills or water towers to extend the range to them, so it would be at least a day before I could do that. The good news was that the farmhouse could be converted, and if the greenhouses could too, it would be worth doing.

Before we made any decisions, they took us out to examine the greenhouses. The group leading us was enthusiastic as they pointed out all the ways they had kept them working. The windows were placed to maximize the sun. There were rocks and concrete pillars inside, all painted black to absorb the heat and radiate it back out. It had been enough for a while, but now they were using a combination of propane and diesel heaters to augment all their heat-trapping methods.

"We have enough fuel for five or six more weeks if we don't get more storms," one of the tour guides said. "We were planning to harvest the furthest greenhouse, then let it die off to extend the growing season in the others."

"The good news is that you built these really well. These buildings can all be integrated," I said after we looked at all of them. "Bryan, do you think you can get your teams building these and standardizing the blueprint?"

"I think so. I might want to bring a team out here and build one or two with help from the people here to learn the process better, but then we could replicate them back in town as well."

"Great, let's head back to the house, and I'll get the info written down so we can see what we're working with and make a plan," I said. This seemed to have real potential. Once back in the house, I started copying the relevant information to my tablet to share with everyone.

"So, here's what I found," I told everyone before using a mini projector to share what was on my tablet's screen.

Custom Farm House

- Integration costs 50 tokens
- Supports 25 people and 0 work pods / 2 pod slots
- Power required 40-400 power units based on weather
- Water required 40 water units
- Safe to -50 degrees base, -125 degrees at full power

Custom Greenhouse

- Integration costs 100 tokens
- Supports 0-work pods / 0 pod slots
- Power required 100-400 power units based on weather and growth cycle
- Water required 50 water units
- Safe to -50 degrees base, -125 degrees at full power
- Produces food for 50 people

"The house and greenhouses are really well built, as the power requirement to keep them running is fairly minor if it's not colder than negative 50 degrees. As you can see, nanotechnology will also greatly improve greenhouse output. It looks like those four houses could feed 200 people a year at maximum output, which would mean you all have a lot of leftover capacity," I said.

"That's about a tenfold increase in what we were expecting," one of the locals said. "You can really boost it that much?"

"The integration will add grow lights and automatic watering that will perfectly adjust with ideal heat to optimize the growth cycle," Vlad said. "There are some other things that speed it up as well."

"The only thing is that all nano housing is currently double-occupied. We would like you to take in 29 more people while we work to get everyone housed. Part of that would be people for the two work pods that would be installed here. Keeping those fully utilized requires 12 people, and we need at least 16 dedicated to that if we want them to have some free time. I'd also like Bryan to send some people here to learn from you and build two more greenhouses, then send others who could help maintain all six. The higher growth rates do create more work, so you might not be able to manage all six with the people you currently have here," I said.

After my long speech, people split off to discuss things. While they handled the complex stuff, I discussed the logistics of bringing building materials out here on the snowmobile. We would be able to bring heavy loads with the snowmobile once I extended the settlements' range out here, so they could load the sled without worrying about power. I was more worried about the time they would monopolize the snowmobile, but it seemed worth it to me.

We were invited to an early dinner, and based on the smells from the kitchen, it was better than what we were getting back at the settlement, so we all said yes. As dinner was wrapping up, the matriarch gave us their decision to accept the help and the conditions.

"We're not used to that many strangers being here, but as long as it goes back to just our family and those we invite when the housing situation gets taken care of, we agree," she said. "We like to stay busy, so everyone out here may start on another house if there is free time. Then the new people can live there."

I agreed to everything on behalf of the council, and then we resumed discussing what came next. By the time we finished eating, it was dark, so we said our goodbyes and headed back to the settlement with a new plan in place.

9

When we got back to the processing portal, I went to find Erin. She was in her office, which was expected. She seemed to spend more time in her office than I did outside. I gave her an overview of the meeting we had on the farm and let her know I would be building two more windmills and two more water towers to connect the farm to the settlement. On the way back, I had considered discussing it with the council, but this was clearly one of the baseline settlement construction issues I told them I would decide on my own. Because of that, I did not present it as a question, but as the plan I was going with. Either she thought it was the right choice, or she did not want to fight about it.

"So that's new housing for 137 people at double occupancy with the three custom houses plus the farmhouse tomorrow," Erin said as she did the math on a pad of paper quickly. "Add in the extra food production, and it will be a good day. A big boost to housing and food, more power, and water. Mainly at the cost of tokens. We have enough of those?"

"We always need more of everything, but material units are still the bottleneck," I said. "I'm thinking about a trip to Bangor, but I'd like at least two communication devices, if not three of them. One to keep here, one to leave in Bangor, and one to have on the trip. I'm not sure how long it will be before I can afford those, though. We might have to do without at first."

"You'll be hearing more about the trip," she said. "Everyone here with family and friends there or on the way there wants a rescue mission. We're trying to hold them off from bothering you until you're ready. It might be worth going without communication devices if affording them is a long way off."

She also gave me information on the service for Eric and the others killed in the storm or by the alien. As I was leaving, she reminded me to check my information sheet. The stashed spheres O'Donnell had been hiding had been brought into town, so I should have absorbed them. When I checked my information, the sphere count was up to 28. I added more enforcer testing to my to-do list, but I was not sure when I could fit it in. We needed at least one more day to recharge batteries before I started draining power for the scans. I let Erin know that and headed out to get some sleep.

The following morning, I started processing a smaller nearby building that had already been gutted for any usable parts. Thanks to all the prework Jason's team had done, it was complete in a single day. With all the additions we were making, I was excited to see the settlement's free space grow like that.

As soon as all the processing and collecting were done, we headed back to the farm. This time, there were six of us in the trailer, as this was also the first load of new residents for the farm. We could only fit four additional people and their supplies for the first trip. That would change once I was done at the farm, and the snowmobile would spend the day moving people and supplies for future greenhouses.

As we took off, Vlad was hovering near Donna while she drove us. He was telling her where to stop so I could place the water towers and windmills. We skipped the final windmill as planned. It would be just 50 feet from the farmhouse, but I needed to convert the farmhouse first so I could fill the two pod slots there. They would be responsible for operating those with the new residents.

When we got there, everyone started filing out of the house. They had been warned that they should be outside for the conversion. I knew we had tested it back in Klawock, but it still made me nervous to have people inside while a building was being integrated. It was cold, but not unbearable for the people outside. I triggered the integration and started moving to the spot where I needed to build the final windmill. As soon as the blue glow faded, I added the windmill, placed the pods, and linked everything up.

I set the two new pods to maintenance. The house had added a chunk to the backlog that needed to be addressed, and the material maintenance was getting out of hand, too. After I added the greenhouses, I would likely need to set some of the new pods back in the settlement to work on material maintenance, even if it would dip into our material unit supply.

"Okay, everyone is safe to move back inside," I said. "The house is now fully connected to the nano grid, and all the bathrooms have running, hot water. The house itself will be comfortable inside on a typical day without the fireplace. You also have power, and the work pods can repair all the finishings and structure that were part of the integration from now on."

Most people went inside, while I headed out to the greenhouses with the people who worked there. They wanted to see the changes and sign off on the conversion after I integrated the first one. The change was relatively minor on the surface. The structure became more uniform, the glass looked a little clearer, and the inside looked more standardized.

The key changes were visible when we went inside. There was a panel inside their door that let them control the watering of each bed, the greenhouse's overall temperature and humidity, and, finally, the change that would speed things up. There were now grow lights powered by nanotechnology, better than anything Earth had seen before.

"This is everything you promised and more," the guy who had been in charge of examining everything said. "Let's convert the other ones, too."

"As I mentioned, I can do two more today, and I'll come do the final one tomorrow," I said. "I'll come out on one of the deliveries of construction materials once I have enough tokens to integrate the fourth one. I need to save enough to convert the three new houses that should be finished in the main settlement today. Also, don't forget the automatic settings will probably be the best, even though you can tweak them if you want."

"Should be best." Vlad clarified. "And they will learn from your adjustments, no matter what the outcome is."

Converting the other two greenhouses took just a few minutes, since they were right there. I reviewed the updated maintenance backlog and decided to split the six pods I had not set up yet from the earlier construction into two each for regular maintenance, material maintenance, and work units. The maintenance was getting out of hand.

Deferred Maintenance	143 units	**Material Maintenance**	78 units

Once the greenhouses were converted, we headed back to the

snowmobile to ride back. The rest of the day, the snowmobile would be used to deliver supplies and people to the farm. When we got back, I just had to wait a few hours to integrate the three new houses as planned. Fortunately, these were well built and did not add too much to the maintenance backlog.

The only downside to the farm expansion was that Bryan decided to keep the next building cycle by that team at three more houses. He was sending too many people off to the farm to learn and could not bump the team to four houses as he originally planned.

"The next group that completes their houses in two days will also stay at three houses after they finish their set," he said. "I'm taking people to start building greenhouses instead. Which makes sense, right? People need to eat and stay warm. Those greenhouses may take more work, too. I'll know more tomorrow, but I am thinking a team can make one every six to eight days."

After confirming plans for the upcoming builds, Donna, Wendy, and I met up to discuss next steps. There was still an alien threat and lots of people who needed our help.

"I'm going to scan more people this afternoon to look for other enforcer candidates," I said. "Now that we know how dangerous this group of aliens is, we need to farm spheres to get more enforcers. Other than that one guy picking people off, they seem to have stopped all attacks on us, right?"

"Do you think they know that letting us kill golems is just powering us up?" Donna asked. That would make the lack of attacks a bad thing.

"That's what I'm afraid of. If the aliens are turtling up, it's going to be harder to take them out. I really want to get their portal and set it up in Portland. That will be the best way to set this region up for long-term success. I'm also really considering a trip to Bangor. I can set up a small base there with power, water, a house, and a clinic, which would help them build something that will withstand the conditions. It's going to be a long time before this little town can absorb whatever is left of its 30,000 people."

"You know that number they gave you is just for the city? The metro area is closer to 150,000 people, or was before all this,"

Wendy said.

My mind stuttered for a second. That many people were so far past what I could consider saving that it was almost laughable. At the same time, I could not let them all die. "All the more reason to help them where they live, I guess. Anything we do will be a drop in the bucket, but I feel bad doing nothing, and I know people in town want to see them helped, too."

"If you get them started, Larry was talking with his team about having them build all their own stuff. Now that there are blueprints for the greenhouse and the regular houses, people are saying we could send people up there to train them. They should have a lot of people to work on stuff, and you could go up every week to integrate them," Donna said.

"That could work. They will still need water and power as we have no way to build that outside nano construction, but that will give us more pods to get more tokens. So, if the Bangor metro area is that large, what am I looking at in Portland?" I asked.

"There are about 70,000 people in Portland and 550,000 in the whole metro area," Wendy said. "I was studying local politics before all this happened, so that's why I know all these numbers off the top of my head."

"Well, that does not change my mission. Save Augusta with the added goal of setting up your town to help everyone else. I don't need to solve it all myself," I said when the idea of that many people needing help threatened to overwhelm me. This was not like Southeast Alaska, where it was possible to save almost everyone left in the area.

"You know your numbers here are just for the city, too, right?" Wendy said. "There were like 70,000 people or more in the Augusta metropolitan area. It's just that they are more spread out here than in the big cities."

I was relieved that I was not responsible for the larger number of people on this mission. Even the number that was my responsibility felt overwhelming. I also felt immediate regret for dismissing the people in towns surrounding the metropolitan area.

Donna agreed to find her husband and talk to Bryan about taking a few people to Bangor to start construction there. Wendy came with me to organize the scanning of people. I had committed to scanning 30 people, so that would take over five hours. I wanted Wendy there to answer questions about the class. I could talk about it, but more people knew her, and she could give her perspective. I knew Eric's loss still lingered, and she would make sure people had a full view of the risks.

Initiating another scan every ten minutes for five hours was boring work. There was some drama when more than one person decided they did not really want to risk becoming an enforcer and left right before their turn. The council had an extensive list, though, and after the first two people declined to be scanned, they sent the next ten to the standby list as backup for people who got cold feet. At the end of the day, we had two more people identified as possible enforcers.

After finishing the scans, it was a rush to get cleaned up and get some dinner before the memorial for Eric. The reality was that we had no place for a large gathering, and it was tough to move large groups in the cold. In the end, we cleared out the portal room for a series of memorials. First was for Eric's friends, mostly other college students. There was an open microphone for people to speak. After his friends and Wendy had a chance to speak, I went up.

"I only worked with Eric for a few days. What impressed me was that he knew the risk of becoming an enforcer, and he did it anyway. He wanted to protect people. Part of that was fighting the aliens so he could get home to Portland and make sure his family was okay. Without him, I'm not sure we could have stopped the alien that was killing your neighbors in the storm, and his sacrifice saved a lot of people. Here's to Eric, who proved he was a hero."

"And we will make sure his family is okay when we make it to Portland," Wendy added.

There were some clapping and some sad smiles as I stepped down. I hoped I had honored Eric without stealing the spotlight. Since I did not know the other people who died in the storm, I headed back to my bunk after Eric's memorial. There was so little room in the portal bay, I did not need to take up any of it for people I did not know.

The next morning was a quick trip out to the farm to integrate the last of the original greenhouses. The snowmobile was currently almost exclusively used to move materials out there for the future greenhouses and a second farmhouse. Even with access to power along the entire route, there was a limit to how much it could haul per load, so many trips were required to move everything. They also knew I planned to take it on a trip to Bangor the next day, so they were piling up supplies.

I also got the first projections on when construction projects would be completed. They hoped to have the next greenhouse completed in seven days, with another completed two days afterward. After a close check of the area, the goal was to have a total of eight greenhouses and one more farmhouse out at the farm before shifting the greenhouse teams elsewhere.

I stayed for about an hour talking to people in the farmhouse. I took that time to confirm they were still happy with their decision to let people move in and start building. There was some lamenting over lost privacy, but aside from the complaints about doubling up the living quarters, they realized this was the only way they could survive long-term.

It also helped that we were not attempting to take any of their supplies. We wanted them to share what was generated in the upgraded greenhouses, but that was all. It would have been nice if everyone in town had been as pragmatic. I knew the council was keeping much of the complaining from me, but I still heard from plenty of people who did not see the big picture.

After delaying as much as I could get away with, I headed back to town to spend the rest of the day scanning people. I had committed to scanning 50 more people, as my planned trip to Bangor the next day would stop the scanning for a day or two. That's also why I was stockpiling resources and not spending them. I wanted plenty available to address whatever I found in Bangor.

I spent over eight hours testing people and just found one more candidate. I had decided to stay out of the selection drama this time, and the council would pick the new enforcer in the morning. Donna and Wendy would be there to provide their input and ensure it was someone they could work with.

Wendy was excited to be part of the decision, but Donna gave me a hard time about passing off the work I did not want to do to them.

"You're right. It's not something I want to do, but it makes sense to pass it off," I said. "I'm going to leave when the mission is over, but all the enforcers will have to work together after I'm gone. Your views on this are more important than mine, and even if I were there, I would defer to both of you. They need to see the enforcers as their own power group, and not just an extension of me."

That did not stop the dirty looks, but it stopped the overt complaining, so I took it as a win. I had eaten between scanning people, so I headed to bed before it got too late. By this point, I was used to seeing Larry and Alex in the room, so we exchanged quick greetings, and I climbed into bed.

The next morning, I made sure to walk Donna through exactly what I was doing. She could collect the pods' output while I was gone if I stayed away longer than expected. She could not change the output settings until she was officially in charge. She was staying behind with Paul, the new enforcer, while Wendy and I headed to Bangor with two builders who could show them how to build custom houses.

"If something crazy happens and I don't come back, you're going to be the one in charge," I said. "I'm pretty sure Paul will defer to you, and Wendy will as well if she makes it back and I don't. I finished transferring my plans and ideas to your tablet last night. So, if something happens, you'll be set."

"You don't expect anything to happen, do you?" she asked.

"No, this should be easy as long as we don't get attacked by desperate or dumb humans. Still, I learned the hard way to be ready for anything. I think there's a foundation here to save a good portion of the people, even without me."

Once we were all done and back at the portal, I checked the information. There were exactly 800 material units and plenty of work units stored up. There were fewer settlement tokens than I wanted. Adding all the stuff on the farm had burned through those. That meant I would not be buying communication devices to take with me. I was torn about that, but hearing how many people might need help up there, I could not wait to get them started on building more housing and food.

While the three new custom houses were getting finished up, I gave Paul the enforcer class and had a very early lunch. About

10:30, the three houses were ready to integrate.

Since the last one I integrated was the tenth house, counting the two existing ones I had converted, I decided to give a quick speech. "This is huge for the whole town. Ten of these houses means 360 people have safe housing at double occupancy. Without you, things would be a lot worse. Even better, two of you are coming to Bangor with us to help them get started. They may have many more people, so the only way we can help them is with more custom houses like this. I hope they work as hard as all of you have."

Most of the people listening looked like they would rather be working than listening to me talk, so I wrapped up, and we headed to the snowmobile and sled. Since it was going to be a long drive and neither Wendy nor I knew the route, I ended up driving. With Vlad directing me, I was not worried about getting lost. Plus, I handled the cold best. Because of the length of the trip, the sled could hold only Wendy and the two builders, with a bare minimum of supplies. I would generate rations as needed to feed people we found along the way.

The sled looked funny with a small tent pitched inside. There had actually been a lot of discussion about that, and for a longer trip, it was decided that would be the warmest option for them. They were also getting one of the nano heaters. They would have to use it sparingly on battery power, but it would let them take the edge off the cold. We were donating the heater to Bangor to help with building construction, over Bryan's objections.

We were on the road well before noon. The plan was to take I-95, which meant a 75-mile trip. At a hoped-for 15 miles per hour, the trip would take five hours. There would be stalled cars and other road obstacles, which might make the trip take longer. The road was near the train tracks most of the time, which allowed us to check the condition of the tracks farther from Augusta. It would also allow me to place a windmill on the tracks at the halfway point. With a planned range of 45 miles with the sled and riders, it could not make it to Bangor on a single charge. That meant a couple of hours' break in the middle of the trip to recharge the snowmobile. There would be no power in the battery at the start, but when we returned, the battery would be full, and we could recharge just by passing by.

There was a small crowd to see us off, and a few last-minute messages shouted at us to deliver to people in Bangor. I had taken a page from prior trips back home, and a blank book had been passed around for people to send messages to family and friends in Bangor. I reminded people of that when they tried to get me to remember stuff for them.

The road was fairly clear, cutting through snow-covered rural landscapes until we reached Waterville. This was another small college town, and there had been some discussion about starting our reclamation efforts there. In the end, it was decided that they were so close that the plan was to move them to Augusta at some point. They were on the list to contact when we could.

There were more stalled cars on the interstate around the town, but there was enough room to maneuver around. As we passed through that town, we returned to rural landscapes. Other than Fairfield and Newport, we saw no signs of human life anywhere along the route, and those two towns were far enough from the interstate that we just saw hints of civilization in the distance.

The recharging tower itself was placed near Pittsfield, right before the train tracks veered away from the road. I attached a sign explaining what it was and how to tap it for power. The plan was to look for people on the way back who could make use of it. For our purposes, I set it so that half of all power generation would be used to charge the battery until it was full, and that the battery would be held in reserve until I needed it. I did not want the snowmobile to wait for a charge on our way back.

The two pods were automatically placed in an open building in the settlement, and I had set things up before I left, so all the pods I built while on this trip would default to settlement tokens. That left us with an hour of downtime while the snowmobile recharged. I went into the tent for warmth, and Wendy stood guard. It was warm enough inside that I took a quick nap, and then when we were ready, I headed back out to keep driving. We had been making better time than expected at 20 miles per hour. If that kept up, we had less than two hours to reach Bangor.

The roads were even more deserted on this stretch of the interstate, and we made it to the outskirts of Bangor in less than two hours. As we got ready to turn off the interstate to make our way to city hall, people started noticing us. We had taken down the tent, and the three in the back would wave to people with their rifles out of sight. I was waving as well, and Vlad was hidden while using the message feature to keep us on track.

I saw a few guns as we traveled, but no one aimed them at us, which I took as a good sign. They must have had some form of communication or runner system and figured out where we were going, as a small security force was waiting for us when we arrived at City Hall. At this rate, I was getting good at summarizing why I was there, and having the nano powered snowmobile lent weight to my story.

The meet-and-greet went quicker than expected. After that, we waited outside before a few leaders joined Wendy and the others in the sled. The historic district was near City Hall, and I hoped to find a house to convert. I convinced them to let me show them what I could do before we dove into the details.

We had to move slowly as the guards were following us on foot. Even with just three extra people in the sled, I had to worry about power levels. With Vlad's help, I found a house near Broadway Park. I wanted to convert a house near some open space to accommodate construction. Without a processing portal, it would be much harder for them to clear old buildings first. Hence, a base of operations near open land was important. The home was abandoned but still in decent shape. It took 46 settlement tokens and bumped up our maintenance backlog, but it was worth it to see everyone's faces as it converted.

As soon as it was done, I placed the water tower and the windmill. Based on the locals' advice, I placed them toward Chapin Park so houses could be built there, too. With that done, we headed into the house to have our meeting out of the cold. Because it was an existing house, the appliances and furniture were still there. The meeting had to be delayed as people realized there were actual showers and laundry facilities. Everyone who had come with us wanted turns in the shower, and they were raiding the clothes left in the house to wear while they washed what they were wearing.

There was a flurry of activity as people were dispatched to bring more people to the house for the meeting, and I was asked to wait an hour before I started explaining the details of my plan. I was also asked to use the snowmobile to pick people up for the meeting, but I had to decline. I explained it was almost out of power and was recharging. Several people who had clearly wanted to drive it looked disappointed, but still headed up to pick up others on foot.

I sat with the team I had brought while people milled around. I made it clear I wanted an actual meeting, not to dole out information piecemeal, which limited the conversation when I would not answer one-off questions. I also had a mission pop-up that needed some review.

Mission Assigned: Bangor

Give Bangor the tools to stabilize itself before 90% of its initial population dies. Successfully delegating will hone your skills for future missions. This mission is secondary to the Augusta Settlement Mission. The current Bangor population loss is 63%. Mission requirements:

- The town population has been stable for ten days
- The town's survivable housing exceeds 20% of the surviving population with regular growth
- Food production exceeds 20% of the surviving population with regular growth

The town was worse off than Augusta had been. I wondered if I was being sent to the more successful surviving towns in a region with alien criminals as a starting point. Like, I was placed in a position where I could easily succeed and focus on building out an entire area. This place needed so much housing and food that I would have been overwhelmed if I had started here. At least the mission was based on the city, not the metro area, so it might be doable.

It's not showing why, but you need to succeed in this mission and fast, Vlad messaged me. We had explained his presence, but he messaged silently about the mission. *I'm almost sure this will unlock a class you need to succeed as the challenges get worse. It's the phrasing of the mission's delegation goal that makes me think that. You can't really delegate without someone who can do some of the things you can do.*

Suddenly, this trip to Bangor was much more important, and I needed to figure out how to make it work not just for these people but for all the missions I was working on.

10

It took less than the planned hour for everyone to crowd into the dining room and the connected living room. I was ready to get the meeting going as soon as they said everyone was there. I even had a microprojector hooked up to display screens for the group. I gave my now routine spiel to everyone about what had happened to our sun and why I was there. With the nanostructures already in place and Vlad to back me up, we managed to skip most of the disbelief that alien spacecraft had caused everything. There were still a few people who did not want to believe the sun would not revert to normal on its own. Fortunately, it was clear their disbelief was just people trying to find a way out of the situation they faced. Other than that thread of denialism, they were too beaten down to argue much. Too many people had died, and they all knew more casualties were coming if nothing changed.

"The fact is, what I can do here right now is limited," I said after answering all their questions as best as I was able. "Still, I wanted to start you on the process of creating something that can last, but before we do that, we need to see where you are now. I got access to a city information screen, which I'm going to share with you now. It's bleak, but we're going to work to turn that around."

Bangor Settlement		**Population**	12,042
Food Supply	37 days	**Heat Supply**	16 days
Housing	25,457 people	**Survivable Housing**	18 people
Food Production	13%	**Secure Food Production**	0%
Power Production	25- 245 units	**Power Draw**	47.5- 250 units
Power Storage	0/ 110 units	**Indoor Pod Slots**	0/2
Water Production	275 units	**Water Draw**	25 units
Production Structures	Large Windmill x 1	Large Water Tower x 1	

Enhanced Structures	Custom House x 1		

"This is just the population of the city itself, so I'm not sure about the greater metro area. Because this location does not have a processing portal, I have to come here to build things. That makes your advancement less efficient than Augusta's and makes it dependent on them. Still, it's not like things are hopeless. We have the start of a plan to help you all survive," I said. "One thing to note as we keep talking is that your city also does not manage its own maintenance of the nanostructures. Augusta will manage all that, but all the nanostructures, including this house, can be maintained by people spending time in work pods. We'll talk about those later."

"There's no good way to spin this," Andy, the de facto leader, said, sounding defeated. "We knew things were bad, but 16 days until we all freeze to death. Can you actually stop that?"

"This is an approximation based on maintaining ideal temperatures and using resources currently available," Vlad said. "I'm sure you are cutting back on heat as much as possible and using non-standard fuel. Both of those things will extend the time you have. The same is true of the food."

"Plus, there are other things not being considered. This house accommodates 18 people. If you really push it, you'll have nearly four times the number of people shoved in here. It won't be fun, but this house uses no fuel, so the more people you put here, the more fuel you save. Also, I'll build two more windmills before I leave. You can hook up power lines to them and use the power to operate legacy heaters that still run," I said. "Finally, these two gentlemen who came with me know how to build houses like this that can be cheaply integrated into the nano network. I'll see if I can find another legacy building or two to convert before I go."

"If you can get us the people and materials, we'll get six teams going in the next couple of days," Dominic, who was a local builder, said to Andy. "With any luck, we can have six more buildings like this done in a week and then scale up even more. I've been talking to the people Devin brought, and the entire process seems far simpler than traditional construction."

"If you cram people in, that's room for almost 540 people in a week. Housing that can handle down to negative 105 degrees with enough power. You should also leave spots in the park with good sun exposure for greenhouses. We have teams in Augusta learning how to build them now, and will bring one or two of them back with me in a week to start building greenhouses that can each feed 50 people per year."

It took a while to go over the details, but most of the people listening grabbed at the chance to do something. We also handed out the book of messages from the people back home. We let them know we could take something similar back when we left, if they had it ready before noon the next day. I also generated the daily food rations and said I would generate another batch the next day. Food for 100 people for one day was a drop in the bucket, but if they stretched it, it would help. Finally, I discussed the medical clinic. I had planned to build one from the start, but seeing how dire their situation was, I was not sure whether to spend those resources on a clinic or on more buildings.

The discussion on that dragged on, and I suggested they tell me about their decision in the morning. The snowmobile had enough time while we talked to get a decent charge, so I asked for a guide to take my group on a tour to look for a house to integrate near the other park and to place two more windmills where they would be most useful for people tapping into them to power heaters.

A few homes could be integrated, but they were scattered and in poor condition. Most of those houses would take too many resources to recover and would not be on the grid to start.

As we looked around, I realized it was a good thing I was not building the clinic until the morning at the earliest. I was down to 55 settlement tokens. With 22 needed for the windmills, I had to find a house that just cost 33 tokens to integrate if I wanted to integrate a house tonight and have some power running. A clinic would be something I could afford in the morning, after Donna collected resources back home.

We finally found a suitable house to integrate three streets away from the other park for 31 tokens, and I added another two windmills as well. I put the four pods from the windmills at the two houses in town and set them all to maintenance.

The rest of the night, the snowmobile was used to move people into the two integrated houses and start staging building materials. One of the builders we brought was assigned to each house so they would be near the two building sites. Wendy and I got bunks in the first house for the night.

When it got late enough, I turned the snowmobile over to the builders. They would be using it to move materials nonstop until Wendy and I were ready to leave. I was a little unsure about letting it out of my sight, but the builders from home would be watching it.

The builders had brought the heater with them to speed up house construction, but that night it was used to heat a neighboring house. I watched as they negotiated who would get the heater and when it would be turned over to a nearby house each evening when construction stopped.

The other thing I did was explain the pods in great detail and stress the importance of having them fully staffed. "Overcrowding buildings like you need to do creates a huge backlog of maintenance," I told them. "These pods won't be enough to keep up, but it will help offset the cost so Augusta can focus on generating the tokens I'll need to integrate the houses when I get back."

"And if the maintenance backlog gets too high, the building will require more power to heat or even stop working," Vlad said. "It's not just aesthetics, it's the viability of the nanostructures. The only reason he is recommending this level of crowding is that you don't have a choice."

The rest of the evening was spent answering questions until I decided I could not stay up any longer. It would be a busy day again tomorrow and the trip home, so I did not want to stay up too late. I said my goodnights and headed to my assigned bunk. They had put up sets of triple bunk beds in all the bedrooms and even in the living room. They were pretty decent for a quick job and already had curtains around them for a modicum of privacy. There were still lines for the showers, so I skipped them even though I wanted one and went to sleep.

In the morning, the discussion about the clinic continued, and I listened while eating a light breakfast. Since we were letting the snowmobile be used for most of the morning, there was no rush to make a decision. I generated the day's rations and used two of my three healing charges. The other was being saved for the trip home.

While the discussions continued, Wendy and I walked around, checking on both building sites and checking in with the people we were leaving behind. The report we got was good. There were more volunteers than needed, and plans were already in place to expand the building crews for the next round. In the meantime, finding and moving supplies would keep people busy while we were gone.

I also learned there had been some disturbances at the other house from people not happy about who was chosen to sleep there, but nothing had escalated to violence. I left it to the people in Bangor to solve, but I mentioned to Andy that having the entire community working together was important.

I also double-checked that the pods were being occupied. The nice thing about pods set to maintenance is that no one needed to collect anything from them. They just needed to keep people inside them. By the time I made it back to the first house, they had decided they wanted the clinic built, so I built that and walked them through the best way to use the two medical pods. They were also using the clinic as housing for eight more people.

An hour before noon, Wendy and I ate a light lunch. Their food situation was way tighter than ours, so we did not want to eat too much of theirs. I answered some last questions as we waited for the snowmobile to be delivered back to us.

"Don't forget the pods and try to have those houses done in seven days. I plan to return in a week with some people to help you start on the greenhouse construction. I hope to have bought some communication devices too, but I'm not sure we can save enough tokens to afford that." I was already mentally adding up all the tokens I would need to integrate things in both locations.

After we left, the ride home was peaceful until we reached the windmill outside Pittsfield. Based on the tracks we found, someone had found it the prior day, and they must have been watching for us. We were waiting in the sled, taking a quick break and planning to follow the tracks to talk to the locals, when everything went sideways.

"There's a large group of armed humans heading our way,"

Vlad warned me as he popped back into existence next to me. He had been scouting the area from inside the snowbanks. "There are eight of them. They look determined, but not in the best of shape."

"Damn, that's more than we can immobilize at once," I said to Wendy. "We can only freeze six of them, and that's if they are generally seen as criminals."

Over Wendy's protests, we unhitched the sled, and she got positioned for a quick getaway if needed. I was still hoping they would be friendly. Being armed did not mean they were hostile. I just wanted to be prepared.

"I've got Vlad and a way to escape if needed. If they are hostile, you could actually die. I don't want another death on my conscience. Hopefully, this is just paranoia, but it's better to be safe than sorry," I said when she continued to argue against possibly leaving me behind.

A few minutes later, the group came into view, and before I could try to use my commanding presence perk to start talking, the first shots were fired at us, and there were yells to surrender. Shooting at us before attempting to talk was a pretty clear sign these were not nice people.

"Go, go, go," I yelled as I raised my hands and moved in front of Wendy. In the few seconds we had after Vlad's warning, we had mapped out a route that dropped her out of sight so she could get the distance needed to be safe.

As the snowmobile disappeared, I tried talking to them. "Look, we don't mean any harm. There's no need to shoot. We were trying to help," I yelled to the approaching figures, but I was not sure they heard anything. They were all yelling at me and demanding I get the snowmobile back.

I kept my hands up as more shots were fired, which was tough. I was still hoping to find an easy way out, but my resolve started to waver when one of the shots grazed my leg. I was not seriously wounded, but it was enough to freak me out. I looked down, saw a smear of blood, and let myself fall to the ground. I resisted the urge to heal it because I still hoped to learn something about the situation. Going out in a blaze of glory would not do much more than make me feel good about myself. If I were not going to fight, a small wound would be a good way to surrender.

After falling, I did not move, and the shooting stopped. I lay there until the group showed up and surrounded me.

"Get that snowmobile back," one of the men yelled at me as soon as they had me surrounded.

"I can't, no way to contact her, and I told her to get to safety," I said. "She won't be coming back."

"Damn it," one of the other men yelled as he kicked snow on me. "That damn windmill is not going to save us if we can't get more food. After last time, the survivors in town are shooting us on sight, and there's more of them than of us. That snowmobile would have made it easier to get in and get out with food without being shot."

Out of nowhere, one of the other guys slammed my head with the butt of his rifle, and I blacked out. When I woke up, they had taken everything other than my clothes. At least they had bandaged my leg. It was a sloppy job, but it was enough to stop me from bleeding out. I was glad my tablet had been on the snowmobile, as it was only locked with my fingerprint. I realized I had to change that in the future. They would have been able to unlock it with my finger while I was unconscious. It contained too much information about Augusta and Bangor to leave unsecured.

My head was still sore, and I had a feeling that without my improved physical score, I would have already been dead. I kept my movements to a minimum while I looked around the area and waited for a report from Vlad. I was locked in a closet, and the gang that had captured me was spread throughout the house they were staying in. It took him 15 minutes of careful searching before he reported back.

It seems this group tried to take over and strong-arm the town into providing them with food and more, Vlad said. *The town fought back and drove them out, and it's been a tense standoff for the last month. There are 14 men in this gang, all well-armed. Neither side can take on the other without big losses. Something is going to happen soon, though. The town has most of the food, and supplies here are running low.*

I was glad that I had sent Wendy away. This group was going to be trouble and having her here would not have ended well. I was already resigning myself to taking out as many as I could so that I could die and get back to Augusta. The downside of sending Wendy away was that I had no way to let Augusta know to come pick me up. I also had no way to get back to Augusta on my own. Escape on foot was not really an option. The upside was that the thugs did not know what I could do, or that I was a lot stronger than I looked.

I also needed to confirm what Vlad had found out. Even though I had jumped right to ways to take some of them out, I needed to talk to them first and see if they were as big a problem as Vlad thought they were. I went ahead and healed my leg under the bandage, then started making noise so they would know I was awake.

It only took a few minutes before I heard something being moved, and then the door opened. I played that I was still hurt and a little out of it as they dragged me out of the closet. They hauled me into what had once been a living room, now more of a sleeping space. I was pushed into a chair against the far wall with multiple guns, including the one I had been carrying, pointed at me. I knew one was still working despite all the cold, so if I stole one back, it would be that one.

"You look like you come from someplace with food," was the first thing said to me. "Tell us where it is and help us get it, and we won't kill you."

I was pretty sure the guy talking was the same one who had bashed my head, so I was not feeling friendly to start, but I tried to stay civil.

"None of us can get there on foot. I'm stuck here just like you," I said. "Maybe you can drop the guns and the tough guy attitude. Then we can see how we can help each other. I could almost see the commanding presence perk make them listen to my words, but all that perk did was make them hear me. It could not force them to be reasonable.

"No attitude," he said, moving toward me threateningly. "If you're like those idiots trying to save everyone in town, you're just as stupid as they are. Only the strong will survive, and when they realize we are the ones with the power, we'll be in control again."

The posturing and threats seemed to continue, with no end in sight. Their conversation was enough to confirm they were as problematic as Vlad had said. I considered trying something while they were all gathered in one place, but decided it would be better to make a plan. If they threw me back in the closet, I could carry out a late-night stealth mission. With Vlad's help, sneaking back out was more likely to let me take more of them out.

After listening to some of the things they said, they all needed to die. After that, Pittsfield, the town they were terrorizing, could be helped. It seemed like this group was about out of food, and they were talking about stealing all the food the town had left. If they were too weakened to get any food, the problem would solve itself, but I was sure they would do something stupid if they could.

Finally, I was thrown back into the closet, and after it was locked, something was pushed in front of it. I had been told I would not be getting any food until I helped them. I knew if I waited until midnight, I could generate a ration bar to eat before I made my escape and assault.

I was pretty sure they hoped hours in the dark, without food, would make me more agreeable to their demands. There were things I could have done for them, from ration bars to creating more nanostructures, but I would offer none of that. I would not be helping anyone who would make the apocalypse worse. Vlad and I spent the time until people fell asleep communicating silently, with him sneaking around inside the walls and reporting back to me. They were keeping two people on watch, but focused on preventing anyone from the town from attacking. The rest of the gang seemed to have relaxed, and one by one fell asleep. None of them seemed worried about me, which was fine by me.

It was around two am, and I had eaten two ration bars, leaving the wrappers for them to find, when Vlad said it was time. The two guards on watch had swapped out, and everyone but the two new guards was asleep. The closet I was in backed up against a bathroom that was out of service because there was no running water, so it was deserted. I carefully used my enhanced strength to make an opening in the closet drywall, leading to the bathroom. With Vlad guiding me, I could go between the studs and high enough up to avoid pipes and wires.

Once I had the hole started, it was pretty easy to make it large enough to step through into the bathroom. After escaping the closet, I waited while Vlad checked everyone was asleep, other than the guards. Then I made my way out to grab the unsecured gun Vlad had identified. I was having a problem thinking about sneaking into a room and killing someone in their sleep. Still, the way they had shot at us unprovoked and bashed my head let me know they would not have been questioning themselves if they got the same chance.

I was steeling myself to head into the first room when my foot caught on a rug and yanked a table, causing a clatter as junk fell to the ground. For better or worse, that would turn things into a firefight, and I gave up any attempt at stealth and headed for the room Vlad had said made the best target.

I got through the door and got a few shots off, killing one of the goons in his bed before the others dived for cover. Neither of them had their weapons, so I could take a few more shots at them before I had to duck for cover myself from people coming from other rooms.

The shots had everyone's attention, and one of the guards had run back in while everyone else woke up. With only firelight in the room, they hesitated, not sure who was who after their initial shot. I dropped them and moved into the most defensible position I could find. Vlad was no longer hiding and was making himself a target to draw their fire.

Even with his help, I was soon pinned down as more people joined in. I was getting hit and had used all three of my refreshed healing perk charges to stay fighting. I knew I was trapped, so I stopped trying to find a way out and asked Vlad where I needed to shoot. With a deep breath, I popped up and took out as many targets as I could before one of the bullets coming my way hit something I could not recover from. For the second time in 24 hours, everything went dark.

"Well, that second chance perk does not stop things from hurting," was my last thought before everything went black. After that, a prompt appeared to return to Augusta or continue to the next mission. I selected Augusta, then everything went dark again.

I was not sure how much time had passed before I woke up with a start, jackknifing into a sitting position. As soon as I figured out where I was, I must have turned beet red. I was sitting on the ground next to the processing portal in Augusta, stark naked. Not much time had passed, so it was about three in the morning. The building wasn't too crowded, but at least a dozen people were looking my way.

"Blanket, please," I shouted before lowering my voice. "Did Wendy make it back safely?"

"She was back before dark," one of the guys I had talked to in passing said as he tossed me a blanket. "She and Donna were meeting with the council to decide what to do to get you back. They planned to make a decision in the morning. How did you get back, and why are you naked?"

"It's not a secret that I'm back, but we don't need to wake everyone up," I said. "If word gets around, tell people I'll be back here at eight to start making plans. In the meantime, I've died once today and really need some sleep."

It was a cold run to my dorm in the blanket, and I got a few looks when I went inside, but most people were asleep. I had not thought things through, though, and even going into my room quietly woke Donna up, who was surprised enough to see me that her husband and son were woken up too.

I briefly explained I had a perk that let me come back to life, and that it was the first time I had used it. "I did not know exactly what to expect, but once I was sure the people who captured me were the bad guys, I did what I needed to do," I said.

"He was quite successful. Based on my observations, five of them are now no longer an issue, and three more will need to recover. That will mean less of an issue if our people can return to deal with them, and would help the town of Pittsfield, who they have been fighting with." Vlad said.

I was glad he censored himself with Alex in the room. We did not need to be too graphic around kids. "Look, I really need to sleep and will give all the details to the entire group at once in the morning," I said, getting into my bed as soon as Donna pulled her sleeping bag off it.

"Fine, but I'm going to find Wendy and let her know you're back. She was really upset that she left you behind, and even if she's asleep, she'd want to know."

I felt bad that I was not finding Wendy myself. I knew if I started talking to her, it would turn into a long conversation I would have to repeat in the morning, and I really was tired in a way I had not been in a long time. I wondered if recovering from dying was like recovering from shifts in the work pods. I barely got any clothes on before I passed out in bed.

When I woke up, it was way later than I had planned, and Wendy was leaning against the inside of the door, watching me. I checked the time, and it was already past 10.

"Don't try getting away with saying 'hey' to me," she said, not moving from her spot as I opened my mouth. "I thought I left you there to be tortured, and here you are, a few hours later, just fine."

"I got shot and died in a firefight," I said. "So, it was not a walk in the park for me. That's why I wanted you to get away. I had an out, even if it was painful. I know you have questions, but if you can let everyone know, I'll be in the portal room in 30 minutes. This time I won't be late after missing the eight o'clock meeting. I'm going to take a shower and use the remote processing before I collect from all the pods and head in."

"Fine, don't be late. Everyone's been talking, and they want to know how you got back here and what's going on. I won't be the only one with questions."

As soon as she was gone, I grabbed another set of warm clothes and decided I needed to get another pair to replace the ones in Pittsfield. As I was walking to the shower, I had a thought and asked Vlad if my old body was still in the gang's hideout. I asked that out loud, and a few people heard me and did a double-take. When he said that my body and clothes were still there, I had a minor freak-out until I was in the shower stall. Vlad never came into the shower stall with me, so I had to switch to speaking mentally, which was for the best.

You mean this isn't really my body? Am I in a copy with the real me back there? I asked as my panic attack got worse.

After all the advanced technology you've seen, this is the part that freaks you out? If you want to be precise, you've been living in a modified body since you accepted the architect class, and it's been modified by nanotechnology each time your physical or mental scores went up. How did you think you were getting stronger? The nanotechnology had to map and improve your body each time.

It made sense, but raised ideas about who I was that I would need to work through later. If I went down that path now, I would never get going for the day. I pushed it out of my mind and finished getting ready. After that, I kept ignoring the existential questions and focused on collecting resources and processing materials. Missing a full day here hurt, as that was about 140 fewer material units since I needed to be near the portal for my perk bonuses to work. At least the settlement token perk worked wherever I was.

I also checked that maintenance was under control, even with the crowded buildings out in Bangor, then headed into the portal room. I had run out of ways to delay the meeting and needed to face all the questions coming my way after using that perk.

11

"So, we're glad to see you safely back, but it seems like there were some things you didn't tell us," O'Donnell said as soon as I sat down at the very full meeting table. I was having flashbacks to the meeting when I first arrived and was being questioned.

"There are plenty of things I have not told you and plenty of things you have not told me. Nothing I keep to myself puts you at risk. I have ways to protect myself that I didn't need to share too early, and as far as this secret went, I wanted to see how you acted when you didn't know I had an easy out if you tried something," I said. "I have a way to cheat death and either come back here or just move on to my next mission. If I were to do that, it would leave you to figure things out on your own. Not that I'd do that unless you all left me no choice."

"It's good to know you don't plan on deserting us," Erin said, breaking in. "Wendy briefed us on everything that happened in Bangor. It sounds like they are even worse off than we are, but you've given them some hope without slowing our progress down too much. I assume you're going back as planned despite the bandits at Pittsfield, since it seems death is not a problem for you."

"Hey now, let's be clear. Dying is not fun at all. I don't plan on making death part of my strategy in the future. Also, I now have the bonus of knowing this is not my original body. My dead body is in the corner behind a couch back at the bandit's house," I said. "I'm still dealing with the thoughts that knowledge brings up and what it means about the soul and.... Never mind, I am not going down that path. Yes, the plan is to go back to Bangor and then possibly contact the town of Pittsfield on the way back. We can help them deal with the bandits. Assuming I understood what's going on, they have been making the town's life tougher. Plus, they are down to nine people from 14. Maybe six if the three I injured don't make it."

There was some more discussion about my plans. I was pushing to make the trip solo next time and see what I could do about the rest of the bandits. As much as I did not like dying, I did not want to put anyone else at risk. Going solo, I could bypass the stop to recharge altogether. That would delay taking people to Bangor who could work on greenhouses by a week, but it might be safer. We had five days to discuss the plan, so I did not need a decision yet. We had stuff to build here and aliens to worry about. My only firm commitment to them was to integrate the houses in Bangor as scheduled. They needed those houses to have any hope of turning things around there, and I needed to complete that mission.

I had gone back and forth on the Bangor mission and Vlad's assumptions about it, but in the end, I told them that Vlad's guess was that we would need the reward from that mission. It was not just about saving them, but about setting everyone up for the future.

There was some discussion about what Vlad guessed we would get from the mission and whether we could trust those guesses, but knowing about the rewards did not change what we planned to do, so we let it drop. After that, the discussion turned to plans for Augusta. Everyone had their ideas, and I listened to them all before I spoke up.

"Klawock has been leveling the greenhouse complex, so it just costs 470 material units to build now. It houses ten people, thanks to the first round of research, 20 at double occupancy, and will also feed 400 people when it's up and running. It feels like food is going to be a big deal soon, so I'd like to get that built and start growing food now," I said. There were no complaints, so I used the building as an excuse to leave the meeting to go outside to build it. I constructed it where the building I had demolished had been.

That dropped our work units below 200, so I put both new pods on work unit production. I limited the work unit increase to that, though. We were building up a good supply of settlement tokens, but I wanted to keep pumping them out. I had a lot of custom buildings to integrate over the next week, and I still needed to buy communication devices. When I got back and saw most of the council had cleared out, I had a meeting with Donna, Wendy, and Paul.

"I think we need to start scouting to the south," I said once we were alone. “A lot is going on, but we can’t let the aliens do whatever they want. I don’t want to always be on the defensive. Plus, we really need to kill some golems to make more enforcers. I can’t move on to my next mission with just three of you here to defend Augusta, and we need to start Portland on the path to being saved. We can’t do that without clearing out the aliens. There are a lot of people still all around here that need help, and the aliens are hindering that.”

Donna and Paul were all for it, but Wendy was clearly reluctant. I could tell Eric’s death and then the attack on the way home had shaken her. I pushed her to speak up, and she said what she was thinking.

“It’s not the same for us to go out there like that. You can come back, but we don’t,” Wendy said. “I’m not sure I want to risk dying again and again.”

“No one’s going to force you,” I said. “But it’s not safe here either. There is going to be a fight with the aliens sooner or later, and I think it’s safer to do it on our terms. That said, if you don’t want to, we can find other tasks for you. Think about it, but I want all of us to train this afternoon and plan for a scouting mission tomorrow. I am hoping hunting them is safer during the day when we’re not in the middle of a storm, but there will always be danger.”

I pulled Donna with me and left the other two to talk. I wanted to ensure Donna could keep anyone from pressuring Wendy. I only wanted willing people on the scouting team.

I spent a few hours talking to people and then eating lunch before it was time to find everyone for training. This time, I hung back and let Donna run the training while I chimed in with what I knew about the aliens. We also discussed additional preventive measures I should have considered, given that the aliens were using guns and traps. Donna had spoken with O’Donnell, and we were all issued bulletproof vests and helmets. Combined with cold-weather gear, it was bulky but could help save lives. A direct hit with a spear like the one that took out Eric would still be fatal, but lesser attacks might be reduced to where I could heal them.

Donna led all of us through five hours of moving together, working with Vlad, and watching for traps. There was even some target practice against drawings of golems. The training continued for an hour after it got dark. Some night training was good, even though we had planned to scout only during the day. Everyone had realized that plans changed all the time. We also spent some time in snowshoes to get used to moving in them.

"I think I'm okay with the scouting run," Wendy said at the end of the training. "It feels like we're more prepared this time, and I guess I'm stronger now, too."

"Glad to hear it, and I'm glad Donna thought of the protective gear. Staying prepared and on the offensive is the way to go," I said before making plans to start the scouting right after breakfast the following morning.

My other task was to check in on the new sleds being built. There was one for use in town that focused on hauling large loads while there was effectively unlimited power. The one for trips to Bangor was lighter than the original, reducing the sled's weight so we could have more range or carry more supplies. It would be a tight fit for three people and modest supplies, but the increased range was worth it.

The next morning, after collecting resources, we all met up to head out. I had decided not to build anything before the scouting. That would leave me the resources to build something on the fly if we ran into trouble. I had deferred to Donna and Vlad to plot our route, combining Donna's knowledge of the area with Vlad's knowledge of the aliens.

We were moving into territory that had not been explored since everything had happened, and the deeper snow meant we were all on snowshoes about a mile outside the settlement. The plan was to head to I-95, then follow it south. We would hike out for four hours and then back for five, assuming we would be tired on the way home, causing it to take longer. The first two hours, from getting to the interstate and then heading down it, were calm. Donna was glad to see our improvements because of the training she had put us through. Thanks to that, we traveled nearly a mile and a half in an hour. It was about two miles to the interstate, and then we started making our way down it. We diverted from our route to check out various buildings, but everything along the route was deserted. It was about the three-hour mark when we saw our first sign of the aliens.

"These were caused by golem attacks, right?" Donna asked Vlad when we found a house with chunks of the walls pulled out.

"It looks like it," he said. "I don't know what else would have done this. We need to be more careful from here on out."

We slowed way down but kept moving forward. It did not take long, another ten minutes at most, when we ran into what must have been a roving patrol. There was a well-trodden path cutting across the interstate that had to have been made by repeated trips by a golem or golems.

"Two golems are coming this way from the west," Vlad warned. "Get ready."

There was enough snow that we could hide ourselves, and we knew from experience that the golems by themselves were not the smartest. Vlad had seen no sign of any aliens with them, so I hoped this would be an easy fight. We were also waiting for them to come to us, so we would not stumble into a trap.

The fight itself was anticlimactic, with both golems falling to gunfire before they were anywhere near us. The downside was that we needed to hike out close enough for my perk to grab the spheres. There was also the issue that the sound of the guns traveled a long way.

"Let's move back and wait to see if that pulls in anyone or anything else," Donna said. "We're almost done for the day, and I don't want to get trapped if we move forward and more golems come down this path and end up behind us."

That made sense, so we backtracked and then headed west. If more came from that direction, we would see them before they got to the area where we had killed the others. That might give us some element of surprise.

We waited longer than planned, but it was okay because we had not gone as far south, so we had less distance to backtrack. Just as Wendy was mentioning going back, Vlad warned us that a group of golems was heading our way.

"Still no sign of the aliens, but this is a larger group, at least five of them, and they are moving more erratically. They might be trying to make themselves a harder target," Vlad said.

"Five's not bad. Even if they are ready for us, I think we can take them," Donna said. "Let's be ready to kill them at range. If we clear this group, it's a good hit against the aliens and seven spheres for the day."

As Vlad had guessed, the golems were trying to make themselves harder to hit. Just two of them died in our first volley, and they were closing quickly as we kept firing. It was not an issue until Vlad yelled that five more were coming from the other direction.

"Donna, you stay with me on the two left coming from the west. Wendy and Andy try to take out the ones coming from the east. Let me do most of the melee if we can," I said.

With the split focus, Donna and I each had to switch to our clubs to take the last two using hand-to-hand fighting. Donna's target was injured a little more than mine, but neither golem was in good shape. I was conscious of the need to finish them quickly and help the others, though. I was judging when to use the incapacitate criminal perk. I did not want to use it too early, before we saw all the attackers.

Vlad was yelling updates, and only one on the other side was dead. The advantage of the clubs was that each attack damaged the plant material, further slowing it down. I finished mine off and just needed a few swings to help Donna finish hers. I was afraid I had gotten both kill shots and robbed her of the points toward a new perk, but we needed to focus on speed.

By the time I spun around and raced to Wendy and Andy, they were already in melee combat with the four living golems. Well, three of them, one of them had been incapacitated. It looked like Wendy had used her charge.

Despite these not being as injured, I stuck with not using the incapacitate perk when we did not need to. We wanted the charges handy when we really needed them. Andy was clearly injured, though, and I called out to say that I would help him. Not only did I start attacking the two golems he was fighting, but I took a second to use my healing perk on him. That was a visible change and burst of energy on his part.

The others looked fine, so I focused on attacking the golems. Hitting them with a club was like beating on a tree covered in pillows. There was some give and bounce when hitting them, but underneath it was like steel, unless you were hitting a thinner limb.

After four hours of walking, then being still and having my muscles freeze up a bit, it was not a fun fight. I was already sore, and I could only imagine how the others felt with their lower physical scores. I tried to get a golem close to death and let Andy have it before I rotated through helping kill the other golems. I was pretty sure I didn't get the final blow on any of these.

Everyone was panting when the fight was done, but no one was injured enough to use another healing charge. We did not want to linger. It was officially past the time we should have left, and we were not ready for another fight. With that in mind, we backtracked so I could get the spheres from the ones we shot at range from the first group, and then headed back to get the solo one from the other group killed at range. After that, we would head home.

I was about to get the last sphere when Vlad yelled for everyone to drop. I was already falling as he spoke, but I caught a glimpse of an alien on another snowmobile. I felt pain as a bullet hit me, but then there was shooting from behind me as someone, likely Donna, returned fire.

"Use your healing on yourself," Vlad said. "That's a severe injury, and Donna has things under control."

I used one charge, then, at Vlad's urging, my last one. I had wanted to save one in case anyone else got injured, but it would not help if I were passed out. Even with the second use on myself, I had not recovered before the shooting stopped. It was bad enough that I passed out.

When I came to, I was draped over the snowmobile they were dragging back to town. I just blinked and tried to look around for a few seconds before Paul noticed I was awake and let everyone else know.

"Thank goodness," Donna said. "I've been using my first aid perk on you, but you have been unconscious for almost three hours."

My waking up seemed to be the signal that it was break time. Everyone looked worn out, and I was too sore to do much more than brace myself upright. Vlad had appeared and immediately headed out to maximum range to scout for us. That left the enforcers to fill me in on what had happened.

A single alien on a snowmobile, armed with a gun, had started shooting as soon as she raced up at top speed. I was the only one who got hit, and Donna had taken him out with her third shot. He was dead before he could be incapacitated. They had decided to grab the snowmobile and drag it back to town. This one was undamaged and looked different from the other one we had captured, so I was not sure how much it would cost to convert it to our settlement's grid. Still, any cost would be cheaper than buying it. As they talked, I checked my information and had a nano matrix in addition to all the dropped spheres. Just five more spheres until the next enforcer could be created.

"Through all that, I earned two personal tokens and leveled up incapacitate criminal twice," Donna said. "We need enough charges so that we are not always saving them. That will make the fights easier."

"I got one token and leveled mine once," Wendy added. "It's a good thing you were wearing that body armor, by the way. The bullet was deflected off your chest into your arm. You got unlucky. The bullet hit just right and nicked an artery. There was enough blood loss to knock you out, but it could have been a lot worse."

I did not mention that what they had seen was after two uses of my healing perk. The wound was probably much worse before that, but I did not want to point it out. We took a 15-minute break and talked. The big takeaway was that, with everyone's perk levels increased, Donna did not want to hold back on using incapacitate as much as we had been. Between the four of us, there were 13 charges. Whenever there was more than one target at melee range for every person on our side, she wanted us to use the perk, starting with those of us with more charges.

It made sense to me, so we all agreed and started discussing how to organize it. We were still talking when it was time to get moving again. I tried to get down and help push, but I was still pretty weak and was told to get back on the snowmobile. My weight did not make it much harder to push, and Donna said watching me shuffle through the snow was more painful than moving the snowmobile with me on it.

We were still discussing updated battle plans as it grew dark, and our pace slowed further. Once we ran out of combat planning to discuss, Paul brought up how much everyone in town would love having a second snowmobile to haul stuff around. I made a little noise that everyone picked up on, but Wendy got what I was thinking first.

"You want to give the second one to Bangor, don't you?" she asked. "It would be nice to have a second one at home, but the benefit they would get would be even larger."

"That's what I'm thinking," I said. "Ride both snowmobiles up so they can use them to move supplies around and then leave one there. I need to limit them to only integrated structures, other than infrastructure. That has them way behind Augusta, and reliable transportation will help them out a lot."

"I'm good with whatever you want to do. This thing belongs to the four of us in my book, and you're the one who got shot and bled out for it. Add to that, it was my shot that killed the alien so that he couldn't get away. I think we can decide what to do with it, no matter what the people back home say," Donna added.

Finally, I could sense we were within range of the settlement, and I told them to stop. This time, it was just 114 tokens to integrate the snowmobile, and I spent them immediately. The snowmobile hummed to life with that same soft noise the other one made.

Everyone was thrilled not to have to push it anymore. Since I was the injured one, I got to drive it, but I kept the speed low so we could stay together. We could have shoved two people on it and made trips back and forth, but even being close to home, we did not want to split up. That meant we were back closer to eight, which was a few hours later than planned, so there were people worried and watching for us. The last run-in with aliens, where we lost Eric, had left its mark on everyone.

I let Donna give people an update, and I headed to the clinic to see if a medical pod was open or about to open. This was really the first time I had tested whether Joey was keeping his end of the bargain. One of the other doctors sent me to the clinic building with the next opening, and I just had to wait 10 minutes for my turn. It was a relatively quick session. I was out of the pod in under 40 minutes, which surprised me. Then Vlad pointed out that my new body was in good medical shape, which stopped that train of thought. I also sparked an uncomfortable conversation with the doctor, who seemed to lack boundaries. His comment about how useful my ability to spawn new bodies would be for harvesting organs made me wonder whether he should be dealing with patients at all.

With a shrug, I decided it was not my problem. I had heard no complaints about him, and Joey seemed to have the medical issues well in hand. I knew they still were working through a huge backlog of issues. At least the lack of medication was no longer a glaring problem, as they used the pods to focus on diseases that required medication.

From there, I checked in with Donna to make sure she had answered all the council's questions before hunting for some food. The good news was that the apartment buildings were still taking turns serving as a communal kitchen for people working on projects around town, or even providing food for people in older housing where cooking was a pain. Just because people could tap into power did not mean it was easy in the old homes, and most appliances were no longer working.

With a full belly and all my aches taken care of, I had a solid night's sleep and was up at my normal time to collect resources. It was not until I got to the portal bay and was asked what new perks I had gotten that I realized I had forgotten about the nano matrix. I used it immediately and got six personal tokens this time. I was tempted to add another level to the second chance perk. The death I had recovered from used one charge that took 30 days to refresh, so I was down to two charges for now. Despite the urge, I placed all six tokens into boosted stamina to get three more levels there and increase the portal processing capacity by 15 more points, adding an average of 13 more material units each day.

As I looked over the settlement, I resisted the urge to switch pods to work units. Material units and settlement tokens were piling up, but over the next few days, many structures in both towns would need water and power. The cold in the area was now high enough that the power draw was always above baseline. Augusta's listed power draw ranged from 2,125 to 9,160 power units per day. The 3,120 power units currently being generated were barely covering the power usage at the current temperature, so I needed to add more windmills before adding anything else that used power. Water usage was approaching the limit as well. Many people were using water from the towers for the old buildings, and I needed to maintain a surplus for that.

With all that in mind, I walked around to add two more windmills and one more water tower. The windmills were installed to expand influence, while the water tower was installed to optimize snow removal. All six of those pods were set to work units after I checked that the maintenance backlog was still slowly dropping. With 86 pods now operating in Augusta, that meant 602 people were required to keep them all active. They were assigning eight people per pod, so there were two extra for breaks and stuff.

The three new custom houses were ready shortly after that, and I walked over to integrate them. The entire process with the houses was becoming an event each time they were integrated, and people moved into them. Each house meant 36 more people were safely housed, without being crowded to the point that the buildings quickly degraded. This round was the one that would get everyone back to double occupancy in the nanostructures, so more people could start moving out of legacy houses. Another 75 tokens later, and the new houses were part of the grid, and people were moving in.

"We're sticking with three houses at a time for another cycle or two," Bryan told me as we watched people move in. "With the stuff at the farm, the plans to add greenhouses, sending people to Bangor, and having to spread out, I think that's best."

"Hey, it's your call. You've got everything on track and know the teams better than I do," I answered. "I'm happy with effectively one new house each day, plus the work on the farm and greenhouses. It's making a real difference in how fast everything is going. Even better, it looks like the experience of building these structures is what will save people in Bangor, too. It's really bad there."

"I can imagine that with all those people, it would have been rough. We were helped because we had a lot of young people, thanks to the college," he added. "I think you should do a presentation on the progress we've made here. It's only been 18 days, so as much as people are complaining, I think it would help them see how fast you are really moving. Letting them know what it's like in Bangor directly might stop the complaining, too."

"Are there many people complaining? It seems like most people are mellow about things. I was surprised there were not more complaints coming my way," I said.

"Trust me, they just don't complain to you. You come across as pretty scary, so people complain to each other and to the council."

I decided to take his advice and spread the word that I would give a settlement update before dinner for anyone who wanted to attend and could cram into the portal room. I planned for it to be standing-room-only so we could fit more people in. I let Donna know I'd need to cut our afternoon training short by an hour to get ready for the meeting. She was clearly unhappy that I was skipping training. Then she let the other enforcers know they would keep training without me if we were going out again the next day.

"As you can see," I said that evening to a packed room. "All the construction that has happened over the last 18 days has made a huge difference. The heat supply reserve has just dropped by three days over the last 18. That's mainly because we need less legacy heat to keep things warm, and old houses that use excess nano power for heating have stretched supplies. Food is dropping a little faster, but there was a bigger cushion to start, and it's dropping less than a day every day. The other thing to note is that maintenance spiked, but it's been constant or dropping over the last few days. As I keep adding more custom buildings here and in Bangor, we will need more pods to work on maintenance. It also spikes up because of overcrowding."

"Why are they overcrowding so much in Bangor but not here?" someone in the crowd asked. "We could have twice as many people in real houses if we matched them."

"It's a horrible trade-off. The maintenance is so bad that it slows construction by consuming the effort of so many pods. Unfortunately, their situation is so bad there's no choice," I said. "If things here get that bad, I'd ask you to cram more people in, but double occupancy seems to be the sweet spot."

After that, I let people examine the sheet I was projecting and call out questions for the next hour.

There was an acknowledgment that the population was still dropping slowly but was mostly stabilized, and that legacy housing numbers were declining as buildings were demolished for materials for the portal or for other buildings. I also talked through what the situation was like in Bangor, which got the reaction I had hoped for. Still, the primary focus was on Augusta for the night.

Augusta Settlement		**Population**	16,147
Food Supply	202 days	**Heat Supply**	28 days
Housing	20, 371 people	**Survivable Housing**	769 people
Food Production	14%	**Secure Food Production**	7%
Power Production	175- 4,575units	**Power Draw**	2217.5- 9,860 units
Power Storage	2,200/ 2,200 units	**Indoor Pod Slots**	86/ 106
Water Production	1,925 units	**Water Draw**	1,445 units
Work Units	407 units	**Material Units**	628 units
Research Units	0 units		
Production Structures	Processing Portal	Work Pods x 86	Large Windmill x 20
Large Water Tower x 7	Large Barn x 4	Class Console	Custom Greenhouse x 4
Greenhouse Complex x 1			
Enhanced Structures	Large Crafting Bay x 1	Dorm x 2	Apartment Block x 4
Medical Clinic x 4	Medical Pods x 8	Custom House x 13	Custom Farmhouse x 1
Deferred Maintenance	146 units	**Material Maintenance**	81 units

12

Erin pulled me aside after dinner to meet with the council. I normally resisted private meetings, but after the public overview of our situation, I let them pull me into one. There had been plenty of transparency, and they had not been causing problems. I knew I had to give in sometimes.

"That overview was a good idea and helped a lot," Erin said to start the meeting. "I'm in the thick of things. Because of all the emergencies we're addressing, I have been so focused on everything that needs to be done that I have lost sight of how much has been accomplished. When I saw your briefing, I realized that's a lot of food and housing that is basically ours forever as long as we don't die, the aliens are dealt with, and we don't screw things up with infighting."

Her statement carried a pointed message to the other council members. I knew there were ongoing internal fights among council members, but I planned to stay out of those fights as long as they did not spill over into the open.

"I'm glad to see how you handled the thugs that caused you and Wendy problems. It seems like we were pretty lucky even before you came. We didn't have any group like that causing problems here," O'Donnell said. "My biggest worry is still about the aliens and when the next storm comes. I'm glad you are scouting them, but you don't seem any closer to a way to kill them or drive them off."

"It's high on my list too," I said. "I plan to spend most days I am not traveling to Bangor focused on scouting for now. It lets us create more enforcers and thin their supply of golems. Creating those is not free, and the spheres are not cheap to replace. If the aliens themselves keep coming at us solo, I'm happy to pick them off and loot snowmobiles, too. Unfortunately, they have shown themselves to be adaptive, so we need to keep pushing them."

"But do you need to spend two days a week traveling to Bangor and back?" O'Donnell asked. "That's taking up a lot of time that could be spent here dealing with the aliens."

"Remember, my goal is to save as many people as possible, not just Augusta. Plus, there's the mission Vlad thinks will unlock another nano class I need to keep people safe. If it's not combat-focused, it likely does not use spheres to grant the class. I know some of you want more people with combat classes, but any class will be a big boost to you and future communities. People with classes are stronger, and a non-combat class will have different ways to get perks," I said.

"All combat-focused classes will use spheres the same way. That's why it made no sense for Devin to take the soldier subclass when spheres are the limiter. Also, there will be large overlaps in who even qualifies for a class when looking at combat classes. That's why a class drawing from a different pool of people and using different resources is so important," Vlad said.

After that, the whole room started talking and asking questions about classes. The prior discussion was more limited, but now that the potential for options was emerging, more questions arose. I also clarified that I was limiting some of the details I was sharing with the public because, so far, it was Vlad's belief. I trusted Vlad's theories, but I did not want the general public to take his guesses as a promise. After that, we moved on to the other topic of conversation that was on everyone's mind. They wanted to know how long I was staying. The fact that I could have moved to the next mission when I died shook some people up.

"It took me two and a half months to stabilize Klawock and end that mission. I want to complete this mission, so I don't plan to leave before it's done, but I'd like to do it in less time," I said. "I don't know if that's doable. There are a lot more people around here, and the aliens seem like a bigger problem. Even with all that, I want to move on faster with each mission. I told you there aren't many people like me. I need to get bastions of humanity started all over the place. You all can save people in the local area over time, but you're not going to help people very far away before it's too late."

I saw everyone doing the timing calculations to figure out how long they would have me around to help, based on that statement.

"Don't worry. I'm not going to leave just to hit a deadline," I added. "I am going to rush things as much as I can, though, while being safe."

Vlad and I both answered more questions for another 30 minutes, and then I headed to bed. The enforcers knew we were heading out again the next day, so they were all getting some rest. We had spread out enough again that Donna and her family had moved out of my room, and I was back to a solo room, which I appreciated. Sharing when I needed to was okay, but having my own space was nice.

In the morning, I had to decide which structures to buy. I wanted to get another greenhouse, but the research on it had reached level nine. I expected it to level up to ten soon to get a bonus. If I built it now, I would have to pay to add the bonus. Instead, I headed out to the farm to build a barn. They had a few animals they wanted to keep, and we could move others out there into the empty space. With the snowmobile we planned to use for scouting, I could get there and back quickly. The greenhouse there was complete as well, so I integrated that and brought some workers back to the main area to start on a greenhouse there.

I knew the three houses back at the main area would not be done until the afternoon, so they would have to wait until we got back from the scouting trip. We planned to use a snowmobile this time to get farther while still making it a one-day trip. We wanted a full day to scout, so I would not be waiting around for the houses.

"Are you sure this is safe?" Wendy asked as we hooked up a sled and got it ready to go. "Won't it be harder to look for traps like the one that killed Eric if we're riding this instead of moving slowly?"

"Vlad will still scout, as will the rest of us, but it's hard to know the risk for sure. We might be so fast that a trap misses us altogether, or the sled protects you from something. It's all a risk, but we're being as careful as possible while still doing what we need to," I said. "Just operating on foot will not cut it unless we want to stay out overnight."

It was not an overly reassuring answer, but it seemed to be enough that we were thinking about making sure everyone was safe. In that same vein, there had been a long discussion about who should drive and who should ride in the sled. Donna wanted to drive as she knew the area better, but I thought it should be me as the driver was the most likely to take an instant fatal surprise attack. In the end, Vlad tipped things in my direction when he pointed out I was the only one he could message silently if he found anything while scouting.

Once everyone was settled in the sled, we took off toward the alien's patrol route we had run into two days before. We planned to head further west before heading south to intercept the route, so we could observe it from the cover there and not be as predictable.

As soon as we were in place, everyone got out of the sled and arranged themselves to watch the patrol path while Vlad scouted it.

It looks like they are still using it, was the message he sent me after a few minutes. *It's impossible to tell how often, but golems have been through since we were last here. Do we still plan to wait until we see more scouts or start following the patrol route*?

The decision had been made to wait for more scouts, but Vlad had been advocating for a more offensive stance, and it looked like he had not let it go. I wanted an opportunity to get more spheres before we went deeper into alien territory. I let him know we were sticking to the plan. We had plenty of time, since the four-hour hike last time was a less than 30-minute snowmobile ride.

There was another hour of waiting in the cold and snow before Vlad let me know a trio of golems was on their way. I made sure we were all hidden, and we were waiting until they passed in front of us, then all three were incapacitated at once. With all three of them frozen in place, it was relatively easy for the enforcers to head down and kill one each with their clubs while I stood watch with Vlad.

"Did you notice?" Vlad asked as we scanned the area and watched the five-minute timer on the incapacitate perk. "The incapacitate perks landed at slightly different times. As soon as the first golem was incapacitated, the other two started to turn. I think they were attempting to flee. That's something new. The aliens must know they need more force to take us on. So, I see two explanations for their actions. They were either told to retreat if there were too many of us, or the golems were supposed to lead us into an ambush."

"We can decide what to do after this fight is over," I said. "Can you figure out where they were trying to flee?"

"Possibly back along the path, but it's hard to tell. They did not have a lot of time before they were frozen, too," Vlad said. "I can't be sure what they were doing, but it looks like they were trying to get away."

As soon as the golems were dead, I grabbed the spheres, and we retreated to the woods. After a brief discussion, we used the snowmobile to follow the trail further west. If they were sending more golems, we wanted to surprise them.

Three more coming, Vlad sent a little bit later. *They are on the same path and in the same formation.*

I passed on the information, and we got ready, but with extra caution. It seemed strange for the aliens to repeat the same attack as last time. I was used to them changing things up, but maybe they had not had time to react to us.

Things started the same way, but the enforcers had just started attacking the golems when Vlad called out that three more were coming. I had saved my charges and used incapacitate on them at range. Despite the noise, I started shooting at them. I was not going to run up to them, and these two groups would be the last ones we wanted to fight before retreating for the day.

I had just gotten a couple of shots off when all three started moving toward me again. I yelled at Vlad, asking him what was going on while using incapacitate on the two I was not shooting at. That was the end of my perk charges for the day.

"There's an alien in sight of the golems but not you. They have a perk to negate your perk," he said. "I believe more golems are coming as well."

By the time he was done talking, I had killed one of the golems, but the other two were free again. With those golems between the alien and me, plus more on the way, I moved back and kept shooting.

"Donna, use your charges on these two," I yelled. "Someone is canceling the incapacitate perk, and more are on the way. We need to kill these and get out of here. Everyone, use your guns. We need speed now."

Donna froze the two still charging us before pulling out her gun and finishing off the golem in front of her. By the time she turned around to join me in firing at the ones she had frozen, they were moving again.

"Damn it, how many charges does their perk have?" I asked Vlad as I kept firing. By then, the original three golems were dead, and the ones from the other side were dead as well. I told everyone to run for the snowmobile. We needed time to regroup and figure out what to do now that they had countered our trump card.

Vlad kept updating us on three new golems chasing us, but we made it to the snowmobile in plenty of time. In this situation, I deferred to Donna's expertise, and she drove while I looked for targets to fire at from the back of the sled.

The snowmobile was faster than the golems, and they had soon dropped behind us, beyond Vlad's range to sense. We still kept an eye out and headed to the two houses I had integrated on the south side of town. We wanted to warn them and use those houses to take a stand if the aliens chased us that far.

Once we were sure we were safe for the moment, we updated each other. I had been in range to get five spheres. We had enough to create another enforcer. Donna and Paul had also each gotten a new perk level. They both planned to put it into the incapacitate criminal perk, since it looked like we needed a lot more charges of that now.

It was just barely lunchtime when we arrived at the integrated houses and started briefing them. Being on the edge of the settlement, they were well-armed and always had people on watch. I was sure that with all of us, we could handle even a sustained assault. That did not stop me from realizing I needed to come up with all-new strategies out here. These aliens either had more resources or had learned from fighting other architects. Most of my strategies centered around the best use of that incapacitate perk, and they were now close to worthless. The other thing I had to consider was that I might face some of the aliens that had fled from Klawock. They would know more about me and my style if they had figured out I was the architect here.

People from both houses rotated on watch with us to discuss

what was going on and offer their advice. Most of them who had not yet been tested for a class wanted a chance to take the test to become enforcers.

"We'd still help out and do whatever you need, but it would be good to have an enforcer type out here more full-time," one of the guards said. "This area is going to remain the edge of town for a while."

"I'll let the council know," Donna answered. "I agree it makes sense, but you know the odds are pretty low that anyone here will qualify, right?"

"Having an enforcer here was my original plan, but it got lost in the shuffle," I said. "We'll see what we can do."

They all realized the odds were low, but wanted to try anyway. We took turns eating and taking breaks for three hours, with no sign of an attack. We wanted to be sure we were not bringing trouble their way and decided to backtrack halfway to where we were forced to retreat. If there were no signs of pursuit, we would feel safe heading back to town. As far as Vlad could tell, they had not pursued us after we got away from them.

"I'm thinking they did not want to risk losing more of their forces by following us too far," I said. "We'll have two days to make new plans while I run to Bangor to help them and see what's happening with those thugs in Pittsfield. I'm also thinking of taking some people back to town with us from the houses and testing them tonight. It makes sense to have an enforcer out here, and the council can't complain if I am doing bonus testing."

Donna did not look confident that I was right about the council's inability to complain, but she did not stop me. I told the guards at the houses that I would test up to ten of them if they came to the testing unit tonight. More than ten people wanted to come. I promised to do more testing later, but they needed to pick ten for now. It made for a caravan of people heading back to the main settlement, and we got a few looks as we headed in. I sent them to wait for me by the class pod while I integrated the houses. The enforcers all split off to brief the council, then meet up later to decide next steps.

It was good that everyone had their marching orders before we got back, since Bryan dragged me over to the completed houses to integrate them as soon as he saw me.

"This is the first time we have had to wait this long after finishing something to get it integrated. I know it's just a few hours, but everyone who worked on them wanted to see it done before they moved on to the next project," Bryan said. "I think some of them were using it as a chance to slack off, but they did a lot of hard work and deserve to see it finished."

This was the last group of buildings in the park for this group. They were heading down to the fields and parking lots around the police station and YMCA next. There was a good amount of room there, and the buildings to the west of that park were being stripped for parts and debris for the materials portal.

Since everyone was watching, I integrated the three houses, one at a time, to make it more of a show. I also confirmed plans with Bryan. That building crew would be beefed up and would have four houses built in six more days if everything went to plan. He also had two builders ready to head to Bangor with me to help them get started on building greenhouses.

With one more check of my resources, I decided I had enough to make the builders' lives easier. I headed out to the middle of the space where they would start building houses and greenhouses, and placed an apartment block. The workers would be able to eat there and use it for staging and to warm up when they needed a break. Even though we were low on work units, I assigned the two new pods to settlement tokens. I had a feeling we would be buying equipment to assault the aliens and would need a lot of tokens for any equipment purchases.

With that taken care of, I headed back to the portal room to do some testing while everyone scrambled to get people moved into the apartment block I had sprung on them. Word had gotten around about the testing, and there were ten people from the council's testing list waiting around to get tested, too, "if I had time in this impromptu session."

It was better than them complaining, so I tested five of them as an olive branch, but then I needed to grab some food and meet with the enforcers. One of the people from the outlying houses was a match, so I told them to stick around in case they were the enforcer I would create that morning. The rest of them headed home.

"So, we all agree with the plan, right?" I asked while I finished the hot sandwich that was my dinner. "Donna and I will be heading to Bangor in the morning. We'll each be on a snowmobile, pulling one of the new, lighter sleds with a builder riding in it and carrying some basic food supplies. That should give each snowmobile the range to reach Bangor without stopping, even with a detour to avoid the gang. On the way back, it will just be Donna and me on one snowmobile to see what's going on in Pittsfield and if we can deal with the gang out there."

"And Paul and I will be training here with whoever gets added to our ranks," Wendy said. "We'll also work on strategies to use against the aliens and see what equipment you can buy to help us out."

We talked about strategies for a bit longer before Vlad interjected to let us know that the region's baseline temperature had dropped. He'd been monitoring it, but he warned that we should expect lower temperatures from now on, even in a warmer phase.

I had noticed the temperature dropping, but thought it was a storm. Unfortunately, it was not a storm, but the cooling thanks to the sun's reduced output was really kicking in. The sad part was that the continued depletion of the warm thermal mass meant it would not heat up in spring or summer. The cooling would only slow, not reverse, as the days got longer.

With that depressing thought, we all separated for the evening. I told Erin my preference was to give Kate from the houses to the south the enforcer class, but I would convert whoever they picked before I left in the morning.

When morning rolled around, I took a longer-than-normal shower, as I would not get one in Bangor, and then had a large breakfast for the same reason. With that done, I gathered resources and went to activate the next enforcer. I was glad to see the council had decided on Kate. We talked for a minute before she got in the pod, and I activated the cycle. I did not need to wait for it to finish, so as soon as it was running smoothly, I headed outside to meet up with Donna and get going.

Before we left, I talked to both the people who were coming with us to teach Bangor how to build greenhouses. It was a husband-and-wife team with family in Bangor that had survived, so they were looking forward to seeing if their family was okay. Neither of them was looking forward to the ride, but with just one in each sled, they could be bundled up below the sides and out of the wind.

The ride went as smoothly as we could have hoped. There was no sign of the gang that had hassled us, and while it was close, there was enough charge to get us to the main park in Bangor, where all the construction was centered. As soon as we showed up, there was a touch of party atmosphere. It was clear they had all been worried that we would not return. We had basically shown up, given them horrible news, a touch of hope, then vanished for a week.

"Before we do anything else, let me get the houses you all have built integrated. The sooner people can move in, the more resources we save," I said to cut through the noise. "Donna and I will leave your two new greenhouse specialists here to make plans while I do my thing here and at the park with the other three houses."

It did not take long to integrate the houses, but it was still only a drop in the bucket compared to all the housing they needed. Over 100 people had died in the week I was gone, but that still left almost 12,000 people needing housing. That was a massive number compared to the official housing for just 144 of them. I had to speed up their progress to complete the mission within a reasonable timeframe. The resources I saved would be used for that, but first, I needed to meet with everyone.

While people were crowding into the new houses, I headed back to the first house I had integrated to meet with Andy and the others.

The space was so crowded that people were sitting on the bunk beds around what was supposed to be the living room. As soon as everyone had a place, Andy started talking.

"Since we knew you were coming back today, everyone has provided me with consolidated reports so that I could brief you on everything. They are all here to answer questions as needed. The main thing is that what you did last time you were here helped, but there was still some work to ensure the resources were allocated fairly. There were a few squabbles, but we got through the fights, and things will get easier each time you come out."

"I was glad to see the houses were all done on time, and the next ones have started. What's the plan there, and do you have people to work on greenhouses?" I asked. I felt a little bad when Andy had to flip ahead in his binder to check his notes, but I was curious.

"The current plan is to build eight houses in the next week and attempt to build two greenhouses," he said. "Since we did not know the greenhouse details, our speed with those won't be confirmed until tomorrow. The snowmobile you are leaving us with will be a tremendous help for all the construction, though. Moving supplies was one of the things slowing us down. I expect that thing will be in use 24 hours a day. Back to the updates, the medical pods have been in use nonstop, and there are requests for at least 6 more, if possible. Also, as the cold gets worse, we are having trouble keeping the few animals we have left alive. You mentioned a barn last time, so there is a request for one here to keep breeding stock alive. Finally, any more power and water you can supply, with a focus on power, is needed."

There were more discussions and clarifications from everyone in the room. Thanks to Andy's summary of their current situation, it was easy to ask good questions. Once that was done, I gave my update.

"The good news is that your heat supply listed in the information sheet just dropped by four days over the last seven. That was before the houses were integrated. Once that happened, your remaining heat supply increased by 1 to 13 days. It will get even better with what else I plan to build before I leave. Food supplies dropped by six days, and you're down to just over a month. I'm going to try to help with that, too. We brought 300 ration bars with us, and I will generate another 300 before I leave. I'll be building a barn to help maintain your animals, and your greenhouses will be coming online next week. More importantly, if we can solve a problem on the route here, the next trip up will be the larger sled filled with food, not people."

I gave updates on the gang we had run into without going into details about how I died and came back. I was not keeping it a secret, but I did not want to rehash the whole thing. That was followed by Donna giving an update on our progress with the aliens. The questions about the aliens went on for a while due to the novelty of discussing them. When the questions started repeating, I cut them off and generated my daily allotment of ration bars. After that, I headed outside to build.

First up was the barn, which I built on the edge of the park in a spot that would not have been good for a greenhouse. People started moving animals into it immediately, and then I had to build another water tower because the barn brought the surplus down to just 20 units daily. While I was at it, I placed three more windmills, scattering them around useful spots and expanding the connected area. All the new pods were located in Bangor and set to maintenance. I was planning to switch some of the maintenance pods in Augusta to other stuff when I got back. I also added one of the requested medical clinics. They were relatively inexpensive to build and could also accommodate a few more people.

"Okay, that's it," I said after building the clinic. "That's almost two days' worth of production from the Augusta portal and pods. I've used up almost everything I had saved up. If you can build as planned, you can make it and save most of the people here. You'll have to conserve as much as you can, but I'll be back in seven days. At that time, you should be able to double your housing and food production again. I'll have resources for at least more power and water. With any luck, I can build a few things on top of that."

With that, Donna and I wandered around, offering what advice we could. They knew we planned an early start the following morning, so we would have time to deal with the gang on the way back. I wanted to leave as soon as it was light. Andy gave me a folder of information to share with those in Augusta who were still alive. There were also letters to take back to Augusta, some for towns along our route, and even some for Portland.

I was very clear that, aside from the letters for Augusta, I could not commit to delivering anything, but no one cared. Having a chance of communication was better than no chance at all. Like last time, we ate little for dinner or breakfast. Instead, we said our goodbyes and promised to return in a week, if at all possible. As we headed out, I could see that their situation had hit Donna hard. She had heard about it from Wendy and me, but seeing it in person was another thing.

At our break outside Pittsfield, I made sure she was ready for what was coming and had put Bangor's challenges behind her for the moment. We double-checked that everything was ready, then headed into town to hopefully find out that I had made the right call in fighting the gang and to get some allies.

13

As we got closer to Pittsfield, we could see smoke rising from a couple of buildings in the center of the town. It was smoke from fireplaces and other heaters, not uncontrolled smoke, so it looked like there were still people here. We were coming in from the north, so I hoped they would not think we were with the gang. We were both decked out in our bulletproof gear just in case, and Vlad was hiding as no one here would know about him.

It seemed they were not guarding the direction we were approaching from. That let us get close to the two apartment buildings where the smoke was coming from before we were spotted. As soon as we were noticed, a group of people came out all bundled up and carrying weapons.

"We come in peace," I called out as we got closer, but I did not stop the slow-moving snowmobile. "We had some problems with the people on the other side of you, close to the interstate, and wanted to get your take on what was happening."

I stopped when we were close enough to talk without shouting. I kept my hands on the handlebars, and I knew Donna's hands were on the sides of the sled. At this distance, I could see what dreadful shape they were in. Everyone looked emaciated, and some of their guns looked like they had no chance of firing.

"Where'd you get that machine?" was the first thing I heard as we came to a stop.

"Is there someone here who can help us?"

I gave a very abbreviated version of events, showed off Vlad, and then convinced them to let us inside. They were not very trusting, but they were also running out of options. After hearing what was happening in Augusta, they wanted any help they could get. The story they told matched most of what Vlad had deduced, but they were worse off than I had imagined. Of the 3,000 people in the town when the pulses hit, only about 200 were left, and they were in rough shape and basically out of food. On top of that, half the people were sick. The gang that had formed had destroyed a lot of the town's resources in the fighting, and some of the strongest people on both sides had died before the stalemate they found themselves in now.

"So that's why we got a break," a person listening to us said when I talked about our run-in with them. "They have not caused problems in the last week. We've been waiting for them to make one last push. If you can help us, we'll do whatever you want."

As soon as he said that, a mission popped up for me, and as I read over it, I asked Donna if she had gotten it as well. She had gotten a different one based on taking out the gang.

Pittsfield Rescue Mission
This community can no longer viably sustain itself even with advanced technology. Rescue as many people as possible by moving them to nearby communities. The mission reward will be based on the number of people saved. Saved: 0 Died: 0 Remaining: 203

I shared the mission details with everyone in the room. There was immediate relief on their faces, but it dimmed when I said it would not be easy. Not only did we need to start by killing the rest of the gang to fulfill Donna's mission, but even 203 people were too many to transport quickly with the vehicles we had. I knew we would find a way to make it work, but they would need to hold on for a while longer. While no one was in a position to help us assault the gang, we really needed intelligence, and they were happy to tell us everything they knew. The gang did not know about our incapacitate criminal perk since neither Wendy nor I had used it. That might make it a lot easier.

That perk was also the final test. Did the community really consider the thugs to be criminals? Donna had pulled me aside to let me know that her detect criminal perk was not picking up a major criminal vibe from most of the people we were talking to, which was a good sign.

As soon as we had a plan in place, we headed to where the gang was located. While we were traveling, I asked Vlad about the mission via messages. It seemed like I should have gotten a mission like that for Wrangell, and I was surprised to see it show up here.

The nano controller is watching all of you and adjusting

missions to help you succeed in ways that maintain the nano density needed for survival, Vlad answered. *Expect missions and rewards to become more useful and survival-focused, even if they are things you would do anyway. Not all the architects are you, and the missions are adjusted using the same templates for everyone.*

With that out of the way, we went back to planning. Vlad would be the distraction for our attack and the one to lure them out if needed. I was not getting overconfident, but I was feeling pretty good about our odds. There was just one thing I was not sure about.

"If this works, we should be able to incapacitate them all, but then we'll be shooting helpless humans," I said. "It was one thing to kill some of them as they were trying to kill me. I think I'll have trouble killing helpless people. How about you?"

"I'm not looking forward to it, but I don't want to see those innocent people die. What else can we do? We don't have the food to put them in prison and feed them. Anything we do other than killing them ends in them dying from cold, dying from starvation, or killing other people," Donna said after a few minutes. "From the sound of it, they've caused a lot of deaths already, including you."

"That does make it a little easier from my side," I said with a weak chuckle. Thinking about my death still freaked me out. "I'm not sure if I want to find the body or not."

It was a quick trip to the gang's house, and there was no time for more discussion. As soon as we were in position, Vlad headed their way and got a reaction. A few shots were fired at him, and we could target the two of them on guard duty to freeze and shoot. Vlad said there were only four left inside. The three I had injured originally had not made it. He also said they were using everything for food. The word "everything" in the message was in bold, and I figured out what that meant pretty quickly. If anything, that made it easier to keep advancing. They had not realized we could freeze them, and they kept showing enough of themselves when taking potshots that we could incapacitate and eliminate them. It was just another ten minutes before Vlad confirmed they were all dead.

The fact that they kept attacking us until the end made the

whole process feel less morally taxing. I was glad neither of us turned out to be unable to do what we needed to. With Vlad's confirmation that the house was empty, we pulled the snowmobile up to the door and did a quick search. It was pretty clear what they had been using for food, and Donna and I both threw up at different points. Mine was seeing what had happened to my body.

After the quickest check of the house we could get away with, we looted anything useful. They had plenty of blankets, a few weapons and ammo, and some books. We took all that and loaded it into the sled. We also moved the firewood outside, well away from the house. After that, we set the building on fire. What was in there did not need to be left for others to find.

Fortunately, the house was isolated enough that there was no risk of the fire spreading. It would not even burn all that much in the cold, but hopefully it would be enough to wipe out what had happened there. With that taken care of, we headed back to town after quickly charging the snowmobile at the windmill. With the windmill's fully charged battery to draw from, we just had to get within range to bring the snowmobile back to full charge. Then we had to let the people in Pittsfield know what was going on and to drop off the first load of loot. Taking care of the gang was a lot easier than rescuing the people.

Once we were inside the apartment building, Donna surprised us with a plan she had been working on. "Devin, I think you should heal some people here and take some of them back in the sled. If they leave almost everything behind, you can fit in four people. You'll have more than enough power for the trip. I'll stay here this time and organize people. Even loaded down, you can make the trip in 3 hours with a clear path. You can be home by six in the evening, swap to the larger sled, and let someone else make the next run and pick me up. We can run four round-trip trips each day that way. We should haul some firewood back here too, so they can stay warmer."

"That makes sense, but I need to build another windmill halfway home. With the extra charging station, we can really load up the larger sled. That will let us take six people on each trip, and it will be along the train tracks, too, so it will be used in the future if we get those fixed. I'll set it to prioritize the battery, so that it can be instant charging on the way."

Once a plan was made, things moved quickly. I ended up taking five people. With two of them being children, they would not weigh too much, even without a recharge from the windmill I would build on the way. I did not want to rely on the one I was building, as it would need time to charge, and people would get cold.

They prioritized people with medical issues who were currently stable for the trip. Even with the lower weight of the people and the number of kids we had to move, if we could move 7 people per trip, that would be 8 days to move everyone if we just focused on that. I would need to get another vehicle to make this possible, as we could not tie up Augusta's only snowmobile for that long. We could waste six hours getting to Bangor to take that one back, but I thought we needed to get something better or get a train running. That was something to think about later.

We could also send food and wood out on the trips to pick up people when the sled would otherwise be empty. That would help the people stuck here survive until we could move them all.

The other thing I realized is that I would also need to come out to heal people for transport on one of the runs each day. The other option was to have one of the enforcers with first aid drive and stabilize one person each trip. There were a lot of sick people, but hopefully, more food and heat would help reduce that number. While I was making plans, there were some quick goodbyes, and then I headed off with my first load of refugees.

Using the resources that had been generated and collected for me that morning, I built a windmill outside Fairfield. We left the highway to place it near the train tracks again, avoiding running into anyone. We really needed to start rescuing people in the surrounding towns, but there just were not enough time or resources yet.

The relief on everyone's face as I got them out of the sled and into the portal bay was easy to see for everyone watching. I was proud to see people step up to help them and explain how things worked. I told them to stay close, but that Wendy would coordinate getting them fed and showered.

"I need to meet with the leaders here and get things figured out for your care and getting you integrated into the town," I told them. “I’ve also got to coordinate sending someone back to pick up the next group of people and to deliver some food.”

The council must have had people informing them of my arrival and the circumstances, as they were already assembling. I was glad they did not try to have the meeting in private this time. I wanted people to hear what we had found.

“Good, everyone is here already. That makes things quicker,” I said, heading to my customary seat at the meeting table. “There’s a lot to go over, and we’re on a timeline.”

I told them I would brief them on Bangor later, but things were stable there for the moment. I passed over the letters and the notebook with information for people who wanted to know who had survived there. Then I talked about Pittsfield. I did not pull any punches with how rough their situation was, and of the 3,000 people who had lived there, 2,800 were already dead. The people who had come back with me chimed in, reinforcing how bad things were there. It won people over, even if rescuing them would require scarce resources. For the people in Augusta, it once again showed them how lucky they were.

I also briefly discussed the elimination of the gang, but, because there were kids in the audience, I only touched on the fact that they had resorted to cannibalism in the vaguest of terms. That was still enough to horrify everyone, including the people I had rescued from Pittsfield.

“So, here’s the plan. I added another windmill halfway between here and Pittsfield. That means we can use the larger sled and transport at least seven people on each six-hour round trip. We can also bring some of my generated rations or other food on some trips, so they have food while waiting for rescue. I’ll build a dorm to start housing them and a medical clinic, since they'll have many medical issues to address. Both of these structures will help us out long term,” I said. “I know this is going to slow down our plans, but it’s the right thing to do. We’ll also have to balance rescuing them with scouting the alien threat and trips to Bangor. I plan to save 500 settlement tokens to buy a six-seater vehicle for the runs as soon as I can. It can’t tow anything, and it’s not laid out to carry much in the way of supplies, but it will be a comfortable trip and leave the snowmobile free. We had one back home, and it was great.”

"I don't see how we could say no," Erin said, speaking for the council. "We're not going to leave them to die, but I am worried about the other communities around here even more. Perhaps that new vehicle can be used to rescue other people after Pittsfield is evacuated."

"That's my hope. There is another thing I have not mentioned. There were quests for Pittsfield. Donna got a mission to eliminate the bandit threat there and now has two more perk levels. I have a mission to rescue as many people as possible from there. I have no idea what the reward will be, but it will most likely be something to help all of us."

From there, everything moved quickly. We got the sled loaded up and sent it back with Wendy driving. She would bring Donna back so we could make plans to focus on the aliens. They would also use their first-aid perks to bring back two of the more severely sick or injured people. As soon as they left, I went outside and built a new clinic. Joey started scanning the people I had brought back in the two pods, and I told them someone would escort them to their new quarters as soon as they were medically cleared.

After that, I found an open spot off the side of the park and built the dorm for them. I was sure they would not mind doubling up. That would hold the first 60 people we brought back, and they could be trained to work in the upper-floor greenhouse.

That construction left me with enough tokens to buy the same nano vehicle we had used in Klawock. First, I wanted to hear what the team had come up with to face the aliens before I used them all on a car. The snowmobile could do runs for now, and we could consider switching to a car the next day.

With all that done, I was wiped out. I double checked that the people I had brought back were being taken care of, ate dinner, and headed to bed. I let Paul know I wanted to meet with all the enforcers the next morning, and that meant having a non-enforcer manage the trip to Pittsfield at six.

Paul had been moved into my room, so his stuff was on the bottom bunk, but with just the two of us, it was not too crowded. I made time for a shower and then slept until my alarm went off at seven the next morning. The first thing I did was check the Pittsfield mission to see how things were going. The number of people saved reached 18, but tragically one person died overnight.

After breakfast, as I was collecting resources, I switched four pods from work unit production back to settlement token production. I needed all of those I could get. I also checked, and the research on the greenhouse complex had reached the tenth level. The bonus effect was that each greenhouse complex would now use 10% less water. It was just 15 units of water saved per day per greenhouse, but it would add up. I hoped they would move on to researching upgrades for the processing portal next. Any boost there would be nice.

I told everyone about the upgrade, spent settlement tokens to retrofit the existing greenhouse complex to take advantage of it, and then built Augusta's second greenhouse complex. Even with the decrease in water usage, the new buildings put us right on the edge. When I integrated the next greenhouse out at the farm later in the day, we would briefly go into negative territory. It was worth it because food was so important. In a pinch, it was easier to heat legacy buildings than to find food for Augusta.

With all that done and people briefed, it was finally time for the planning session with the enforcers. O'Donnell and some of his people were invited to sit in on it and give advice on how to take on the aliens. We even opened it up to the public. Some people were worried about spies, but I did not think we could keep secrets all that well, regardless. Secret meetings would have just slowed down the information leak and cut out a lot of people who might have had good ideas.

The problem with using the nano shop for supplies was the cost. There was a nice protective suit in the shop for 250 settlement tokens. It would provide more protection than the bulletproof gear and keep us warm, too, but that was 1,250 tokens for the five of us. A better option seemed to be weapons.

"Our current weapons are not designed for this cold," Wendy said. "They are taking more work to maintain, and we run the risk of them failing at a bad time. New weapons can also be added as resources allow, while maintaining what we have for as long as possible. There's a high-powered pistol that would be easy to use and only costs 250 settlement tokens, plus one settlement token per 100 rounds of ammunition."

The pistol got a round of agreement, but I looked at Vlad before responding. I wanted the enforcers to give their impression of the gun's usefulness, but I also wanted Vlad's perspective.

"The weapon idea is a good one, but I think you are overlooking the nano inhibitor," he said. "It's much cheaper at 100 settlement tokens and can hold a charge with unlimited shots in range of a power source and built-in storage for 20 shots when away from the settlement. You can even buy 50-shot, single-use clips for one token each."

"We looked at that, but would it be that useful against the aliens?" Wendy asked.

"Not against the aliens, but it will be more damaging than your current weapons or that pistol against the golems," Vlad said. "One to three shots should be enough to destroy a golem, and you can hit them anywhere. No need to hit important spots or worry about damaging spheres. It won't do much against the aliens, but there are far fewer of those, and it can still be effective to disrupt their equipment."

There was a long conversation about what to do, and people were on both sides of the argument. There was a faction of people who liked the lower cost and the fact that the new nano inhibitors could not be used against other humans. Others, like O'Donnell, saw that as a drawback if they needed to defend themselves against gangs, as we had run into by Pittsfield.

"Really, I think gangs making it to you is something so unlikely as to be a non-issue," I said. "If people have not attacked you by now, they are not making it here without having access to nanotechnology. In that case, if they do have nanotechnology and go rogue, the nano inhibitors might be more useful. Also, after getting a new vehicle, I could afford one of those right now. I can't afford the pistol, and we really need to start saving up for communication devices as well."

There was no rush, so I let the conversation continue for a while. More snowmobiles were brought up as another way to make attacks on the aliens easier. Unfortunately, at 250 tokens each, they were also expensive and felt more like a nice-to-have.

As lunch approached, I forced a decision. I wanted to buy the vehicle in time for it to head to Pittsfield with the snowmobile on its next run. I would need to delay the next trip by 15 minutes or so to integrate the greenhouse at the farm and bring some people back, then head back to Pittsfield to use my healing perk and ferry more people to Augusta. The plan was for me to get the nano inhibitors before our next scouting run. People could keep coming up with ideas until then, and if they had a better idea, we would listen to them.

I purchased the vehicle and watched the tokens I had been saving drain away. I gave a brief tutorial on its use and told people to pack it for the trip back to Pittsfield. Kate would be driving it this time to learn the route while following me. My trip to the farm was fast, and the first batch of workers who needed to come back hitched a ride in the sled.

As soon as I was back, we headed out to Pittsfield. The trip had been cut down to a little over two and a half hours heading there, lightly loaded, and just under three hours coming back. That made four trips a day possible, even with the time to load and unload, or for things like my trip to the farm and the healing I would be doing once we got there.

It was refreshing to enjoy the ride to Pittsfield. There were no aliens or gangs to worry about. Vlad was scouting as usual while I paid attention, but there was no looming threat. I enjoyed the low-stress ride through the snow on a mildly overcast day. Now and then, I caught sight of Kate's face in my mirrors, and she looked to be enjoying the ride too. As we got close to the town, we passed by the windmill to recharge the vehicles.

As soon as we arrived at the two apartment buildings, people saw the new vehicle, and faces pressed against the few windows that had not been covered to block out the cold. When we were inside, I explained the new vehicle and why we had bought it.

"We just can't tie up the snowmobile for these runs, so we added that nano car to the fleet. It will run four trips daily and be much more comfortable and safer for you. It's climate-controlled inside, so people won't have to struggle for warmth in the sled. It just has seating for six, so that's five seats besides the driver, but you can squeeze in, and the kids will take up less room. We should still get six or seven people for each ride. We'll try to schedule two snowmobile trips a day as well. Six trips per day will move 40 or more people. It will slow down toward the end, though, as people in poor condition might need to take two or more seats for safe transport. I know from one of these I had back home that we can fold down the seats on the right side of the vehicle to have a kind of single bed to transport really sick people."

While I was healing people, we talked about organizing groups for the two vehicles and that I would try to come out when I could, but that we also needed to think about taking care of the alien threat. There were no complaints about the plan. We had already rescued almost 20% of the remaining people. I was healing people for the trip each day, and despite another person dying, they were getting the food they needed. It had gone from abject hopelessness to everyone knowing they would be somewhere a lot safer in just days.

Once we were back in Augusta, it was time for me to relax. The next day would be my down day. There were plenty of things to build and integrate, but I needed a day at home before we tried another scouting run the day after that.

After a good night's sleep, the first thing I did in the morning was to make sure the overnight pick-ups had gone smoothly. With 67 people extracted, we had already moved over a third of the people. It was getting crowded in the nano housing, but with more houses coming online today, there would be more room. Most locals' complaints about having to wait longer for a nano powered home had faded as they saw how bad off the people being brought in were. Joey was also pushing for another clinic as they had a lot of medical issues, but I had to tell him no.

My first order of business was to use most of the material units to add two water towers. With the housing coming online today, we needed two to get out of the hole we were in and have some surplus. Building them also added four more pods, set to generate settlement tokens. I was tempted to increase my perk to generate more of those, as they were scarcer than I liked.

After that, it was just a matter of waiting for stuff to be ready for integration. The snowmobile was hauling supplies back and forth, so I hitched a ride whenever I needed it. A little after lunch, the three houses were ready to be integrated, and I spent 75 tokens on them. All three were allocated to the people from Pittsfield. We kept them together as much as possible to minimize disruption during their recovery. Then, in the mid-afternoon, the second farmhouse out on the farm was ready to be integrated.

With some of those construction workers coming back to town to help build stuff here, this group of builders was going from three houses to four the next cycle as well.

"I've got to say, knowing what I'm doing and having that research behind me is helping a lot," I said as I met up with people in mid-afternoon. "That's already room for 1,000 people officially, over 2,000 the way we are crowding, and we have even shoved more people in. It's only been three and a half weeks to do that."

After bragging, we made plans. I would be doing the evening run to Pittsfield, then sleeping until we tried another scouting run the next day. I planned to have nano inhibitors purchased for both Donna and Kate by then. We decided it made the most sense to see how they performed when used by the most and least experienced of the enforcers. I was not planning on buying one for myself until we had more tokens than we needed. I did not want to be killing golems or aliens when the enforcers would get perks for it. They were all looking forward to trying them out.

The evening trip to Pittsfield was routine getting there, but then there was a hard choice to make. One of the people I had already healed once had taken a turn for the worse and was in bad shape. The reality was that I was not sure if all three of my healing charges would stabilize him, and even if they did, it would take a few more days for him to be well enough to travel. I was trying to be delicate as I explained the dilemma, but he spoke up right away.

"All my family has already passed thanks to this cold. Heal the ones that can make the trip, and if it's meant to be, I'll recover enough to get a ride home at the end. If not, I was not meant to leave this place," he said in a faint voice.

"You're a good man," I said when it was clear no one was going to speak up to try to save him. "I'll do my best to help you after helping the others."

After that, it was time for the trip home. When this group left, they would be consolidating into one building. They were also staging some personal items they hoped to have moved. While there was no room to take them while saving people, they wanted stuff ready to take to Augusta when we had the capacity.

With everyone coming on this trip loaded up, we drove back in the dark. Cloud cover had rolled in, and snow was coming down. Vlad had not seen signs of another cold snap, and I hoped the snow would not keep falling into the next day. It made scouting a pain as it impacted us more than the golems.

14

The next morning, I was excited to see three research levels from Klawock that improved the processing portal. I immediately spent the three tokens to apply the research to our portal. That would be two or three more material units each day. We needed every available material unit we could get because we were still woefully short. I also checked the status of the rescue mission. It had gone well overnight, but one more person had died. Still, well over half the people were now rescued.

I rushed through the morning chores, then bought us two nano inhibitors so we could get an early start on scouting. We were going to see whether there were still patrols on the track from before and decide what to do based on what we found. When we got there, that path looked filled in and unused. From there, we slowly moved deeper toward Portland. Shortly after noon, we ran into a lone golem. Kate killed it with a single hit, but there were no follow-up attacks, and it had popped out of the snow. As far as we could tell, it was just a sentry to let the aliens know where we were.

"After all the attacks, this feels wrong," Donna said when nothing else happened. "They must be planning something."

"This group does seem to be better at planning and laying traps. It's late enough that I'm not sure I want to press forward if this is a warning so they can mass forces. We should be unpredictable too and leave instead of pressing on," I said.

All we had to show for the day was a single sphere, but we had tested the new guns, and they worked better than we had hoped. Still, I was frustrated. I needed to clear the alien threat, and I did not have a clear path to do it. I was tempted to try a full assault with a team of O'Donnell's people supporting the enforcers and me. It was far more dangerous for them, but I was also starting to feel stuck. I filed that under things to consider as we made it back to the settlement. I did not want to put more people at risk if I could build up the ranks of the enforcers. We made it back in time for Bryan to use the snowmobile to move some supplies before it was time for the evening run to Pittsfield.

As I feared, the man I had not healed the previous night had passed away. There were also increasing numbers of sick people left who would have a hard time with the trip. The food and supplies we brought up had only slowed the rate of illness, not reversed it. I got two people to the point where they could be moved, lying down in the vehicle, with one of the enforcers providing first aid. Those two runs would each transport two fewer people overnight, since they had to have three seats turned into a bed. At least it would leave room for a few of the personal items they wanted to bring and reduce the number of very sick people left to move. This was also going to be the last night the sled would be used to move people. There were just too many sick people left to expose them to the cold like that. I would come out with the sled to heal since I could not use first aid on the ride back. That meant I could retrieve one load of personal effects each night without taking up a car slot.

After I explained the plan, we headed out. There was evening snow again after it had died off during the day, and it was thicker this time. Vlad said the weather was "unpredictable" at this point. There could be a rough storm moving in or not. I hoped it would hold off for a few days if it were coming.

The following morning, I was glad to see there had been no deaths overnight and that another research level had been added to the processing portal. I also shifted more pods to working on settlement tokens. I had a lot of integrating coming up, including four new houses here in town. They were coming online just in time as the crowds of arriving refugees filled the spaces.

They would not be ready until the afternoon, though, so we did another scouting run. This route was more directly south and along the river. We ran into two more sentry golems and dispatched them easily. We were all getting nervous because we could not figure out the purpose of the golem sentries, which kept giving us easy spheres. We even tried to look for one more on the way back, but had no luck there.

"Low risk spheres are nice and all," I said. "We need 18 more of them to make another enforcer, though. Something has to give soon because we can't spend the time to collect a few spheres each day with the cost of each enforcer going up."

"I still think it's the best they can do for early warning, and we should trigger as many as we can before they come up with something else," Wendy said.

She seemed fully past her hesitation over Eric's death and was leaning into the attacks on the aliens. She was right, and we all agreed to do a longer scouting run the next day to either figure out what was up with the golems or collect more kills and spheres.

The houses were ready as soon as we got back, and I integrated all four while reviewing future construction plans with Bryan. We were still talking when Vlad interrupted us.

"Power is getting tight," he said. "I'm still not sure about the weather, and with more buildings coming online tomorrow, I'd get some windmills built now and get the batteries charged."

I took Vlad's advice and put up three more, extending the grid to cover more of the city. I also built a sixth medical clinic at Joey's urging. The people coming to us from Pittsfield were overwhelming the current pods. Even after their issues were all addressed, he assumed we would be bringing in sick people from other villages. He had a point that we did not want to evacuate people here just for them to die.

I also started testing people during my free hour before I headed to Pittsfield. It allowed me to test a few and keep the line moving. We already had some options for the next enforcers, but people who wanted a class were frustrated that I wasn't making more time to do testing. I knew it was important to people, but with a couple of options for enforcers already, it felt like a waste of time to identify more. In the end, I scanned five people with no matches before I left for Pittsfield for some more healing and hauling stuff back.

The trip there and back was typical, but as I got close to Augusta, people waved their arms to get my attention. I pulled up to the closest one while waving the other vehicle forward.

"What's going on?" I asked the guy who had been waving at me.

"The farm set off flares, the ones O'Donnell set up for emergencies," the man said. "Donna, Wendy, and Paul headed there on foot. As far as we know, Kate is home on alert at the houses to the south."

"No other alerts or flares?" I asked as I hopped off the

snowmobile to unhook the sled. "How long ago was this?"

"About 30 minutes ago, and there have been no other signals, good or bad."

"Make sure the guards stay on alert here," I yelled as I sped off. About halfway there, I turned off the headlight and navigated by the faint light from the partial moon and the stars. Vlad was scouting to the limit of his range without being told. I also bought another nano inhibitor and two clips before I left the portal's range. We did not know if it was because of aliens, but it seemed like a safe bet. If there had not been any more flares, there were two options. First, my team was all dead, which was unlikely, or they were still fighting. If they were fighting, I would want a better weapon.

Stop here and follow my directions, Vlad messaged me.

I stopped the snowmobile before getting off, as quietly as I could, and followed Vlad's messages on how to move through the woods toward the farm.

There are at least two aliens and a mass of golems out there. I can't get too close without risking them figuring out I'm here. Fortunately, my range is improved inside the settlement, Vlad messaged. *It looks like they are using the greenhouses as cover to keep people pinned down. These golems can fire projectiles from their bodies to damage the houses. Other golems are damaging the greenhouses. It looks like they have just started on that. The two aliens I see are moving up and firing on the main farmhouse. The other farmhouse seems to be dark. I think the humans consolidated in the original one.*

Can you direct me to a spot where I can see both aliens and have a minute before the golems get to me? I messaged. *The people in the farmhouse are returning fire, but they can't do much with all the incoming fire. If I can give them some breathing room, I've got to hope they can keep the golems from overwhelming me. At least the greenhouses are all lit up, so there is plenty of light.*

It took another five minutes of careful positioning before I was ready. It was hard not to speed up when I heard a scream from the farmhouse, but I just had one shot to do this, and I could not rush it. Finally, I was in place. I checked with Vlad, steeled myself, and popped up. I used an incapacitate criminal charge on both the aliens before firing at the golems. Vlad warned me there were at least 16 of those, meaning both aliens specialized in golem control.

I was not surprised when half the golems swiveled to focus on me. I was firing at them and watching the aliens for any sign they had broken my incapacitation. I was hoping they had burned all their perks to counter my incapacitate before I showed up, but that was not the case. Both started moving, and I reapplied the perk to them.

Even with that distraction, I killed two of the golems charging me and avoided all the shots fired my way thanks to the very thick fallen tree I was using for cover. While I did that, Vlad was at the edge of his range, yelling instructions to the people in the farmhouse. In the seconds it took for the aliens to break free again, my team must have listened, because the gunshots picked up and were aimed at the aliens.

Since the nano inhibitor would have disrupted my incapacitate I had not been firing at the aliens, just the golems. I went to use my last incapacitate criminal charge before focusing fully on the golems when the alien I was targeting was shot in the leg and collapsed. I switched to the other one and used my last charge, then focused on the golems that were getting way too close for comfort.

It seemed they lost most of their strategy with both aliens occupied. They were no longer using cover. It was a mindless charge at me. With two extra clips, I was not worried about aiming. Speed was more important than precision, and I did not mind wasting a couple of shots for every hit.

As soon as I noticed that one alien was not getting up, and the other was trying to get away, having broken my incapacitate again, I ignored them and focused on the golems. I dropped another four of them, leaving three of the original nine charging me, but then I had to retreat. I was on my second and last clip, following Vlad's directions as I backed up, in and out of cover, still firing.

"You're out of places to retreat to," Vlad said as the last two got closer. "Get ready to fight the hard way. I'll try to help distract them."

"Damn it," I muttered as I kept firing with one hand, pulling my club off my back with the other. I did not want to block their attacks hand-to-hand, but Vlad was right. I could not retreat any farther, and they were about to come around the tree I was using for cover.

I used the club to block the two attacks. The last one landed before the nano inhibitor finished off the golem. Then the fight was suddenly over. It took me a few moments to realize no shots were being fired from the farm either.

"That's all of them that were coming after me, right?" I asked as I slumped against the tree, catching my breath with the nano inhibitor still out. I checked the clip and saw it was full, and the gun was still fully charged.

"Yes, you are safe, but there were injured people at the farm. You need to get back," Vlad said as I straightened up and started moving. "Impressive job counting shots and switching clips, but you forgot you were inside the settlement's power grid the whole time. You never needed the clips. I'll guide you to the full one you threw on the ground mid-fight."

With Vlad scouting for me, I retraced my steps quickly as I headed to the farmhouse. I was keeping my eye on my information, and the spheres were dropping into the sheet. Shortly after I detoured to grab the clip I thought was empty and had dropped, I got two nano matrices from the two aliens who had been killed.

"The aliens and golems have all been accounted for," Vlad said. "I've been tracking your information, and you got all 18 of these spheres."

I yelled to the farmhouse that I was coming up. I did not want to get shot by a trigger-happy guard, now that the threat had been taken care of.

"Thank goodness you're here," Donna said from the porch. She was armed, but not pointing it at me. "We've got a lot of wounded inside. We're trying to rotate the first aid perk on people, but it's a losing battle."

"Vlad says all the threats are dead, but stay alert. It's after midnight, so that means I can heal again," I said, then paused as I stepped into what looked like a trauma center. There were over a dozen people injured and bloody, some of them children. There was also one person with a blanket pulled over their face and blood pooling below.

"Someone tell me who to heal first," I yelled.

People looked around, then the woman, trying to bandage a crying kid's side wound, waved me over. "I can't stop the bleeding here," she said. "Can you fix this, then I'll take you around to other priorities."

It took two of my perk charges to stop the bleeding. I abandoned my other plans and used one of the matrices as I moved to the next patient. These aliens were stronger and gave more points. I got eight personal tokens for this one and used seven of them to raise the medical effect perk to level ten.

"Paul, take my nano inhibitor and go get the snowmobile," I said, handing him my gun as I moved to the next patient. "I need someone else to get a sled to transport people lying down. That will be a safer way to move people to medical pods."

People got moving as I used the other eight healing charges, but many were still badly injured. I helped where I could and identified two people who could make the trip and one who would need Wendy's first aid perk.

"Get those three ready to move," I said. "We're taking them back to town, where I'm building another clinic. We'll need it to work through these injuries. Donna, keep things stable here. I'll come back with medical staff, and we'll plan how to get everyone else into a pod as quickly as we can."

We carefully moved the three identified people onto the hastily assembled sled. Everyone was bundled up and ready when Paul pulled up on the snowmobile. I sent him to help guard the farm, then headed back to town as soon as the sled was hooked up. Donna had set off the flares to let the town know the threat was neutralized, but there had been casualties.

All the council members were waiting for me, but I ignored them to talk to Joey. "There's one dead and at least 12 wounded pretty seriously, and that's after I leveled up my perk and used all ten charges," I said. "I'm making you a new clinic now, then I need to know when we can bring more people here and who I can take back with me to help stabilize people."

It just took a second to walk to an open spot where I could put the clinic and will it to form. As soon as it was done, Joey was directing people into it.

"We can have another pod open in addition to getting all three of these people into pods by the time you get back, and we'll have six beds open across the clinics by then as well," he said. "I'm sending three people with emergency kits back with you while I coordinate things here."

I nodded and motioned for them all to get on the sled for the ride back. The person Wendy had been stabilizing with her perk was now in a pod, so she was coming back with me as well.

When we got back to the farmhouse, there were moments when I was sure we would lose someone else while we worked to stabilize and move everyone over the next few hours, but other than the initial casualty, everyone made it.

Once I was sure everyone was safe, I announced I was heading to bed, but there would be a lot to discuss in the morning. I also made sure to thank everyone for the great job they did in holding off the aliens and driving back the threat with minimal casualties.

I could tell that Vlad wanted to talk about what had happened, but I was wiped out. I asked him if anything had to be handled now, and he admitted it could wait. I did make time to take a very quick shower. I had a fair amount of other people's blood on me and was just grimy from the trip and fighting. From the time I finished my shower to the time I was asleep was less than five minutes.

The following morning, I woke up on my own, no alarm this time. I was still the only person in the room, so either Paul had come and gone while I slept, or he had not made it back here. Either way, the space was mine, and I took a few minutes to look through my information and the town's information.

"I'm guessing that maintenance is one of the things you wanted to point out last night?" I asked Vlad about it as soon as I noticed it. The material maintenance backlog had gone from 73 units to 198. Regular deferred maintenance had increased from 135 to 411 units.

"Yes, the golems damaged the greenhouses extensively. Until they are repaired, food output will drop and resource usage will spike. You are going to have to allocate many more pods to address that. The sooner, the better. You also unlocked the first aid perk for getting your medical effect perk to the tenth level.

I'm not sure it's useful to you, but it's there," he said. "You also impressed a lot of people. I was listening in on conversations around you, and your focus on saving people, coupled with your taking on the aliens solo, won you a lot of praise. You're not just the guy with cool tech, but the guy willing to do anything to save people."

"Popularity was not the goal, but if it helps keep people from causing me problems, I'm all for it," I said. "Now for the fun part of this, I have another nano matrix to absorb and perks to level up."

This matrix was worth seven personal tokens, taking me back up to eight. I had been considering increasing boosted mind for a while. More settlement tokens would be nice, and now that so many pods were being reallocated from that to maintenance, it would be even more useful. I spent five tokens to take that to the tenth level as well. I also added one point to the second chance perk. The one respawn I used had not refreshed yet, and I was regularly putting myself in danger.

I used the last of my points for the incapacitate criminal perk. I had used it five times in the fight, thanks to perfect timing, with midnight occurring after my first use, but I could not count on that timing in the future. I needed more charges if they were going to be able to counter it.

It was coming up on noon, so I rushed out to switch pods to maintenance and perform a delayed resource collection pass. Once again, a council runner was waiting for me in the hall, and I told them I'd like to meet with the council and the enforcers over lunch shortly after noon.

I appreciated the influx of settlement tokens before I swapped 38 pods for maintenance, with 36 of those swaps coming from settlement-token pods. My token production was going way down. I also upgraded the portal to level six with the research Klawock was working on. Maintenance in the settlement would take a while to address, but the increase in dedicated pods focused on it would reduce the backlog. Unfortunately, it would also burn through some of the material units we were generating, as much of the maintenance was material maintenance.

I had enough resources to do some building, but nothing was an emergency, so I decided to wait. I wanted to have options in

Bangor when I headed up there the next day. I had wrapped things up in the portal room, so as soon as I was done, I sat down with the council members who had been watching me and started eating while they gave updates.

There had been no changes overnight, and while it would take several more days to use the new pods to get everyone healed up, no one was in danger of dying from their injuries. Once the injuries were addressed, the two new pods would speed up resolving all the medical issues for Pittsfield's citizens.

I was still talking about the injured when Donna and O'Donnell pivoted and started talking about the assault. For all that O'Donnell could rub me the wrong way, he did know his stuff, and he seemed to be helping Donna organize her thoughts.

"Our best guess is that the golems we have been finding one by one were part of a spy network. The setup was almost perfect. They lured Wendy, Paul, and me out there, then sprung the trap when everyone could be pinned down in one location. They knew how we would react and what we could do, other than the nano inhibitor. Even one of those helped and made them slow down and be cautious," Donna said.

"Talking through the assault with people who were there, I have some guesses as to what they were doing," O'Donnell said. "These are just guesses, but it seemed as if they were focusing on causing mass damage, in addition to killing whoever they could. I'm guessing that the resistance we provided was harsher than they had planned. If it had not been, they would have ruined what they could, killed who they could, and been gone before the counterstrike. They were clearly not expecting you or your recklessly effective attack from behind."

"We drove them off with minimal casualties, but they did a lot of damage. Even after stopping them, I had to redirect over half our work pods to repair the greenhouses and farmhouses. That's a lot of settlement tokens we won't be earning while fixing that," I said, ignoring the backhanded compliment. "If they had a little more time and gotten away, it would have really set us back. The good news was that we surprised them and killed two more of the aliens. Killing off golems slows them down, but each alien is a loss they can't replace, and these were two that specialized in controlling golems. I'm just sorry I was not there in time to stop the one death."

"The golems basically sneak-attacked a guard on patrol, from what we were told," Wendy said. "No one could have done anything. They were dead almost instantly."

"We have enough spheres to create another enforcer, and I'm guessing you all leveled up some perks in the fight, right? After my trip to Bangor, we need to plan another offensive against the aliens," I said. "Has anyone checked to see if they left us more snowmobiles? They might have used them to get close before starting the assault."

I was surprised no one had thought of that, and Donna excused herself and the other enforcers to hunt for any abandoned snowmobiles while I kept the briefing going. I highlighted the updates I had made to myself to heal more and generate more settlement tokens. I also told them I was planning to hold off on building more in Augusta until I saw how Bangor was doing.

"I've already used all my healing perk charges today, but when I head to Bangor tomorrow, I should be able to get everyone left in Pittsfield ready to come back. That evacuation should be all wrapped up by the end of the day tomorrow," I said. "And I know you want me to build more stuff here, but we are doing okay at the moment. I want things to be moving faster, but no one is in danger of cold or starving here yet."

I could tell a few of the council members wanted to argue, but the crowd around us was nodding in agreement with me, so they let it go.

"Even with everything that happened last night, both greenhouses planned for today should be done by the time we're done here," Bryan said. "We're really getting into a groove on those and the houses."

"We need to generate some research tokens to start researching something with the custom greenhouses," I said. "That will let Klawock know we need them to help out on them, but that's got to wait until we get maintenance under control. I can't pull any pods off the settlement token creation right now."

From there, it was just a matter of listening to people as they tossed out ideas. I had learned the value of listening to people, but also the value of cutting it off. After about 30 minutes of that, I wrapped things up and headed outside with Bryan to integrate the greenhouse here in town. The other one was at the farm, and that one could wait until the snowmobile was back. That integration was not so much of a rush that I had to walk out there.

We were talking about future building plans when Donna pulled up in the snowmobile, dragging another one behind it. She had left the sled and the others at the farm to get the snowmobile back here. It was a larger, two-seater, and it required 164 tokens to make it usable on our grid.

"That's great," I said, looking at it. "I've got to save tokens for all the conversions here and in Bangor, but keep it safe until I'm back."

While she was securing the new snowmobile, I took the other one out to the farm to integrate the greenhouse and pull the sled back. After that, I left it to Bryan to get the workers he needed back in town to start the next greenhouse.

While he handled transporting people, I created our new enforcer. I also made sure everything was ready for my trip to Bangor the next morning. After that, I had a meeting with the enforcers to talk through the fight. We had all debriefed, but it was another stressful situation, and I did not want to leave it to Donna to make sure everyone was okay.

Some of them had problems with the death and injuries they had seen, but it did not seem to have affected any of them too badly. I still talked through it and let them know they should lean on each other or me if they had problems with the aftermath of that fight or any other.

15

The following morning, I collected resources and changed the work pods' output again. Even though we still needed to work on the maintenance backlog, I moved 20 work pods back to settlement tokens. I did not have enough tokens to integrate all the buildings if the team in Bangor had finished their work by the time I left. Having enough would depend on people collecting from the pods for me while I was gone, and I wanted some extra in case Bangor finished more buildings than planned. Material units took a big hit over the last day, with nearly 60 units used for maintenance. I updated the portal with the new research, since it was just a few tokens, and in the long term, we needed material units.

After that, I had breakfast and made sure Donna and the other enforcers felt prepared to handle things on their own for two days. We went over strategies for a variety of scenarios if the aliens attacked while I was gone. We hoped we had time while they developed a new plan, but we still wanted to be ready.

By the time we were done, the sled was loaded up with food for Bangor. I was not taking any people, and with just 12 people left in Pittsfield after the current trip, they did not need more food. I would heal the eight of them who needed help, and then they and their four caretakers would all be moved to Augusta by the end of the day. We were still at just four dead, and I was happy with how well that entire process had gone. Four people dying was horrible, but without us, it would have been so much worse.

People were already talking about the next place to rescue, but I had asked them to wait until I was back. One day to use the vehicle for other stuff would not hurt, and I was not sure whether we only got settlement quests if I was there.

"Keep everyone safe," I said as I got on the snowmobile. "I should be back in less than two days. I plan to make this as quick as I can. Make sure you all collect from the pods, so I have enough resources to do everything I need up there," I said.

"We'll be fine, get going," Donna said, pointedly turning and leading everyone away.

The trip to Pittsfield went as planned, and I was able to get everyone ready for transport with all ten healing charges. There would still need to be an enforcer or two on each trip with the first aid perk to be safe, but they were mostly stable.

"Don't forget, have the load of items you want me to bring back tomorrow organized and labeled in the main room," I told them before I left. "At the very least, I'll get another load of stuff each week when I go to Bangor, so if you have time, organize everything you want picked up."

"Most of us thought you were full of bull... bull crap," the man, talking, corrected himself when his daughter, who was taking care of him, hissed. "But this has been faster than you promised. I don't think you'd go to all this work to sacrifice us to some aliens, so it's looking like you're saving us, and we got lucky."

"Even the Scaled Syndicate does not demand sacrifices," Vlad said, sounding scandalized. "We evolved past that long ago. At worst, they would work you to death."

His genuine outrage at the idea of sacrifices got a laugh and seemed like a good note to leave on, so I said goodbye and headed out.

I enjoyed the rest of the ride to Bangor. It gave me some alone time to enjoy the scenery and make sure I did not get lost. I probably would have gotten off track a few times on my own. That was not really a possibility with Vlad, though. He was like the world's only remaining GPS after visiting a place once.

I checked the information for Bangor as I got closer and was glad to see that fewer than 200 people had died in the week I was gone. On the one hand, I felt bad that 200 deaths were a good sign, but I knew it was a turnaround from before I showed up.

They had been waiting for me, and a scout who had been watching the road waved to me and pulled out a whistle. I could hear the three notes he blew before waving again and settling back into his scouting spot.

It only took me a few minutes to make it to the park from there, but Andy had a whole reception waiting for me by the time I arrived.

"We're all glad to see you," Andy said as soon as I pulled the snowmobile to a stop. "We all knew you planned to come back, but the builders you brought told us all the things that are going on with the aliens, and we knew there was a chance something would come up, so we were worried you would be late."

"It's good to see you all," I said as I got down and started shaking hands. "The sled is full of food this time, and I'll be able to generate rations today and tomorrow as well, so let's get that sorted while we make plans and start integrating houses. I checked, and with the food I brought, your food supply only dropped by five days during the week I was gone, and the heat only dropped by three. Both those numbers should spike back up as soon as I integrate some buildings."

"The good news is that we put a lot of resources into building," Andy said as he led me over to the greenhouses. "We got three of the new greenhouses built, not two, and we still managed to build all eight houses that were planned."

"Okay, I can do the three greenhouses and two of the houses right now. We had some alien attacks, and I had to spend a lot of tokens and focus on maintenance work pods. Because of that, I have to wait until morning to integrate the rest of the houses. Getting food production up and running as soon as possible is your new priority, so let's get those done first."

Following Andy's request, I integrated both the custom greenhouses here and a custom house. Then we traveled to the other park to integrate the greenhouse and a house there. From there, we headed back to the meeting room, still full of bunks, to debrief.

I went over everything that had happened in the past week. The alien assault, the rescue of Pittsfield, and the gang we wiped out. A few people asked why we moved people from Pittsfield to Augusta but left everyone in Bangor. Others in the room quickly told them to stop asking dumb questions. One person in the room pointed out that the trip was twice as long and that there were over 80 times as many people in Bangor.

"That's right, it's just a matter of scale. The other thing is, you are large enough to justify a whole new infrastructure grid, while they weren't. If we moved you, there would be just as much building in Augusta, plus the danger of moving everyone," I said.

They gave an update on how they were doing. Having power and knowing more housing was coming online, they were crowding into fewer legacy houses. That allowed them to stretch their heating supplies further, even though the crowding everywhere was causing problems of its own.

"We're planning to deviate from the plan you gave us," Andy said. "I hope that's okay, but we are focusing more on greenhouses now due to the lag time of getting them up and running. We hope to have five more done when you are here next, and just five more houses. We need both, but getting the food growing is more important. We're also hoping for another barn and more power from you this trip."

"That makes sense. My plans were focused on getting you all started. I'm here less than a day each visit, so you know what you need better than I do," I said. "That's a cost of 625 tokens for me to integrate five of each when I come back. I'll do my best to save up for that next visit. As for the new buildings, I'm going to build what I can here before I leave tomorrow. including more power and water. When I integrate the rest of the houses tomorrow, you will not have enough water for everything."

The meeting went on for a few more hours with status updates and questions. It took me longer than it should have to realize they were trying to make sure I saw them as working hard and worth supporting with a return trip. I did not address it directly, but I tried to be as encouraging as I could. They did not need the stress of worrying about whether I would return, on top of everything else. That was also when I passed out a batch of letters and picked up the ones they wanted me to take back. The only thing I was pressed on was the need for more clinics by the guy in charge of health for Bangor. I told him I would see how things looked in the morning.

After that long meeting, I met privately with the people from Augusta who had helped get their building teams up and running. I wanted to make sure they were happy and check if any of them wanted to return. They were all enjoying their time, even though the conditions were not ideal. They had bunks in the new houses, and those with families in Bangor were getting a chance to help them.

With all that taken care of, I got into the bunk they had assigned me and got some sleep. I knew the next day would be a long one with the trip back to Augusta to look forward to after a round of integrating and building.

Over breakfast the next day, when I once again kept my portions small, I saw the morning resource collection appear on the information sheets. I used that as an excuse to cut breakfast short and go outside to integrate the rest of the buildings. My group had to walk between the two parks because the builders were taking full advantage of the second snowmobile for transportation and hauling until I left.

As soon as the integration was done and people were moving into the houses, I managed to snag my snowmobile to put up another water tower and windmill. The windmill was used to expand the town's grid, but the watermill was used purely for snow clearing.

With the basics complete, I checked my resources and went big. They could wait a week for another barn. Instead, I built another water tower, a greenhouse complex, and their first dorm. After that, I did all the healing I could before getting ready to leave.

"Getting the greenhouse complex now lets you get stuff growing," I said. "It also adds a little more housing. My plan is to add a barn next time, but you all need to really try to speed up the housing and greenhouses. Try for eight houses and five greenhouses before I get back next week."

With the current population, a 20% coverage of housing and food was 2,345 for each. Housing and food were at 328 and 683, respectively. Food was important, but if I wanted to finish this mission, I needed to keep the two somewhat balanced. Plus, their heat supply was getting dangerously low.

"We'll do our best," Andy said. "We know it's not comfortable, but each house has 72 people who don't need to burn fuel to stay warm. You will be back in a week, right?"

"That's the plan. If I'm not here, I'll be back as soon as I can, so keep building. If there are ever spare tokens, I'll get us some communication devices so you don't have to wonder about my schedule, but I have no idea when that will be."

It was overcast on the ride back, which slowed me down some, but I still made good time to Pittsfield. As soon as I was in range of the town, I got a mission completed notice. It looked like something I needed to study, and I figured I could do that inside the now-abandoned apartment and grab some lunch. They were supposed to have left some food for me, and I was looking forward to an actual meal after eating light in Bangor.

As soon as I started the fire and had some food, I pulled the message up to review.

Pittsfield Rescue Mission: Variable Rewards

This community has been successfully evacuated. Final rating is 179 (199 saved and 4 dead). Suggested reward allocation: production, defense, and defense. Accept the reward allocation or request a modified allocation.

At least the math was simple for the scoring. I was awarded one point for each person saved and penalized five points for each person who died. The reward allocation stumped me, though.

"Do you have any idea what this reward allocation is or what it means?" I asked Vlad, "And why is defense listed twice?"

"I don't know any of the details," Vlad said after a moment. "The suggestion seems to make sense, and the nano controller probably knows what you need better than you do. I'd accept it this time. If it's messed up, you can blame the nano controller. If you change it and it's wrong, you'll have to blame yourself."

With no other information to go on, that was as good an idea as any. I accepted the allocation, and a new screen popped up, while a blue gem about three inches across appeared in my hand.

Pittsfield Rescue Mission: Allocated Rewards

- Material unit enhancement device level 20 (100 points) - device may be placed on or removed from a portal by an architect. Adds 20 material unit production points to the assigned portal per day. May be upgraded
- Enforcer cost reduction (50 points) - cost to assign enforcer class decreased by 5 spheres
- Sphere generation (29 points) - 29 spheres added to inventory

"Wow, that's a great mission reward," I said. "A material unit boost I can take with me, a permanent reduction in the cost of enforcers, and more spheres. I know it sounds mercenary, but I am going to try triggering more quests like this."

"I believe it's a sign that the nano controller is using resources to speed things up. Which could be a good or bad sign," Vlad said. "At least it will make this mission easier."

With the quest completed, I packed up the sled and continued home. While traveling, I was talking to Vlad about potential locations to try to rescue next. We would need to talk to the people back at the settlement. Vlad was going off maps, not the personal experience they would have. We would also need one of them to come with me to reach out to the next town and vouch for me.

We now had the equipment and procedures in place to carry out an evacuation, so there was no reason not to continue. Even better, if we picked a closer town, everything would go faster. I also needed to plan more testing sessions. With the quest rewards, I could create another enforcer, and that would exhaust our list of candidates.

Planning our next steps kept us busy until we reached the edge of the settlement. Once there, I started waving to people as we got closer to home. It was early afternoon, so I had made good time. I turned over the snowmobile and sled so the supplies could be distributed to the evacuees they belonged to. I also let Bryan know that even though the final greenhouse at the farm was ready, I was out of settlement tokens, so it would have to wait a day.

"I'll get to it tomorrow," I promised. "For now, I'm going to take a shower and change, then meet with everyone in 30 minutes, if that works?"

He headed off to collect people, and by the time I was showered, changed, had used the remote portal effect, and made it to the pod room, everyone was waiting.

I gave a detailed update on Bangor and passed out the letters I had received this time. My runs up there and back were a type of mail service on top of everything else. Once that was done, I shared the mission rewards for saving the people in Pittsfield.

"I know saving them was worth doing just to save them, even though it added more people to take care of," I said. "Getting rewards like this means that, in addition to saving people, we're boosting the town. The extra material units will be very helpful. The real winner, though, is the reduction in costs for enforcers, and the bonus spheres are even better in some ways. We need to clear out the alien threat, and adding more enforcers is a huge part of that. I'd like to see if we can start rescuing another town tomorrow. Vlad and I were thinking Sidney might work. Do we have people with ties to that town?"

"We'll discuss it and have someone ready to go with you tomorrow," Erin said as she took some notes.

"You'll need to start more testing to find more candidates," O'Donnell pointed out. "After you empower our next enforcer, that is."

"Yes to the testing, no to the enforcer. Until we get ready to launch an offensive attack, I'd rather wait and try to finish more quests like Pittsfield. The cost to create another enforcer is down to 20 spheres, but if it were lowered by another five, I'd have the spheres to create two enforcers. We can formalize the list of who will become enforcers next and have those candidates train with the enforcers. If needed, I'll convert them early, but let's try to maximize the spheres we have by waiting," I said.

There was some concern about not having enough enforcers if the aliens launched an attack. Still, even O'Donnell had to admit that it was unlikely one more enforcer would make that much of a difference. I committed to doing a better job at fitting in at least 20 enforcer scans per day until we had a backlog of five people. That meant three and a half hours at the class pod every day I was in town, but it was a needed sacrifice on my part.

With the briefings wrapped up, I went over to the portal and figured out how to attach the enhancement device. That turned out to be as easy as all the other nanotechnology. As soon as the device was close to the portal, a socket formed to hold it. We did some testing. While it looked like it had just been set there, no one else could move it.

I also spent the tokens to upgrade the portal after the Klawock research there hit level ten. Not only were there now ten additional processing points each day, but the level-ten effect also allowed us to trade up to 10 settlement tokens for material units each day. The trade was five material units per token, so a boost of 50 per day. Even though we were very low on tokens, I made that trade. I was not sure whether we were lucky with the research effect or if the nano controller was tweaking things in our favor again. Either way, I was not complaining.

After finishing all that, I grabbed an interesting-looking book from the shelves that people had placed in the portal bay. I sat down next to the class pod to start testing people to fill my quota for the day. I was pretty happy when we found one match out of the first 20. It had been a while since the last match, and I was glad to start with a win.

When I did my rounds the following morning, I shifted ten more pods back to settlement tokens. I could not integrate all the work completed today, but that would help. The greenhouse left over from the prior day meant there were two greenhouses and four regular houses ready to integrate. That was 300 tokens, and I was about 140 tokens shy of what I needed.

I used the tokens I had to integrate the greenhouse at the farm. That ended the planned construction there. I also integrated two of the four completed houses. With those added, we were getting low on power again, so I added the 24th windmill.

The rest of the morning was spent scanning more people and talking about our next trip. The consensus was that Sidney was the right choice. It was closer, and we could probably make seven round-trips each day without needing a windmill for recharging. There had been a lot of discussion about who to send with me. None of the enforcers had many contacts there, but no one wanted to send a non-enforcer. The compromise was to send Kate with me, who at least had a few friends there.

Once lunch was over, we loaded up the sled with food and basic supplies, and then Kate and I headed out. We had several plans for how to approach people, but I warned her that much of it would have to be played by ear. I was driving, and she was riding in the sled, but if things went sideways, she knew to jump on the snowmobile, dump the sled, leave me, and get out of there.

At least the turnoff to town from what was left of the interstate was hard to miss. The huge quarry along the side of the road stood out, even covered in snow. As we headed west toward the town, we slowed down. There was no real downtown area, and the 4,500 people were spread out before the event. Finding where people were congregating was a matter of looking for smoke. Our first plan was to head south as soon as we were in town. That is where we would find the school building, which everyone thought was most likely to be a gathering spot.

"I think our guess was right," Kate yelled from behind me. "That looks like a lot of smoke coming from the same place, and I think it's where the school is. There are other bits of smoke scattered around the town, but there was a definite clump of smoke coming from the school."

I took it as a good sign that we were not stopped or challenged as we made our way to the school. It seemed that whoever was left was not on edge, suggesting that no one was being threatened.

Even so, I was surprised when I made it to the door without being noticed. Vlad was hiding, and Kate was on the snowmobile, ready to flee if needed. It felt strange to be knocking and yelling, "Hello, is anyone here?" It was all very pre-apocalypse.

I heard a lot of movement spark up inside, and then the blanket over the small window panel on the door was pulled back before the door was opened, and someone came out. There were people with guns piling into the hallway, but they stayed there as the door closed.

"Wait, is that a vehicle that works?" was the first thing that was said.

After I arrived in Augusta, I was surprised by how little travel there was between places. They were not on islands as we had been, so I expected more travel. After talking with Vlad, we developed a theory that the latitude and the mountains back in Klawock had helped vehicles survive the pulse.

In addition to fewer vehicles here, it was also dangerous to go any substantial distance in the cold with legacy vehicles that could break down at any moment. There had been some travel at the start, but people soon realized that everywhere was problematic, and then even more things stopped working.

"Yeah, it's some nanotechnology that works in the cold," I said. "That's actually why I'm here. That's my friend Kate. We're from Augusta, and we're trying to help people around here and let them know what's going on. Is this the primary site for Sidney if I wanted to talk to people?"

"Yeah, I guess so. There are some people grouped up in the nicer farmhouses, but most of us who are left are trying to make it work here until it starts warming back up," he said. "If it's just the two of you, I guess you can come on in and tell us what's going on."

Nothing seemed off, and Vlad was messaging me from where he was sneaking around in the walls, saying that everything seemed to be on the up and up. I waved Kate forward, and we followed our guide inside.

Once we were in the school, the smell was overwhelming. I tried not to show it, but our guide saw our reaction to the wave of smells that hit us.

"There's not really water for showers, and most of the remaining livestock is living here. We've got goats, sheep, chickens, and even rabbits in various classrooms and the gym. We've had to eat all the big animals already," he said. "You get used to the smell."

There were some disbelieving snorts from the people who had fallen into step around us. It seemed not everyone could ignore the smell. As we made our way down the hall, I could see that classrooms had been repurposed as living spaces, just like in Craig. Finally, our guide opened the door to a smaller classroom where people were working.

As we were introduced to everyone, my eyes roamed over all the stuff on the walls. They were organized. I could see lists of resources, people, work rotations, and more. It looked like a strong organization, but even at a glance, I could see the resources were dropping, as was the population. There was also a timeline trying to stretch resources until the spring. They were not going to like what I had to say about that.

"You mean it's not going to warm up, ever?" one of the people in charge of resource organization said with a hint of desperation. "Everything we have been doing has been based on keeping some of us alive until this crazy cold snap ends, and now you're saying it won't end until long after we're dead?"

"I'm sorry, I know it sucks, but at least there's a way to make sure that people survive. We're building stuff that will last so our great-grandkids can see the sun fixed, and the world come back," I said. Vlad had been part of the show-and-tell and was now visible, nodding along.

"How does this amazing technology in Bangor and Augusta help us, though? It sounds like you are tapped out on resources," someone else said.

Apparently, that was the trigger for me to get the mission for Sidney, and I held up a hand for a minute while I read it before sharing it with everyone else.

"That question triggered a mission for me. I was given the option of leaving you here. The message says, 'Leaving you here to die,' to be precise. It also gave me the option to save you all by building out a nano powered settlement here. Finally, we could move all of you to Augusta," I said. "First, you should know there are rewards we get for saving you all. The nanotechnology controller wants Earth to be saved as much as possible and rewards us for saving people. The reality is that the third option is the only viable one, though." I said.

"Why can't you help us like you're helping Bangor?" several people called out.

"Setting up a whole nano infrastructure takes a lot of time and resources. We're already skating on the edge supporting Bangor, and you don't have enough people to justify a new grid. Plus, you are small enough and close enough that we can evacuate you effectively."

"It helps that you have a good setup here for the short term," Vlad said. "As we relocate people, there will be room for people on farms to move into the school and wait without being at risk."

There was a brief discussion as I started generating the ration bars for them to pass out. The end of the discussion saw some people say they would be heading to Augusta no matter the decision. That ended things for the people who wanted more time to consider.

"I guess we're agreeing to move, at least the people in the school. We'll have to talk to everyone else in the other buildings," was the reluctant decision.

"I'm not trying to force anything, but that is the best option I can see," I said as I triggered that choice and then typed out the updated mission so I could share it with the others.

Sidney Rescue Mission This community can no longer viably sustain itself. You have decided to relocate them to Augusta. Some people may decide to remain for now. They will not impede mission completion or alter the mission score. Rescue as many people as possible by moving them to Augusta. The mission reward will be based on the number of people saved. Saved: 0 Died: 0 Remaining: 583 Not Participating: 0

People gasped at the remaining number of survivors. They thought there were more people still alive, but it looked like the people outside the school were not doing as well as they thought.

"We knew the cold and the various illnesses were catching up with people, but just 15 percent of us are left?" the lead organizer said. "If those numbers are right, we need to go around and talk to everyone. Leaving is the right choice."

"The clinics we have will clear up medical issues, and I'll heal people when I come out here, so they will be ready for the trip I said.

From there, we talked about logistics. They had a little more time than Pittsfield before they were in trouble. They had not lost resources and people to infighting, so the plan was to take five people at a time in the vehicle or five on the sled. That would allow people to bring some personal items. We would also let them use the snowmobile to visit all the people still grouped in houses in the area and start consolidating those willing to move. If enough people moved, we would start moving animals, too, when there were not enough people left to maintain them.

With a plan in place, they helped empty the sled, then we loaded five people and their belongings onto it for the trip back. With seven trips a day in the nano car and three with the snowmobile, we could evacuate 50 people each day. Bryan needed the snowmobile for moving supplies, and I would need it for the enforcers and me to do more scouting, so it would just be used for three daily evacuation trips. Still, even if everyone wanted to move, it would just take 12 days.

"That's a lot of rewards with that many people," I said to Vlad as we left. I was already thinking about the boosts we would get.

"Don't assume the rewards will be the same," he said. "The

nano controller is helpful, but there are limits. They won't let you game the system, and this mission seems far easier than the Pittsfield one."

"Either way, it will help," I said. "I'm already thinking ahead to the next mission if the rewards stay as useful."

16

Kate and I dropped off the first five people from Sidney when we got back to Augusta. I hoped that the evacuation could go smoothly, without requiring me to travel out to heal people too often. I was happy to help people, but trips back and forth would eat up a lot of time. I felt I was running out of time to get everything done as it was.

"We've got to speed things up," I said to Vlad that night as I patrolled the area I had volunteered to take first shift for. "I've been here for 30 days already. In eight days, I will have been here half the time I had spent in Klawock, and I really wanted to do this quicker. I feel like that's all but impossible."

"That's one way to look at it, but it's the wrong way. Sure, you are not going any faster here, but across all the towns you've helped so far, that's about 30,000 people. The two settlements back where you started had about 7,000 people. Even if you spend as long here as you did there, you will have quintupled the number of people you can help in 77 days," Vlad said. "That's not even counting whoever is left in Portland. You're also setting yourself up to move faster in the next mission. That material unit enhancer alone will be a noticeable help, and it will just get better if you get similar rewards from saving Sidney."

"I guess so. I just see how bad a lot of these places are and think how many other towns are in the same situation and getting worse. How many other people are like the ones in Sidney? People hoping it will warm up, and it won't." With that depressing thought, I kept patrolling and running numbers in my head until it was time to pass the patrol route to the next person.

The following morning, I started by checking the status of the Sidney evacuation mission. It looked like the transfers were running smoothly, and six people had declined to move. I was not sure how that worked, but I knew they could change their mind at any time, even after the mission ended. The council had already committed to checking in regularly with anyone who stayed behind.

The lack of settlement tokens remained a problem, but I did

not reduce the number of maintenance-focused pods again. My only change was to adjust the type of maintenance they were working on to reduce both backlogs. I wanted to avoid sitting on the upper edge of acceptable maintenance backlogs in either category now that I knew the aliens could spike it. I was going to get them both to the teens and keep them there. The upside was that I did have lots of material units and was going to take advantage of them.

I started with the leftover buildings to integrate before I started my planned nano construction, though. The greenhouse and two houses were all integrated into the grid for 150 tokens. Next up were two more windmills and two more water towers. All eight of those pods were used to generate more tokens. With 11 water towers scattered around, we were starting to get the local snow under control in town.

Every time I considered switching to a larger version of either of those, I realized a larger structure might be more efficient, but there were two problems with that approach. The windmills and water towers were the drivers of pods, and the research on the windmills would have to be replicated on a new version of them. I was concerned about getting enough pods in use without them and having to buy batteries while waiting for research. With those built, I debated between another greenhouse complex or an apartment block and went for the greenhouse again.

Even better, I saw that someone back home had read my mind and was already researching improved resource generation for the custom greenhouses. It was just level one so far, but that meant our current greenhouses would feed an extra five people per year once the research reached level ten. That would be huge if they focused on that and we got a ten percent boost to all those greenhouses here and in Bangor. It would be a lot of tokens to level them all up, but it would be worth it.

With all my chores taken care of, I met up with the enforcers for a scouting run. We had done nothing like that in the four days since the alien attack, and we needed to check the borders. We did not want to give them free rein to plan another attack. We were also taking the two enforcer candidates with us to start their training. It made for an interesting group in the sled behind the snowmobile as we checked the edges of Augusta to the south. I was looking forward to having the spare tokens to get the other snowmobile running, but it would take at least a few days.

To my surprise, we found and killed golems. It was the same individual fights as before. They were the same scouts or triggers that we had seen before. It seemed like they had been moving in while we were busy elsewhere. I was worried there was something we were missing, but we found and killed seven of them, which was a nice boost to spheres. We let Kate get all the kills, except for one that Donna had to step in for. That gave Kate a chance to level her perks.

As we headed back, Vlad mentioned he wanted to spend some time looking at the golem locations we had found so far. He said there was some pattern he was trying to figure out. I was not used to Vlad needing time on anything, but I hoped it would be something we could use for a plan. He had plenty of time to think things through as I settled in for a late afternoon round of testing people again. It was another fruitless round of testing, but we were bound to find more enforcer candidates soon.

Since there was time, I joined one of the runs to Sidney to use my heal charges out there. There were a few people whom Kate was worried about moving, and I had the time while Vlad was still working on his idea. The trips were faster and easier because they had enough food and heat. The trips out were not hauling food and firewood, as we had been doing on most runs to Pittsfield.

On the ride back, Vlad almost had me jerking the snowmobile off the route when he popped up next to me and yelled that he had figured it out.

"What exactly did you figure out, and why was it so exciting?" I asked.

He started to explain that the semi-random distribution of golems indicated a distributed net he could trace back to their base with more data points.

"I might be able to project the location of the scouts with enough data points," he added. "We could sneak in without triggering their alarms."

"There's not really anything we can do about it tonight, right? It's great you figured it out, but I think we should go over it with everyone in the morning while I'm doing more testing. I need a map in front of me while you explain how this all works, but having a target will change everything," I said.

Vlad had a couple of people he wanted to talk to, so we got them into the portal bay, and then he spoke with them while I hung out with the other people in the bay. The math they were talking about while marking spots on maps was beyond me. I knew I would ask questions if I paid attention to their discussion, and I did not need to slow them down.

Finally, I heard Vlad thanking them for their help, and I wandered back over. "Got it all worked out? Still have a plan to share in the morning?"

"I think I do. Everyone helped a lot, but I have some more calculations to run. I'll be ready to brief everyone while you scan more people," he said.

I had already left instructions for people to meet us the next morning, so there was nothing else to do before bed.

That morning, I reduced the number of maintenance pods. It was nice to be building back some cushion of settlement tokens. I was up over 200 again, even after spending 20 to raise all the local greenhouses to match the research being done in Klawock.

Before I sat down to talk about strategy while testing people, I built two more windmills. With four more houses coming online, we were again too close to the power limit. By the time I made it back inside, there was a crowd waiting. O'Donnell and some of his people were representing the council. All the enforcers were there, as well as the mathematicians Vlad had been working with. I had to imagine they were excited to be using their skills to help the town. Surrounding that group were other people who had heard what was going on and were curious. Finally, a group of people waited in line to be tested.

Once I had the testing started and sat down, Vlad launched into his explanation. It took a lot of math to show that the golem locations were meant to look random. However, it was a distribution that maximized coverage, with coverage increasing toward a key point while still making it appear there was no pattern.

"The math seems right," one of the mathematicians said. "It took a while to fit it inside the mathematical notation we use on Earth, but it's elegant and fits the model. The induced randomness would have made it almost impossible to see without these formulas or a lot more data points."

The conversation continued for another hour. Some people O'Donnell brought seemed to grasp some of the math and asked questions. O'Donnell and I were on the same page for once, both somewhat lost but glad it made sense.

"So, I'm not going to pretend I understood most of the math and patterns that were being thrown around. It looks like everyone who does understand it agrees?" I asked. When I got nods, I continued. "I trust Vlad, so if this is true, what are the next steps?"

"If this is correct, they are based somewhere near Lisbon. Maybe around Beaver Park," one of O'Donnell's aides said, pointing to the area on the map between Portland and us. "That's about 30 miles from here, so there will need to be plans on how to get there. Before that, though, we should consider more scouting runs. The team can extrapolate where other golems will be found, and then we can test that. We should collect more data points and then plan the assault."

"We can do that, but we have to make it look like we're encountering them randomly as we sweep the area," Vlad said. "We don't want to give away that we have figured out their pattern. It's also possible that the pattern is accurate but is a trap. It could be purposely pointing us to the wrong location. I doubt that, but it's possible."

"Even if everything is right, we have about ten more days at the current pace to finish evacuating Sidney. I want those bonuses before we create more enforcers and attack. If I can get another snowmobile running, we can cut that time down by several days, but let's give ourselves a week to confirm the pattern, make some plans, and get people ready for an assault."

"We need more weapons, too," Donna said. "The nano inhibitors are great, but if we are facing a group of aliens, I want nano guns too, not just our old weapons that are succumbing to the cold."

Everyone agreed, but I pointed out that it might slow us down more. There was just too much demand for the tokens. Still, we had a plan at last. We would start with large, random patrols in the afternoon to map other golem locations. By the time everything was decided, I had almost finished scanning the 20 people for the day, having found another candidate, and it was lunchtime.

After eating, I integrated the four new houses, bringing us to 31. Bryan also let me know that the next round would grow again, with five houses completed, as he continued to ramp up construction teams. I used most of the remaining material units to add another windmill and water tower. We did not need them yet, but I wanted to create more settlement tokens, so I built them in advance for the pods.

The afternoon patrol was interesting. Vlad gave us a general area to search, but then let us plan the route. We didn't fully understand the math to determine exactly where to look, so our patrol route would appear random if the aliens were watching. He knew where to expect the golems, but did not tell us until we were almost on top of them. We found two in the four hours we were out there, and Vlad seemed smug each time we found one, so I knew his formula was working.

As soon as we returned to the settlement, there was a meeting where Vlad and the mathematicians he was working with plotted the new golem encounters.

"See, right where predicted when accounting for the localized randomness. I've identified this area next to continue confirmation scouting," Vlad said as he pointed at an area on the map, "but I am not seeing any reason to revise our formulas based on this data."

While they discussed things, I tested a few more people's suitability for becoming enforcers. Knowing there would be a math debrief after each scouting run, I volunteered to scan five or six more people after each of them.

"It sounds like the plan is scouting runs the next two days and then a break while I head to Bangor?" I asked as they were wrapping up.

"Yes, but we have to be wary of our own patterns. This is your fourth trip there, and each time we stopped patrolling for two days. If they are paying attention, it would be a good time for them to attack. We'll plan to step up security while you're gone this time."

I had not even thought of our patterns like that, and was glad we had people watching for that kind of stuff. It was clear I needed to learn as much as possible about strategy when I had the chance. My next mission might not send me to a town with a good team to support me, but it looked like I would have to deal with aliens, no matter where I was sent.

The next day, I spent the tokens to activate the captured two-seater snowmobile. That, plus three more research ranks for the greenhouses, cost me 194 tokens. It was worth it to let us speed up the evacuation of Sidney. That was the last time I could spend a large number of tokens on anything other than integrations before I headed to Bangor. If they had built everything they were working on, I would be spending another sizeable chunk of tokens there. To help build a token reserve, I built three more windmills and allocated all their pods to more tokens.

After that, I had a good morning of testing, identifying another enforcer candidate, followed by a scouting run that netted us two spheres from golems, where Vlad expected them. The next one was different, though.

"We've got another one," Donna yelled as the snow moved to our left. Half the group focused on it with the ease of people who had been practicing their response. Everyone else was watching for threats from other directions. Even though this process had become routine, people remained on edge, looking for surprises. That paid off this time.

"Everyone down," Wendy yelled as she scanned the woods to the right of the golem. Everyone dropped down at once, but Kate was a little slower than the rest of us and got hit. There were machines like the spike trap that got Eric, but this time they were shooting larger discs that cut through the air toward us.

From my spot in the snow, I could hear Donna swearing as she fired at the golem, which was still moving our way. Two more volleys of blades whistled overhead, and I was glad they seemed to be automated devices that could not target us on the ground.

I was already crawling over to Kate before Vlad gave the all-clear. She had been hit on her shoulder and back as she dived to the ground. There was a lot of blood, and she was not conscious, which might have been for the best. I saw there was a lot of skin missing on the top of her back and some muscle on her left shoulder.

"Wendy, get your first aid perk on Kate," I yelled as I felt the familiar pulse as I activated my healing perk to help Kate. Even eight charges of the perk did not fix everything, but the bleeding had stopped, and she seemed stable with the help of the first aid perk.

"The golem's dead, and the snowmobile is fine, but the sled was hit a few times," Vlad said.

I looked over and saw that the sled had been hit more than a few times. It was basically destroyed. Based on the locations and firing arcs of the disc launchers that had been tossed at us, they had been targeting us for the first wave. When we ducked, the blades mostly hit the sled. It looked like the targeting had not been adjusted after the first volley. Thankfully, the way I had stopped the snowmobile meant the sled took all the damage, and the vehicle was fine.

Once we were sure the area was secure, the rest of the team tried to salvage what they could of the sled. We were about to turn back and were nearly five miles from the nearest part of the settlement, which left us a bit trapped. I could hear them talking while Wendy and I monitored Kate.

"I think this is the best we can do," Donna said after 20 minutes of messing with the sled.

They had made a flat sled with short walls and room for two people. The plan was for Wendy to drive with Kate in the sled, with one of the enforcer candidates watching her. The other seven of us would start walking back with Vlad's help to avoid any golems. It was just a little over an hour until sunset, and with no moon tonight, it was going to be a cold, dark walk home until Wendy could return with a new sled.

"Take your time. We'll be okay if it takes a little longer to come get us," I told Wendy as we got Kate settled. "Don't bounce her around too much and make sure she's safely under Joey's care in a pod before you leave. I don't think your first-aid perk will be needed, but let's be sure. We can handle ourselves out here for a little while, and we've got the flares if any emergency comes up."

"I'll be as quick as I can while keeping Kate safe. Be careful out here," Wendy said as she slowly drove away.

Everyone stood around watching her head off into the distance until Donna spoke up. "Okay, that sucked, but we're all alive, and Kate will be fine. Even better, no valuable equipment was damaged. Let's check the area one more time and head out before it gets too dark.

After Vlad said it was safe, we inspected the traps the aliens had set for us. They were very basic, likely to keep Vlad from sensing them in advance. There was a small box that aimed the launchers at us when they popped up, but it had burned out.

"If this had not burned out, you might have been in more trouble," Vlad said. "It could have re-targeted to your prone position. I would recommend firing the nano inhibitor at traps like this next time, in addition to taking evasive action."

While everyone else was talking, I was thinking about the need to save more tokens to get more nano inhibitors. I was trying to figure out how to boost those totals more as we started walking back. It had been almost an hour, and it was getting dark, when we saw Wendy returning with an undamaged sled. We were all glad to see it, but the enforcer candidates who had not yet taken the class were the most excited to have a break from the cold and walking. We let them sit down out of the wind while Donna, Paul, Matt, and I stood and scanned in all directions. With Vlad doing long-range scanning, our help seemed unnecessary, but it was better to be safe than sorry.

Wendy called back to let everyone know Kate was safe, but that the damage was extensive, and she would be in a pod healing for a little more than a day. Everyone had seen how severe the damage was, so hearing that she would be fully recovered in barely more than a day made everyone feel better. It was comforting to know that any injury that did not kill you could be fixed with perks and pods.

By the time we made it back, a large group was waiting for a debrief. I knew how important it was to get the information out to people who might be patrolling and run into something similar, so I was glad they had set it up, even though I was tired. Donna led the briefing with Vlad's help. There was some grumbling when people realized that nano inhibitors could be used to disable targeting devices.

"Can't you get more of those for us?" one of the guards called.

He was the only one who spoke up, but I could see that others were thinking it, too.

"Not in the near future. We still only have three of those total for the people directly hunting the aliens," I said. That was not a question to leave Donna to answer. "As time goes on, we will get more of them, but the hope is that the enforcers and I can clear out the alien threat, and then those would not be needed. They are only used to fight the aliens, and once they are gone, they will be useless. Plus, we don't have the tokens now. It's all about building new stuff and integrating the buildings the teams are working on."

"Also, while everyone needs to know about these traps, it's unlikely anyone patrolling in town is going to encounter them. I don't think they could get them near our normal patrol routes without getting caught," Donna said.

That was enough for now, but I know the calls for more weapons would grow if people other than the enforcers started running into traps. I hoped we could push the aliens out before it came to that.

The briefing wrapped up, but I stayed there testing people and eating dinner for a while longer. I was not planning to make a trip to Sidney that day. With just two healing charges left, it was not worth the trip, and they were not in dire need of healing to get people here.

Once the last scan of the night had been finished with no evening successes, I stayed for one game of checkers before heading out. I stopped by the clinic to check on Kate and was assured she was healing well and would be out of the pod in a day. I had seen just how much damage those blades had done, and I was glad the pods could fix all the injuries.

The other high point was seeing that the extra snowmobile was speeding up the evacuation of Sidney when I checked the following morning. There were still no deaths, and 182 had been moved. Not counting the 15 that wanted to stay so far, there were 386 left to move. Just four more days would be needed if everything continued to go well.

As I got busy, I needed more tokens as usual. The custom greenhouse research reached level 9, and I spent 30 more tokens to upgrade the ones in Augusta. The tokens were so low that I would have to wait until my second day in Bangor to integrate everything that was scheduled to be ready for me. Because that trip was coming up, I did not build anything in Augusta. I wanted to have options in Bangor.

"No more enforcer candidates were found during testing today," I told everyone over lunch. "Is everyone ready for another scouting run? We need to see if they are laying more traps and get better at spotting them if they are."

"We're ready," Donna said. "I even worked with some people to add some plating to the sled we use for scouting. It will give some protection against blades like the ones we ran into without adding too much weight."

There was now some galvanized steel cladding on the sides of the wooden sled. I was unsure if it was worth the added weight, but if Donna said it would work, I was all for the protection.

"Check the maps and decide where you want to scout as a group while I go integrate the two greenhouses," I said. "Vlad does not want to pick anything about the scouting for the next few runs, not even where to hunt, so what we do looks totally random."

I left them to it while Bryan and I walked over to integrate the two new greenhouses. He was hoping to increase the number of houses being built next cycle, but had been focused on greenhouses this time. I let him know that thanks to the research upgrades, we were now officially producing enough food for more than 2,500 people. Of that, food for 654 people was from the greenhouses his teams had built so far.

With that taken care of, I went back to the team. They had decided to go much farther east and south than usual. They wanted to prevent another attack on the farm, which was still our most vulnerable location. Even though we spent a full four hours scouting, all we found was a single golem and no traps.

"Based on the pattern, that one seems to be the edge of what they are monitoring," Vlad said as we headed back. "There were a few spots we passed further east where we would have seen golems if they had extended the pattern, but those spots were empty. We're also finding locations where they have replaced golems, like the one we killed today. They are trying to rebuild their scouting network. We'll have to see if they are really just putting golems in the same spot and hoping we won't notice, or if they start randomizing the starting point of their net to try to fool us."

From what Vlad said, that would make it more complicated to chart a path to their base if there were scouts deployed on two different nets. The good news was that the spheres were continuing to pile up, and I had high hopes that we would be able to add three or even four enforcers after Sidney was evacuated. Nine enforcers would be enough for an assault once we were all appropriately armed.

Once we made it back to base, I had time for some more testing and dinner before I headed to Sidney to get some healing in. Erin had asked me to leave early to talk to some people who wanted to stay in Sidney. Those groups were getting cold feet about staying as more people left, and her counterpart in Sidney wanted me to answer their questions.

Since I had time, I made the trip up and did the healing before picking up a guide to find the house where most of the people who wanted to stay were living.

"So, you're the one trying to get everyone to move down to Augusta," was the first thing I heard after some introductions.

"No, like I told people, you all can do whatever you want, but you've seen the weather, you've seen the lack of technology. Vlad says that even if people figure out how to start rebuilding, there will be more pulses, and it will just keep getting colder. There are not enough resources to give you the infrastructure to survive here long-term, but with people leaving, you can hold out a long time if you want with what's left."

"But we've heard the stories. You're going to crowd us into cookie-cutter housing and assign us all jobs. We get heat and food, but you're in control."

"It's the council that's in control. My control is limited to deciding what is built while I'm there and working with the enforcers on safety issues and fighting the aliens," I said. "I think you have the wrong idea, though. We are still short on housing, which is why people are crowded in. If you want to find a house like this, or a couple of houses like this, and keep doing your own thing, just with access to power, water, and medicine, you're welcome to. The long-term plan is to have housing for everyone, with no one having to crowd, but that's a long way off. I foresee all the big cities I visit trying to help people in towns like this, so they will have a steady influx for a while. You'll be expected to contribute somehow, but it's not going to be someone micromanaging you."

They asked many more questions, and it was clear that some people in town had just been giving everyone a generalized answer that left people uncomfortable with what was happening. I was upfront that I saw them moving into nano housing in the long term. They might stay here until things got so cold that it was the only option, or they'd get tired of being out here on their own.

"After a certain level of cold, it won't matter how hard you work. You'll accept the nanotechnology or freeze. Even before that, illness or accidents will happen, and out here, that might be fatal, where it could be easily cured in town."

No decisions were made before I left, but the mood was more accepting of our offer, and people were thinking about the real implications of what was happening. The fact that I was okay with them staying here as long as they could made them more comfortable about moving. I understood people wanting to stay independent, but I did not see how it could work out for them. The conversation had run longer than planned, but I still made it home before it was too late. The group I was hauling on the sled was all waiting for me when I got back to the school, which helped speed things up. I dropped them off and headed to bed for some sleep before the next trip to Bangor.

17

The following morning, I would have liked to have said I was up bright and early. Unfortunately, it was more like I was up early, and it was cloudy with a dusting of snow. Vlad said a small front was moving in, but the trip to Bangor would be fine. I wanted to leave right after I collected resources at eight, so I could get to Bangor with more time to help out there. The sled, one of the ones that had not been reinforced with metal, had been loaded the night before and was ready to go.

While I was getting ready, I saw the greenhouse research upgrade had reached level ten, granting a welcome bonus. "That's an awesome upgrade," I told everyone in the portal bay as I shared the bonus effect from the custom greenhouse research.

Improved resource generation. The selected blueprint will produce 1% more of the selected resource (1% more than the maximum amount for variable resource generation) • Custom Greenhouse. Level 10. First added effect: each custom greenhouse supports enough small herbivores to feed an extra five people per year.

"It looks like that extra five people fed is modified by the 10% bonus from the levels of the research. Now, each of those greenhouses is feeding 60.5 people instead of the base 50. With how many we've built, I wouldn't mind seeing that bonus go up more," Bryan said. "I'm glad we've been focusing on those."

Upgrading the local ones took 12 more tokens, and then I was ready to head out. The snow was still drifting down, but I had Vlad, so I was not worried about getting lost. I just had to hunt down Donna before I left. She had wandered off to talk to Wendy before I could talk to her.

"I know I'm repeating myself, but make sure the resources are collected, and keep people safe. I'm worried about the aliens attacking while I'm gone, so don't let people here do anything too brave that gets them killed," I said.

"We've been working on a patrol schedule. Go, have fun on

your vacation, and we'll keep things going here. You do remember we'll have to handle this all without you soon, right?" Donna answered.

"Yeah, yeah, I'm going," I laughed before getting on the snowmobile and heading north. By this point, the trail to Sidney was well-traveled, and there was still a pretty good track to Pittsfield. After that, it was guidance from Vlad and the landmarks I could remember that got me the rest of the way.

Once again, a scout was waiting for me and looked excited that I had made it. The snow was still coming down, so it made sense they would be worried if I showed up this time.

"Hey, are you staying here or can you go back now that you've reported I'm here?" I asked after he had used his whistle to alert people I was coming.

"This time, I was just here to let them know you made it. I know it's cheesy, but everyone wants to make sure you're pleased when you show up to a big welcome. We all know we need your help," he said.

"First, I don't care about being greeted, but if it makes people happy, go for it. Second, hop on. There's room, and the snowmobile is charging from the grid here, so more weight won't hurt," I said.

He hopped on and enjoyed the ride as I made my way to the meeting point. By now, it was somewhat of a well-oiled machine. As soon as I pulled up, I was greeted while they started unloading all the food I had brought. Andy was giving me a general overview of all the work they had gotten done, and I let him talk as I looked around. People all seemed to still be in good shape, even if they were still losing some weight. They were definitely on reduced rations. When he got to the report of what they had built, I was thrilled. They exceeded the target with eight houses and six greenhouses.

"That's really impressive for seven days," I said. "Because of stuff going on at home, I can only integrate some of them today, but I'll be able to do the rest tomorrow before I leave. Plus, I needed to set aside 30 tokens to upgrade your first three greenhouses with the new research upgrades."

That sparked a whole side discussion about the upgrades that had come in for the greenhouses. Everyone was excited to hear about the basically free upgrades to the greenhouses they had built. It was enough food for 84 more people, 168 people at half rations, with no further construction on their part. The upgraded greenhouses would also pick up the overflow of animals from the barn.

I cut off the conversation to get started on my work. Over the next 15 minutes, I upgraded the three existing greenhouses and integrated three of the new ones. I also integrated six of the eight new houses. That put the water supplies in the negative, so I added another water tower. All of that had left me with 24 settlement tokens. I was already resigning myself to a noon departure the next day to finish integrating buildings. My other chores were to generate ration bars in their storage space and use healing charges to help injured people.

Once that was taken care of, it was back to the meeting room for a rundown of everything that had happened in the last week in Augusta. There were many questions about the aliens and our plans for them. I kept the strategy at a high level up here. They were so far away that they did not need to know the details. The information about the two towns we were evacuating brought up jealousy in some people again, but I reminded them it just would not work for them.

"Things are looking good here, you've really slowed the drop in heat and food supplies," I told them. "I'll update the group on the status tomorrow after I get everything built and integrated. We're going to have to wait that long for me to have the supplies to finish integrating everything, so it's going to be a long ride home for me tomorrow."

"It looks like you might be staying longer," Vlad said, popping back into the room. "The weather is turning bad beyond my projections. You might be stuck here for a few days."

"Damn, well, we knew that was a risk," I said. "I'll prioritize the houses in the morning if the weather gets worse, and then windmills if needed, before thinking about the other greenhouses. I recommend staging people here to move into the houses so you can use the heated living spaces as soon as possible. It looks like you have been keeping the windmills' batteries fully charged, which will help if it gets cold. With the new buildings, you were sitting on the edge of barely having enough power in town. I'm going to build two more windmills now and set those pods to tokens until I leave."

Hearing that a big storm was probably heading their way ended the briefing. Everyone had jobs to complete to help prepare for the storm. I offered to help, but was told I would be in the way. They were happy to have a second snowmobile to move things around, though. I ended up hanging out and talking to people as they took breaks from their jobs to warm up. I was worried about everyone in Augusta, but Vlad said if the weather changed as he expected, the approaching storm would be obvious in the morning. That would give them time to prepare.

Finally, around midnight, Vlad confirmed the storm was moving in, and I was going to be spending an extra day there at least. I made the decision to go to bed in order to prepare for the morning and try to manage their heat issues. With the heat supply so low, I needed to make sure the storm did not use up too much of their reserves while they were building out their housing.

There was a lot of noise in the room as people came in and out of the bunk room all night. I kept waking up, but it seemed like everyone else was used to it, as no one else woke up when I did. I still got enough sleep and was dressed and ready a little before eight a.m., when they would be doing a full round of collection back home.

Fewer material units were generated back home thanks to the lack of my perks. I also ended up with ten more tokens because they weren't being converted to material units. That research effect was not limited to me technically, but it was limited in practice. I was the only one who could spend tokens since they all appeared on my sheet when they were collected.

Once I had all the resources I was going to get, I integrated the two houses, and I moved on. The power drain was still too high, so after checking resources, I built five more windmills. That left just enough material units to add an apartment block as well.

"That's it," I said after building the apartment block. "I'm tapped out on material units now. I could integrate the two waiting greenhouses, but that would drain more power for food production that could be used for heat. With that apartment, though, you can stack almost 2,400 people in the nano housing and clinics."

"What about the greenhouses? Can we use those for housing now that they are set up for animals?" Andy asked.

"Just a minute," Vlad said as he froze. "Yes, that does make them suitable for housing once they are upgraded with the latest research. The unused floor space is fairly narrow and limited, but you should be able to cram 15 or more people in each one."

I winced internally, thinking of all the maintenance that would pile back up after I had just got it under control, but getting another 100 people into a nano building and not burning fuel to keep them warm was worth it.

"Give Vlad a list of who should be moved where," I said. "Then work up a list of people you want me to check up on or deliver supplies to. My class and perk points mean I can handle the cold better than most people. I'll spend the day outside as much as possible, taking care of stuff so that more people can stay inside."

I proceeded to bundle up while they decided which buildings were the least efficient for heating. Those residents would be moved to the six completed greenhouses. As soon as I had the list, I headed outside to clear the snow off the sled and start picking up people. One look at the heavy snowfall was enough to make me change my plan, and I went back inside to ask where I could find a tent or something to cover the sled.

"Even for short trips, it's going to be cold and full of snow if we don't put a cover on it," I said. "Vlad's projections call for up to four inches an hour at some points, and some of these people are outside the range of water towers, so there is snow everywhere. Not that the water towers can even keep up with clearing all the snow in this storm."

A few other people bundled up and helped me rig a cover on the sled, then I headed off to the first house I was evacuating. The outside temperature was just over negative 60 degrees. When I made my way inside the house, I found 22 people crowded in the main room around a roaring wood stove. The air was heavy with hints of smoke, and it was still just in the 40s inside.

"Hey, I don't know if you've seen me, but I'm the guy from

Augusta. We upgraded the greenhouses, and now people can sleep in them," I said by way of greeting. When it looked like I had stunned them into silence, I kept talking. "It will be tight, but it will be warmer, and the air will be clearer while this storm is going on," I said. "Get some bedding and the minimum supplies you need for a few days. I can take seven or eight people at a time, and each greenhouse can hold up to 20. You'll need to decide who will be in the neighboring greenhouse."

There were some questions and confusion, but everyone was ready to get out of the house and go someplace warmer, so I cut the discussion off quickly. I divided people up so they could fit into three trips, with the most capable left to the end to keep the fire going, and then safely taper it off before they left.

It took about 15 minutes per trip, and then I came back to make sure the fire was safely out before heading to the next house to evacuate. The whole process to fill the greenhouses took six hours, but with at least one more cold night before the storm broke, it was worth it. I had also used eight of my healing perk charges by the time the moves were done. There were some sick people in those colder houses.

After a quick break to eat a small meal, I spent another four hours checking on people and moving supplies around as needed. By the time it was a few hours after dark, the temperature was approaching negative 70 degrees with more room to drop.

"Cold like this is not that bad, we know how to survive it," Andy was saying as I ate another small meal. "The problem is not having a few warm days to recover and running out of heating fuel. There's only so much wood to burn, and stoves can only handle the heat for so long. The supplemental power your windmills supply is our only backup, and it's not enough."

"I'm thinking I'll add more power tomorrow, but save enough that I can build another apartment block the day after," I said. "Part of that will depend on what Vlad thinks the storm is doing. We still have most of the batteries fully charged. That's about 1,200 units of power to tap if things get worse, or to reduce wood usage once we know this storm is ending. I know it's not ideal, but it looks like you're going to have to keep people living in the greenhouses, with the hit your fuel reserves have taken. Even then, it's going to be tight."

Everyone was too tired and stressed to talk much, and I slept well that night. It was too cold for people to move around, so the house was actually quiet that night. It seemed everyone slept well and woke up early, though, so I was up with them at six.

The good news was that Vlad thought the storm was already passing. I would not be leaving for another day at least, but the temperature was no longer dropping, and there was less snow. I passed on the good news, but said I wanted to see at least some warming before tapping into the batteries.

While I was waiting for all the resource collection to happen back home, I checked on the Sidney mission. It looked like the enclosed vehicle was keeping up with the evacuation. Just the one vehicle in use slowed things down, but it was progress. There were fewer than 200 people left to be moved.

Not getting my perk bonuses for the processing portal back home hurt the day's material units, but I had enough resources to build two more windmills. At least I was not running short on tokens now. Those were piling up.

I got the windmills placed and let Andy give me a list of whom to tell to use more electricity and less wood. By the time I was done with that, temperatures had risen five degrees, and we started using the batteries to augment power as well. As I went to more areas to check on people, I saw the effects of the cold and how they were on the edge with resources. There were two houses where it looked like a chimney backdraft had left the residents frozen before they could get the fires going again. There were also three house fires where most of the people looked to have died. Those were caused by the stove overheating or chimney fires. Then there were just people who succumbed to the cold or the smoke. There were not as many of those as the most vulnerable people had already been moved to nano housing or had already succumbed. There were still a few who did not make it, though.

There was nothing I could do about it at this point, but seeing it up close was sobering. When I asked Andy about it, he said it was just something that happened. As soon as it warmed up enough, people would rotate between houses. They would let the stoves cool slowly, then clean them and the chimneys thoroughly.

"When we have time, we can keep things safer," Andy said. "In these storms, though, we can't move people around and have someone cleaning chimneys. The cold-induced backdrafts are even harder to fight. No matter how well the airflow is managed, this cold is dangerous."

"It'd be nice if we got more help here instead of you helping everyone else while we freeze," someone shouted from one of the bunks. I saw Vlad start to respond, but I waved him off.

"It's not easy for me either. I'm trying to save as many people as possible," I exclaimed. "I don't always make the right decisions, but I'm doing the best I can. I've got some people in Augusta asking why I've helped you, Pittsfield, and Sidney. If I'd just focused on Augusta, they would be in a lot better shape."

"People are just frustrated," Andy said into the sudden silence. "We know almost everyone would be dead here without your help, but it's hard to see even more friends and family die."

The silence after that was not hostile. It was more resigned. No one knew what to say, and I was ready to avoid it all with a long night's sleep. It had been an exhausting day, and if the weather were even a little better the next day, I would be taking off. We could not afford to keep missing my portal bonuses.

The next morning was warmer, which boosted everyone's mood. Already feeling better, I almost laughed to see the 1,015 settlement tokens built up. That problem was taken care of for at least a day or two. When I stepped outside, the snow had stopped, and I could feel it was warmer. Nearly up to negative 50 now. If the temperature kept rising, I'd be heading out before noon, but before then, I had buildings to build and integrate. I also had more plans to make before I could head out.

I started by integrating the three remaining greenhouses. That took the water into the negative, so I followed that up with another water tower and yet another windmill. Then it was time to meet with people. The town's population loss had increased from 64% to 66%, which was far below the mission limit of 90%, but I would not mention that. Saying that another 24% of their starting population could die before I failed my mission just sounded cruel. Instead, I shared the updated sheet with them to review and talk about next steps.

Bangor Settlement		**Population**	11,372
Food Supply	21 days	**Heat Supply**	5 days
Housing	23,481 people	**Survivable Housing**	582 people
Food Production	9%	**Secure Food Production**	9%
Power Production	150- 3,890 units	**Power Draw**	2,245- 11,105 units
Power Storage	94/ 1,870 units	**Indoor Pod Slots**	50/ 75
Water Production	1,650 units	**Water Draw**	1,410 units
Production Structures	Large Windmill x 17	Large Water Tower x 6	Barn x 1
Greenhouse Complex x 1	Custom Greenhouse x 9		
Enhanced Structures	Custom House x 24	Dorm x 1	Medical Clinic x 2
Medical Pods x 4	Apartment Block x 1		

"First, to discuss is the heat supply. I know it looks bad, but you are doing great. It's just gone down 11 days in the 24 days since I first came here. The rate of decline in the reserve is even slower now. By quadrupling the official beds, adding beds in the clinics, and adding beds in the custom greenhouses and barns, there are nearly 2,700 people in nano housing, not using firewood or any other fuel. There's also about 1,000 excess power units a day to power legacy heaters if you're careful now," I said.

"Even in the best case, we need to extend that supply," Andy said. "What we have will run out in two weeks, and we won't have enough room for everyone by then. All the food you bring and generate has helped, but we'll need to focus on that, too. Even at half rations, we are producing less than 40% of what we need."

"And we can't stay at half rations forever," someone yelled from the crowd.

"You've got a lot of people trained on building now. You need to go all in on it for when I get back next time," I said.

"And collect more firewood while cannibalizing other structures," Vlad said. "Those 5 days listed do not count all the burnable material that has not been collected yet."

I had another hour or so to make plans while confirming the worst of the storm was over. They were determined to build 12 more houses and six more greenhouses in seven days when I returned. That would be housing for almost another 1,000 people, the way they were cramming in.

I decided to give up on buying communication devices anytime soon. To integrate what they planned to build in a single week would require 900 tokens. I would need to save that on top of what I was spending at home. I also had to plan for more infrastructure builds the next time I returned.

Finally, I was ready to go and reclaimed my snowmobile from the people using it to haul supplies. A few last messages were given to me to transport, and then I headed home. Despite the late start, I stopped by Pittsfield to pick up more of their personal items. It was after dark when I made it home, and everyone was happy to see me. They had weathered the storm with few issues, and there had been no attacks by the aliens. They were glad to see they could handle stuff while I was gone, but preferred me around as a backup.

After checking in, I started my chores by getting people to use the bonus processing portal capacity from my perk, then checked which buildings were ready for integration after the storm. According to Bryan, the storm effectively delayed everything by two days, leaving only four houses and two more greenhouses for me to integrate.

"Easy come, easy go," I said as I watched the settlement tokens tick under 400 after having briefly been over 1,000. "I feel like we are building a lot slower than Bangor here, though."

"They are all focused on building," Bryan pointed out. "Here we've got enforcers, guards, and a lot more people in pods. I am upping the building rotation, though. These groups will be going to five houses and three greenhouses for this next cycle."

As we were talking, I was looking over the numbers and saw that there were research updates on the greenhouse complexes. Their resource generation increased by 2%. With a base of 400 people fed, each level meant it could feed four more people. That would help too.

With all that taken care of, it was time for a longer debrief. While there had been no emergencies, the cold snap had been painful for some people. There were a fair number of veiled and outright complaints about the speed of new housing and food coming online. After days in Bangor, where people were not getting enough food and were crowded far beyond what was happening in Augusta, I was pretty blunt about how good they had it.

I also clarified that we would continue to help other towns. We needed the mission rewards, and it was the right thing to do for those people. If Augusta got to a point where people were at risk, that would be a different decision, but as long as it was mostly just discomfort, I would not change my plans. That included more scouting and more testing. As soon as Sidney was evacuated and we got the mission reward, I wanted to take the fight to the aliens. If we could loot a second portal, I needed Portland on a recovery track sooner rather than later. If Portland had a large number of people who needed Augusta's resources and there was no portal, I was not sure what I'd do.

Donna said she'd have an afternoon scouting run planned, and I was told people would be lined up for testing at eight the following morning. I finished my huge dinner, took a shower, and called it a night.

In the morning, I realized I had forgotten to adjust the pods the day before. With all 50 pods in Bangor set to maintenance, I could shift all but two of our maintenance pods to token production. I had been thinking of building another greenhouse complex, but if Klawock was leveling that blueprint, I would wait on that. Instead, I built another apartment block and a windmill.

I was excited for the next night. It looked like Sidney would be all cleared out by the next morning, and all the holdouts had decided to move. There would be ongoing trips for a few more days, as there were still animals and other valuable items to bring to Augusta. They would need another two days to move everything important before we could think about rescuing another town. That also meant I would need to take a trip out there the next day to collect the mission rewards.

The good news kept coming in the morning testing session when I found another enforcer candidate. That meant there were five of them waiting in the wings, and coming with us to train while scouting. We rechecked some of the close-in areas we had already checked and encountered golems in spots we had cleared before. It looked like they had used the storm to reposition themselves. The fact they were moving to the same spots as before made us all worried. It seemed like a dumb move on the alien's part, so I feared there was something we were not seeing. The only hiccup came late in the afternoon when we found another golem a little further out.

"Trap!" Vlad yelled as the golem rose from the snowdrift. "Fire southeast, now!"

Following our plan, the three enforcers with nano inhibitors fired where Vlad directed, and the people with regular guns started firing at the golem, which I incapacitated as I moved the snowmobile to be protected by the sled.

It went far better than the last trap. All but one of the launchers were disabled before it could fire. The golem died, and a single blade struck the sled. It went through the upgraded siding far enough to hit one of the candidate's body armor, but there was no substantial damage, and the bruising was healed with a single charge of my healing perk.

"It's nice not to come out of one of those traps without a whole layer of skin and muscle missing," Kate said once everyone had calmed down.

She sounded as if she were joking, but also like what happened was still bothering her. I was making a mental note to check up on it when Donna caught my eye and gave a subtle nod. If Donna was handling it, that was one less thing for me to worry about. We cleared one more scout before heading back, adding five spheres to my collection.

"I just can't figure this out. Either the aliens are worried about an attack and are willing to throw away golems for an early warning, they are trying to lure us into complacency, or there's another angle I'm not seeing," Donna said on the way back. "I'd feel a lot better if I knew what was going on."

"Hopefully, we'll make our move before whatever they have planned happens," I said. "The other thing Vlad mentioned, heading back from Bangor, is that it all may be a delaying tactic while they focus on Portland."

"I hope that's not what's going on," Donna said, which got general agreement from everyone else.

Once we were back, I hurried things along to make it an early night. I planned to head to Sidney to pick up some of the remaining supplies at about five in the morning, so I could make that trip without messing up the rest of the plans for the following day.

18

When I headed out of my dorm at five the following morning, the snowmobile and sled were waiting for me. It was early enough that I regretted getting up and driving there in the dark and cold, even though I knew I needed to get there early to stay on schedule. At the same time, I was excited to see what we got as a reward for saving the town.

As soon as I entered the town, I received a mission completion notification. I waited until I reached the school to read it. That way, I could get out of the cold and review the message while the waiting group prepared the animals for travel on my sled. This sled had been enclosed, and one of the nano heaters was inside. The animals were harder to keep safe than humans, as they tried to move around the entire trip. A small group was stationed at the school to keep the heat on and help with the final animal transfer. They were all from Augusta, so that the town residents could be moved and the mission completed, while giving us time to transfer animals and other valuable items back home.

"Give me a few minutes here before we start loading up the sled," I told the group waiting for me in the heated garage we were using for transfers. "I won't be able to wait until I get back to see what the mission rewards are."

I sat down and pulled them up. Everyone else was curious, so I read them off as I looked at them.

Sidney Rescue Mission: Variable Rewards

This community has been successfully evacuated. Final rating is 291.5 (583 saved and 0 dead). Suggested reward allocation: production, defense, and production. Accept the reward or request a modified allocation.

"One point per two people this time," Vlad pointed out. "That's half of what you got last time, but this was far easier due to the distance and the fact that they were not yet in dire straits. Even with the reduction, it's still a lot more points than the prior mission. The message suggests you select production twice. The nano controller must see that as a more pressing need."

"After seeing how Bangor is faring, I can't argue with that. I'm taking its suggestion again," I said as I accepted the reward and watched the next screen pop up.

Sidney Rescue Mission: Allocated Rewards

- Material unit enhancement device level upgrade 30 (150 points) - device may be placed on or removed from a portal by an architect. Adds 30 material unit production per day to the assigned portal unit enhancement.
- Enforcer cost reduction (100 points) - cost to assign enforcer class decreased by 10 spheres
- Material unit generation (33.5 points) - 1,655 material units added to Augusta

"Whoo-hoo, now that's an awesome mission reward," I shouted when I got to the end. It was perfect. "Enforcer class cost is back to its starting point of 10 spheres. I can empower four more right now. On top of that, the upgraded device will add 350 material units per week. That's a huge boost over time. And that one-time boost to material units is enough to build three big buildings with some left over."

Everyone else was excited about the award, too. It would cover a lot of the food and housing needed for the people we evacuated from Sidney. I talked to them a little more, then helped load the sled and turned on the heater. The sun was peeking over the horizon on the trip back. It was pretty, but it was right in my eyes most of the way. That slowed me down a little, and it was just before nine when I was back helping unload the sled and collect resources. With that taken care of, I had a lot of construction to do.

With the device, my bonuses, and the token-to-material-unit conversion feature, we were generating almost 500 material units daily. That was a new apartment block or greenhouse complex every day if I wanted. My limitation now was the work units, but those would be easy to boost. Before building anything, though, I upgraded the greenhouse complexes with the latest research. After that, I found Erin and explained the mission rewards and what I was building. I was not in a rush, and it seemed worth getting her thoughts on what I was going to build.

First up were two new apartment blocks to house the people we kept adding. Erin was on board with any new housing, since that was the chief complaint she had to address. I built those with her blessing, then moved on to the less glamorous stuff. I added another barn for the animals that were still coming from Sidney. That made us tight on water and power, so I added two windmills and two water towers.

As I headed back to the portal area for a council meeting, it was nice to see people scrambling to fill the new buildings. It was rare that we saw positive surprises like this. New housing was planned a week or so in advance, and people knew when their turn would come. These unexpected buildings bumped things way up, and I would be adding another five houses later in the day as well. I could see how excited people were to be getting out of the legacy housing early. I also knew our rough plans to patrol today would likely be set aside to activate the new enforcers and get them used to using their perks.

Everyone was smiling when I sat down for the meeting. Erin had already shared the mission rewards, but I projected them up for people to see while I took care of the first thing I needed to handle.

"Do we have the list of which four of the five identified enforcer candidates we are initiating today? I'm only a few spheres short of initiating the fifth, so that person should be ready to get the enforcer class tomorrow or the next day. I want to get them all done this morning so we can work with them late this afternoon if they are recovered and go scouting tomorrow." I was looking at Donna while I was talking. She was now officially part of the council, and I wanted her to have plenty of say in this.

"We've ranked the list, and they're all standing by. We weren't sure how many could be converted today," Donna said as she handed me the list. "You know the recovery time on them, though. It will have to be a really brief training in the early evening."

"Great, I'll be back as soon as the first one is started," I said as I headed over to the pod and got the first candidate, Roger, started. Then I headed back to talk about the mission and what the bonus meant for the settlement. "This should be enough resources to let me build a large building every day for a while, plus the additional infrastructure we need. I'm going to try speeding things up here and then create some resources to give Bangor a boost before their situation gets even worse there."

"What about more towns we can rescue for the mission bonus?" O'Donnell asked. "Those seem to be useful for everyone, and there are a lot of towns around here we could be rescuing for missions."

"There are at least three more days to finish clearing out all the useful stuff in Sidney and hunting for any small groups still alive on the outskirts of the towns we've helped," Erin said. "Unless we are getting more vehicles so that we can expand operations."

"Not yet, every spare token is going to be spent on weapons soon," I answered. "Those are the focus after construction until we take care of the aliens. Right now, only a third of us have nano weapons, and that needs to change. If Donna agrees, we will train, scout, and prepare for next week. When I get back from Bangor next time, we'll launch our attack on the aliens."

As for timing, the rest of the council deferred to Donna and O'Donnell, and they were both on board with my timeline as long as the training and scouting went well. I had checked with Donna ahead of time, so her agreement was expected, but O'Donnell's quick agreement was an unexpected surprise.

"Since we're getting ready for real, I'm getting one gun now," I said, spending 255 settlement tokens at once to buy the nano pistol and 500 rounds before handing it to Donna. "Everyone should train with it, even me. I'd like to have three of us armed with this and six with the inhibitors before we leave, but I'm not sure we'll get that many bought in time."

When it was time for me to start the class process on the second candidate of the day, people took that as an excuse to end the meeting. We had covered everything we needed to, and the boost in housing meant work to keep things organized and lists up to date. O'Donnell also needed to plan for Augusta's defense. When we left, defensive patrols would all fall to his team. We would be taking both snowmobiles, so he'd have legacy weapons and basically no transportation. There was always a small chance that we were being lured away so Augusta could be attacked. The transportation situation was even worse because almost all the legacy vehicles had given out during the last cold spell, and they no longer had anything running reliably.

Those enforcers not out working or patrolling all migrated to Donna, Vlad, and me as we sketched out a basic plan to assault the aliens, assuming Vlad had identified their base using the pattern he had found. Talking through all the scenarios we could think of took the rest of the morning. Then, after lunch, they went off to train while I met up with Bryan to integrate the next five houses.

"So, the foremen and I have been talking," Bryan said when we were done. "We want to take a crack at making our own version of the dorm. We can model it after the ones you've been building. If we can clone it and it costs twice as much as the houses or less, it would be a popular choice. Not everyone needs the house vibe, and we like that they have some food production alongside housing. It seems good to have a mix for the long term."

"How fast they get built and how much they cost to integrate will determine if they would be worth it," I said. "If you've got people motivated for it, you should at least try it."

When he said he thought it could be done in ten days, I was all for it. I knew the speed was partly because of the nano processing that occurred during integration and to the fact that the maintenance pods were fixing many errors, but it was nice either way. If they could do it at that speed, it was the same three official spots for people created per day as the house, but with bonus food production. The single people and the college students did not mind the bunk situation, and it would be a useful blueprint for me in the future if it worked. With my buy-in, Bryan pulled one team off building a house for the next cycle and shifted them to the dorm.

"If they can perfect it, the dorm blueprint would be even more useful for Bangor," Vlad pointed out as we headed to the enforcer training area. "It's a good thing you have me to keep track of some of these timelines with the various teams in two cities building three different blueprints now."

"No kidding. I have them on the tablet, but this was a lot simpler back in Klawock. Still without all this new stuff, we'd be in trouble." My point about how the changes from my first mission were helping was driven home as I watched the enforcers train with the nano weapons. They were a vast improvement over the weapons we had for the last alien assault I was part of.

"You ready for some target practice?" Wendy called over as I walked their way.

"Yeah, I should be ready to step in, even if I want you all to be the ones to fight and get the personal tokens. If I could get them for killing the golems and the aliens, it would be great, but I'll have to stick to using the nano matrices we find," I said as I got in line to test out the nano pistol. "We've got four days of training and scouting after this, and then I'll make the trip to Bangor before we try this for real. I'm going to see how many tokens I can set aside for more weapons in that time."

"We're prepared to use legacy weapons and clubs, too," Wendy said. "The old guns are failing fast whenever they are out in the cold, though. At least we have plenty of ammunition left."

We kept talking until it was my turn to try out the nano pistol. It was easy to fire, with almost no recoil, and the sighting mechanism made it simple to pick the target. The best part was that the ammunition was variable based on the pistol setting. It could be a more typical shot that went through a target or one that quintupled in size right before impact to do more surface damage. That could be useful for fighting the golems when an inhibitor was not handy.

Donna and Vlad were talking while I was practicing, and when I made my way over there, I learned I had been signed up for more work. We were going to place some fake traps in a few spots for the team to react to. Those traps were the current primary threat, and Donna wanted us to get some realistic practice against them. It would not help me, as I would know where they were, but it would help everyone else.

Vlad knew what I needed to set things up, so when we found Bryan, he listed off the supplies we needed. The rest of the afternoon was spent collecting supplies and setting up the fake traps for the next day. By the time I started work on the third one, I was having fun. I had done little building since starting this mission, and I made a note to get some more work that was not fighting into my list of things to do.

That evening, a schedule was set for patrols focused on trap detection and practice in trap disarmament. The team was large enough now that the enforcers would be divided into two groups. Donna and Wendy would each lead one of the patrol groups. One team would be with me each day for patrols and practice. The other team would stay back to guard the settlement and practice target shooting. I was going out every day, though, not because they needed my presence but because they needed Vlad for scouting.

We also moved my time scanning for enforcers earlier in the day, as Donna wanted us to have eaten and been out scouting by eleven, so groups could be out for six hours without too much darkness on the way back. With my next four days planned out, I went to bed early. After a slower start, the apocalypse was getting tiring again.

At least there were still plenty of resources in the morning to have fun building things before a day of trudging around in the snow. Another apartment block went up, and then two more windmills. After that, I had to head back inside to finish the scanning I had started before leaving to collect resources.

That afternoon was the first attempt to deal with the traps we had set. It did not go well at all, and somehow ended with one of the new enforcers shooting Donna in the leg. It was not a severe injury, and I healed it with a single charge of my perk. She was not happy, though.

"What was that?" she yelled at Roger. "You were supposed to be focused on securing the area. Not aiming through me at the trap, your weapon won't even disable a trap."

"It's just, everyone was yelling traps, and I freaked out. You told us there were some fake traps, but there were real ones too, so I was supposed to treat them all as real," Roger said. "Vlad yelled to fire to the right, and I did."

"That's why we practice," I said, trying to calm things down. "Still, you have to be more careful than that. A mistake like that in an actual fight could end up with people dead. You can't do that again."

"Forget in a fight," Donna said. "Put that weapon's safety on, and we'll continue. Try to act like you would if you could fire, but we'll work around you not being able to actually fire if we run into something real."

Donna was the one who was shot, so I let her decide how to handle it. The good news was that, aside from that issue, the group reacted appropriately to the trap. That was about the only excitement we faced that day. It seemed the sentry golems were no longer being replaced as quickly, and this was a freshly cleared area. There were no other traps besides the one we had set up. That did not stop Vlad from occasionally calling out that there was a trap.

When nothing moved, it was less realistic. However, people still got practice targeting and firing the nano inhibitors. We kept the shots down enough that we did not have to use the clips. We did not want to start dipping into the clips for practice if we could help it. They were cheap, but there was no reason to waste them. The three golems we cleared earned me three more spheres, but I still needed eight more than that for the next enforcer. I had told no one yet, but that would be the last one I created here if all went well. I wanted to save up more spheres for the next mission.

The next morning, I constructed another apartment block, a windmill, and a water tower. The most exciting thing was that the greenhouse research hit level ten, and I could upgrade our greenhouses. The bonus effect here was similar to that for the custom greenhouses. In this case, it added a base 20 food production by providing space for herbivores. This one had space for small to medium-sized animals, not just small ones, so we could add enough goats or sheep to feed 20 extra people each year. With that and the bonus production, greenhouse complexes were now feeding 462 people each year, up from 400.

I also noted that the upgrade took the production research track to 3,800 of 5,000 research points to unlock the next tier of options. That put it just as close as the blueprint branch did. I was looking forward to seeing new research options after the portal branch had not gotten any new options when it reached tier one. Vlad had told me the processing portal was just too powerful and also too limited to have research options at every tier.

After a round of building, it was back to scanning, with one success, before a quick lunch and a long afternoon with Wendy's team. There were no friendly fire incidents this time. From what I could hear, Donna had worked on that with both teams all morning while I was testing people. She had worked on it enough that I heard people complaining about the extra drills, thanks to Roger. While the scouting went well, we only found two golems this time.

"They're placing them to maximize tracking us with fewer golems," Vlad said as we were heading back. "I might be able to project which nodes they will populate out here. My best guess is that we have drained their resources, and making more spheres is getting tough for them. The other option is that they wanted to stop giving us spheres and are building up a massive defensive force."

"Let's hope it's the first option," I said, to general agreement from the team. "We still do not know how many of them are left. Maybe they all fled already, and the golems we are seeing are on some programmed timer to keep us busy."

I knew it was unlikely the aliens were gone, but I wanted one option that made people feel good. The conversation continued until we were back, and I could drop everyone off before heading to find Bryan. There were two greenhouses ready to be integrated, and I wanted to get them done before it got any later.

"Those people we brought in from Pittsfield seem to have recovered, and they are motivated," Bryan said after we had integrated both of the greenhouses. "I've got four teams on this cycle now, so this cadre will have four of these bad boys done in six days instead of two."

"That's great. We still need a massive increase in food production, and that will help a lot. If both sets of teams could each do four or five at a time, that would be around 500 more people fed each week just from that."

"We'll get even more teams going. People are realizing there isn't much time left, and they need to get stuff built. I'll keep ramping up as we train more people, but the limit will be the availability of supplies at some point. We have tapped all the easily lootable local supplies, so it's now all scavenging. More vehicles to haul in supplies from the hardware stores in deserted towns would be helpful if we want to keep accelerating," Bryan said.

"I'll put it on the list for after the aliens are dealt with," I answered. "Until then, spare tokens are focused on arming people, but with any luck, we'll be going after them this week."

We talked a little more, but Bryan needed to do an evening sweep of all the teams, and it was already late. I let him take the snowmobile, and I walked back as my day was done.

The following morning was my last big build before I saved up some resources for Bangor. A repeat of the prior day, plus I saw what Klawock's new research was focused on. Research on custom house insulation reached the eleventh level. With 40 custom houses here, upgrading them required a lot of tokens. I did not mind the cost, as even a 1% reduction in power usage added up across that many buildings. That reduced base power usage by ten and maximum usage by 100 in the settlement.

It was the second training day with Donna's group, and this time we found a real trap, in addition to the last fake one Vlad and I had made. Things went smoothly in both cases. Roger had been drilled in being careful and had no issues. It helped that it was his day to practice with the null inhibitor, so he was the one to fire at the traps and could not hurt other humans if he misfired. I was pretty sure he was not one of the enforcers who would be getting a pistol for the assault.

It was another day with just two golems to fight, even though we pushed the patrol in attempting to locate more. That left us four spheres shy of making another enforcer, and I was not sure I would make it before I left for Bangor.

"We'll just do it when you get back," Donna said. "We're going to carefully try scouting without you and Vlad while you are gone. Some of the time on foot to practice those skills that have not been getting any use on the scouting runs with you."

"Just be careful without Vlad there to scan for traps and stuff," I said.

"We will, but we can't always count on him," Donna said.

There were some joking comments about how she looked for any chance to create more work and training for everyone, but despite the jokes, it was clear she was well respected by the team. She had dived into building a group that would survive, and no one questioned her authority. We had spoken a few times about the potential conflict between O'Donnell and her when I left, but she seemed to think it would all work out fine.

"We're changing things up tomorrow," Donna reminded everyone. "We're taking both snowmobiles, and everyone is heading out as one large group. I want to practice coordinating two groups like that."

"I'll do the shorter scanning round and be ready by ten so we can do a longer day," I confirmed as we pulled up to the portal bay. Several of us lived near it, but the rest would use the snowmobile to get dropped off at home before it was turned over to the scavenging teams.

I found no new enforcer candidates before I headed out to join the massive group going out the next day. I did not realize I would not be driving one of the vehicles. Donna and Wendy were each in charge of one, with the rest of us split between the two sleds. I had really spent no time in the sleds on these scouting missions, and riding in them was a new experience. There was more protection with the steel-plated walls, but I missed being in control.

Standing up and not getting jostled around too much was tough, as the unexpected turns and bumps seemed to be magnified in the sled. I was in the sled Donna was driving, since they needed Vlad in the lead sled for scouting. They were trying to find golems and traps on their own, but Vlad was the backup if they missed anything.

That slowed us down, and even with the extended scouting time, we only found three golems and one trap. It was frustrating being one sphere away from getting another enforcer, but after Donna extended the hunt for an extra hour with no luck, we turned back. We did not want the snowmobile batteries to be drained too much.

Before we split up for the evening, I bought three more clips for each weapon, just in case they were needed while I was gone. When I handed them over, Wendy asked for more for the pistol. That one did not have unlimited ammunition in town if aliens attacked. It was a good point, so I bought another three clips for that one. I had the tokens to spare at the moment, but I knew the trip was going to be expensive, and as soon as we split up, I had to meet Bryan.

"Still on track?" I asked him as we went around, integrating the five new houses and upgrading the existing ones to take advantage of the new insulation level.

"Yup, these people are on top of it. I'm keeping the teams working on five houses and adding a dorm here and taking the greenhouse production from three to four per cycle," Bryan said. "I still need an actual truck designed to haul things sometime soon, though."

"As I said, we'll see after we take out the aliens. This just blew through nearly 500 tokens. Vlad and I looked, and there was a kind of snowmobile pickup with a cab for three people and a four-foot-by-eight-foot bed to haul things. It's just 600 tokens, but it's designed for on-grid use. It's got horrible range without shelling out another 200 tokens for a battery pack."

"That sounds about perfect," Bryan said. "I'll be waiting for you to buy it for us. Once we get the other group back up to five houses too, I'm not adding more teams until we can get more supplies."

As I was walking back to my room, Vlad got my attention and told me to check the mission update.

Augusta Settlement Mission: Update

Earth's rapid cooling has been progressing since the solar incursion. Secure this community to survive up to 200 years in this altered environment while defending against criminal incursions from off-world. Beware: The global temperature is expected to continue decreasing at a more gradual rate before stabilizing. The larger population at this location will require prompt, decisive action to address their issues. You may migrate to the next mission at any time, but the success of the prior mission will determine the starting resources for the next. You have limited time to save outposts of humanity and survive as a species until remediation of your star is possible.

- Food supply marginal
- Water supply marginal
- Power supply insufficient
- Housing supply insufficient

"Those greenhouses just tipped you over the 20% mark on sustainable food production here," Vlad said. "That seemed to be enough for a marginal rating. You need almost 1,200 more housing slots to meet that requirement at a marginal level if the threshold stays the same. I'm not sure about the power situation."

"I'd like to get them all past marginal to secured, but it's good to know what I'm shooting for," I said.

I stopped by the council's office to remind the person there that I needed the letter and notes to take to Bangor in the morning. After that, it was time for a huge meal. A big dinner, then breakfast before I headed to Bangor, was now a tradition.

19

"The weather's looking good, right?" I asked Vlad the next morning when I woke up. "I don't want to get stuck in Bangor again if I can help it."

"It's been stable with the gradual cooling of a degree or two each week," he confirmed. "There's been a little more snow than the usual flurries the last few days, but no signs of anything more."

"What I wouldn't give to see rain again," I said as I headed to the showers for a long soak before I collected resources and started eating. I had gotten up early so that I could spend some extra time in the shower.

I ran two more scans for enforcer candidates over breakfast and started a third before I left. As usual, the sled had been packed full of food for Bangor. I said my goodbyes, reminded Donna to be careful in their scouting, and headed north.

I once again had to rely on Vlad. The road and signs of civilization before the big freeze were getting harder to pick out. Even with a guide, the trip was taking longer. There were frozen snowdrifts to drive through or around when they could not quite be driven over safely.

"I know we've not had the time to work on it, and it's expensive, but I think they are going to need the train long-term," I said as I realized how much longer the trip was taking me. "There's no way this will remain viable in a few years, and I don't think a network of water towers just to clear snow makes any sense."

"No, that would be far too expensive to maintain. They will need those to clear the building snow that will fall and blow into settlements. Without snow removal, the nanostructures will just get covered in snow, and people will need to get around in enclosed walkways. It's good that you've been able to delay building those here so far, but at some point, you'll need those here too. At least this environment had people more used to extreme cold with proper outdoor equipment," Vlad said.

Our usual scout was watching for our arrival as we headed

into town, but looked even colder than usual from his bundled-up location.

“Sorry, we got in later than normal,” I said as he hopped on top of the sled. “The route here is getting more challenging, and that slowed us down.”

“As long as you’re here, a little cold is fine. Things are getting rough, and everyone has been waiting for you,” he said.

“Well, the good news is I brought a lot of resources from Augusta this time, and the people back home have been doing some research that will help you all, too,” I said. I could pull up the information on Bangor now that I was here and saw that things were not going well. There were nearly 700 deaths while I was gone. The only upside was that the remaining resources would last longer with fewer people using them. It felt bad to think that, but it was true.

“We've had problems with people burning things they shouldn’t and dying from the smoke. Then there was a virus that ran through a few buildings,” he said.

I wanted to ask more, but we were at the park, and people were waiting for me. I thought it made sense to integrate the buildings as soon as possible, so I held off on the debrief after saying hello to Andy and the others.

Andy exchanged a few words of greeting while the loaded sled was taken care of. He and the heads of some of the building crews led me around to integrate the buildings.

“With everything going on, we have been going all out,” Andy said. “We’ve got 14 houses and six more greenhouses ready for you. It’s been rough, and people are working themselves to the bone trying to improve things.”

“I’ll be able to integrate them all and supply some more buildings,” I said. “There are also some research improvements to reduce the power spent on buildings and increase food output. It cost 48 tokens to upgrade their existing houses with the two researched levels, and the one greenhouse complex needed ten tokens to rank up. I explained those benefits as I bought them. I followed that up by integrating all their new buildings.

“That’s food for 425 more people at full rations added in a week,” I said when we were done. “Even better, that’s housing for almost 200 more people at baseline, or 800 if you stuff them in there. Unfortunately, before I build anything else, we need two more water towers and four more windmills to get those numbers back up. I plan to build another apartment block after that, and then tomorrow we can add a few more things before I go."

They were on board for more housing. I kept bringing food, but warm places to stay were the bigger issue. With all the integrations and upgrades, and with people being stuffed into the apartment block, almost another 500 people were moving into nano housing on top of what they had built for integration.

Once all that was done, I headed inside for the debrief. All the new buildings had boosted the mood somewhat, but people were still looking pretty downcast.

"As I'm sure you've seen, it's been a rough week," Andy said when we were seated. "There have been losses because of illness, fire, toxic smoke, and a few people who just gave up. It feels like we're running out of time."

"I saw the losses. I'm sorry it's happening. I can tell you the heat supply dropped from five days to three, and the food supply from 21 to 18. Everyone here is stretching everything, and the improvements are stacking up. You have marginal housing for at least 40% of your people, which is stretching the remaining legacy heating. You can also feed 30% of your people on half rations just from the nanostructures. Plus, you're getting the food supplies and ration bars from me every trip."

"That's all good, but we're just building enough housing for 1,000 people a week, all crammed in," Andy said. "That's six more weeks just to scrape by, and we don't have the supplies to keep that pace up. Can we last long enough to build stuff out for everyone?"

There was murmuring from people around the room at that question, and I could see much more skepticism this time than on my prior visits. The rush of excitement from the new buildings was being drowned out by math.

"It's going to be rough, but I think it's doable. I'm hoping we get some good bonuses from driving the aliens off when I get back. That should free up some resources. I'll be building what I can to help here as well. I know it was just one apartment block this time, but there were also six infrastructure buildings, and I'll add a little more tomorrow. Your teams added housing for a little over 1,000 people, and the stuff I built is another 500 this time. It all adds up."

As I was talking, I was trying to figure out how to fit in another apartment block, but there just were not enough material units. I could build one, but I also needed another windmill and water tower. I could add in a dorm, but that was it.

Am I doing the right thing here? I messaged Vlad. *I could be diverting more resources here than to Augusta. Things here seem so much worse off than back home.*

Augusta had more starting resources, and you got there earlier, so there was more time to build stuff out. I don't think you could have diverted more resources here before now. You needed people to guard against the aliens and be ready to fight them back home. Now, once the alien threat is handled, you can push them to work harder instead of depending on your buildings. Here, the only enemy is the cold. You're going to have to triage the issues in places like this on each new mission, Vlad messaged back.

I still was not feeling good about the whole situation, but I felt reassured that Vlad did not think I was on the wrong path. It still left people here in a bad spot, but I needed to remember how much better off they were thanks to the stuff I had helped build.

That night, there were more stories and talk about the aliens and the rewards from evacuating Sidney. There were lots of questions about what would happen after we cleared out the aliens and about the trip back and forth.

"I should be fine getting here on the snowmobile," I said. "Long term, the train tracks can be upgraded, and you can have a nano train going between cities. That's going to be needed as the snow and cold build up. We've looked into it, and it's too expensive now, but after the area is stable, it will be a way for you all to stay connected."

"How expensive?" was asked from multiple directions.

"It's basically the same number of tokens to upgrade 2 miles of track or integrate a greenhouse," I answered. "Then you need to purchase the train and power sources. I have already built two windmills for train recharging, but there might need to be more, or train batteries."

We talked about that and other options for a few more hours, and then I begged off for bed. Even with a recent path to follow, I had an early morning to finish building stuff here and then a long drive back to Augusta.

By the next morning, another level had been researched for the houses, so I spent 38 tokens to upgrade all their houses again. Any bit of power saved was more power to heat legacy houses. While I was waiting for the resources to be collected back home, I asked people here what they wanted. I had a plan, but I decided to let them have some input.

"I have enough resources to build a windmill and a water tower, or a windmill and a dorm," I told them. "If I build the dorm, you will be two water units short and will have to ration water some until I come back, but that's more beds and food. I'll need to know in 20 minutes when I have the resources to build."

It only took them a few minutes to reach the same decision I had. I waited until the material units were available to me and built the last two structures of this trip: a windmill and a dorm. A quick round of goodbyes and reminders to collect the settlement tokens followed. They now had 60 pods working on maintenance, which was enough to keep the backlog stable, so I set six of the new pods to be full-time settlement token generators. Then, I was off to Pittsfield to pick up more of their possessions before heading the rest of the way home.

The blowing snow and scattered flurries had filled in most of the signs of my passage from the prior day, but it was still a smoother trail to follow home. At least the snow meant I was not leaving much of a trail for people to follow, which was good on some level, but did not seem needed, since there were no people around here who could travel much.

I was worn out from the trip home, but I made it there before it got dark. As soon as I was there, Bryan found me and led me out to integrate the four houses his teams had built. As I was doing that, I upgraded all the other houses with the new research as well. That gave everyone else time to gather for my post-trip meeting. I had noticed five new spheres in my inventory, so they had done some successful scouting while I was gone, and one more enforcer would be coming up soon.

"I'll start with the scouting so we can get that out of the way,"

Donna said. "We'll need to go more in-depth on plans later, but I'll go over the important parts now. We had a few injuries, but the pods have already taken care of them. We killed five more golems and faced one trap that caused the injuries. Tom is waiting over there by the class pod to become an enforcer, too. As soon as the settlement stuff is done, we want to begin planning the assault on the aliens."

"Thanks, that briefing covered what I needed," I said. "Give me a minute to get Tom's process started, and then we can dive into Bangor and what else happened here, as I can tell you are all bursting to talk."

It just took a few minutes to get that started, and then I got back to the table and dug into the food set out for me while Erin started talking.

"We've finished getting all the important stuff out of Sidney and found the next town we'd like to rescue. Readfield is about as far away as Sidney was, and we've sent the vehicle out there already to chat and bring some people back. We need you to go there to get the mission. We want to start that before you leave."

"We also asked, and the lumber store there is well stocked," Bryan chimed in. "We want to evacuate them and haul supplies back. They had just received a huge shipment of building materials for some local development when this happened, and it's a goldmine of supplies. Rescuing them will be good for everyone, especially if I can get a real truck to haul stuff."

"I can check for a mission there, but we won't be getting you a truck before the assault on the aliens," I said once again. "There's just not enough tokens for that."

"I know," Bryan said, "but I'm going to keep asking. Lack of supplies is what's holding back construction speed now."

"I want to help more people, but you all need to understand my priority. Bangor has been working hard. They are building almost as fast as people here, which is great, but they are barely keeping up with their dwindling fuel supply. On top of that, most of them are on reduced rations to keep from running out of food. I'm saving up resources for them until my next trip, so the only thing I am building here for at least a week, if not two, are the water towers and windmills so the grid can keep up with what you build."

"That seems extreme," O'Donnell said. "Why the shift?"

"They are sleeping four or more people per bed in the nano buildings. They are sleeping on the floors of the greenhouses, building faster than I thought possible, and they just have enough fuel supplies for three days left. They are stretching that with all the crowding and finding more to burn, but the best-case scenario is that half their population freezes to death in two weeks with no further help. Even with their construction going as fast as it is, it won't save everyone. Then, even if half the people live, half of that group starves to death in a few months to half a year. I'm going to turn that around."

"That's hard to argue against," Bryan said. "It sounds like they have been taking advantage of the larger city's depth of supplies to build faster. The supplies are the issue here, not the people willing to work."

"It's not an attack on the work ethic here, but we need to get Bangor on track, and soon. I have a feeling Portland is going to be consuming resources too. Just plan for more buildings to integrate here for now. I'll try to get Bryan something to haul in supplies so building can continue at this pace or speed up,"

That led to an overview of salvage efforts and the current structure build-out. There was a lot of hope for the potential to switch to building dorms instead of houses and even to speed up their construction to get more people housed more quickly, while I was focused on Bangor.

Questions about various building issues kept coming up, and I could see Donna getting more annoyed about the delay in getting to what she wanted to talk about. Finally, I told them I was getting tired, but that we needed to discuss plans for the alien assault so that we would focus on that, and they could leave if they wanted to.

"I know that stuff's important, but we need to get our plan in place too," Donna said when I turned the floor over to her. "We spent a lot of time over the last two days talking about what we are comfortable with based on where Vlad thinks the aliens are, our supplies, and timing around your other commitments. Here's what we want to do."

"We're planning based on their projected camp location, so a change to that changes all this," Wendy continued the train of thought, rolling out a map covered in marks. “We’ve got a roughly 25-mile trip to face them. The plan is to use the snowmobiles to get about ten miles in, then hike the rest of the way. The snowmobiles will return here after dropping us off. They will have a skeleton crew that will try to trigger and clear a golem heading east to throw them off our track.”

“That leaves nine of us,” Donna said, picking the thread back up. “We’ll have a long, slow trip to travel the remaining 15 miles. The goal is to use the routes Vlad has mapped to slowly maneuver around all of their scout positions for a surprise attack. We know they can likely sense us as we can sense them once we get close. Once we are a mile or so out, it will be a mad dash for their base so we can clear it before they can recall all their sentries to swarm us from behind.”

Vlad and I traced the planned route and timing before asking a few more questions. It seemed they had thought through the plan, but there was a significant risk.

“If this goes wrong, we could all be trapped,” I said. “I’m the only one with an escape perk. What if the aliens are not there, or there are too many of them to take out before the golems swarm us? It seems like a high-risk way to go about this.”

“It is high-risk, I pointed that out to them repeatedly, but several things are pointing towards this being what needs to be done,” O’Donnell said. “Timing is a big issue. We know you need to move on at some point, and our current attacks on their golems do not seem to be affecting their long-term defense. There’s also the question of total risk over time. These scouting runs that accomplish little are not risk-free. Someone is going to die on one of them, but they will die not having made a real impact on the aliens. This gets all the risk out of the way at once.”

“Plus, everything points to Vlad being right about this. Even if they are not there, we should be able to turn around and fight our way out. It will be a lot of spheres to collect,” Donna said. They had clearly planned their arguments out. “We also wonder how many aliens are left. They have not been seen since we killed those two, and there have been no more substantial attacks. They have been in a holding pattern, so maybe we’ll get lucky. Either way, we want to hit them before they come up with a new way to attack us, or you leave."

"It's not the worst plan," Vlad said as he examined it again. "It's dangerous for everyone other than Devin, but if it works, you can kill or drive them all off. It potentially leaves a lot of golems scattered about, but they will be leaderless and easy to clear out. An effort to methodically clear out the golems and fight our way to their base would be slow and would warn them of our approach. There might be far more risk because they know we're coming, and they might be able to replace golems faster than we can kill them. Even with the scouting, you're barely making progress, and we believe there are layers of golems to go."

"Fine, it seems like you've thought it through, and it has the advantage of fitting inside the general timeline I wanted to work on," I said. "Make sure the whole team knows the risks and understands everything. I'll make the trip to Readfield in the morning, then I want to meet with all the enforcers one-on-one after lunch. Everyone gets a private talk and can say if they like the plan and want to take part, with only Vlad and me hearing them. As soon as I'm sure no one is feeling pressured to do this, I'll sign off, and we can leave the next day."

Donna and Wendy were all grins at that. They had no worries about people backing out, even when given a chance in private. I wanted to believe there were no reservations. Still, I needed to give people that option before taking them into a dangerous situation.

"That leads to my other bit of good news," I said as I started buying weapons. "I have been generating tokens just for this. I'm buying two more pistols and three more nano inhibitors. I'll buy more clips before we leave, but what you have now should be enough for training. I think we'll have enough tokens for two communication devices at last. Plan some emergency rendezvous spots for us to be picked up if something goes wrong, that will work for everyone. Assuming everything works as planned, we'll leave the day after tomorrow. Get that training, packing, and planning done."

That wrapped up what needed to be discussed in the meeting, but everyone was wired from having a plan to deal with the aliens. They wanted to keep talking. There was also discussion about starting a Portland information book and collecting letters for people in Portland. I stuck around for an hour, then had to tell them I needed a long shower to clean off the grime from my trip, followed by some sleep. We would leave at nine the following morning in a caravan of vehicles to try triggering a mission in Readfield and start evacuating people.

"I assume there will be a mission," Vlad said as we walked home. "The council should not count that as a guarantee, though. They seem fixated on mission rewards, but you might want to remind them there are no guarantees. Are they still going to save those people for no reward?"

"I can tell you right now they will be," I said. "There is no way we are showing up to save them and then saying, 'nope, you can stay here and die because we won't get enough out of it.' I'll make them rescue them if that happens."

The following morning, I got to drive the nano car while Donna and one of Erin's aides took the snowmobiles. We got started a little earlier than planned after I collected resources and reminded the enforcers that I wanted to see them when I got back.

I knew I could handle the cold better than the others, but after the trip to Bangor and back, I took the car anyway when it was offered to me. The warmth inside was a nice change, and I just had to follow the others while Vlad popped in and out, checking the countryside and building up his map of the area.

It was another small town, and we stopped in front of what was the Readfield Family Market, according to the sign. From what I had heard the night before, the market, plus the fire station and post office, both a block over, were where most people had congregated, unless they had a really well-built house.

There were few people left in this town. Many had tried to get out when everything happened and had not been heard from again. The word was that they had tried to head south towards Portland. I assumed they were frozen somewhere, but it explained why those who were left were basically okay for the moment. There had not been a drain on resources as people died off.

"Well, we have a mission again, and it looks like they have fewer people than Sidney did, but the same type of mission," I said, quickly sharing it with the group.

Readfield Rescue Mission
This community can no longer viably sustain itself. You have decided to relocate them to Augusta. Some people may decide to remain for now. They will not impede mission completion or alter the mission score. Rescue as many people as possible by moving them to Augusta. The mission reward will be based on the number of people saved. Saved: 0 Died: 0 Remaining: 413 Not Participating: 0

Everyone in Readfield was expecting us, since Augusta had already visited. They had even been smart enough to bring people from Pittsfield and Sidney to discuss how their evacuations went and what Augusta was like.

The advantage of all these small communities was that people knew each other from before the freeze, which lent a lot of weight to what they heard from other locals. I had been helped by the same phenomenon back home. Vlad and I, well, more Vlad, were the center of attention for a while as people asked us questions.

Everyone was glad to hear a mission had been granted, but the number of people surprised them. It was 21 more than they expected, which meant they had missed some people in their last check of everyone in the town. Around 300 were living in the three buildings in the center of town, and the rest were in various farmhouses that could withstand the current cold but were burning through their wood supplies.

The plan was to evacuate the outlying areas and all their valuable supplies, such as food, before starting on the center of town. They also needed to figure out where the missing people were. They had not yet agreed to the move, and if they were that off-grid, they might not want to. Still, they needed to know about the offer. After meeting with everyone, we headed to the first farmhouse, and I was impressed with how well-built it was.

"I can't spend the resources now, but this could be integrated, and with a windmill and water tower here, it could be a way station and charging point for people exploring deeper northwest," I said. "Keep that in mind after we clear out the aliens and contact Portland."

Just the mention of Portland got people excited. Everyone had friends or family who had tried to make the trek there when this all started. While they knew it was unlikely that any of them had survived, everyone still hoped to find them and be reunited.

People here were all fine to travel, so I had used most of my healing charges back at the store. The two I had saved were used to heal people with minor issues, and then we started packing up. We were taking all 11 people who lived here, their chickens and rabbits, and some of their stuff. The next run would get the rest of their things into the sleds, while the car would be used to pick up people and animals from the next house on the next trip. Things would slow down as the alien assault force was dropped off the next day. We would use the snowmobiles for that, and when we needed a ride back after defeating the aliens.

The trip back was interesting as the people in the car with me talked nonstop. It had basically just been the 11 of them for months at this point, and someone new to talk to was a target they could not pass up. I was glad to have Vlad with me to pick up the conversation while I pretended to watch the road. It was an easy way to avoid talking. There was only so much conversation I could carry on, and I wanted to stay focused on what I was doing.

"Okay," I said to Donna when we were back, and I had turned the car over to be unloaded and prepared for its next trip. "I'm going to grab some lunch. Start sending people to my room in 30 minutes. I don't care about the order, except that you and Wendy come by last. Plan on 15 to 30 minutes per person.

My room was soundproofed, and Vlad and I would be the only ones to hear what everyone had to say. I hoped the privacy would take any pressure off them to agree to the plan so they could be honest about how they felt. It was also a chance for me to talk to the enforcers I had spent little time with. I wanted to know the people I would be fighting side by side with.

20

"I'm not going to say I'm excited about it. It sounds dangerous," Matt said as I got into the meat of my fifth conversation with the enforcers. "I knew that becoming an enforcer had some danger, though, so I'm okay with the plan. I think this is our best shot to keep everyone safe, and I'm looking forward to not wondering if I'll die in an alien attack every day once we've driven them out."

"So, you're okay with the plan that's been put together?" I asked for confirmation. There had been some buildup and conversation, but this was the main point.

"Yeah, I'm good with it. It needs to be done, and this seems like the best way to do it," he said. "I just want to be past it, you know?"

We talked for a few more minutes before I thanked him and told him to let the others know I needed a quick break before continuing.

"He seemed to be okay with things, too, right?" I asked Vlad.

"No one is looking forward to this fight, but they all think it's for the best. Their answers have all been unique, so I don't think they were coached, although they have clearly heard the same reasoning to justify the plan," Vlad said. "They may have been influenced, but at the same time, they understand the risks and want to move forward."

I headed out for a quick bathroom break. As I did, I let Tom, the next in line, know it was his turn as soon as I got back to my room.

The rest of the meetings were the same until I got to the final two. The meeting with Wendy was far more casual, and I focused on getting her take on things after bluntly asking if she was cool with the plan. The final meeting with Donna was to get a feel for her thought process behind the plan and to make sure she was not under too much pressure herself.

"Larry and I will do whatever we have to do to protect Alex," she said. "I've seen what it was like in Pittsfield and know what it's like in Bangor. We know how lucky he is to be here, where there's new technology and a future. To keep him safe, we must do this. I'm still not sure how I ended up being the enforcer in charge of things, but I'm going to do it the best I can. I'm not the only one doing my part. Larry's been doing his best as well. He shares stories about what I've seen to motivate the builders. He's been driving people to really speed up the construction efforts. We're going to get this done. The fight and the infrastructure."

"For what it's worth, I think I got lucky, and all of Augusta got lucky that you were the first enforcer picked," I said. "I'll be following your lead tomorrow, but Vlad and I will speak up if needed, based on what we know from prior fights with the aliens. You all have already heard the breakdown of the fights I had back home, though, so I doubt that will be needed."

The rest of the meeting was spent going over the supplies for the assault. We needed to pack in the tents and equipment to survive multiple nights in the cold and snow. Even with the improved ability to survive the cold, as people with classes, we needed to be prepared. She also went over the list of what equipment she would like from the store to augment our supplies, and I said I would consider it in the morning.

I made sure to wrap up the meetings before dinner. All the enforcers and I were under strict instructions to get a good night's sleep. None of us had patrol duty, and, as a treat, everyone heading out the next day had unlimited shower time. I also reminded them to eat well. Once we left, it would all be ration bars. They were filling, but not the tastiest.

I checked in the morning, but none of the greenhouses scheduled for completion that day had been completed yet. They would have to wait until I returned. I spent 45 tokens to upgrade the custom houses to the next researched insulation level, though. There was just one more level, and then the next tier of the blueprint research tree would open up. I was looking forward to seeing what tier two was like. After that, I finally spent the 400 tokens to get two communication devices. We would have to limit their use while in the alien's territory, but I wanted a way to call for a ride and check in as needed.

After that, I worked my way through Donna's list of items the team wanted, buying what we needed. Single-use mini-heaters jumped to the top of the list. Because they were single use, they were smaller and lighter. They would cut the chill overnight if needed. Then it was stuff like improved snowshoes, lights we could trust to keep working in the cold, and some high-tech blankets that could augment our other camping supplies. The last part was stocking up on more clips and ammo than I thought we could go through. It was better to have them than to run out.

The entire team was there as I bought supplies and distributed them among the assault team. I also gave a quick walkthrough of the two communication devices. The people giving us a ride would have one of them. Once they were back in town, they would need to monitor it 24 hours a day until we were back.

Everyone who was coming had friends and family crowded in the bay to see them off. There were a few tears, lots of prayers, and well-wishes. I let them have their moment and checked in with the council. They all knew the hierarchy of who would take over the portal if I did not return. They also knew that I would likely return even if everyone else died, so that was not as big a deal yet.

"Good luck," O'Donnell said. "It feels wrong sending random people out to fight because their genetics matched alien nanotechnology, but I can't argue with their perks. Heck, I can't even argue about their improved tolerance for cold. Try to bring them all back, but if you can't, make sure their sacrifice matters."

On that somber note, I signaled to Donna that it was time, and she began rounding up people. We loaded into the sleds for our mission and took off. The morning was spent successfully making it to our drop-off point before the snowmobiles turned around. They would get closer to town before they started laying the false trail for the day's scouting pattern. They would be carefully hitting a few golems each day, far from us.

As soon as they were safely out of sight, we started moving forward. Donna and I were side by side at the front of the line, and the rest of the team was spread out. If we found a trap, we did not have sled walls to hide behind. We needed to spread out so we would not all be targeted, and we would have room to dive for cover.

The deeper snow made it easier to keep everyone on the same

path, but it was tiring to push our way through it. Donna and I had the worst of it, being in front. We took turns going first. If I were a few steps behind her, that would not restrict Vlad's range too much. Also, I walked to the back of the line every time we took a break so that Vlad could scan as far back as possible for anyone following us. If I had not leveled my perks so much, it would have been tough to keep up with the group while moving around a lot more.

Vlad's directions to avoid the sentries worked, but it was slow going. Even though Donna and I had studied the map, we still needed him to tell us where to go. Neither of us could navigate in the woods without GPS. All I knew from reviewing the map, even if I did not understand the math, was that the aliens' sentry net got tighter as we approached the center. It reminded me of a spider's web in some ways. We were also well off the beaten path, and there were a few times when we had to backtrack to find a different route between the sentry nodes. Vlad knew where we needed to go, but the maps he had seen did not account for terrain obstacles. That contributed to our traveling just five more miles, with about ten to go, by the time we lost the light and decided to make a very small, quiet camp.

Because we wanted to avoid traveling in dim or nonexistent light, we planned to spend 12 hours in camp. After subtracting time for setup, meals, and teardown, we were left with about 7 hours of sleep for everyone and 4 hours on guard, in groups of three.

We repeated the double-tent layout that had worked so well for me before, but this time we used candle heaters to warm it instead of a fire. With the upgraded inner and outer tent, which I had purchased with tokens, combined with our body heat, it was tolerable and kept light from leaking out. We had five single-use heaters in reserve, but if we did not need them, we would save them. Dinner was the same as lunch and snacks: more ration bars. I could generate more of them than the nine of us could eat, so everyone had a few on hand for emergencies, but just asked me for them as needed.

"The cold and activity must be burning the calories," I said as I passed more of the bars out. Three of them were considered enough food for an adult each day. Most of us were already on our sixth or seventh.

"Having basically unlimited food for no additional weight is a huge advantage for us," Paul said as he ate his way through another bar. "I've done cold-weather hiking and camping before, and I was always hungry because that was easier than carrying tons of food. This may not be the tastiest, but it's got the nutrients we need to keep going. I am curious where they come from, though. Saying nanotechnology is kind of like waving your hands and saying magic."

"They come from air and nearby materials that won't be missed," Vlad said when I looked at him. "The matter is captured and restructured at the molecular level to become the food you eat. It's just a variation of how buildings are made, except that the raw material is provided by the portal, which breaks down debris into the perfect building blocks to be reassembled into different forms. Here, it's Devin's perk that stores and processes various materials to create the bars."

"I'm not sure that really answers the question," I said. "It's the best answer he can give, though, so if it's not enough, then magic."

That got a laugh, but a quiet one, as we were all trying to limit noise. Shortly after that, I headed to bed as I was on the last watch shift of the night. With my perk level and resulting physical score, it made sense for me to be on the coldest shift. Donna also wanted Vlad to be active for that shift, as she felt it was the most dangerous. I did not complain about the chance to sleep for nearly eight hours and burrowed into my sleeping bag, or at least my sleeping bag for two shifts. We only brought six sleeping bags, as the plan was always to have at least three people on watch. Sharing the sleeping bags saved on room and weight we had to carry.

I was woken up for my shift and felt a moment of relief that I was not being woken up because of an attack in the middle of the night. I was already feeling grimy and wishing for a shower, but that would not be coming until after we captured the alien base or returned home.

The cold in the middle of nowhere, with the wind blowing at four in the morning, chased away the last remnants of sleep. There was a light snow again, which muted the sound. That was both good and bad, but I appreciated the quiet. Vlad confirmed that the weather remained stable, and we began the patrol path. The three of us were pacing in circles at various distances from the tent, with two of us going clockwise and one counterclockwise. Vlad and I had the outer circle as expected. In addition to the layers of sentries, we all varied our speeds to be unpredictable.

As the light grew, another group came out to relieve us so we could eat and get ready for the day. The last group handled the camp breakdown.

"I know we're all tired from yesterday," Donna said as we gathered around. "The goal is to stay undetected and make it to a spot about two miles from where Vlad thinks they are located. Once there, we'll find a protected place to camp. We want to attack them when we're fresh, not at the end of a day of pushing through the snow."

"As we get closer, my scouting will be far more limited," Vlad reminded everyone. "At five miles from the projected base location, I'll start pulling back so there's less chance I'll be detected. I'll still be able to guide us around the golems even if I'm staying close to you all. The sentry locations are getting closer together, so be even more careful today and expect backtracking. They have no issue placing themselves in rough terrain, but you don't have the same advantage."

The day was slow and frustrating. There were more spots where we had to backtrack as the day went on, and then we had to angle north around Lisbon to reach the target. We could all see there were no signs of smoke where the town was supposed to be, but with the clouds and snow, it was hard to know for sure. We did not want to risk encountering any humans who might inadvertently raise an alarm.

Our first scare came during a brief lunch break, when we slowed down but did not stop moving. While we were eating, one of the new enforcers stumbled down an incline.

"I told him not to move at all. He's close enough to a golem spot that any movement could trigger one if they are there," Vlad said to all of us after popping in next to where Cody was lying and then back. "We need to extract him in a line directly back to this spot."

As he was talking, Vlad stepped a few paces back on the path we had taken. It sloped down to Cody there as well, with a few trees in the way. We had a hurried discussion, knowing that every minute he lay still in the snow, he grew colder, and we risked discovery.

The eventual plan was to have me tied off with two of the strongest enforcers, slowly feeding me rope as I moved down so that it would be a controlled descent. The rope was tied off around me, with a tail long enough to tie off around Cody. Once that was done, we would both be pulled back and up the slope to safety.

The trip down was nerve-racking. I had to stay on a mostly straight path down while dodging trees and not losing my footing. Twice, the rope got caught on trees, and I had to carefully backtrack to get it free. After nearly 15 minutes, I reached Cody. We did not want people yelling, so Vlad had been passing messages, but when I saw him, I could tell Cody was in bad shape from the cold caused by lying still in the snow. On top of that, he was sure he had at least sprained his ankle.

I used three charges of my healing perk on him before he said he felt better, so I figured it was probably a broken bone rather than a sprain. After that, it was the slow process of tying him off and pulling him back a dozen feet before he stood up as well. Then we made our way back up the slope with the assistance of the others pulling on the rope so that we would not slip.

By the time we were safely back on the path, 45 minutes had passed during the rescue adventure. As soon as we were sure Cody was okay, Donna had us moving again. We had been behind schedule before that happened, and now we were even further behind where she wanted us to be. I was glad she did not try to speed things up, though. That would have added too much risk. It was getting dark when Vlad called a halt to talk.

"I've been barely moving away from you all since we moved inside the five-mile range, but there is a house to the north, just out of your view. It looks deserted, and we can get there while avoiding any golems. I know we're about three miles out, not the two Donna planned, but you are all tired. I don't think it's safe to keep going, and a structure might be the safest place to spend the night, even if we're further away than planned," he

said.

Donna looked annoyed that we had not made it as far as she wanted, but almost everyone else clearly wanted to sleep in a house and be done for the day, so she agreed. We carefully made our way there, then scouted the outside before heading in through the unlocked door.

Inside was well-maintained with no sign of a struggle. It looked as if people had packed up and left in a hurry. There were blankets over the windows, and even what looked like foam mattresses used as insulation on the inside of some exterior walls.

"We need to check the windows to make sure light is not leaking out," Paul said after we looked around. "Check inside to make sure windows are covered with lights on low so that Devin can walk around and check for light leakage while Vlad passes messages back for us to turn up the light with each pass.

We spent ten minutes making sure we could use light inside the house without exposing our location. It was not safe to use the fireplace, but we pitched the tents in the living room after pushing furniture aside, then used the candle heater to warm it up. The extra layer of being inside the house made it relatively balmy compared to the previous night.

It was no longer safe to conduct large patrols. So, people were positioned in other rooms with views outside, making it easier to stand watch. However, it was colder because there was no movement. I went to sleep early, but some others hunted around the house while I was sleeping. When I got up, there was a vibe going on.

"What's happening?" I asked, confused. No one was being woken up, but people seemed pissed.

"Wendy was hunting around on her shift and found a diary," Donna said. "It seems like the aliens are close, and they were collecting humans. They let people here know that when they ran out of food or fuel, they could turn themselves in to the aliens. According to the diary, no one who went to their camp ever returned. A lot of people tried to attack them or just refused to go, but this family went. The diary was from a teenager. His younger sister died due to the cold and hunger before his parents gave in."

"Hopefully, that means we can rescue some people. Either way, the aliens are dying," I said. I was not sure what else to say.

Once the three of us, who were starting our shift, were ready, Vlad let the others know. All the lights were turned out as we left the safe room, and the people who had been on shift returned. I headed to my assigned station and started watching for any movement in the darkness.

This is different, I said to Vlad. *Do you know what's going on*?

I would need to look at the whole diary, but I'm not sure why they would want to capture people. You should be ready to deal with the fact that they may have just wanted an easy way to kill them, Vlad said. *Based on the dates I saw in the diary, it seems they did not announce themselves for about a month after they arrived. That must have given them time to build a position the humans could not get past. Hopefully, your advantages will allow your team to succeed tomorrow.*

Our ability to get past the golems and our weapons gave us a good shot at making it past their guards, which the locals could not.

Once everyone was up, the strategy session lasted longer than I had expected. The last entry in the diary was just a couple of weeks prior. People were wondering if we could pretend to be surrendering and make it further in.

"That's a big guess about the alien's response to base a plan on," I said. "If this were just a way to get people to give themselves up to be killed, we'd be in trouble. Also, can we pull off the unarmed, worn-out, people surrendering look?"

"Devin's right," Donna said. "We'll never pull it off, and we're not leaving our weapons behind. Up close, they might be able to detect nano signatures. Even so, if we get caught by a golem, we should give it a chance to herd us to the alien base instead of attacking it immediately. If people were actually being taken to their base, the golems should not just attack, and I have faith we can fool one of those."

There were a few more details to hash out, but the general plan remained the same. Keep following Vlad's directions, now routed through me, as we were so close. If, or more accurately when, we triggered a golem, see if it tried to guide us in instead of fighting.

We had been warned that as the net got tighter, there would be no perfectly safe path. We would have to depend on some empty nodes to get through, and that was unlikely this close to their base.

Once the plan had been made, everyone had eaten, and we were ready, we filed out. We left a lot of our supplies in the house so we would not have to drag them into the fight. When we started moving, it was a slow process. It took nearly three hours to move another mile closer, thanks to the terrain. By noon, we were about a mile out when Vlad let us know we could no longer avoid the sentry nodes. Our best bet was to head directly for one and hope it was empty, and the ones on either side would not trigger. That was not what happened, though.

As we stepped forward, the spot we approached shivered, and a golem burst out of the snow. As soon as it appeared, the nodes on either side exploded into showers of snow, and they all moved to surround us.

"Hold your fire," Donna hissed as some hands moved toward weapons. She had people keep them holstered, which was wise, as I am sure at least one person would have fired if they hadn't.

The golems moved in, then froze in place around us. After a few tense minutes, there was a crackle coming from the golem in front of us.

"I thought you humans in this sector had all surrendered or were dead. Nevertheless, welcome to your new life in the Scaled Syndicate. If anyone failed to follow the instructions, discard any weapons now. Bringing weapons to the base will result in your death and the death of two other humans, per the warning. Step forward when you have complied."

We all looked at each other, and then I stepped forward without dropping my weapon. Everyone else did the same. The golems started moving, keeping us boxed in, and the voice was heard again.

"You will be met for processing. Do not attempt to leave your guides. They can't understand you, and I can't hear you. If you fail to comply, you will be eliminated along with two other humans as specified."

It took 20 more minutes of walking before the base we were heading to came into view when we crested a small rise. It was far larger than I had expected.

What's going on here? It looks like a whole settlement, not some outpost in the woods like the last aliens we ran into. How many of them are there here? I asked Vlad. He could see through me, but had no other external views.

You might want to make your move before you get too close, while there is some cover. They have not removed the trees near the buildings, but there are lots of golems out here. I have not seen any aliens, though. Have you? he responded.

I saw what he meant, and we were about out of time. We had remained mostly silent as we did not trust that we were not being monitored, but now I needed to talk.

"It's almost your birthday, right, Donna?" I asked. "I think we should have a party with games like 25 steps and hide and seek in the woods. You'd like it. It's one of those games that everyone starts one minute after it's announced. I love group party games. Doesn't everyone here love a good coordinated party game?"

Everyone around me was confused for a second or two, but it quickly cleared up, and everyone looked to Donna as their hands crept to their weapons.

"That's a great idea," Donna said. "It will be fun to play some games together."

People's heads were nodding, or fingers were tapping as we all counted down to the one-minute mark together. As soon as Donna yelled, it was time. Nano inhibitors emerged from holsters, and all three golems were killed instantly. Nothing happened for a few moments, and then all the patrolling golems in the open area between us and the base pivoted and headed toward us.

A group of over 20 golems charging us looked scary, but with nine of us and advanced weapons, they were all killed before they could get close. Vlad stayed hidden, and we were not using perks yet. The three people with the real nano pistols, though, had made some noise as they fired.

As soon as all the golems were dead, we waited. We had not yet seen aliens or humans, but the settlement buildings were dead ahead.

"Humans, you have been warned of the consequences of challenging us. The humans here will be killed to ensure your compliance. They came here of their own free will, so there is no need to attack. Surrender, and we will allow you to live and serve us as well." The message came from some hidden loudspeakers, but we could see no one.

"Still no sign of any aliens or more golems. Let's move up and use that building as cover," Donna said. "I don't think hiding in the trees is going to do us any good."

Vlad agreed and said the outlying golems were likely being called in. We made our way to within 500 feet of the nearest building, then sprinted across the open space to use it as cover.

"Vlad, we need your scouting," I said. "I think keeping you and our nanotechnology a secret is pointless as soon as they look at how we killed their golems."

Vlad shimmered into being and phased into the building next to us, bypassing the door, before coming right back out. "The captured humans are in there. They are in pods that trap a sentient being inside to supply resources full-time. That's how they have been able to field so many golems and build so much. It makes sense now that I... watch out, they're coming," he yelled before he started to flicker and phase out.

"They're jamming Vlad somehow," I said loudly enough for everyone to hear. "Based on where he was looking, they're coming this way."

As I pointed around the western side of the building, we were using as cover, Wendy called out that golems were swarming in from behind us.

Donna divided us up in seconds, with three people left to defend our rear and the rest of us preparing to come around the corner of the house, where we thought Vlad was warning that the aliens were approaching.

21

"There are at least four aliens and some golems coming from this side," Donna yelled from the side Vlad had been facing as some shots whipped past her. "We've just got a few seconds. Devin, take Tom and Roger through the building. See if you can get behind them as they come for us. Paul, watch the other side. Everyone not with me, get those golems behind us cleared out so we don't have to worry about them."

The door in front of me was locked, but I shoved my way through it, breaking the lock. My raised physical score was good for more than dealing with the cold. Once inside, I shuddered at the pods containing people. They looked sickly and pale, but I had no time to worry about them. The sounds of combat behind us pushed me through the maze of pods. They were piled in the building, covering the space to the door on the other side of the room. There were no windows, so I could not see out, but I could hear the gunfire.

"I miss having Vlad here to tell me when to move," I muttered to the others. I made sure the door was unlocked, but did not open it. We needed to make sure we could come up behind the aliens and surprise them.

"There are too many of them, all right here on both sides," I heard Donna yell.

That was totally not like her, but it was a good signal that we needed to move.

"Roger, you're with me. Tom, take the other side. Use incapacitate, but be ready for it to be shrugged off. Call if you need help." With that, I used raised fingers to count from three to zero before bursting out of the door and heading to the right.

There were no enemies in sight, so they had to all be on the sides of the building, just like we planned. I peeked around the corner and saw four aliens and three golems still upright. There was one alien and two golems already down.

I said I had the aliens, as I tagged them all with incapacitate, only for it to be shrugged off as expected. I used my other two charges only to have them countered, just as Rogers' attempts were. While that was going on, I was firing my nano inhibitor at the golems, while Roger used an old firearm to shoot at the aliens.

I heard a cry of pain from our group, but ignored it as I focused on killing the golems. We had the enemy forces trapped between our two groups. We could fire on them with no worries about friendly fire as long as we did not shoot straight down the wall of the building.

As soon as the last of the golems died, I swapped my nano inhibitors for a gun, but as I was doing that, I was shot by one of the aliens. I had to pull back and use three healing charges on my arm before I could get back into the fight. Having a bullet wound in my right forearm was not something I could shrug off. It had to be healed if I was going to be firing a gun with any accuracy.

I was firing around the side of the building when Tom screamed from behind us. "Keep the pressure up from back here," I told Roger as I rushed to where Tom had fallen and was holding his leg. I used heal on him twice before the alien he had been firing at came around the corner. He was not expecting me to be there with a pistol. It took five shots, two of which missed their targets in the heat of the moment, but then the alien fell, half on Tom.

"Yes, but there's another one, and Paul needs help," Tom said when I asked if he was okay.

I maneuvered around him and started taking shots at the other alien on this side. As soon as my gun clicked empty, I switched back to my nano inhibitor. Paul was using a gun, but there were two more golems on this side. If I could take them out, it would let him focus on the alien.

I was on my second energy clip when the last of the golems went down. I pulled back to check on Tom again and to reload my pistol. By the time I was ready to peek around the side again, the alien there was dead.

"I'm helping with the incoming golems," Paul yelled. "Help the other side. They're still fighting."

In the short time the fight had been happening, I had heard at least two screams from behind the house. They were far more out in the open, even if they were only facing golems from behind, as far as I knew. I resisted the urge to run through the house to see if anyone needed my healing perk.

"They have some sort of shield," Roger said as I moved back over to where he was. "Try to take them out with the nano inhibitor. That seems to block the shield for a brief second, and then a real gun can get through. We've killed two of them that way. The last two are proving to be tougher."

I swapped weapons again and peeked around the corner to start firing. It felt like the fight went on forever, but it was probably just another minute before both aliens collapsed. Donna yelled it was clear, but they needed my help. I started down the side of the building and was almost to the back, where the fight against the golems was still going on, with Roger right behind me. Out of nowhere, shots from another building rang out.

I saw Donna go down with a bullet through her leg and dove for her, starting to spam my heal perk on her. I had burnt five charges when I heard Roger yell in pain behind me and turned to start healing him. As I was turning to heal him, I felt a bullet tear through my chest and then blinding pain in my head. I had just enough time to think, "Not again" to myself, and then the prompt I had seen before flashed up, giving me the chance to advance to the next mission or return to Augusta. I selected Augusta as fast as I could. I was already thinking about the next steps.

This time, as soon as I blinked back into existence, I grabbed the blanket that was stashed next to the portal. After showing up naked the first time I used my perk, I stashed a blanket and spare clothes near my spawn point. There had been a game of people hiding it, but they had left it there for me when I did anything dangerous.

"Get both snowmobiles ready for a trip and get some people who can fight. We need to head out to rescue them," I yelled into a room that had burst into activity and questions when I appeared. If I had died and returned, they knew something had gone wrong.

With the blanket draped over me, I hurried over to the person with the communication device. "Has there been any word from them?" I asked.

When he shook his head, I took a minute to grab the clothes I had stashed here and get dressed. I had seen people run out, and the entire council would be on its way here soon. It was as I was getting dressed that I realized I still had not seen Vlad.

"Vlad, where are you?" I asked the empty air. "Damn it, you get messed up like this too easily."

Here, you need a medical pod. I have information. Do pod before decisions, he sent me. It did not sound like him. I could feel that something was wrong in the way the message felt.

"Hey, someone find Joey and let him know I'm going to need access to a pod to fix Vlad right away," I said, watching someone else run off.

It had only been minutes since I appeared, and already people were rushing in. I gestured for the man watching the communication device to bring it over and sit next to me as I waited for people to show up.

Not only was the council showing up, but the enforcers' friends and family were, too. I saw Donna's husband come in with their son. Because people were worried, I started by describing the situation when I left the fight.

"We had made it to their base. They have other humans trapped there, but the important part is that we were holding our own. We were fighting off aliens and golems from two directions, and then there was a wave of golems coming from behind," I said. "I think we had about won. I checked, and I have five new nano matrices, so all five aliens are dead. There are 32 spheres, so most of the golems that were close must be dead. Roger and I were regrouping with Donna's team when someone hidden in another building shot at us. Donna was hit in the leg, and I was healing her when I heard Roger yell. I was turning to help him too when I got shot in the chest, and I think in the head," I said. There were kids around, so I tried not to be overly graphic.

I then briefly covered the pods we had found, the diary at the cabin, and the fight as I had seen it. I said a few times that when I left, everyone was still alive as far as I knew, but that I needed to get back there.

"I'm getting a team together. We can be ready to go in 30 minutes," O'Donnell said. "I'm coming too, and will get the sleds ready."

"I need to get into a medical pod before we go. They messed up Vlad, and I need to fix that so he can help chart our course and deal with what's going on. He sent me a message saying he had information, but then he cut out again. I'll do that while you get people ready. It looked like they were recalling the golems to the base, so we will have to be ready to fight. Even with Vlad's help in plotting our course, they may be in new locations."

I was getting up to take care of the medical issue so we could get moving as soon as that was done. Then I heard Donna's voice come through the communication device.

"Hey, is Devin back there already?" She asked before continuing when she got a yes. "Devin, I just want to say it was really weird having to roll over your almost headless body to get this walkie-talkie thing to talk to you back in Augusta."

"How is everyone?" I asked, grabbing the device.

"We lost Roger. Wendy and Tom are in terrible shape. We can't find any medical pods here. We really need you to get back here to help. There are still golems out here, but the shooter was the last alien as far as we can tell. The golems are fairly aimless unless they get too close to one of us. We're picking them off as we can and are holed up in the house the aliens were using as a base," Donna stopped talking for a minute to listen to something in the background. "Paul says, based on beds and stuff, we got them all, but we're carefully checking the other buildings. It's mostly those pods with people trapped in them, but we're not touching them until you and Vlad are back. We're leaving the portal here alone, too."

"Speaking of Vlad, I need to get into a medical pod to fix whatever they did to me that broke him. I'm not sure how long it will take, but as soon as that's done, we'll head out with some people who can handle aimless golems. Keep people safe and alive until we get there. I'll let you brief the others while I hop in the pod."

Joey led me out to the nearest free pod. He was going to check the readout and tell me what the expected time was before triggering the pod. I was not sure why rebuilding my body had not fixed the issue, so I asked Vlad, but I got no answer.

"I can't see what the issue is, but it says 47 minutes to completion when I activate it," Joey said when he opened the lid.

I told him to do it, and I went unconscious as normal when the pod went to work. When I opened my eyes, the area was crowded, and O'Donnell started talking, but was quickly cut off by Vlad reappearing.

"The issue was not fixed when you were rebuilt by your perk because the problem was me. The rebuilding only moves me, and it moved the damaged me," Vlad said, answering my earlier question. "If you want to save all the people in pods out there, bring four medical personnel with you, and bring the nano car, not just the sleds."

"They've had another injury and need you out there right away," O'Donnell said as soon as Vlad stopped talking. "I'll have someone get the nano car, but it might take another 15 minutes. We can send it after you, but they need you out there."

"It's not safe for it to travel alone. We'll take one of the snowmobiles now, and the other one can follow with the car," I said. "They'll catch up quickly if we clear golems on the path."

While I was talking, I was getting dressed for the cold again and taking the gun O'Donnell was handing me. I also spent tokens on a third communication device. I told Erin to keep it and to update us on when the others left to follow us.

After grabbing a few more supplies, I let Donna know the plan. I passed the communication device off to O'Donnell's three people, who would be in the sled. Vlad and I would need to follow the same route as before and watch for stray golems. The somewhat good news was that it had been more than 30 days since my last death, so I still had three second chances stored up after this death. We made sure we left a trail the others could follow and tried to balance speed and safety. The other vehicles left about 35 minutes after us, but caught up to us after 2 hours.

Even balancing caution with speed, we were going five miles an hour, which meant five hours to reach the team. I was tempted to speed up, but then we started running into a few random golems in the second hour, and I fought the urge to risk going faster. Based on the messages the people in the back were passing on to me, everyone was alive and stable under the first-aid perk. I decided it was better to get there than to rush and have something happen.

Plus, while I was paying attention to the route, Vlad was briefing me on what he knew and what he guessed about what was going on, and we were making plans on how to handle things. We followed the same path back, passing by the house where we had left our supplies. I pointed it out, but we kept moving and stuck together. Right before the base, there were still golems milling about, and we slowed down to coordinate with the enforcers there. They used the nano inhibitors to clear a lane, and we headed into the compound and were led to where the wounded were waiting.

O'Donnell's team spread out, supporting the enforcers and relieving people who needed a break after being on alert for most of the day. Joey's team followed me in to check on the wounded, and I used my remaining three healing charges as directed before standing up.

"I need three guards to come with me to check out their portal. Vlad's got some ideas about what's going on, but I need to confirm things before we do anything or make any plans," I said.

Donna wanted to come with me, but she was administering first aid to Wendy, and the medical team wanted her to continue. I had Andy and two of O'Donnell's team follow Vlad and me. He knew the location of the portal.

We were there for nearly half an hour examining the base and options. Then we went to one of the buildings full of humans in pods before returning to the main room for a debrief.

"Sorry for the delay," I said once we had gathered everyone we could spare from guard duty. "This situation is all new for Vlad and me, and we needed to check some things out. When we took over the last portal, we just sold off all the structures so I could claim it. That's really not possible here without killing the people in the aliens' pods, which we are not going to do. Instead, I can spend tokens to claim all these structures. They are within my extended range from Augusta's portal. While I could build here, it also means I can effectively keep all the structures here at a discount. Once all the buildings are linked to the Augusta portal, I can claim this portal to move it to Portland."

"There are ten windmills, four water towers, three common

rooms being used for pods, two houses, and the portal bay," Vlad said. "They are all a little different from the buildings in Augusta and have different names, but it will be standardized to our builds when Devin claims them."

"What about all the people in the pods?" one of the medical team asked.

"The aliens were using them to create resources like food and spheres. That's why there's no food production here; the process slowly kills them. We've turned that process off, so they are not getting worse, but they're still all trapped in the pods for now. They're stable, but we can't take them out without having a plan," I said. "

"That's going to be a slow process. Devin needs to claim the base and make medical clinics. Each person will need to come out of the pod and spend anywhere from a few days to a week in a medical pod to be back to normal," Vlad said. "This is an outlawed life force extraction process, and it was how they managed to create so many golems. There were likely humans who were used up and discarded."

"How many people?" Donna asked. She had seen one of the rooms and knew there were lots of people there.

"There are 120 pods across three buildings, and 107 are occupied," I said. "If I convert all the buildings here, that's room in the two houses for a team to guard the place and start cycling people through the medical clinics I'll build. Then, as the team cures people, they can be sent to Augusta. There's a good amount of food here, and although the pods are not creating the resources the aliens were using, there is a stock of it that can be used to create more rations before I claim the portal. There will be plenty of food."

I opened the floor to questions, then had to shut it down again. "Are there any questions that would impact me converting this outpost, building medical clinics and pods to heal the injured people, and then starting to heal the people in the pods?" I clarified. "The other stuff can wait."

When no one spoke up, I went outside and started spending tokens. It was not too bad. Each building required 10 settlement tokens to convert, totaling 210 across all buildings. There were also two more snowmobiles next to the new portal, but they required 113 tokens for the one-person version and 127 tokens for the two-person version to convert. They could wait.

Next up, I built three clinics, each with two medical pods, and let people know to rotate all our people through them to fix everything that had built up from the trip and the fights. In the morning, Vlad would show them the process to start freeing people from the pods they were trapped in.

Once I was done, I pulled up the information for the base.

Alien Outpost		**Population**	0
Food Supply	314 days	**Heat Supply**	Unlimited
Housing	0 people	**Survivable Housing**	20 people
Food Production	0%	**Secure Food Production**	0%
Power Production	100- 2,300 units	**Power Draw**	370- 995 units
Power Storage	1,100/ 1,100 units	**Indoor Pod Slots**	2/ 23
Water Production	1,100 units	**Water Draw**	956 units
Production Structures	Large Windmill x 10	Large Water Tower x 4	
Enhanced Structures	Medical Clinic x 3	Medical Pods x 6	House x 2
Medium Common Room x 3	Large Crafting Bay x 1		

Because the portal was no longer part of this base, it was not listed. Once I had it back in Augusta, I needed to get people to feed it materials to build up its reserve of material units for when I moved it to Portland. I also saw that there were only two real pods, and I needed to get people into them as soon as possible to build up some work units associated with the portal for the move. I asked for volunteers to use them until I collapsed the portal in the morning. I wanted to check my quest completions and then go to bed. The nano matrices and spheres could wait until I had a good night's sleep.

I had been assigned a hastily cleaned room in one of the houses. My roommate had not arrived yet, so after cleaning up,

I got into bed and started reviewing the messages I had received. The first was a repeat of the one I had received when I last helped clear out an alien foothold.

Hidden Mission Completed (Repeatable)

Reclaim stolen resources and reuse them for approved purposes. You receive four settlement tokens and a personal token.

The first time I received that award, it was a big deal. The personal token was still nice, but the four settlement tokens were a drop in the bucket. I also knew from experience that did not mean all the aliens in the area were gone. I needed to remind people they had to stay on alert in case one had been away from the base.

The next notice that popped up was a new mission, but it covered what I was doing anyway.

Drone Rescue Mission

A large number of humans were enslaved and turned into resource generators at the expense of their health. Free them and restore their health. Saved: 0 Died: 0 Remaining: 107

"I'm glad the nano control is prioritizing recovering them, but I don't think the mission will be complete before I leave," I said as I did the math.

"Missions initiated here will continue after your departure. You will not get the rewards, but whoever is in charge will," Vlad said. "You will also be able to recycle those pods for resources. There is no humane use for them, so you will be expected to recycle them as soon as they are emptied."

"Hey, why did you have us bring out the nano vehicle? That's the one thing I haven't figured out yet," I asked.

There was a pause before he answered. "I made a mistake. I thought the process of extracting people from the pods would be simpler, and you would need to take them back to Augusta in a protected environment for healing. You really could have left it at home, but you will need it later to transport them to Augusta. Even after they are cured, they will need some time to get back to normal."

I could tell Vlad was embarrassed to have been wrong, so I let it go with a nod instead of commenting on it. In the grand scheme of things, it was not worth giving him a hard time over.

I checked a few more things, then forced myself to get some rest. I had to get everything set up the next day because I was supposed to head to Bangor the day after that. There were also plenty of structures in Augusta that needed to be integrated. I had not even thought about that when I respawned there.

The next morning, I was up early to set everything up. The first good news was that when I made it to the living room, which had been repurposed as headquarters, I learned that all the enforcers had cycled through the medical pods and were cleared, except for Wendy, who had a few hours left.

The first order of business was to discuss how the base would be used and who would be living there.

"My suggestion is to have three enforcers and six of O'Donnell's team here full-time to provide security," I said. "That should continue at least until all the people in the pods are freed and cured. There will also need to be four medical staff here, plus a couple of people to monitor the communication device and run errands. At least there are no normal pods here after the portal is removed. They were depending on these drone pods. Say 15 people full-time.

"For supplies, I'll convert one of the snowmobiles before we leave, which will be assigned here with a sled we'll leave behind. You should get one of the communication devices, two nano inhibitors, and one nano pistol."

"That should cover everything we need to support everyone other than food. There is more power production here than we could use, and enough water even though the usage seems really high," Donna said.

"The resources extracted from humans were being processed into raw materials that could be converted into rations. It's connected to the portal, so before Devin powers it down for transport, he can use some of the resources to generate food for 2,000 people. That will cover three or four months before you need to think about building a greenhouse here or importing more food. The rest of the resources can be used to jumpstart food in Portland later," Vlad said. "The excess power was to process those resources, and the pods people are trapped in each take four units of water per day to operate. The water usage will drop as people come out of those."

"Well, the plan sounds good. We'll decide who is staying and who is going back with you today," Donna said. "Since this group will be able to talk to Augusta, it will be easy enough to swap people out as we send vehicles back and forth to pick up the people we rescue from the pods. I do want to keep another team of three here to explore the area, killing golems and letting any survivors know the aliens are gone," Donna said.

"We should also let any survivors know about the people in the pods. They can be seen through the covers, and people will want to know their loved ones are safe and will be recovered," one of the medical team said. "Also, can we get started on moving the first five of them to pods now?"

Since Vlad was needed to explain the process, I had to go, and then everyone wanted to see how it was done, so it was a group field trip. We went to the building that I had damaged. People had patched it, and the maintenance pods back home were working on it now that it had been integrated into the Augusta settlement. Vlad had explained that we should clear the buildings one at a time so they could be reused once the pods were emptied and recycled. I was not sure it mattered, but it was as good as any other way to pick who to rescue first.

There was a process to trigger the opening sequence on the pods. Then, 15 minutes later, the cover would slide open, allowing the person to be extricated.

"They will be unconscious for roughly ten minutes after extraction," Vlad said as we loaded the first person onto a stretcher that had been made for this purpose. "The whole process will be easier on the victims mentally if they are transferred to a medical pod before they wake up. Don't take them out of the medical pod until every issue is addressed, no matter how long it takes."

While the first victim was being moved to the medical pods, I recycled the 14 empty pods. Each one earned me three settlement tokens and 50 material units. From there, I generated all the food I had promised, and we filled storage everywhere with it. That just left converting the one-seat snowmobile into something they could use and collapsing the portal.

The portal was once again not too impressive, but it was slightly better than the one I captured last time. It allowed for remote utilization just like the one in Augusta, and I planned to use that for the few days it was in Augusta.

Settlement Processing Portal

This portal serves as the basis for the architect's class. Feed materials into this portal to add to the settlement materials inventory to build other structures. All materials for blueprint construction will be pulled from the settlement inventory. Settlement Processing Portal efficiency is set to 75%. Daily capacity is limited to 150 processing units. Portal has four work pods. Up to 50% of the processing limit can be utilized remotely.

There was a fair number of resources stored up, with 3,142 material units and 470 work units waiting to be used. If I collect additional work units before I head to Portland, I would have the resources needed to get the new settlement off to a good start. I watched the portal fold into a cube and loaded it for the trip back to Augusta.

It was approaching noon when we were ready to go. We were leaving the nine guards this time, but we still had enough people to drive the three vehicles back safely. They would bring more people back on the next trip. I said goodbye to everyone and promised to be back soon on my way to Portland after the Bangor trip. Getting the base set up felt rushed, but I needed to head home. This time, we stopped at the abandoned house to pick up the supplies we had left there before continuing on.

22

Once we left the vicinity of the base, we did not see any other golems for the entire trip home. This route was not guaranteed to be totally safe until the area had been thoroughly cleared, but it was already safer. I hoped that after a few trips we could use it with minimal risk. Vlad warned that there were likely more traps even if we had found all the golems. It would require a long-term project to check all possible nodes in all directions around the base.

"They are like landmines," I said as Vlad reminded us of the traps. "Can you map out all the places they might be located so people can hunt for them?"

"I can, but it won't be super precise. Teams will need to proceed carefully if they can't find anything about their locations back at the base."

"We'll pass all that off as a project for Augusta to take on after we leave," I said. "Hopefully, we'll find some information on the traps."

I knew people were carefully searching the base for any maps or notes the aliens had left behind. They would not be able to read any notes, but they could sort any notes they found and save them for Vlad to review. I was also looking at the spheres and matrices on my sheet as we talked. There were 93 spheres and six nano matrices listed after the fight. I wanted to save all the spheres for the next mission. I knew some people would push back on that, but this mission had shown I needed to recruit enforcers quickly when I got somewhere new.

I also decided to use all the nano matrices for myself. Between the six of them, I got 38 personal tokens. With the one from the quest, I now had 39 of them, which was more than I had ever seen before. I started by spending 12 of them to increase boosted stamina to 20 and improve the portals' processing power. Next up was to use six points to increase the extended range and incapacitate perks to level ten. I wanted to see what new perks might be unlocked, and both were worth leveling to at least ten.

The range perk reaching the tenth level did not open anything new, and the incapacitate perk just opened detect criminal. I was not interested in that, so I increased the system integration perk, raising the range I could interact with nano buildings and devices to 250 feet from the 25-foot range it currently had. That opened nano inhibition as a perk. It was similar to the nano inhibitor weapons, but as a built-in power.

Nano Inhibition: Expel a targeted nano inhibition beam. Offense score unlocked. Usable once per day. Level 1

My offensive score started at rank four, which seemed low based on everything I had been through, but now I could start increasing it with this skill. With just 11 personal tokens left, I spent eight of them to increase boosted materials to level 22 and add ten more material units daily. That left me with three tokens to save for later.

Because I was staying focused on the terrain and looking for traps, I could only partially focus on my perks. That was why working my way through everything took most of the trip back. At least I was riding in the second seat of the snowmobile and not driving, or I would have gotten nothing done on the trip to Augusta. It was just before dinner when we were back at the processing portal. I decided to get everything done before I took a break to eat.

First up was getting the second portal placed and getting the pods occupied. I had people clear space for it in the portal bay, cutting into the free space there, and then spent 30 tokens to activate it with four pods, all set to work units. I had a quick conversation with Jason about keeping that portal processing capacity utilized each day as well. That was followed by a conversation with Erin about keeping the work pods full while the portal was in Augusta.

"We can meet later over dinner," I said when she tried to ask me questions. "There are buildings that have been waiting to be integrated, and I'm going to do that with Bryan now so they can start being used before it gets too late today."

We started with the eight greenhouses and five houses, saving the first custom dorm for last because that was the one we had questions about. As I integrated things, I saw our power and water reserves drop, as well as my token stock. I needed to build the minimum here while making sure I had enough for Bangor. I was ignoring the research upgrades for now. I could not spend the tokens to upgrade buildings on top of everything else.

"Water and power are in the negative now," I told Bryan. "Let's build some more water towers and windmills, then get that dorm integrated."

We grabbed a snowmobile to save time getting to the locations for six more windmills and two more water towers. After that, we circled back to the completed dorm, and I triggered the integration before sharing the details with Bryan.

Custom Dorm

- Integration cost 40 tokens
- Supports 30 people and 4 pod slots
- Power required 30-300 power units based on weather
- Water required 25 water units
- Safe to -40 degrees base, -115 degrees at full power
- Top-floor greenhouse
- 50 power units
- 50 water units
- Produces food for eight people

"It's better than I thought it would be. The capacity is an exact match for the original. It uses about 50 percent more power and water, and it can't handle quite as much cold. Still, all that for 40 settlement tokens instead of 150 work and material units is a useful option to have," I said. "I don't want to add learning something new to Bangor's plate this trip, but think about who could go train them on my trip there after this one."

Bryan promised to get some people ready to train on building the dorms for next time. He was disappointed when I told him I would be integrating none of the houses the next day, even if they were ready before I left. It was unclear whether the Bangor trip would be two or three days to integrate everything there. I wanted to save tokens for the trip to limit it to two days if possible.

With the integrations done, I had no more excuses to avoid the meeting that was waiting for me. No one was particularly getting on my nerves, but I was just ready for a break before my trip the next day. Unfortunately, I needed to go over an entire list of things that had happened and set plans for the future.

"Okay, time for a quick debrief and planning session before bed," I announced to the group. "I've been watching the mission for Readfield, and it looks like more than half the people have already been rescued. That seems fantastic, given how we were monopolizing some of the vehicles to fight the aliens. I saw there was one death, though?"

"We've been prioritizing the evacuation. I want to get the rewards so we can get more enforcers," O'Donnell said. "The death was an accident. Some kids were horsing around in one of the sleds on the trip back and fell out and down an incline. By the time people got to him, there was no way to save him. New rules have been put in place to stop that from happening again, and the kids seem to realize the risk now."

"We should be done creating enforcers," I said. I knew I might lose the goodwill I had built up with him, but I needed to be clear. "If the aliens really are gone, I need to prioritize saving spheres for the next mission. I didn't bring enough when I came here, and I don't want to repeat that mistake next time. Next up is my trip tomorrow and getting the base set up with the right personnel."

There had been ongoing communication with the base, so a plan was already in place. When five people had completed their recovery, the nano car would go out to pick them up and drop off supplies. They had not found any more aliens, but had continued clearing out golems. They planned to start looking for survivors the next day.

I told everyone I planned to take the third communication device to leave in Bangor so that all the major settlements would be connected.

"I'm hoping to do an up and back, but I have blown through the settlement tokens," I said. "I want to make it a normal two-day trip so we can head to Portland as soon as possible, but no promises yet. At least it gives you plenty of time to plan who should go with me on that trip. This could be the most massive city I've seen since this all happened, so I'm not sure what to expect."

“We’ve been working on that. It could be a hostile environment, so we’ll have to plan carefully,” O’Donnell said. “That’s why it might be a good idea to create more enforcers.”

“I don’t plan to create more preemptively,” I said, shooting that down before pivoting. “Finally, here are the topline numbers for Augusta before I head out again. Of the 16,611 people here now, the food production in nanostructures can feed 3,801, and that number is growing quickly. We will need to keep rationing food to stretch current supplies until production catches up, but we’re in a good place. As for housing, there is official space for 2,310 people. Right now, with everyone doubled up and some staying in places like the doctor's office, that’s 4,700 people in nanostructures not using up the remaining legacy heat supplies.”

“And the new custom dorm will speed things up even more,” Bryan said before discussing the details of the new building his team had designed. “I plan to convert most of the house teams to dorm teams as we get more people. They are a more efficient use of supplies, and they provide more food, so we’ll make a burst of those before going back to houses.”

“Yes,” I said in answer to another question. “I’m hoping to get Bangor to a moderately sustainable position in the next two trips so they won’t be a drain on the resources I could be using here, but we’ll have to see where Portland is by then. Now, if no one has anything else I need to address right now, I’m going to check in with the base, make sure Wendy has recovered, and then turn in so I can be ready to head out in the morning.

I did not get away as quickly as I had hoped, as there were still many questions about the aliens and the fight. They wanted my take on what had happened and to hear more about Roger’s death. They were planning a memorial for him timed to coincide with my time not on trips. After another 30 minutes of conversation, I ended the meeting for real.

Wendy had gotten out of the pod shortly after I left and was now the one in charge of the base, as Donna had returned to Augusta with me.

“I’m fine, and everything is mostly okay here,” Wendy said. “We’ve had the first two people come out of the medical pods. Even with the pods’ help, they are still not dealing with things well. We need to think about bringing a mental health professional down here, in addition to lining up support in Augusta for them. We're also going to have an issue because there are whole families and groups of friends here. People will not want to leave until their family is out of the pods and healed. I don't think we should force them to leave."

"I had not thought of that," I said. "I agree we don't want to force them, so double up on space as needed. I'll build a dorm or something if I have to, but I'd prefer not to spend the resources on that. It would be a waste if people are not staying at the base long term."

After finishing up that conversation and remembering to do the remote portal processing after Jason asked if he needed to dump stuff into the portals, I headed back to my room to get some much-needed rest.

When morning rolled around, I used remote processing on both portals and ensured all resources were collected. I would need to shift some more pods to maintenance soon. The base buildings I had added were not in great shape, but that was for after the Bangor trip.

I made sure the sled was packed with food and also picked up the message bundle. I expected the number of messages to drop, as the council was already discussing how to allocate time for community use of the communication device so people could stay in touch. I also enjoyed having my system integration perk at level ten. Collecting and controlling portals from 250 feet away made life far easier.

"I'll see you all in two or three days," I said as I headed out. The snow was still falling more often, and with no rescue missions to the north anymore, the path was filled in from the start of my trip. Even with Vlad's help, I was later than the last time, but my greeter was there again, and we talked on the way into town. He warned me that tempers were once again flaring, but people would do their best to hide it while I was visiting.

I made a note of it and hoped there would be enough housing built to relieve the pressure. With that in mind, I kept things brief when I got to Andy. I explained how to use the communication device and that I would be leaving it for them.

"It will let you talk to the council in Augusta whenever you need to and ask for help if something happens," I said. "I had to buy them for the assault on the aliens, but now that we've handled the ones around here, they are available for all of you. I'll take Dominic and start integrating stuff and building infrastructure as needed."

The communication device distracted everyone, and I caught Dominic looking at it a few times as we walked out to start integrating buildings.

"Everyone has been motivated to get stuff built. They all know we're running out of everything," Dominic said as we walked. "The good news is that there are 17 more houses and seven more greenhouses if you can handle all that."

"I can get most of it today, and the rest tomorrow," I said. "I've also got a lot of material units to build stuff. Let's start with the houses and four of the greenhouses."

We rode around and integrated the first house. As I saw the mad dash for the people assigned to get inside, I quickly turned over my snowmobile to help transport people and their stuff. Dominic walked me around the other building sites to integrate the finished structures. It took longer walking, but we had time, and I would have to do much less briefing now that I had turned over the communication device. I was sure the council in Augusta was keeping them busy.

"Great work on all the construction," I said as I burned through 825 tokens to integrate the buildings I could. "Now we need four more water towers and six more windmills. I've also been upgrading the other custom houses as we walked around."

Six more levels had been researched on them, with just the expensive level left to hit level 20. That was 252 more tokens I had to spend, but it cut around 100 off the base power usage for the town, and the next level would improve how much cold the buildings could handle. We wandered around some more to place the windmills and water towers where they would be most useful.

I was down to 24 tokens from the 1,111 I had started the day with, but I had plenty of material units, so it was time to build two more structures. Since fuel was the immediate problem. We went back to an open area, and I built two apartment blocks.

"If you all pack into those four deep, that's another 880 people in nano housing and not using legacy heating," I told Dominic as people started scrambling to move into the two new structures.

With my supply of tokens down to just two, I headed back to the meeting room to see how much they had learned over the communication device.

It seemed they had covered a lot. Andy and his team handed off the communication device to people who had been waiting for a chance to talk to family and friends in Augusta. During that time, they asked me questions about the aliens and the pods we had found.

"Are the aliens gone now?" Andy asked after I discussed the pods we were freeing people from in more detail. It seemed that seeing some people had it worse than them was good for morale overall.

"We think all the aliens in the area are gone," Vlad said. "There are plenty more around the world to face, but unless there were one or two out on a mission or in hiding, we got rid of all the ones in this area. Any of them left are really limited in what they can do with all their supplies now co-opted by Devin."

"I'm really hoping they are all gone so I can be totally focused on getting people here set up before I move on," I said. "I plan to come back here at least one more time, but I'm not sure after that."

That started a round of panic among people, which I had to calm down quickly. "If it's not me, there will be someone who can integrate things. The progress will continue."

"I know it's not a surprise, but things are getting really bad here," Andy said. "Even with all the construction, I'm not sure what's going to happen next week. People are really on edge and not sure how to make this all work."

"It's rough, I know, but I saved almost all the resources from Augusta for you this week. I built two more apartment blocks tonight and should be able to build two more tomorrow. If you pack people in, that's almost 8,000 people in nano housing, leaving just 2,600 or so to use the remaining fuel and wood to augment their heat. There's a real chance that by the time I return, everyone could be in nano housing. Then the construction can focus on food and relieving the overcrowding. I know people are scared, but look at what has been done in 38 days. You all will make it."

"We'll keep up the speed on the houses for one more week," Dominic said. "Devin was telling me about new dorms they are perfecting in Augusta that we can start building after next week. It will be a better use of the remaining resources and will also contribute to food production. We may focus on that and greenhouses soon. Once everyone is housed, morale will improve."

"Research will improve things, too. All the research Klawock has completed has unlocked a new research for blueprints that I am guessing they will start working on next," I said as I read it off to everyone.

Improved Building efficiency. The selected blueprint will require 1% less electricity and water due to improved design. Cost 50 research tokens for Level 1

"That's a huge reduction that will allow you to build even more structures without needing as many windmills and water towers," Vlad said. "If they research the custom houses next with that track, getting to level ten would be a significant reduction in custom house power use from that, and improved insulation. The point is that you've about rounded the bend. People need to hold on for a few more weeks."

"Yeah, your days of heat remaining only dropped by one day in the week I was gone, food dropped five, but we can start shipping more in if needed, and when I generate food today and tomorrow, that will be a small bump as well, plus three more greenhouses are coming online," I added.

It felt like Vlad and I were doing some cheerleading, but it seemed to be working. The overall mood in the room, already boosted by the return of some communication, had gone up even more. It felt cheesy, but it was all true. I was also watching the ratios for the Bangor quest. Given the current population, I needed food and beds for 2,093 people. That meant that after tomorrow, I would only need 159 more units of food production to hit the first threshold. That was all but guaranteed in the next week. I would still need 301 beds, but that was all but assured as well. I felt like I was jinxing myself, but one more week should be enough to finish this mission and see if the reward was as good as Vlad thought it would be.

I kept answering questions and keeping one ear on the people using the communication device. When there was a break in those conversations, I broke in to check in with Augusta and the base, which was at the edge of the range we could contact directly. Bangor would not be talking to Portland with these devices.

I had a later night than usual, talking to people and trying to boost morale even more. I'm pretty sure Andy realized what I was doing from the grateful looks he sent my way. When I started yawning, I headed off to bed.

Since everyone had heard my plan the night before, people were ready to move into the new buildings the following morning, which I had created before integrating the remaining greenhouses. While people were using my snowmobile to move stuff around, I used the last of the material units to build one more water tower and three more windmills.

"There's just 90 spare water units per day now, so be careful with those. I think you have enough people in nanostructures that you'll be fine. The power is a bit lower than before, but I'd rather have you cram 440 more people into an apartment than keep the power at the same level. The net power usage is lower building things out that way," I said.

Once I had delayed as long as I could to let them continue using the snowmobile, I checked in with Augusta and then headed back home. My usual stop-off in Pittsfield took longer than expected, as the cold and neglect were taking their toll on the apartment where their effects were stored. I cleaned up what I could and picked up another load. I needed to tell the team back home that it might be time to get the rest of the important stuff from there. If we waited much longer, it might be too late.

All that combined meant I made it back to Augusta later than planned. That did not stop me from integrating the five new houses that were ready. Bryan let me know that two of the teams had shifted to work on the dorms, so there would be only three houses the next time that team was ready. I held off on upgrading the houses because I was short on tokens and would not have any excess for a few days.

After a long day, I was ready to get food and head to bed. There was no genuine need for me to debrief thanks to the constant communication, and with the longer-than-normal trip, I was glad not to spend time on a briefing. I would go over the high points and the item retrieval at Pittsfield in the morning.

The next morning, as I was collecting resources, I looked at the 654 settlement tokens I had. I knew there would not be enough to cover everything I needed to spend. Although I needed to shift some pods to work units and maintenance, I postponed it again.

From there, it was time to meet with the council. The status updates were good. Readfield would be evacuated by the next morning. Then they would focus on clearing out supplies and personal items in Readfield and Pittsfield with the vehicles for a few days before considering rescuing another location. The recovery of the people in the pods was going well from a medical perspective. They had already cured six of them, but there was an ongoing trauma for the people who had been trapped. Due to some incidents, one of the medical pods was kept free for emergencies even after all the guards and enforcers had been cured, which slowed things down somewhat.

"More medical pods would make things worse," Joey said when I asked if they wanted more. "Now that the work pods are not draining their life, leaving them in there is not hurting them. We need time to help those who are cured. Having five medical pods focused on that is almost too much. We can't handle more right now. If they were getting worse waiting their turn, I'd have a different answer, but my understanding is that's not an issue."

"No, they can wait there as long as needed," Vlad said. "Devin has made it impossible for the pods to extract anything from their occupants, so now it's more like stasis."

After a few more updates, the rest of the morning was spent planning the trip to Portland. The plan was to leave the next day. No one had any idea what the situation would be like, so we tried to plan what to do if the city was doing well and had many people in need of help. Its proximity to the heat sink, which was the Atlantic Ocean, made that at least somewhat possible. They would likely have been warmer there by a noticeable amount.

O'Donnell also had us game out how to deal with a city that

had broken into warring factions. With that many people there, that was also a real possibility. It would complicate things, but we needed to be ready for it. Another option was a city hollowed out by the cold and the lack of food. I thought that was the most likely option. It was heavily urbanized, and I did not see how it could survive without technology, even if the cold were not quite as bad. Yeah, a cold snap of negative 60 or 70 was better than one at negative 80, but it was still really bad without technology.

While the planning was all useful, and I was glad to be thinking things through ahead of time, it was also frustrating to get too caught up in the hypotheticals. I was excited around lunchtime when Bryan let me know today's buildings were ready to be integrated, and I could escape the meeting with a promise to be back later. I realized I had not hidden my relief when Erin gave me a disappointed look as I hurried away.

Four greenhouses and a dorm took nearly two-thirds of my available tokens, but left me with enough to finish upgrading all the custom house insulation to level 19 as well. That helped with power usage, but I still needed to add two more water towers and four more windmills to keep the infrastructure covering all the costs.

Even though that brought me back down to two settlement tokens, I split the new pods between work units and maintenance to start catching up on all the maintenance backlog that had been building. After that, it was time to head back to finalize the plans for the trip to Portland the next day. We would route through the base to recharge the snowmobiles and to recycle pods for resources along the way. That meant a straight shot of about 20 miles to the base on the new route and then 25 miles to Portland from there.

The plan was to use the nano car and driver to get me to Readfield to finish that mission, letting me sleep both ways in the early morning, then be back in time to head to Portland at 8:30. Now that there was a cleared path to the base, we could make it there in three hours, leaving five hours to make it to Portland before it got dark. The entire team would rest in the car on the way to the base before trekking to Portland using the snowmobile.

I planned to purchase another communication device before

we left. Two would have been nice, so we could leave one and have one for the trip back, but that was not reasonable with all the other demands on tokens. I would need to spend a lot in Portland to get them up and running, too. At the start, their pods would need to be mostly work units with a few focused on maintenance. Augusta would be supplying all the settlement tokens for them.

"I'm glad you'll be handling the team for this trip," I told Donna over dinner that night as we finalized plans. Her husband, who had joined us, did not seem happy that his wife was heading into danger again, but he was not complaining.

"You, me, the three enforcers with the most ties to Portland, other than Wendy, who needs to stay here to run things, and one person the council is sending because they have ties to Portland," Donna confirmed. "We'll make full use of your leadership perk to set things up, but you'll be leaving soon, likely, so Erin wants someone to be our representative."

"I know, and I agree. I'll make a few trips there before I leave, but I don't need to be in charge. I wish they would believe me when I tell them I don't care about all that, but I guess the political types can't grasp someone who doesn't care," I said. "I think we're as prepared as we can be. We'll have to see what the situation is before we decide what to do."

After we wrapped up, I made sure I had everything I needed for the trip packed and ready, and that my blanket and extra clothes were ready by the portal in case I died again. After the last two times, I was not discounting that possibility.

23

Three in the morning rolled around way too early, but I got up and dressed in 15 minutes and was ready for my pickup. There were a few pillows in the car, and I settled in and dozed off for the ride to Readfield. Being chauffeured around like this was wild, but I dozed right off. Since there had been constant trips back and forth for days, the path was well known and easy to follow. I noticed no bumps, though I knew this particular nano vehicle was great on the roads and in the snow.

Once we arrived, I woke up and got out of the car to help the last of the residents into the vehicles. The two sleds behind the snowmobiles were loaded up with the residents' possessions, and the four remaining people got in the car with me once that was done. That triggered mission completion, and I let the driver know we could leave while I reviewed the mission.

We had earned a total of 196 points. It looked like half a point for each of the 412 people saved, and negative ten points for the one death. The suggested rewards were the same as last time, and I accepted them after dithering about putting rewards into defense again.

Readfield Rescue Mission: Allocated Rewards

- Material unit enhancement device level upgrade 20 (100 points) - device may be placed on or removed from a portal by an architect. The device adds 20 material units per day to the assigned portal. May be upgraded
- Enforcer cost reduction (50 points) - cost to assign enforcer class decreased by 5 spheres
- Material unit generation (46 points) - 2,300 material units added to Augusta

It turned out just as I wanted. The cost to create new enforcers was back to the baseline of ten. It looked like it could not go lower. That was perfect for going into the next mission. The production device was also improving, adding 70 points to the material unit's daily production.

Are you sure there's not some way to swap it between portals during the same day? I asked Vlad.

You've already tried it, and it does not work. There might be a way to upgrade it to do that, but it's such an edge case now, it would be a waste of an upgrade, Vlad answered. *You can't find a way around all the rules.*

I cut my internal conversation with Vlad short to talk to the last of the Readfield refugees in the car with me. I could have told them I needed to sleep, but instead I answered their questions about how the nanotechnology worked. At least I answered what I could, and Vlad filled in the rest. I was surprised to realize how much technobabble I had picked up from Vlad since he arrived. I actually knew a fair amount about nanotechnology at this point, even though I had known nothing about it before Vlad showed up.

The other part of the conversation was asking me to look for people in Portland. I told them to get their information into the next book and to use the communication device once it was set up.

"The focus is on getting them started building stuff to survive, not contacting people," I said. "Plus, I'm just not good with names and hunting people down. You will get a chance, but please don't count on me to be the person remembering these messages."

They understood and were curious about the entire mail system set up with Bangor. The plan was to deliver letters back and forth to Portland as well. People would have multiple ways to keep in touch since there was only so much time that could be allocated to the general public on the communication devices.

As soon as we were back in Augusta, I hopped out of the car to get my breakfast and to be ready to collect resources right at eight. I wanted to do that before collapsing the portal for the trip. Everyone going with me was already there, packing the sled for the journey to Portland.

With five people in a single sled plus supplies, there would not be much room for food and other stuff on this trip. At least I would have my daily generation of ration bars to pass out. I could also generate a lot of food with the remaining resources in the aliens' portal.

We talked about last-minute logistics while I ate. The rest of the team had already eaten by the time I got back from Readfield, so it was a good time to go over things while I mainly listened. I collected Augusta's resources and then shifted two pods to maintenance. We were still not quite keeping up with maintenance, and we were overdue for a cold snap, though Vlad said there was nothing on the horizon.

After that, it was time to review and collapse the portal we would be taking with us. First, I double-checked that no one was in the work pods associated with it. The 4,734 material units were enough to build a lot of stuff, but we would be hampered by only having 1,070 work units saved up. With no way to transfer work units between portals, that would be the limiter for the first round of building. By the time I was done, a whole crowd had gathered to watch the portal fold in on itself until it was a small cube, ready for transport. It was grabbed to put on the sled, and then I joined the rest of the team for our relaxing ride to the base in the car. The two trips were the longest time I had spent in the car since I had arrived here. I forgot how much nicer it was than riding on a snowmobile or bouncing along behind one in a sled.

We had a quick lunch when we got to the base, and I recycled the 13 pods that had been freed up. That was 39 more settlement tokens and 650 more material units. I tried to funnel the material units into the Portland portal, but it didn't work. They all ended up in Augusta's portal. I also picked up more spheres from what had been collected, clearing out more golems in the area.

Checking in with people did not take long. I was mainly making sure things were on track, and they needed nothing from me. I also talked to a few of the rescued people waiting for a ride to Augusta. They were still having a rough time, but they thanked all of us for saving them.

I would have stayed longer talking to them, but we needed all the time we could get to make the trip to Portland and start figuring out what was going on there. Because the area south of the base had not been as thoroughly cleared, we would need to watch for golems and traps the whole way. That meant I was driving again with Vlad scouting as we went. Our goal was to reach the edge of Portland proper between three and five, then decide whether to camp for the night or make contact the same day.

We only ran into a few golems on the way south. The terrain was more of an issue than the golems, but the few more spheres were enough to get me to 176 stored up. With the cost to grant the class reset to 10, that was a lot of enforcers I could make. Thanks to all the terrain slowdowns, we were only at the very outskirts of town a little after five. We saw many deserted and burnt-out houses and buildings, but no sign of people. The destruction made us hesitant, and we decided to find a defensible position and spend the night so we could start fresh in the morning light.

"Even Pittsfield was not this bad, and they were fighting each other," Donna said as we made camp in a building that had too much concrete to have burned badly. "This looks like arson, not people being careless trying to stay warm."

"I know, I'm starting to think that O'Donnell's worst-case scenarios might be the ones we're facing," I said as I helped get the double-layer tents set up inside the building for the night. We had all the leftover supplies from the assault on the alien base. We even used one of the single-use heaters since someone was here without a class, so we were pretty comfortable despite the setting.

As soon as we were secure, we had a more detailed check-in with the people back home. We had been letting them know we were okay every 30 minutes on the trip out, but this was a detailed debrief. Everyone back home was disappointed to hear what we had found in Portland so far, but they knew things were likely to be bad, so no one was giving up hope yet.

"So, there's no way you are back tomorrow, right?" Erin asked.

"No, we knew that was unlikely even in the best case, and I'm sure it's not happening now. We'll be back in two days at the earliest," I said. "It depends on whether we can get things set up tomorrow and leave the following morning or not."

There was more questioning and planning, but Donna cut in and told us to wrap it up. She wanted people either on watch or sleeping so we could get an early start the following day. She was right, and we said goodnight and started the rotation she had laid out for us.

In the morning, we had to make a decision. The snowmobile and sled gave us speed, but they would stand out. We were close enough to the city that we could start exploring on foot, which might give us a better chance of blending in. Everyone had their thoughts on it over breakfast, but in the end, no one was willing to leave all of our stuff behind for someone else to loot.

"My primary worry is the portal. I don't think anyone else could use it, but we're not going to lug it around by hand. Someone could steal it, and then we'd have to try to hunt it down. Just because of that, we need to take everything with us. It's not like we're going to hide where we are from for long anyway, and it lets us retreat quickly if we need to," I said.

That settled the issue. I was not officially in charge of the mission. That was Donna, but people listened to me. With that settled, we stashed the rations I had generated the night before that we had not eaten and did not have room to take with us. We could tell people where to find them if we met up with anyone. I would not skip generating food just because we could not use it. The bars could survive the cold, so in the worst case, it would be a cache here for later.

With enough light to really check the area out as we traveled, we headed toward Payson Park. I did not know the area, but the park was right on the water, and people thought it would be a suitable spot to build if there were survivors in the area. If not, we could follow the road around the bay to the peninsula containing the downtown area. That was likely to be the warmest part of the city, with water on three sides. There was even a waterfront park along the edge of the peninsula that could be better for building if it stayed warmer.

We spent nearly two hours making our way through the city. There were cars dead on the street, and everything was covered in many feet of snow. As we got deeper into the city, the destruction lessened, but it was still totally deserted.

It was not until we were approaching the park that we saw smoke to the east, and we slowed down further. The advantage of the piles of snow everywhere was that Vlad could scout without being seen. We moved toward the smoke, with Vlad ranging as far ahead as he could and feeding information back to me.

"It looks like there are some hotels and apartment buildings in this area being used as housing for a group," I passed to everyone after reading the messages Vlad was sending me. "They've added fireplaces all over, but it doesn't seem like a lot of people for the area. Maybe 1,000 total based on the smoke and buildings."

Vlad had seen a few people watching from the windows, obviously making sure they saw any approaching threats, but not overly concerned. They were armed and indoors, so they were likely still operational weapons.

Vlad could not get any more information unless we got close enough to be seen ourselves. After a quick conversation, we all tried to look non-threatening, and I drove us toward the occupied main building. Vlad stayed hidden ahead of us to gather information while they were focused on us. I saw the moment the guard facing our way saw us and reacted. I waved hello and kept the snowmobile heading that way at a moderate pace.

"The good news is that he's not firing at us," I said, even though the others could see just as well as I could. "The bad news is that he's panicked and yelling for people. Stay alert."

It did not have to be said, but Donna was ready to jump out of the sled, push my body off the snowmobile, and drive away if I was shot and killed. I got to be the first target again.

I pulled us up right in front of what looked like the building's entrance and a restaurant, and waited. I might have been more nervous, but Vlad was relaying the conversation inside the doors to me in real time. They were trying to figure out which faction in the city we were from and if we were a threat. The consensus seemed to be that we were a new player, and they wanted to make a good impression. They planned to be armed and show they could take care of themselves without pissing us off.

There was a lot of speculation about the snowmobile. It was clearly not a gas-powered vehicle, but nothing battery-powered worked that they knew of. I fought back a grin at that. We were running low on power and would need to recharge soon. If I did not deploy the portal, I would need to build a windmill linked back to Augusta.

Finally, the door opened, and three people came out to talk to us. I let Donna know it seemed safe enough, and she came up to start the conversation.

"We're from Augusta," she said in response to the first question. "It's a long story, but Devin here was sent to help humanity survive the ice age caused by alien cops chasing criminals through the solar system and weakening the sun. He was given a way to build nanotechnology-powered devices, like this snowmobile, and structures that can keep people alive as the planet gets colder."

I let her talk some more, nodding along as needed. I was used to the disbelief my story caused and enjoyed watching someone else fight their way through it. While I listened, I was waiting for the signal to let Vlad know to show himself. Either she did not explain what Vlad was enough, or people were trigger-happy. Someone tried to shoot him as soon as he appeared. That was not an issue, but the gun was obviously not in great shape, as it basically exploded in his hand.

I stepped away from the snowmobile and toward the idiot who had fired. I used two healing charges on him to stabilize him, then healed the two people nearest to him who had been hit by the shrapnel. While we had not planned it, the alien hologram, followed by my apparently magical ability to heal people, was enough to quiet most of the doubts about Donna's story. We were all invited inside. We accepted, but left two enforcers to guard the snowmobile and its contents.

My impression from listening to them talk was that they were unprepared for a conversation like this with people they did not know. They were ready to deal with other city factions, not a new player with working technology, which was understandable. They were also clearly trying to work the situation to their advantage by presenting themselves as the only option for us to work with. They did not know that when I pretended to dismiss Vlad to save power, he was moving through the walls and spying on people in the building.

The picture he painted was not as rosy as the people in front of us were presenting. They were part of the group in charge and seemed to be doing well. The rest of the people here did not seem to be abused, but they were second-class citizens. They looked to be getting fewer resources and looked like they had the beginnings of malnutrition, while the people in front of us looked well-fed.

"But where can we meet these other groups for ourselves?" I asked when Donna's polite questions about other factions hit another brick wall.

Before the person who had been deflecting all of Donna's questions could answer, one of the other people at the table spoke up. "Why do you want to meet them? All they do is throw their weight around. If the cold had not set in and everyone's cars had finally died, we'd still be fighting."

There was a beat of silence as I internally thanked my commanding presence perk. I was pretty sure that was what led to the outburst.

"So, tell us where they are and let us decide. We need to find the best spot to save as much of the city as possible," I said when no one else spoke up.

After that, we got the information we needed, but it was laced with numerous warnings. We took the warnings to heart, even if they had a personal motive to make the other groups look worse. We would be foolish to discount what they were saying. At the same time, we would not let it color our opinion too much.

"Sorry to take over like that," I told Donna as we pulled away. "They were going to keep talking around us, and I knew I could leverage my perk to get things going."

"I was going to shoot someone if they didn't give me a straight answer, so it's a good thing you stepped in," she said. "It was good practice for me, even if they ended up stonewalling."

"If the next group we meet is not someone we're going to go with, we'll need to find a place to put up a windmill and recharge the snowmobile," I told people as we made our way around the bay toward the city center.

The locals on the team were shocked to see the whole bay frozen over. We considered cutting across, but Vlad confirmed it was not frozen to the bottom. The thought of going over ice with water underneath, no matter how thick the ice was, freaked me out, so we went around. There were almost no signs of life, but as we neared the city core, everything seemed to be in better shape. The ruined buildings all looked to have been looted for parts, but there were no signs of arson. The burnt buildings we saw looked to have been caused by accidents.

Once we were around the bay, we headed to the middle of downtown and to the city's largest apartment building. According to the people we had spoken with, it had been taken over as housing for the city core that had survived. It had used up the remaining fuel and then had stoves and other heat sources installed.

The group we were talking to discussed the lack of sanitation in an enormous building like that and how people were sleeping in the halls and fighting all the time. Plus, there was no place nearby to grow food, and they must have been running out of food in the city.

We passed a few other buildings that looked inhabited, but no one gave us any problems, so we kept moving to the Casco building. Stovepipes were sticking out of windows on all eighteen floors of the building, and it looked like a mess. I was surprised that there had been no fires yet. With over 250 units, I could believe they had around 2,000 people shoved in there. All that body heat would help.

As we got closer, I could see how they were handling waste. There were piles of frozen waste all around the building. It looked as if stuff had just been thrown out of the windows. The one positive of the cold was that it froze everything solid, keeping it from smelling.

They had obviously seen us from a distance, and a group was waiting for us as we approached. Despite the warnings we had received, they looked no more hostile than could be expected.

"Well, that answers that," I said as a mission popped up. "This is the group we are going to have to work with, according to the nano controller. Let me read it to you."

Mission Assigned: Portland

Portland has splintered and is failing. Empower the primary faction to bring the city together and survive while upholding your moral code. Persuasion will hone your skill for future missions. This mission is secondary to the Augusta Settlement Mission. Success criteria

- All factions united
- Single viable plan for the future
- Primary faction is an ally to Augusta

"No more hunting around. It sounds like we'll need to make them see things our way, though. Let me start again, but help as much as you can with your perk," Donna said to me, and then it was time to start talking.

Donna took the lead and gave the same brief overview. I could tell she had already adjusted her pitch after seeing the reaction with the first group. We were immediately offered a place inside out of the cold. There was a garage they could still open, which had room for the snowmobile and the sled. If the mission had not popped up, I would have been hesitant to trap ourselves like this, but since we wanted to make this work, we took the risk.

The people here seemed more like jerks than the other group, but also more aware of their long-term survival prospects. That was making them polite, though it was clear it grated on them. Things stayed civil as Donna went over the nanotechnology at a high level, but they were growing impatient. Finally, the guy who seemed to be the leader spoke up.

"So, what's the deal here? You have a way to save some of us, or maybe even all of us, but you want something from us, or we wouldn't still be talking."

"I'm the only one who can operate the nanotechnology until I leave, and then I will pass it to someone else. You need to bring the entire city together, whoever is left, and make it work for all of you. I know there has been fighting over limited resources, but that will be a thing of the past. It will take a while, but there will be enough for everyone. Things will be cramped at first, but over time, the buildings and resources will keep growing," I said.

"So, you save us, but you can take it all away at any moment," he shot back.

"Look, I get rewards for saving people. Everything I do is based on that. As long as you help, I won't cause any problems. You're clearly the top dogs here. Use that to get everyone pulling in the same direction and treat everyone equally. That's all you have to do," I said.

"What if they cause problems or don't work?" was the immediate response.

"Don't be a pushover, but don't be a jerk. I'm not going to be here to police the letter of the law, just be a decent person," I

said.

The whole time I was speaking, I could feel my commanding presence perk flaring. It was working, but I had genuine concerns about how long the agreement would last after I headed back to Augusta. This group seemed as if they were entirely in it for themselves. I hoped my perk at least gave Donna a window to get things set up so things would remain smooth after I left.

That exchange seemed to cement the plan, and then it was time to talk logistics. There had been no buildings I could integrate as we traveled through the city. Over time, the stuff was just too damaged for that. While there was plenty of space at the promenade water park, it was on the edge of the city, which was problematic.

Finally, everyone decided on Deering Oaks Park. It was over 50 acres of open space. The trees had been mostly cleared early on, and it was near major roads to make it easier to bring in people and supplies. With a place selected, a small group accompanied us to the park to see whether what we were promising was real.

As soon as we arrived, I picked a suitable spot and placed the portal. When it was active, I built a large crafting bay around it and erected a windmill and a water tower. The processing portal had surprised people, but watching the other structures form from the typical blue light over the next ten minutes convinced everyone. Once everything was built, I invited people inside.

"There are two restrooms here. Feel free to take advantage of the hot running water. This building doesn't have a shower, but I know even using the sink to get clean can be a relief after a while," I said. Two people darted off immediately, but I kept going. "One of the main things I can't supply, and you are short on, is work units. You need to get people in these pods right away so I can build more stuff this trip."

I explained the process a little more and made sure they knew no one could sleep in the crafting bay. Then Tom took one of the leaders back to their building and started moving people to the park. I told them to get 20 or so people out here because I was going to be building more, and they would need people for the second shift, too.

While that was being done, I stepped outside to build a dorm to house the people who would be working in the pods, and a barn for the few animals they had left to start breeding more to improve the food supply. That required two more windmills, and then I headed back inside. I lost more of the group that had accompanied us to the actual showers in the dorm, though. That was fine, as I used the remote processing on the portal to clear out some more land and use up the last of the work units I had stored for one more dorm and one more water tower.

I placed the water tower leading to the apartment building so travel back and forth would be easier, as it would absorb the snow. I was also building the windmills that way so they could more easily tap into the spare power.

I then had to explain how they needed to feed the portal debris each day to generate material units. When they realized they could put trash in it, they were excited, but I had to tell them to keep that in check. Dense, finished products provided the most material units, and they needed to focus on that for a while.

"Keep the trash and waste processing to about 20% of the total for now," I said, explaining why we did not want to overdo it.

With my building spree for the day done, I started using the resources stored in the portal to generate food. I started by providing enough food for 1,000 people for a day. That might not have sounded like a lot, but it took up a lot of space. We also claimed one of the rooms in the newest dorm for our team. It was just until we left, but I heard Donna negotiating to have it set aside for us full-time, as we would be sending people out to teach them how to build stuff. I left them to talk and headed back to the building to generate my rations for the day. I had gotten into the habit of trying to generate them somewhere they would not have to be moved. They were snatched up and distributed immediately before we turned around and went back to the park.

Donna was waiting for me with a request. "If we want them to make a genuine effort to connect with all the other groups, they are going to need a snowmobile. Do you have the tokens to make one for them?"

My tokens were dipping quickly again, but it made sense, so I spent 250 of them to buy a snowmobile so they could get around the city. We were letting them use our snowmobile as well, but only to move people and supplies between the new buildings and the apartments, with an enforcer as the driver. I did not want to risk it being stolen. Even if I could locate it within the range of my system integration perk, I did not want it to be too far away.

After another update, we let people use the communication device to talk to Augusta. While that was going on, we continued discussing plans to start them on their own building projects, to clear the area around the park, and to extend the buildings to other cleared areas as the park filled up. In the morning, I would build more, and we would go over the city information in detail before heading home.

24

With all that taken care of, we spent a few hours just talking with everyone. There were lots of questions, as always, and I used my perk when answering them to make things easier for Donna going forward. There were also many questions that only Vlad and I could answer based on our firsthand knowledge of what had happened.

I got the vibe from a few of the people we were talking to that they were interested in getting to a more settled place where things would be easier. It would be important to keep them from having more than one or two vehicles and to make sure they could not assault the Augusta settlement in force. There had been no overt threats, but their city was way behind Augusta. Some people in Portland were already jealous. The team was not bragging, but it was clear the people in Augusta had it easier based on how they talked about it.

Trying to figure out motives and what to worry about was all way too complicated, and I was wishing I had not bought them a snowmobile as quickly as I had.

Vlad, is there a way for people back home to track the snowmobile I just bought so Augusta will know if it's heading their way? I messaged while keeping my conversation going.

Yes, you can install a nano tracker for 50 more settlement tokens. It will only report location when it's on the grid, but that would give you some warning. It would help just knowing if it has gone off grid, he answered, knowing what I was thinking.

I asked him to make sure I did that before we left, just in case they tried something stupid. This group left me worried. They were intense in a way that the people in Bangor were not.

Finally, as it neared midnight, Donna told us we needed to get some sleep. We would be up early for the final instructions, building more stuff, and our trip home. Because we had a single room in the dorm to share, we felt secure and had privacy to talk once the door was closed. I went over my worries and plans to put a tracker on their snowmobile.

"Thanks, I don't want to assume the worst, but I'm not getting the best vibe either," Donna said to general agreement from the others. "I think they will be fine if we can get them stable, but until then, they could be trouble. Some may not want to wait, and this is a discreet way to protect ourselves. I think the leaders would ditch the city in a heartbeat for more luxury."

"Don't lie, but don't make Augusta sound like it's perfect. It may be a lot better than what most people are experiencing, but everyone there is working too," I said.

There was some more debriefing to go over as everyone got ready for bed, but no one had anything else important to report. We all used the bathroom, but no one got a shower. The locals were monopolizing those, and I couldn't blame them. We all could wait until we got home.

The following morning, we went over what they needed to do while we were gone. They needed to keep the pods occupied. The portal had to be fed every day, and they needed to clear space in the park. They could not do the remote processing I could, so they had to do it manually. We also left a list of supplies to be staged for the custom dorms and greenhouses. The plan was to focus on those when we brought the builders back.

"We will let you know when I can get back out," I said. "It will be pretty soon, but at least four days, probably a couple more. I have to travel to Bangor to help them before I can come back, and that's a two-day trip in itself. Next time, we'll have at least two people who can help you with constructing buildings for integration. That will also give your portal and pods time to gather resources for lots of new buildings. Now, let's use up the resources you have to set you up for the next few days."

Once I could collect the latest batch of work units, it was time to start building. I started with three more dorms and a clinic with two medical pods. That left just enough resources for three more windmills stretched toward the apartments. It did not extend the grid there, but they would not have to run power cords far to tap into it.

"As long as there's not a cold snap, you should have about 400 excess power units each day," I explained to the leaders. "I would advise you to charge the batteries. I've set them so that if I am not here, you can control when they discharge. I would save them as backup for emergencies and not let them be discharged for day-to-day use. You'll be able to pull up all the information on the screens, but let me walk you through it now. It looks bad. It always looks bad at the start, but it's not quite as dire as it appears."

With that, I pulled up the information for Portland to discuss it with everyone.

Portland Settlement		**Population**	22,963
Food Supply	89 days	**Heat Supply**	34 days
Housing	76,451 people	**Survivable Housing**	150 people
Food Production	32%	**Secure Food Production**	1%
Power Production	50- 1,370 units	**Power Draw**	530- 1,750 units
Power Storage	57/ 660 units	**Indoor Pod Slots**	32/ 37
Water Production	550 units	**Water Draw**	315 units
Work Units	20 units	**Material Units**	3,228 units
Research Units	0 units		
Production Structures	Processing Portal	Work Pods x 32	Large Windmill x 6
Large Water Tower x 2	Large Barn x 1		
Enhanced Structures	Large Crafting Bay x 1	Dorm x 5	Medical Clinic x 1
Medical Pods x 2			
Deferred Maintenance	3 units	**Material Maintenance**	1 units

"That's a pretty good survival rate for the city so far, and your stock of food and fuel is impressive this far in. I'm not sure where you're producing food in buildings that are not nano powered, but you might need to fill us in. The remaining days are worst-case, and if you ration and find additional food and fuel sources, those totals should grow. Plus, we'll quickly ramp up building production. There's a lot of material units already processed for building once there are work units to go with it," I said.

"We'll keep things on an even keel and not waste anything,"

said the group's leader, Davis. "There are a lot of sources for materials, so we'll have supplies laid out to start building."

"It sounds like a plan. Keep in touch, and we'll let you know when we'll be back," Donna said. "Don't forget to take care of people and start combining forces. The pod's staffing demands will explode. Long-term, you really need eight people assigned to each pod to allow for some breaks. You'll want a lot of people to keep them full."

With that, we headed out. We needed to get going to make it back to Augusta at a reasonable hour. We also needed to stop by the first group we had met to tell them what had happened. They would need to contact the primary group and be open to working with them.

Since we were watching out for other people, we kept our conversation to a minimum. Watching for survivors and then for golems meant we would not be able to relax until we left the base for Augusta, which was hours away.

This time, when we approached the buildings at Payson Park, the people there came out to meet us, without guns, which was a step in the right direction. I started the meeting by generating the ration bars for them to use as they saw fit. I thought about telling them where to find the cache, but it would not have been safe for them to hunt it down. We would pick it up on the way into town the next time.

While the reaction to more food was positive, hearing that the group downtown had access to the nanotechnology and would reach out to combine forces was not.

"Look, I get that you have problems with them, but they are the most centrally located and the most likely to save as many people as possible here," Donna said. "We will not force you, or any of the people here, to work with them, but that's where the long-term survival will be. Devin has built weatherized accommodations there, and it will continue to build out quickly. There's room for 150 people there right now, more if they cram in."

"Like we can trust them," was the response. "They'll use their power to take over everything, and then we'll be alive but not in charge of ourselves. We told you they were the wrong choice."

"Devin and I are still the ones who decide what gets built and when. You'll have to learn to live together, but they don't have unlimited power. They have to work to help everyone. Find a way to make it work. This technology will continue to advance, and its growth will accelerate. In time, there will be enough space for everyone if we can keep from fighting each other while we get things in place," Donna said. "You should be rushing to get everyone here to survive and helping other towns."

I had to fight to keep my mouth shut when someone asked why they should waste time helping others if they had not finished helping their own people. Donna was quick to respond, and I could tell the question had touched a nerve for her, too.

"Seriously, are you saying it was stupid for us to try to help you? We can take that portal back and speed up building out Augusta," she snapped. "I feel like we got lucky with the towns we've helped so far. They've all dug in and been grateful. Everyone here is pissing me off. We have to get going, but think about what you want to do. We'll stop back here next trip, and I hope you all are working together before more people die. You know, that like 55,000 people in the city proper are already dead, right?"

People tried to explain or make excuses, but Donna said we needed to leave to stay on schedule and herded us all outside to get going. I felt Donna had made her point without pushing things too far, and enough people had seen the confrontation that it would spread throughout their entire community.

"Nice work back there," I said as soon as we were out of earshot of the group she had just told off. "I think that will make them reconsider their attitude. It was great to sit back and let you handle it. Letting someone else be the bad guy is way more fun than I imagined."

"I don't want to be doing all this, but you're right, we can't leave it all to you when you're getting ready to go help a new group of people," she said. "I'm not sure how you are going to handle doing this over and over."

"The nano controller will continue to help architects by starting them in a favorable location. There was a reason he started in Augusta and not one of these other cities near the aliens," Vlad said. "It won't be easy, and there won't always be a good option, but his starting location for a mission will be one he can integrate with more easily."

As I kept driving, I realized Vlad had a point. My starting location for this mission could have been a lot worse. I was glad to meet people in Portland after stabilizing Augusta. At least the rest of the trip to the base went off without fighting any golems or contact with other humans. We were ahead of schedule and had time to eat with everyone quickly while I recycled the three pods that had been freed up. That was 12 people who were healed of the physical damage caused by the alien's pods, with another five in the medical pods on their way to being cured.

I talked about converting the remaining snowmobile the aliens had left, but we decided to take it to Portland for them to use on the next trip, so there was no rush to burn the tokens until we were heading back. We requested that the team at the base get a sled together for the trip and start collecting stuff to send to Portland next time.

With all that taken care of, I convinced Tom to take over driving duty for the rest of the trip home. The route was relatively safe, so having me as the lead target was not as important, and piloting the snowmobile while dragging a sled through potentially hostile territory was exhausting. I was ready for a break after the morning's trip.

The downside of communication devices everywhere was that people knew when to expect us and were waiting for us when we arrived. I was used to having at least a few minutes to sneak away before everyone realized we were back.

"I need to head out with Bryan to integrate buildings before it gets any darker," I said when people told us the meeting room was ready. "I'll let you get started and join as soon as I can."

Donna glared at me as I headed out with Bryan. The glare was clearly a warning not to drag out the integration to avoid the meetings. It seemed she had figured out all my tricks. I started by using the portal to clear more debris to make way for more buildings, then we integrated the five houses and four greenhouses.

"I was up to almost 1,700 settlement tokens," I said as I integrated the last of the completed buildings. "Now I'm under 1,200, but look at all those new buildings. You are all speeding up. I need to build two more water towers and four more windmills to make sure there's enough water and power."

"You forgot to check the research," Vlad said when I had finished building more infrastructure. "They finished the insulation research on the houses."

I immediately pulled that up to look at the bonus effect.

Improved insulation: The selected blueprint will require 1% less electricity due to superior insulation. Cost 50 research tokens for Level 1

- Large Custom House. Level 20. First added effect: each large custom house's base and maximum supported temperatures are increased by ten degrees. Second added effect: each large custom house's base and maximum supported temperatures are increased by ten degrees.

"That's awesome. With 60 custom houses here, that's a base savings of 300 power units a day. Even better, the temperature has to be negative 40 now instead of negative 20 for the houses to start drawing more power to stay warm. Also, thanks for looking out for me, buddy. Reminding me at the end of my building pass is an excuse to travel around and upgrade all the houses that Donna can't complain about." I said, grinning at Vlad.

That startled a laugh out of Bryan, but he promised not to rat me out when we went around upgrading all the houses. Despite his promise not to rat me out, Donna still looked like she was annoyed at how long I had taken when I finally showed up.

"So, some good news. Vlad reminded me to check the research before I came in, and the house insulation research hit level 20. I went back and upgraded all the houses, and it's a huge reduction in overall power usage. On top of that, those houses can now comfortably handle up to negative 115 degrees with enough power."

My news distracted people and put them in a good mood, which was what I had hoped for before my part of the meeting really got going.

"Between Donna and the communications with the people in Portland, we have a pretty good view of how your mission went," Erin said. "Things have been stable here, but Bangor has been checking repeatedly to make sure you will come up on time. They are really riding the edge still and want to get some sort of cushion built."

"I've been saving a ton of resources for them," I said. "This should be the last big push to get them stable and finish that mission, which has dragged on far longer than I had hoped. How's the resource extraction from the nearby towns going?"

"We're keeping up with building demand for now, but we could really use that truck Bryan asked for," Jason said. "We're having to spend more time dismantling buildings and going further for the easy-to-get stuff. I wonder how long it will be until all the old buildings are gone. They'll either be repurposed or fed into the processing portal. Some of them should be saved as museum pieces."

"Realistically, there will come a point where you will just feed waste into the portal," Vlad said. "There are so many fewer humans now that you will not come close to needing to repurpose all your old construction."

"Since we've moved to the depressing portion of the meeting, I have genuine issues with the people you trusted in Portland. They are using the communication device to collect information, and we're having to watch everyone who talks to them. We were pretty free with people just talking to Bangor, but this group is trying to get information. They're even using innocuous questions between friends to figure us out," O'Donnell said.

"I agree some conversations are suspicious," Erin said. "On the other hand, we can't tell everyone here not to trust their friends and family in Portland."

I was impressed that they did not try moving this meeting to a more private location to discuss that. People were milling around and listening. I gave myself a moment to be proud of ingraining a more open approach to meetings in the team here.

"I don't trust them, and I don't think any of us did. Based on the mission I got, that faction is the one to help recover Portland. They may not be the ones to lead it though," I said. "In fact, I was worried enough that I took some precautions."

"Donna told me about it, and we have someone monitoring that situation," O'Donnell said. "That was good thinking, but I still fear this is a long-term issue you've left us."

"I agree, but I'm not sure we would have found anything better, and it would have taken a lot more time exploring the city and not starting to build," I said. I was glad the tracker seemed to be a secret, as we did not want them to know about it and find a way around it. I did not let myself dwell on what might have been hypocrisy around secrecy.

"Plus," Vlad broke in, "the mission Devin got is a good sign they were the best choice. That could be because the other options are worse because of personality and location, but even if they're still the best choice, you can't assume that means they are a good choice. Remember, they can be the best choice and also a horrible choice."

"With what we knew, it was the best decision at the moment," Donna said. "We'll monitor the situation and do what we need to."

There was some more general conversation when I broke the news that everyone had been expecting, even if they were not excited about it.

"I'm really trying to move on to the next mission sometime within the next two weeks," I said. "I've been here 57 days, and two more weeks will take me over 10 weeks here. That's just one week less than the last mission. I won't leave if things aren't ready, but if we can evacuate one more town, and if everyone can start wrapping up their guides for where I end up next, I'd appreciate it."

"No one's looking forward to you leaving," Erin said. "The drop in resources alone will hurt, but we're on a path to being stable pretty soon, and with our help, the cities around here should not be far behind."

A few more people said nice things about me, then we got down to what I needed. The top of the list was updated manuals for all the new buildings and building methods. I wanted them in both hard copy and digital formats, so I could transfer them as needed and keep a backup. At some point, I would need to replace my tablet with one bought with settlement tokens, but I was not there yet.

After assigning everyone tasks, I did not do much the following day. Other than integrating the three new houses, my only other project was to start organizing what I wanted to take on my next mission. I did not want to scramble at the last minute and forget something. I started boxing stuff up with master lists taped to each container and a copy on my tablet.

After a solid night's sleep, I was ready to head to Bangor with more supplies and lots of resources for their build-out of structures. That was all in addition to the one builder who was packed into the sled to train them on building dorms. I felt like this trip would finally deliver on the promise I made to Bangor when I first showed up.

"I've got 2,044 settlement tokens, 4,766 material units, and 4,480 work units. I really should've gotten some more work units, but this should be enough," I said to the enforcers who had shown up to see me off. "Keep an eye out for problems from down south. I have a feeling O'Donnell is right to be suspicious. Do what you need to do to keep people safe."

I had plenty of time to think about my plans for the next two weeks as I headed north. I tried to speak with the builder Bryan sent to help them transition to building dorms, but he refused to speak with me. He was bundled up in the sled, out of the wind, trying to stay warm, which made conversation impossible.

The route to Pittsfield was easier to follow this time, as the salvage team had made a few trips up here to gather readily available building supplies. It also sped things up, and I was in Bangor by mid-afternoon. The speed increase surprised them somewhat, even though they knew I was coming.

Once we were in the main area, I introduced Jim to everyone before he headed inside to recover from the ride up. The trip was tough on people who did not have a class. Thanks to bringing him and his equipment, there were fewer supplies in the sled this time, but people were still there to unload and distribute them.

With that done, I followed Dominic around to integrate all the structures his teams had built. He was practically bursting with pride that they had built 18 houses and seven greenhouses.

"This shows an awesome dedication by all your teams," I said as we went around integrating them. I also spent the 59 tokens to apply the research to the custom houses that had already been built. "I think the dorms Jim will help you build will speed things up even more."

Once that was done, it was time to balance the infrastructure to support the new structures. We needed four more water towers and six more windmills, so we kept riding around on the snowmobile to get them all placed. I wanted to get the town's baseline before I started burning through my resources to build more.

I checked the stats. The new buildings provided food and housing for over 20% of the remaining population, but the mission had not been completed.

"Vlad, I have been so focused on building that I have not paid attention to the other part of the mission. Does a stable population for ten days mean no deaths for ten days?" I asked. "The population has dropped by almost 50 in the week I was gone, and I don't know that I can get it to zero for 10 days."

"The population has to drop by less than 0.5% over the course of ten days to qualify. Having no deaths is unreasonable in a large population, but 0.5% is. If no more than one other person dies today, you will achieve the mission tomorrow."

That earned a raised eyebrow from Dominic, but I did not let it stop me from continuing to build. They all knew the mission's definition of success would not work for them long-term, and I would not stop at the 20% minimum. First, I added two more apartment blocks. Then I followed it up with their second greenhouse complex and a windmill before I ran out of work units.

"Okay, time to go give everyone the good news," I told Dominic as we headed back to the main house and turned over the snowmobile to the mobs of people moving into the new buildings.

Once I was in the main room and had everyone's attention, I shared Bangor's key information for everyone to see.

Bangor Settlement		**Population**	10,417
Food Supply	11 days	**Heat Supply**	0 days
Housing	20,102	**Survivable Housing**	2,346 people
Food Production	5%	**Secure Food Production**	27%

"This is the important part," I said. "You can look at the other parts later. The nano controller thinks you are out of heat because it assumes you have 8,000 people living in old buildings. Andy, with what I integrated and built today, everyone should be housed, right? I know it's crowded, but with four people per official housing spot, that's 9,384 people in nano housing. The other 1,033 people should fit in the clinics, barns, and greenhouses where the nano controller lets people sleep. That should be doable, right?"

"It's really uncomfortable, but yes, that should be everyone moving in," Andy said. That announcement got a small cheer.

"The good news is, no one is going to freeze," I said. "And it just gets better from here. Every single new building will reduce crowding. Think about that. This represents the worst your housing situation will be. Every single new structure built makes the housing situation less crowded. Food still needs some work, but at half rations, you all produce 64% of the food you need. I can't tell you what to do, but I would focus on greenhouses and learning how to build dorms. With the resources I collect before I leave tomorrow, I plan to build one more clinic and then as many water towers and windmills as I can. You have enough power now, but there's not much margin in a cold snap."

While I said I would not tell them what to do, they wanted my input, so we discussed the building plan for next week. There were already eight houses under construction, so they would finish those while learning to build dorms by starting on two. That would leave enough people to work on ten greenhouses at the same time.

While the food supply was listed at 11 days, that was assuming everyone was eating full rations. If nothing changed, it would be enough for about four weeks. With new production coming online continuously, I expected they had at least five weeks to handle the food issue. More deliveries from Augusta, along with adding ten greenhouses a week, would let them survive indefinitely on half rations within four weeks. The more they built, the more they could increase the amount of food people had to eat above the half-ration baseline.

"This is all good, but you're talking like you might not come back. We can keep building houses and greenhouses, but how will we power them? You're the only one who can build nano structures up here from scratch, right?" I heard someone ask.

"You'll have two options," Vlad said before I could speak up.

"Research to free up water and power. Klawock's research has unlocked the 'Improved Building Efficiency' research. For 950 research tokens, you could level the custom houses to level ten in that research, reduce power and water use by 10%, and build eight more houses without needing any more power. You can also learn to make windmills and water towers by hand and integrate them, but that will be a lot of work."

"And I plan to be back one more time. Other than the clinic in the morning, the rest of the buildings this trip and next will be power and water, so you are set up for the future," I said. "It will cover you for a while until other options come online."

That seemed to address most of the concerns, and people were still hyped that they all had warm housing. The rest of the night was a party atmosphere, just without the alcohol. That had all been used up weeks ago, and there was not enough food to even think about making moonshine yet.

I went to bed later than planned and was then woken up around two in the morning.

"Devin, you need to come to the meeting room now. Donna is on the line and needs to talk to you," the person who woke me up said.

I was groggy, but I had gotten used to strange wake-up times, so I was pretty much awake by the time I made it to the main room to hear what was so important.

25

"What's happening?" I asked as soon as I had the communication device in my hand.

"It's the group in Portland," Donna answered. I could hear others in the background as she talked. "The tracking on the snowmobile showed it leaving the city, then it was picked up a few hours later on the east side of the base heading toward us before it vanished into the dead zone. They're coming here for sure, and they knew about the base and avoided it. If there had been an emergency, they would have called or stopped there."

"All you can do is watch for the tracker to reappear when they get close and intercept them. Make sure you've got the vehicles and enforcers on standby," I said.

"We already took care of that, and we've plotted out where they might show up. There are enforcers stationed at each location, with the rest ready to rush out. Is there any way to use that tracker to disable the vehicle?" she asked.

"Not from here," Vlad answered for me. "Also, remember that the incapacitate criminal perk has the same restriction as the find criminal perk. 'The entity must be seen as a criminal by you and the majority of the community.' So, it's unlikely to work on these people until they attack. Even then, it might be tough for the community as a whole to consider them criminals. It's not like you can wake everyone up and tell them to consider these people to be criminals."

"So, we can't count on a clean way to disable them," O'Donnell said in the background. "The people standing guard need to know and be ready to take action."

"Do we shoot on sight?" Donna asked. "Should we try to contact them and see what they say?"

"I told everyone that I think if the people on the snowmobile had the communication device and are not using it, that's an answer in itself. If they left it behind, then what can we learn from the people there, and could we trust them?" O'Donnell said. "It's already suspicious that they said they were turning it off for the night earlier."

"I agree, there's no point in trying to contact them. At best, you'll give away that we know what's going on. My advice is that you need to be ready to defend yourselves at the first sign they're hostile," I said. "You need to do what you all are comfortable with, but protect yourselves."

"We'll do what's needed," O'Donnell said, with Donna agreeing with him in the background.

"It's your city, and your relationship. Focus on the threat and keep me updated when that won't distract you. I will be here until everything's resolved.

"We'll let you know what happens," Donna said. "The soonest we could have contact is in three hours, more likely four or five. You may want to get some sleep until then."

I wished them luck once more, then freed up the line and looked around. The excitement had woken a few people. I was expecting questions about Portland and what would happen, but the first question was about their snowmobile.

"No, I did not install a tracker in yours. I had not thought of it until we ran into people in Portland who seemed sketchy. As I said, they were almost fractured gangs. The people we worked with were the best option according to the nano controller that issues missions, but I was not comfortable with them," I said. "It looks like tracking them was a good idea, though. I hope no one on our side gets hurt, and we can figure out a path forward with Portland after this. This is going to be messy no matter what the outcome is if it's an attack."

"It sounds like you have some time before anything happens," Andy said. "You can lie down on the couch here and rest. We have the communication device monitored for messages all the time."

"Thanks, I want to be here when there's news. Wake me up for any updates, but I'll see if I can get enough sleep to head home tomorrow. I'll need to help clean up stuff there," I said.

I went back to the bunk I was using and got my bedding for the couch. It was somewhat strange to be sleeping with all these people here while I was out in the open, but I had gotten used to a lot in the last five months. The bigger issue was trying not to think about what was happening or about to happen.

I woke up to hear the report every hour for the next three

hours. There was no news, and each time I would fall back into a fitful sleep. The fourth time I was woken up was shy of the next hour's check-in, and it was right around six in the morning. This time, it was not Donna checking in.

"Devin, the tracker showed up just where we suspected it would," Erin said. "As soon as it showed up, four of the enforcers and O'Donnell with five of his people went to confront them. We have two enforcers and some of O'Donnell's guards here just in case they are smarter than you all thought and are using the snowmobile as a distraction somehow."

It was a very long wait for an update after that. Erin and I talked, but we had no way of knowing what was going on. We were still talking almost an hour later when I heard a commotion and then Donna's voice.

"No one on our side is dead, but it's a good thing we had Joey clear some pods. We have six people with gunshot wounds. It was a mess, but everyone on our side is alive thanks to the warning from the tracking device and the first aid perk stabilizing a few people."

"I'm not sure how they did it, but they had automatic guns still working in the cold. We thought we had them outnumbered, then they pulled out three of those and did a lot of damage," O'Donnell said, breaking in. "All five of them are dead. The initial attempts to incapacitate them did not work, from what I was told. When they did work after the fighting started, my people gunned them down before we knew they were helpless."

"I hate to say it, but it's probably better they're dead. We need to make sure the people who were part of the attack have a chance to talk to someone, though," Donna said. "I think some of us are going to have to talk through what just happened. Also, so you know, we learned that trying to use incapacitate on an invalid target wastes a charge. We also learned that with enough bullet strikes, a nano snowmobile stops working, but does not blow up."

"I'm glad everyone will be okay. The maintenance pods will repair the snowmobile, so drag it inside. Do we know who it was?" I asked.

"It was Davis and his main crew. They brought the communication device with them, too. So, who knows what's happening back in Portland?" Donna said.

"Damn, so it's a mess there for sure, and we can't contact them. Make sure the portal is fed today and resources are collected. I'm going to try to sleep for two more hours and then head back as soon as I build some more stuff here. We're going to need a team to go back to Portland tomorrow and try to straighten this out before it goes more off the rails."

Someone had taken my bedding back to my assigned bunk while I was talking, so I went back and fell asleep, though I knew I was forgetting something even as sleep claimed me.

Vlad let me wake up and check for any updates from Augusta before he reminded me of what I had forgotten.

"Devin, the mission here is complete. It didn't matter last night, and I didn't want to distract you, but you can now receive the reward."

I immediately pulled up the mission to see what the reward was.

Bangor Stabilization Mission: Reward

You have provided Bangor with the tools to stabilize itself, with only 69% of its starting population dead. Successfully delegating stabilization of a settlement on the brink without direct access to a portal is a vital skill for the future.

- Builder Sub-Class unlocked
- Builder Class unlocked
- Two known structures may be placed in Bangor for no cost

"A new class, based around building stuff, seems like a fantastic thing," I said. "Can I use the current class console to see who qualifies and grant it? What all does it do?"

Vlad said I could use the console just like with the enforcer class, and it would be even rarer than the enforcer class. "It will show up as an option on the class pod in Augusta and back in Klawock. As long as they are checking it regularly, like you told them to, they will know they have a new class they can test for too." Vlad said. "You can pull up the class information here to get an idea of what it can do."

Available Classes
Enforcer: This class begins with two available perks related to finding and subduing criminal elements. Other perks related to protecting their settlement are available. Next bestowal 10 spheres
Builder: This class begins with two available perks related to building and maintaining structures. Other construction-related perks are available. Next bestowal 100 settlement tokens

"Well, that's a little more information, but not enough for me to take it as a sub-class. I need to find someone to test it on and then decide. At least this one does not take spheres. Using settlement tokens seems like a good fit for builders," I said.

"I would recommend bringing a group of potential builders back to Augusta with you today. Having a builder here would give them more autonomy when you leave, and you don't need to pick up supplies in Pittsfield anymore," Vlad reminded me.

We talked some more while I got ready and packed my stuff. As soon as I got to the main room, I gave people an overview of the new class and asked for five volunteers to come to Augusta for testing. I told them it would likely be a week before they could return, and that there was a good chance none of them would qualify for a class.

"It's actually quite unlikely. If I had to guess, less than 2% of the general population will qualify, but you can improve the odds by sending people who would fit the idea of a builder based on skills or inclinations," Vlad said.

Dominic started complaining that it sounded like he was going to lose five of his best workers for a week, but I tuned him out as I checked in with Donna. There had been no changes or signs of a response from Portland. They were preparing to head back to Portland with a larger team in two snowmobiles as soon as I was back.

"Now for the other bonus. I can build two known structures here for free. I'm planning to add two more greenhouse complexes. That's food for over 900 people, so about the same as building 15 regular greenhouses. As they ramp up, that will give you a significant boost to food production here, and they add a little housing too," I said. "Then I'll use the rest of the resources from Bangor to pump up your water and power."

While the buildings were free, I still had to pay for the pods, but 20 tokens for two greenhouse complexes and four pods was well worth it. Next up were four more water towers. Finally, I had just enough work units for 12 more windmills.

"There you go," I said. "You've got surplus water and power for a few more buildings. If Klawock isn't researching ways to lower water and power usage, switch some pods to research and do that yourself if you can't get more towers out here. I don't want to do a long goodbye, as I hope to come back once more, but if I don't, it's been good working with you all. Portland is proving just how good it was that we came to help you first."

There was a brief round of goodbyes and thank-yous, but Andy kept it from dragging on. After I had one final check-in with the people back home, I made sure the people coming with me were secure in the sled and headed back to Augusta.

The trip back was always faster because I had my own trail to follow. The snow flurries were not enough to cover my tracks that quickly. We stopped briefly in Pittsfield so people could get out and take a break, since there was still firewood in the apartment. It was also where I recharged the snowmobile, even though I was not picking anything up.

When we got back, the portal bay was a hive of activity as people looked at maps, checked gear, and packed two sleds that had been pulled inside. I had multiple people trying to talk to me at once and had to shout to get them to let me talk.

"Hey, here's the plan. I'm going to go to the building sites and integrate the finished dorm and greenhouses. Our guests from Bangor will share one of the new four-person rooms. Then I'm going to come back here and start testing them and the people you have lined up for the new class while we make plans for the trip tomorrow. Don't forget they will be tested for all classes at once, so people being tested for the builder class will also be tested for the enforcer class. Unfortunately, people who have already been tested for enforcer have to be retested if they want to try to be a builder."

Surprisingly, that was enough to get everyone back to work and leave me alone, except for Donna, who said she was coming with Bryan and me so she could debrief me while I was integrating stuff. The one dorm and four greenhouses did not take long, even though I had to go farther and farther to get to them as the construction spread out.

There was not much new in Donna's debrief until she talked about the fallout from the fight itself.

"So, there are a couple of enforcers that are done being enforcers?" I asked her after she described their reaction to the shootout.

"At least for now. They could handle fighting golems and the occasional alien. Now that it's fighting other humans that may just be trying to survive, they aren't sure they can handle it."

"As I've said before, we don't want someone who does not want to be there fighting with us. Let's let them move to Bryan's team full-time. Their improved strength and ability to handle the cold will make them good workers for him. They can scavenge or work on building stuff," I said.

"I have been using them when I can for jobs, but having two of them working for me full-time will be great," Bryan said. "Once Portland is straightened out, it might make sense to give me more of them. Building, not fighting, will be the way forward then."

"We can discuss that then. We also have one of them, Tom, who might have the opposite problem. He's become more gung-ho and seems to enjoy the firefight," Donna said,

"That's far out of my realm of knowledge of how to address it. I guess watch him and ask O'Donnell for advice," I said. "I don't know how to handle that or what to watch for."

After confirming there was enough water and power for now, we left Bryan to finish making rounds and checking on his teams. At the same time, Donna and I returned to the bay to work on a strategy for the Portland trip.

"I know it's going to be annoying to have me walk over to the class pod every ten minutes," I said after getting the first scan started. "But I don't know how else I'll fit scanning in, and I really want to see what this class is all about."

"That's fine. I think we're all curious about it too," O'Donnell said. "For now, we need to make the plan for tomorrow. We don't know anything beyond the fact that they were here to attack and that they had a map of Augusta with routes to this park highlighted. Our best guess is that they wanted to take over by force and rule the whole area. I can't see why else they would have done this."

"And with no communication available, whoever they left in charge doesn't know what happened, if they even knew what was going on. We have to figure out who we can actually trust in that faction and try to get them building stuff, not plotting coup attempts," I said.

"We're also going to take some precautionary steps," O'Donnell added. "We're going to have a small additional team stationed at the base, with more patrols along the town's southern border."

"And full-time protection for the portal area," Donna added. "That will make everyone feel better."

"There's one other thing Vlad told me I could do," I offered. "The power grid at the base. It will be set to require the approval of whoever is in charge there for vehicles to be recharged. They took advantage of the fact that they just had to get in range of the base to recharge last time. This will limit their ability to make it here with a full sled. And for those wondering, yes, I can bypass the restrictions for myself and whoever I'm with."

"Snowmobiles are the other thing. We want to take a group of ten out there, so if you can fix the snowmobile that got shot up, we can take it back. Then, if you integrate the other one at the base, we can take three down and have two that will get us all back," Donna said.

I agreed to focus all the local maintenance pods on fixing the snowmobile so that it would be ready for the morning. After that, I ended the third scan and started the fourth. It was a welcome surprise when Sean had a 91% match with the builder class.

"This is great. I want to keep doing the scanning while the meeting is going on. Sean, when I start packing and getting ready for bed, we'll do the one-hour class process on you. If you still want it and don't mind sticking around tonight," I said.

"Dominic would hunt me down if I said no. Plus, being the first person to get this class would be cool. I've seen what you can do, and if I get perks to help build faster, it will help everyone. My family and I will get off half rations and stop being crowded on the floor of a greenhouse sooner," he said.

I started up the next scan and saw the benefit of having Sean and the others in Augusta. The casual way they talked about the situation back in Bangor had an even greater impact than if people had heard it over the communication device. It would be another boost to local morale to hear how much better off Augusta was.

With that taken care of, I went back to the meeting where we were planning out how to clean up the mess in Portland. Part of that was making a list of everyone we had interacted with and our individual impressions of them to get a sense of who might be worth working with.

The conversation was useful at the start, but as it went on, I started thinking about how to end it. As always, there was a point where it got too hypothetical to be useful. That is when Vlad spoke up.

"Not to complicate things further, but the weather is changing. There's a significant chance another storm is coming in," he said. "If you're going to Portland tomorrow, I advise you to leave early."

"Okay, so you have no idea how long it will last," I said after we questioned Vlad more. "So, either we leave Portland to spiral for who knows how long, or we risk being trapped there for who knows how long."

That decision dominated the conversation for the next hour. There were many opinions about what we should do and what was safest, but, as we had seen all night, there was a lack of information. We were guessing at the situation we would run into, so every course of action was a risk. Finally, I had to speak up and make a call for myself at least.

"I'm not making decisions for anyone else. We all know I have a get-out-of-jail-free card, but here's what I'm doing. As soon as the next scan is complete, I'll start the process to give Sean his class, and then I'll pack. I need Jason to be ready to feed the portal by six in the morning. I will be building some more windmills, as there's not much spare power capacity now, and then I'll be heading to Portland no later than 30 minutes after that. I can go by myself or haul a sled with people. It's up to all of you, but decide by morning. I need to get ready to head out again."

The timing with the class pod was just about perfect, and when I was done talking, I headed over to it and got Sean positioned there. I warned him there would likely be some pain, then spent the 100 tokens and started the process. No one else had qualified, but I saw the cost jump from 100 tokens to 200 tokens for the next builder.

"I hope it's 100 more each time, not double each time," I told Vlad as I headed back to my room to pack. Since I was not sure whether there would be a sled for my trip, I carried a backpack and some bags to place on the snowmobile.

By the time I had showered and packed, it was time to retrieve Sean from the class pod. He looked fine as he got out, and he was excited about the changes. He ran to the door to look at something and then returned, still excited. I did not even have to prompt him to share his sheet.

Sean Ward		**Age**	47
Class	Builder	**Sub-Class**	N/A
Perks	Form Materials L1	Convert Structure L1	
Debuffs			
Physical Score	11	**Mental Score**	8
Personal Tokens	0		
Personal Perks • Form Materials. Any non-living materials may be converted into materials needed for a structure that the builder is actively working on. The number of materials created depends on the material's complexity and perk level. Level 1. • Convert Structure. Any structure may be converted to an official nanostructure. The number of perk applications to achieve the conversion will vary based on the structure size, similarity to the nano blueprint, and perk level. Level 1			

"I've got an intuitive sense with both of them," he said. "When I looked at one of those custom dorms, I could tell it would take about 47 convert structure charges to convert it to a regular dorm. Until I level up, that's a lot, but it still seems like it could be useful. There will be no change to a structure until I've used enough charges on it, and others could help apply charges, too. For the form materials perk, I can look at something, and think about what materials I want, to see how much I can create."

"Once we know how your class gets personal tokens to level up, we'll know how to make it even stronger. It's not overpowered, but it will be useful. You can figure out a custom windmill blueprint, use form materials to create the hard-to-find parts to build it, then convert it to a normal windmill to get all the research bonuses," I said.

"This class will also be better at using the portal," Vlad said. "A person with no active class pays 400% of the base cost using it to build nano structures. Enforcers pay 200%, while builders pay just 150%. They're going to be in demand."

"Do I have to worry about people creating more of them and jacking up the costs to the point where I can't make more wherever I go?" I asked. That had not been an issue with enforcers, as there were basically no sources of spheres once I handled the alien threats.

"No, when you leave, the cost branches and travels with you. Once you move on to the next mission, their actions won't boost your class-granting costs. They will be on their own path," Vlad said. "When you reset the cost for enforcers here, that did not change it for Klawock, for instance."

"Okay, this has been some awesome news, and we'll find more people to grant this class to, but maybe after I leave," I said. "In the meantime, experiment with your skills and keep track of everything so we can figure out how you earn personal tokens to level up those perks. I am off to bed. Let me know in the morning if anyone is coming with me."

I knew I probably sounded rude, but I needed some sleep before heading to Portland the next day. I also knew I had to be ready for part of the trip to be made amid a storm. The council was still discussing what to do, and Donna shot me a pleading look as I left, but I couldn't bail her out. They needed to decide what to do without me weighing in.

I woke up when my alarm went off, but I was still tired and in a bad mood from lack of sleep. I needed to be more even-keeled to deal with Portland, and that was going to be hard with the upcoming trip. Vlad confirmed the storm was still moving in, but that I could probably make it to Portland before it got too bad. When I made it to the portal room, everyone from the night before was already gathered.

"We're going with you," Donna said. "Same plan as before, even with the storm coming. It just took everyone a long time to decide that."

"That's good to hear. I didn't want to go solo," I said. "I'm going to go build some windmills. It looks like the storm is coming, so people here might want to triple up again and move into the greenhouses if needed. If you triple up, you can fit half or more of the people here in nano housing."

There was no need to save resources, as I would not be building in Portland using Augusta's material units or work units. Any structures built with Augusta's resources would be on a different grid, and that was not worth it. With that in mind, I spent basically all the resources to add 13 windmills. It would give them a large buffer, and all the custom structures coming online would soon burn through the excess power.

As I added pods, I increased the number of people working on maintenance and work units. I also asked Vlad again whether we had to worry about the pod cap anytime soon, but he thought we could have at least 500 active. Between Augusta and Bangor, the pods associated with that portal were only about to hit 400.

My other purchase was another communication device. We were taking the one I had bought for Portland back to them, but we needed one for the expeditions to carry while traveling. I gave the second one to Donna for the trip, and then we got ready to head out. Donna and I were riding in the sleds on the way to the base, and then we would drive for the rest of the trip. We had talked about sending the nano car as well, so some people could sleep, but we did not want to waste it for that alone. It was needed in Augusta to move people around in preparation for the storm.

With one last round of advice from O'Donnell, we headed to the base. About halfway there, the snow and wind picked up, but Vlad said the snow would end soon, and then it would just get colder and colder. I was not sure whether the cold was better than snow, but it would make navigating easier.

When we got to the base, we just stopped long enough for me to integrate and fix the other snowmobile by spending 127 more tokens. Once that was done, Wendy and Tom got out of the sleds and rode it as a two-seater. We wanted to lighten the load in the sleds as much as possible.

In total, it was just a 20-minute stop, and then we were on the way. The snowfall was slowing, but the cold was getting much worse, and we needed to keep moving to reach Portland before it got too cold.

26

The cold was getting so bad that it was bothering even me during the last hour of the ride into Portland. At least we did not run into any golems on the way in, and there were no signs of humans other than smoke rising in different parts of the city. We briefly discussed options and decided to start at the building near Payson Park. It was on our way, and if they were still on their own, I could at least get them some power for heat. We thought about grabbing the food cache for them, but the sled was already loaded down.

There were no guards this time. The few people we could see seemed to be trying to get supplies to stay warm. Once they saw the snowmobiles, there was a moment of fright until they realized it was us. If they feared snowmobiles, that meant the people who attacked us probably gave them trouble, too.

"I'm glad you all came back. Those thugs you left in charge threatened us after you left, but did not help us at all," Aaron, their spokesman, said once we were inside.

"Yeah, well, they came north and tried to attack us. They won't be causing problems again. We're on our way there to straighten things out, but I wanted to check on you on the way," I said as I focused on accessing the Portland portal, not the Augusta one. I wanted this construction to be part of their grid.

The sight of a windmill forming right next to the main apartment building, where most people were gathered, was enough to stop everyone who was dragging stuff inside to burn.

"This won't solve all your problems, but you can hook power cords to the windmill and power stuff in here if you dig up pre-event heaters that are still working. In the future, nanostructures within the windmill's range can use this for power. I'm also leaving you half the food I can generate today. We'll check in when we can." I said.

Giving them a source of power earned us enough goodwill to offset the threats from Davis's team. We answered a few more questions and promised we would give them an update when we left the city. Then we headed off for the real challenge of this trip. I wanted to be at the portal to see what we were working with before things got too cold.

As we got to the buildings I had constructed last time, I was happy to see they were still standing. It even looked as if people had collected materials to start construction. There were still a woefully small number of buildings for the cold that was already here and getting worse. Still, we needed to confirm what was going on before I started building. I was not going to throw up buildings without knowing who was in charge.

People here took longer to notice us, but when they did, they seemed excited. No one came to talk to us, but there was waving and people running into buildings, which we assumed was to let others know we were here. There was no sign of hostility or weapons as we approached the portal building. A group came out of the dorm and met us inside the portal bay. There was a bit of shuffling around before one of them spoke up.

"I'm not sure you remember me. I'm Karen," she said. "I was in the background when you were here last, but when those idiots left to attack you all and did not come back, we hoped for the best. I'm the head of the new council that replaced them. Since you're alive and have their snowmobile, I guess you captured them."

"They tried to attack us," Donna said. "It didn't work out well for them, and they're all dead, so at least they won't be a problem in the future. We are here to figure out what to do with all of you. The timing to address this is horrible with this storm moving in, but I guess it's always a bad time to kill people you were trying to help."

"Fair enough. The only people who will care they are gone are their family members and some friends," Karen said. "I was in most of the meetings you had with that crew, so I passed on what you had said to the council. We've actually been following the requests you made for how to organize things and want to work with you, for real, now that Davis and his friends are dead."

"We have time to sit down and talk. Since there seems to be some reliable leadership in place, Devin is going to do what he can to get you ready for this storm," Donna said. "He'll need some people to feed more stuff into the portal now that he's here, and his perk boost increases its output."

I took that as my sign to get started and told them how much to feed the portal and how many points to leave free for remote usage. Then I headed outside to start building what I could. While there needed to be a balance on what was built, the only food-producing building would be another barn. I checked, and they needed more room for animals. I wanted to keep as many of those alive as possible through the cold snap. Other than that, it was all about getting more beds and extending power and water to the downtown building, where we knew a lot of people were stashed.

The three apartment blocks and the barn I built appeared in their customary shower of light. Then I ducked back inside and told Karen and Donna I needed someone to relocate people into the new buildings.

"Get a couple of people who can organize waves of people. We can start with your main building or anyone else who will have trouble with the cold," Donna told Karen. "My people can use the snowmobiles and sleds to move people out here. Devin, how much did you build?"

"Three apartment blocks, so room for 330 people at standard density. Given the way things are, we should move in at triple density and put people in the new barn as well. Plan for 1,000 people moving into these buildings. Oh, and you can have two of the snowmobiles to use for that right now. I need one for a little longer to place the water towers on the route to the other building, and then the windmills. When I get back, let me know if I need to place windmills near other groups of people as we did near the park."

It turned out I had to place six more windmills and two more water towers to ensure there would be enough resources for the already-constructed buildings. That also left some water and a noticeable amount of power left over for legacy buildings. There was enough of everything left to add one more apartment block if needed, but that depended on how many people we could safely move and if I needed to build more windmills.

The new infrastructure buildings were enough to clear the snow halfway to the downtown apartment and get power close enough to hook them up without long runs of power lines. With all that taken care of, I went into the apartment building to explain how they could hook up to the power to help with the heat, then picked up some people who were ready to move into the new buildings. Despite people there trying to keep things organized, there was a lot of confusion. People were worried about what was going on, but they seemed to follow the people in charge.

"Do I need to head back out?" I asked Donna as soon as I was back in the portal room.

"I've got a map from Karen here. There are three concentrations of people who could use a windmill. The second one should get two windmills. Also, can you add one or two more clinics here?"

"Yes, I'll build the clinics now and then head out to these places," I said. "As long as Vlad can read the map, I'll be able to get there. That will come close to tapping us out on building resources, though."

"It's down to negative 70, even with the sleds being enclosed and people using everything they can to heat them, I'm not sure we can keep moving people, so we'd be wasting resources to build more anyway," Karen said. "We've not even filled the current buildings."

"These are loans," I said as I checked my resources, deciding I could spare the settlement tokens for once, and created two nano heaters. "These can each keep a sled tolerable for the trips. Once you've finished moving people, they can supplement heating in any building on the grid. It will not do a ton in a large space, but it will help. Now I'm going to build this stuff you requested and get back here before it gets too cold."

I built two medical clinics, then headed out to build windmills for the various population groups identified for me. That took longer than planned because I had to stop and talk to people to explain how things worked. At least Karen had sent people out to talk to these groups after Davis and his group had left, so I did not have to start my story from scratch. The three buildings I helped with were all positioned so that it was easy to set up a windmill nearby, making it simple to run power to them. I also had Vlad make sure I did not get lost while maneuvering around the city. There were many abandoned cars everywhere, which made travel harder. They were definitely going to be fed into a portal at some point.

With that done, I headed back inside to get warm and figure out what Donna and Karen had worked out. They seemed to be collaborating well, but the mission I had received for Portland had not yet been updated, so there were still things to work through.

"Devin, can you take the two heaters back to the apartment building?" Donna asked before I could take off all my gear. "The temperature is dropping so low we can't transport people even with the heaters, but we want them there. You should be able to handle the return in the cold."

I really wanted to say no, but even if the portable heaters were limited in how much they could help, they were a better use of power than legacy heaters. "Okay, but then I am staying inside," I said as I bundled back up. "Vlad said we are getting near negative 80 degrees. I can't handle too much out there after a long day."

I dropped the heaters off and glimpsed how they were trying to stay warm. These temperatures were far below freezing, and I was worried about everyone. I also knew that the people still alive had figured out how to survive at least to some extent. I hoped the temperatures would stabilize when the sun came up, so they would not get any colder. It was so cold that there was no cloud cover, so at least the sunlight would bring some warmth in the morning.

This time, when I returned, no one asked me to go back out. Instead, they called me over to review what had been discussed.

"As I detailed with Donna, I don't think Davis ever intended to help the other groups in the city, but he used your arrival as an excuse to get a census of people," Karen said. "The known large concentrations are on this map with details we know. There are a lot more small groups, but it gave us a start for passing out information and bringing people in. All the locations marked with a star we contacted after Davis left. I've given Donna an overview of their reactions. We need to build more structures, but it sounds like we still need to wait for some instructors from Augusta to start construction. While waiting, we're collecting supplies when it's not too cold."

"There's a good plan in place for how to move things forward and create a few pockets of construction in the city. It will allow them to make use of open space and let there be a few independent groups all under the same umbrella," Donna said. "I think it can work. I agree with Karen that we need to leave some of our people here as guards. It will keep us up to date on what's happening and give Karen's newly formed council more weight."

"That's the sort of decision you all need to make," I said. "For what it's worth, though, I think it's a good idea."

There was not much for me to weigh in on after that. Donna managed the discussions. She was taking charge, and I was mainly kept informed, with occasional requests for input. I raised the point that they should plan to have a builder in the city and consider having one created locally when I left.

"Since the increase in cost splits with each new city, if I am not around, waiting for me to leave makes sense. One has already been created in Augusta, so if you create your own class portal with me here, your starting cost will be 200 tokens; if you wait until I leave and start from scratch, it will be 100 tokens for the first one in Portland. I carry the increasing cost with me to each new settlement," I said. "At least I get missions that will reset the cost, so it balances out."

I sat around and gave more input as two enforcers and one of the guards from Augusta were selected to stay in the town. They would get one nano pistol and one nano inhibitor. The plan was for them to be in charge of protecting the council from any of Davis's buddies who might be hiding and waiting for revenge.

As the conversation was winding down, Vlad alerted me to check my notifications, and the mission for Portland had updated, so I shared it with everyone.

Mission Assigned: Portland

Portland has splintered and is failing. Empower the primary faction to bring the city together and survive while upholding your moral code. Persuasion will hone your skill for future missions. This mission is secondary to the Augusta Settlement Mission. Success criteria

- All factions united
- Completed: Single viable plan for the future
- Completed: Primary faction is an ally to Augusta

"Is anyone else disturbed that this nano controller is monitoring things closely enough that it could mark those two criteria complete?" Donna asked.

I had been thinking the same thing, so I nodded along and looked at Vlad. "Want to explain that, buddy, and explain why the mission did not tell us to put Karen in charge from the start?"

"The nano controller is collecting some information through me. It is not yet able to accurately predict human actions, so missions are created using best guesses. I assume it thought Davis would be an issue, but did not know that until he acted as he did," Vlad said. "It would not want to accuse people based on incomplete modeling and data."

"So now I have to worry about this AI nano controller figuring humans out and taking over? I think I'll ignore that, or I won't sleep at all," I said, noticing a nod from Donna and a horrified look on Karen's face.

"There are nano controllers on all advanced worlds, and that's not a problem. It will become more accurate with its predictions and will use that to improve how it supports you, but free will is always respected. At most, it will refine missions to guide you to decide the best path," Vlad answered, getting that slightly huffy tone that signaled he felt attacked.

"Okay, seeing as I'd be dead along with everyone I knew without you, we'll call that a good thing," I said. "I am wiped out. Is there anything else we have to do tonight, and is there a room assigned for us?"

"It turned out that just about 500 people had been moved over before it got too cold, so the team from Augusta had a three-bedroom apartment assigned just to us. That was still three or four people per room, but it gave us privacy and security as a group. I took a super brief shower and had two ration bars to replace all the calories I burned in the cold, then fell asleep as soon as I crawled under the covers. The internal temperature was around 48 degrees to save power, but there were plenty of blankets, so I did not mind.

I had not set my alarm the night before, but I still woke up around seven the following morning. All the other beds were full, and it was still chilly inside. When I checked with Vlad, the sun was out, and the temperature had climbed to almost negative 70 degrees. A check of the settlement information showed the batteries at zero and all the power being used as fast as it was created.

I got out of bed and quickly added a few layers of clothes now that I was out from under the covers. As soon as I left the room, people were waiting for me.

"Good, you're up," Donna said. "I know the trips you were making outside took it out of you, but the temperature is barely high enough to start moving more people. We were hoping you could go pick up the heaters and build some more windmills."

"It's still pretty cold, according to Vlad, but I can do that after I get some food. I would suggest using a single, well-insulated sled with both heaters now. Let's see if some people in the smaller groups want to evacuate before we focus on the larger groups again. Oh, and rotate out a different enforcer for each trip," I suggested. "It's cold in the driver's seat of those snowmobiles."

I also asked her to make sure the portal was fed, and I would use the remaining processing points remotely. Even though it was still bitterly cold when I went outside, it felt better in the sun. I hooked up a sled and went to pick up some people. That turned into a small fight when I got there. The people who had the heaters did not want to give them up. I thought it was going to get awkward, but the other residents solved the issue for me. They knew if they kept the heaters, no one would get a ride to the nano houses. That created enough peer pressure to get the heaters turned over to me and to crowd the first family of six, with the bare essentials, into the sled with the heaters.

As soon as I dropped them off, I collected resources from the local pods, then went into the portal room to warm up before heading out to build more stuff. While I was warming up, I received an impassioned plea for another clinic and to link them together somehow. I promised to look into it once I was ready to start building again.

I started by looking at the clinics. I had bunched three of them near the bay with the processing portal. It was really too cold to walk between them, and I spent a minute planning the layout to maximize space. I also had to pull up the blueprint information on walkways, since I had not thought about them in a while.

Sealed Walkway

- Unlock 5 tokens, purchase 1 token
- 10 material units, 10 work units
- Ten-foot sealed walkway
- No weather effects or wind if ends are connected and doors are closed
- Power required 0-10 power units
- Safe for limited exposure to -50 degrees base, -100 degrees at full power

With just 90 feet of walkway, I could connect the three clinics to one of the apartment blocks and the portal bay. That would let people get around more easily. Nine enclosed walkway segments later, I had the buildings connected with room for another clinic. That clinic would address cold-related issues, then transition to general issues when the temperature warmed back up.

Even though we were having problems moving people in this cold, I decided to build a final apartment block for this trip. They needed the space for people in the long term, and if this cold held on, they would need to keep moving people. After that, it was a matter of building more windmills.

I built one more by the apartment building downtown to give them more options to plug in, then went back to warm up before starting a line of windmills toward the next-largest concentration of people. There was a park on the way, and I wanted people all on the same grid as soon as possible. The four windmills I could afford in that direction were not enough to link everything up, so I built three toward that group to feed the main grid, and one near the other building to feed their grid until everything was linked up.

On my way back, there were not enough material units to build anything large. Instead, I extended the sealed walkway to link two more apartment blocks to the rest of what I had already connected. I really needed to talk to Bryan and Dominic about starting those in Augusta and Bangor as well.

By the time I made it back inside the bay, one whole side of it had been turned into a planning area, complete with a full map of the city that looked like it had been projected and traced to fill a whole wall.

"Perfect, you're here," Donna said to Vlad. "Can you come point out the locations of windmills and water towers so we can start planning out where Devin needs to build and what we need to link areas up and reach the other parks?"

It looked like they just needed Vlad's help, so I sat down off to the side and reviewed the information about the town and relaxed without falling asleep. I was watching Vlad point to spots on the map while Donna marked them with different-colored markers when there was a bang at the door. A person, so bundled up in clothes that they were impossible to identify, fell through the door as soon as it was opened.

"We need help," he said. "The fires can't keep up at our building, and we're freezing. We need some help."

Karen got the information on where he was from, and the medical team hustled him off to a medical pod. He had hypothermia and frostbite that needed immediate treatment.

"It looks like this is a house within range of the newer windmills you put up," Vlad called out from the map. "You might be able to run power to them or take one of the heaters over to help out."

"I'll see what I can do. I can't build anything else today with the material units all used up," I said. "I'll get another heater to keep me warm and to give to them if I can't get them connected to power. I don't want to slow down the evacuation by taking one of the other heaters, and it sounds like there are fewer than 20 people at this house, so there's probably not much space to heat.

It took me a few minutes to get bundled up and figure out how to place the heater on my lap to take the edge off the cold. It was somewhat wasteful, but if I was going to be stringing up legacy power lines, I needed a way to keep from freezing.

Vlad directed me towards the building, and I tracked the distance from the windmill to the house. There was no way I was getting power lines put in to connect stuff, and it was too cold for anyone else to do it.

"It looks like it's the heater or evacuating them," I said to Vlad. I was glad he did not really need to hear, so that I could talk into my mask. I could also hear him even with my ears covered in layers.

"At least there are still some fires burning," Vlad said as we got closer. "I can see two working chimneys, so it can't be that bad."

I pulled up, saw someone peeking through the heavily insulated window, then the outer door opened, and I was waved in. I grabbed the heater and came into the entryway. As with most houses still in use, there was a multi-step process to get inside to save heat. The enclosed porch had been sealed off from the wind, and then the entryway had been cut in half with thick hanging blankets. That provided another barrier before you opened the door to the heated space.

Vlad was double-checking the power lines to see what could be used, so I had no warning when I followed the woman who had let me in through the door into the main space and saw four guys with guns holding a tied-up family hostage.

"I'm so sorry," the teenage girl who had led me in said. "I had to do it, or they were going to kill my little sister."

"Shut up and get in the corner," the guy who was acting like he was in charge said, waving his gun around. "Now, as for you, mister friends with aliens. If you're here, then Davis is dead. I told him attacking your base was stupid, but now I have lured you here, where we have the upper hand. We're going to tie you up just like them. Then we are going to take that fancy heater and vehicle and kill everyone who gets in our way. I'm sure there's enough stuff built by now for us and a chosen few to live out the apocalypse in style."

"If you behave, we might not put out the fires before we leave," one of the other guys laughed. It was clear they planned on killing all of us.

"You think you can fool my friends? They'll know something's wrong when I'm not driving," I said. That started an argument about whether they could outsmart my team. I did not care about the argument. I was buying time for Vlad to make sure it was just these four I was facing. As soon as he confirmed it, I used four charges of incapacitate criminal to freeze all four of them. I had been worried it would not work on them, but taking all the people around you hostage seemed to make them sufficiently seen as criminals. I was glad I did not have to go with plan B. That was getting shot, using my healing perk to survive, and getting a gun I could turn on them.

I just had five minutes before they unfroze, and I used that to disarm them all. They could not even move to talk. They could make noise out of their mouths, but they could not shape their lips to make actual words. The noises they could make sounded pissed enough. With that done, I started untying the hostages. That about used up my incapacitate time, and I used another round of the perk on the hostage takers. I asked the two guys who looked like they had some muscle to help me tie them up and get them into the entryway.

"What are you doing with them?" one guy asked while doing what I asked.

"They're going outside," I said once I was sure none of the kids could hear me.

"You're going to kill them?"

"There's no choice. I'm not going to tie them up and keep them fed. They almost killed whoever it was they sent to bait this trap, and they were going to leave all of us to freeze to death."

The people we were carrying tried to yell for help, but we ignored their grunts. "You'd better all go back inside. Keep the fires going and turn up the heater I brought in. I'll be back in a few minutes," I said.

It looked like the guy who had protested might argue, but his friend pulled him back inside and closed the door behind him. I was running out of time, so I pulled the first guy out onto the porch. Then I tossed him to the side where the snow would not insulate him, and he would feel the wind. My improved physical score made things like this possible. I could not have done it that quickly before. By the time I was bringing out the third guy, the first one had stopped moving. Between their lack of cold-weather gear and movement, they would not last long. With the wind chill, it was negative 110 degrees.

This whole situation was brutal, but I was not sure what else I could do. Even being disarmed, all four of them were in good shape. I did not see another choice unless I wanted to shoot them while they were frozen.

As much as this made me sick to my stomach, I was not going to risk those kids dying because I was trying to be the nice guy. I had to use one more incapacitate charge on the last guy to make sure I could get him outside before he started moving.

"Vlad, warn me if they get up, and let me know when they are dead," I said, turning back to the porch before twisting to the side and pulling my face covering free just in time to dry heave. The shock of the cold stopped that quickly, and then I headed inside.

When I got back inside, everyone seemed shell-shocked, but they had listened to me, and the heater was blasting. The room was at least slightly warmer, but everyone still looked stressed out. I generated ration bars for all of them to eat before grabbing one for myself and biting into it after rinsing my mouth out with some water. I wanted everyone to have more time to process everything and avoid going into shock.

I went to speak, but was immediately interrupted by one of the little kids. "Is Chad okay?" they asked.

"If he's the one they sent to get me here, then yes," I said. "He was pretty cold when he got to us, but we have medical pods that can heal anything, and we got him in one right away. Now we have to decide what to do here. Vlad, any estimate on how much longer this cold snap will last?"

"Sorry, no," he said, sticking his head through the wall for a second. "It could end tonight, or it could be a week."

"With that in mind, I think we should try to get you all back to the main camp, where there are buildings that can handle this cold. I think if I back the sled up to the porch, we can get all of you in there safely. If we fit all eight of you around the heater, it should be okay. It uses nanotechnology, and the surface does not get hot, so you'll be able to push up against it," I said. "The only thing is you can't take much. A few small backpacks in the sled, and I'll wear one with more stuff you absolutely need. You can come back here when it's not as cold and get the rest of your stuff. The other option is I leave you here with the heater, and we hope it's enough for however long this storm lasts."

The discussion did not take long. All the people in the building were ready to be somewhere where they were not at risk of dying from the cold because of a single mistake. They also wanted to see Chad and be there when he woke up. Once a decision was made, everyone started bundling up while I set up the sled. It was one of the ones they had been using to move people, so it was covered and as insulated as they could make it. I also positioned it so that the kids would not see the four bodies as they got in.

Once they were about ready, I moved the heater into the sled to take the edge off the cold. Then it was a coordinated effort to put out the fires and get everyone into the sled as quickly as possible. Once they were all aboard, we headed back to the park as fast as I could go while carrying eight people in the sled.

27

Vlad was hovering in the sled, keeping me updated on how everyone was doing on the trip back. I wished I had the second communication device to let Donna know what was happening, but it was with the apartment block in case there was an emergency there. I knew the people inside the sled were cold, and I was feeling it too without the heater.

As soon as we got close enough to the portal, Vlad phased inside to get help. I was off the snowmobile and pushing the sled up to the door as soon as I could. If there had not been kids listening, I might have let a few swear words out from the cold. The fact that I was worried about swearing in front of them, not about basically executing criminals in front of them, seemed like a reflection of the world we found ourselves in.

Once we were all inside, a few people with medical training checked everyone over while I filled them in on the details of what had happened.

"I knew there was one more group of Davis's friends out there that I warned Donna about," Karen said. "That must have been them, so I feel a lot better about actual threats now. I never thought they would go that far, though."

"I'm hoping that's it for excitement," I said. "I'm heading to the team's room in the apartment after I make sure that the families are okay, and after I generate the rest of the rations for the day. It's only the afternoon, and I'm already wiped out."

"Just show people how you used the heater to stay warm while driving, please," Donna said. "We're still moving people around, but even swapping out drivers is not enough to fight the cold."

I showed people how I used it to fight the worst of the cold and headed back to my room. There was not much left for me to do, with no material units, and the cold holding steady. I used the time to catch a nap, then just talked to the people hanging out in the apartment's common areas. Everyone seemed happy that Davis was gone, and no one had any problems with Karen, aside from the usual complaints you might hear about anyone in charge.

As usual, there were plenty of questions for Vlad and me. People seemed to understand what it would take to stay alive and were not shying away from the idea of working. Many of the questions were about what they could do to speed things up and improve their chances of survival. It was a relief to see people trying to be proactive, and I said so.

"It's a relief for us too. Other than scavenging, which we all knew was only delaying the end, there's been nothing we could do," one of the people I was talking to said. "At least now we can help build homes that will survive and get some greenhouses going. How soon can we get people out here to show us what to do?"

I told them the plan was to send people out the day after it was safe for us to travel home. Once we got back to Augusta, one or more of the snowmobiles would turn around and bring out the construction trainers for them. When the conversation died down, I headed to the next apartment to talk to people again. I wanted to gauge the mood in town, and I could do that while Donna was making plans with Karen.

When we reconvened that evening, the map on the wall was covered in even more notes, but Donna looked satisfied.

"I think we have a plan," she said. "Working with a group that wants to get stuff done here is nice. It will not be easy, but I think we can make it work. We need to get people out here to help their teams start building, though."

"The bad news is that I checked with Vlad, and there's no sign this storm is dying down. He can't find a pattern to project the storm, so the end could be tonight or next week," I said. "I'm thinking of designating you or Wendy as the one who can use this portal as well, so you can adjust pod use. I'll still try to get back to purchase the cheapest buildings before I leave."

"That's great, but we are stuck here, and the building trainers are stuck there," she answered.

"That's the other thing. If it's not safe to head out tomorrow, I'll buy another car. That can make the trip without us freezing. If it's too cold, I might have to build a windmill to recharge, but six of us can get back. Then it can be used to transport people between the settlements. With it getting colder all the time, we should shift the snowmobiles' usage to transporting materials and using cars to move people," I said.

"I heard about that builder class," Karen said. "Can we start selecting people to get tested for it?"

"The class pod is fairly cheap, and you're going to need one here," I said. "You can buy it after I leave, so we won't waste two day-long trips moving people back and forth," I said. "You'll just need to wait to start scanning people until there's excess power, and I need you to wait to buy it or to grant the class until after I leave."

The wind was even worse overnight, and the storm was clearly not letting up. When morning rolled around, I bought the nano vehicle for 500 tokens before the sun was even up. That way, I could let the team here take it to move people around for a few hours before we headed out. I had breakfast and made sure the portal capacity was all used, then decided what I needed to build before I left. I also swapped most of the pods to maintenance and tokens.

In the end, I built three more windmills. They were enough to link the grid up to that other apartment complex. There was way more power than was needed for the nano buildings, but it was still being drained for legacy systems.

Then it was time for one last meeting before we headed home. They had set up a projector, so I started by projecting the exact text of the Portland mission for everyone to see.

Mission Assigned: Portland

Portland has splintered and is failing. Empower the primary faction to bring the city together and survive while upholding your moral code. Persuasion will hone your skill for future missions. This mission is secondary to the Augusta Settlement Mission. Success criteria

- All factions united
- Completed: Single viable plan for the future
- Completed: Primary faction is an ally to Augusta

"Once the weather clears up, this should be easy enough to finish. Even before that, after the car returns and we can get around safely, it might be enough to finish uniting the town," Karen said. "It sounds like there will be a reward that will either help us directly or indirectly through you, correct?"

"So far that's how it's been," I said. "I'm not sure how much longer I'll be here, but if it's finished in the next week, that timing would be perfect. Now, here's the status of Portland right now. It still looks bad, but everyone should know where you are, so you can understand what needs to be done. As far as we can tell, this is just based on the actual city, not the metro area."

I displayed the settlement sheet on the screen next. I did not mention that the population count had dropped by 1,500 since the last time I was here. Between that and the construction, food and heat reserves had actually gone up.

Portland Settlement		**Population**	20,478
Food Supply	92 days	**Heat Supply**	37 days
Housing	76,197 people	**Survivable Housing**	590 people
Food Production	30%	**Secure Food Production**	1%
Power Production	100- 5,380 units	**Power Draw**	909- 4,191 units
Power Storage	113/ 2,640 units	**Indoor Pod Slots**	82/ 83
Water Production	1,100 units	**Water Draw**	780 units
Work Units	3,990 units	**Material Units**	45 units
Research Units	0 units		
Production Structures	Processing Portal	Work Pods x 82	Large Windmill x 24
Large Water Tower x 4	Large Barn x 2		
Enhanced Structures	Large Crafting Bay x 1	Dorm x 5	Apartment Block x 4
Medical Clinic x 4	Medical Pods x 8		
Deferred Maintenance	63 units	**Material Maintenance**	35 units

"You've got a surprising supply of food and legacy food production," I said. "That gives you time to build a lot of greenhouses and maybe more barns as you breed animals. Just keep using that portal to collect material units. Also, remember that after I leave for my next mission, whoever is in charge of the portal will get the settlement tokens and add them to their sheet. Keep that in mind for collecting them to integrate buildings when that starts."

As much as she wanted to get home, Donna was staying here, but I was taking five of our team back with me. We packed up, and I grabbed the second communication unit. The car would turn around the next day to bring back the builders and the communication device. That way, Donna would have one for her trip home.

The trip was far nicer in the enclosed, heated car, even if I did not keep it as warm as I would have liked to save power. We stopped by the same apartment on the way out of town to update them on the news and pass out my daily allotment of ration bars. A few people knew Karen, and there was a consensus that they could work with her once the weather cleared.

When we stopped at the former alien base, there were 29 more pods to recycle. That was a nice boost to tokens and material units, but the completion of the mission to cure everyone seemed a long way off. Not that it would speed up the mission completion much in the long run, but I used most of my healing charges on the person slated to be moved to the next open medical pod. That would save some time.

The overall visit was not long. We wanted to get back before it was too late. We just made sure everything was good before we continued our trip to Augusta. There was still no snow, but the wind was enough to cause problems and slow us down so we would not tip over. The normal tracks were all covered as well, thanks to the snow, and I was making use of Vlad's navigation basically the whole trip.

We checked in with O'Donnell and Donna on the radio frequently, as both locations wanted to know where we were and how we were doing. That meant they were waiting for us as soon as we showed up, even though it was getting dark by the time we made it back.

"We're doing some building integrations before all the boring meetings start," Bryan said as he stuck his head in the door as soon as the car came to a stop. "The rest of you can get out while Devin and I do this. We have some of the buildings completed despite the storm, but the next round will be delayed. We'll need some more water and power built too as soon as these are added."

"We might not need as much water and power as you think," I said as he got in the car and everyone else got out. "Eight levels of improved building efficiency have been researched for the custom houses while I was gone. That's another 8% reduction in water and power usage for them. It's going to cost 504 tokens to buy the upgrades, but it will pay for itself in the long run."

I made a larger loop of the area to upgrade the existing custom houses while integrating the three new houses and four greenhouses that had been finished while I was away. I followed that integration up with two more water towers and five more windmills.

"Well, there goes over 1,000 tokens and most of our material units," I said when we were all done. "Great work on getting stuff finished even in the cold. Do you already have a team picked out to go train the building crews in Portland?"

"They are getting all packed and leaving in the morning. I think the four of them are fighting over who gets to drive this thing," Bryan said. "From everything I've heard in the meetings, they're going to have their work cut out for them when they get there.

"The drive is not all that fun in the wind, but they can take turns or something. As for the work, once they are there, they have a lot of materials stacked up, so I think they'll get a good start on building. They also have groups of motivated people who want to get more built quickly. Everyone there knows they need to build fast, and no one messes with Karen down there," I said before we wrapped up the building and upgrading, then headed inside.

"I was telling Bryan, I think it's time we started building some enclosed walkways to connect buildings here," I said before anyone else around the meeting table could start talking. "The designs I brought are far more energy efficient than the ones I can build using the blueprints. I'd rather get ahead of the problem here and not build on the fly like I had to down in Portland. This is the one case where the custom-built stuff is flat-out better all around."

Bryan started talking about the benefits of connecting

buildings and how he wanted to do segments to connect building clusters while also leaving paths for vehicles between the clusters. The conversation quickly spiraled into planning the walkways and deciding what to prioritize.

The discussion went on for almost 15 minutes before Erin stepped in. “We can plan that later. What many people here want to know is what your plans are. It seems like things are moving along quickly, and you keep mentioning leaving. What’s the updated plan, and how long do we have left?”

That question made the entire room go still. Even the people sitting and standing around us, listening in, fell silent at that question. They had been watching me recreate their world, and even the people who had not left Augusta knew how much I was doing for the surrounding towns as well as them.

“Right now, I think one more trip to Bangor to build them a few more things, then a final trip to Portland. After that, it will be time to go,” I said. “I’ve been here for over two months now, and it’s just getting colder. Pretty much every piece of legacy equipment has stopped working at this point, so everywhere without nanotechnology is going to get worse fast. Plus, we need to get housing here to at least 20% of the population, so that's about 700 more beds. I’m going to have to take a marginal rating on the main quest again if I want to get moving.”

“I know you want better scores, but this is not supposed to be easy,” Vlad said. “If you can hit the marginal success and move on with plenty of resources, take the win.”

“Speaking of that, I also need to save up as many settlement tokens as I can. I know that hurts you all a bit, but it will help the next place I end up. I’m still building and integrating structures, but I won’t make any more purchases using settlement tokens unless it’s an emergency. Finally, I’d like to do one more rescue mission. More levels for the material unit token I can take to the next mission would be perfect.”

“Well, that’s easy enough. We’re going to Belgrade next,” Bryan said. “They’re small, but they have a lumber company I want to acquire supplies from. It sounds like I still won’t get my truck, but we’ll make do until you leave. Anyway, they had a little over 3,000 people when this all started, so it’s the right size to save. We planned to travel there as soon as the storm let up enough to make it safely."

I checked with Vlad, but he still had no update on the storm. The pattern did not match prior storms, so he was at a loss. "It doesn't seem to be getting worse, so it should start slowing down, but I'm not sure how quickly that will happen or how long it will take," he said when I asked for more details.

After that, we completed the plans for Portland. The new car would take a group there and then would return, picking up people who had been cured at the base. Other than the person driving the car on the way back, the other enforcers and guards from Augusta would stay there until the weather cleared enough to use the snowmobile to bring back the people who were not staying as guards long-term.

With all that taken care of, we moved on to talking in more detail about what I needed before I left. I wanted to review all the written guides I planned to take with me as soon as they were done. In addition to the technical documentation, I asked all the council members to write letters offering advice to the people in charge wherever I was sent next.

Around noon the following day, Vlad announced the storm was tapering off. It was still cold, so we decided to wait until the following day to make the trip to Belgrade. The team had headed to Portland in the morning, and the other car had been used for some errands around Augusta. We could have made the trip in the car, but Bryan wanted the two snowmobiles to bring back supplies as well. Now that the weather was changing, we commandeered everything for the trip to Belgrade the next day.

The storm wound down rapidly, and by early evening, the wind had died, and temperatures were back up to negative 40. With the confirmation that the storm was over, we received updated building completion times from Bangor. Their timelines were three days behind because of the storm, and they needed another five days before they would be ready for me.

Given the rescheduling, we planned to visit Belgrade the next day. With any luck, we could trigger the mission and evacuate them quickly using both nano cars once the one from Portland was back. I had to tell Bryan no on the truck once again.

"The amount I will spend on integrating and upgrading buildings takes all the spare tokens I have," I said when he glared at me after I told him he was not getting his truck. "Once I'm gone, you'll have plenty. You will need to start working on research, though, too."

"I get it. I'm not happy about it, but I know why you have to do it. I've seen the charts someone on Erin's team did about how much the tokens you brought to upgrade the portal helped us," Bryan said. "Just don't stop integrating the buildings we are working on."

"Maybe right at the end you'll have to wait a few days, but no more," I promised.

My other project was to continue packing for my departure. I had to repack things every time I added something. I was also keeping things modular in case I could take more or less than this mission.

The trip to Belgrade the next day included the car and two snowmobiles. The temperature had spiked overnight and was just a little below negative 25 after the sun came out. So, it was perfect weather for the trip. It was warmer than normal after the storm moved through. We let Bryan drive the car on this trip. He wanted to check out the lumber mill and organize what needed to be brought back, as they had capacity.

The lumber mill was on the way to the town, so we stopped on the way into town to give him a chance to look it over. I hopped into the warm car while I had the chance. I could tell he was excited about the supplies. He came over again to ask about the truck, and I had to tell him no. Once his inspection was complete, we headed onward and found this town in about the same shape as the other small towns like it. These towns all seemed to have only a few hundred survivors left hanging on.

The difference this time was that they were living in individual houses, as indicated by the smoke we could see. The school looked as if they had tried to use it, but there was no smoke coming from it, so there was no way anyone was inside.

It was clear that there had been some efforts to insulate the school before the vehicles and the fuel stopped working. Dirt had been pushed against the walls for natural insulation, and some construction to improve insulation was visible. It had clearly not stayed warm enough, though, and people were clustered in houses all around the school. With multiple houses to pick from, we selected one and went to knock on the door. It looked as if they had used the lumber mill supplies to improve all of them, and a few had flashed up as possibilities for conversion into nano houses.

I would let Erin and the council know about the houses for the future, but I planned to ignore their conversion potential for now. I was not setting up a small enclave with its own infrastructure in a spot where it's easy to move the people. The exception would be if I got a different mission or there were a ton of people there.

The look on the person's face when we knocked and they opened the door was priceless. They had no lookout and just expected it would be a neighbor. They did not know what to do with a group of people who showed up in working vehicles. Once they were over that, we were invited inside, and there was a quick conversation. Then one of them was sent with me to drive around and pick up the de facto leaders of the community who were in various houses.

I was happy to do it, as Vlad could collect data to help make a map of the town later and plot evacuation routes. It took two trips to get the six people we needed to represent the community. While I tried to tell them all their questions would be answered at the meeting, I could not help answering them, so everyone I picked up knew at least a little bit of what had gone on.

Visiting them just after a cold snap like the one that had barely ended was enough to get them on board with the evacuation idea. It also helped that the Augusta team had a clear explanation of what was going on, delivered with well-practiced precision. The particular challenge was getting people from each house to reach a consensus. The community had not come together at a single location like the others we had encountered. They were not fighting, but each crowded house was its own little fiefdom. Despite that, people were surprisingly open to the move, and I got the expected mission shortly after the meeting started.

With a plan in place, one of the sleds was packed with the first evacuation group's possessions. While that was going on, I returned other people to their respective houses, prepared rations to hand out, and used my healing to cure those I could. When we were back at the first house, the eight people traveling to

Augusta with us crammed into the nano car with Bryan. Even though it was not too cold, there was no reason for people without classes to be outside.

The final sled was empty for now. It would be used to pick up supplies at the lumberyard. One of the guys evacuating with us on this trip worked there before everything happened, so we would all stop at the lumber mill so he could help Bryan plan the extraction of building materials.

While we were sitting there waiting for the rest of the trip, I was running numbers. If we used both cars, crammed full of people, and one sled for personal possessions, it would take only three days to complete the evacuation. That was assuming we crammed seven passengers into each car moving forward and could fit in seven round-trip trips each day. Since we were fitting eight in the car this time, that seemed more than possible.

Belgrade Rescue Mission

This community can no longer viably sustain itself. You have decided to relocate them to Augusta. Some people may decide to remain for now. They will not impede mission completion or alter the mission score. Rescue as many people as possible by moving them to Augusta. The mission reward will be based on the number of people saved. Saved: 0 Died: 0 Remaining: 277 Not Participating: 0

No one seemed in horrible health, and no one sounded like they wanted to stay, so I expected we would be able to get credit for all 277 people. I was on the snowmobile pulling the sled full of possessions, so I got off and joined Bryan and the others in checking out the resources we could loot for construction. It was enough to keep the teams building at their current pace until well after I left.

With no other pressing plans, I used the next two days to head to Portland and back so that both portals could receive my bonuses for those two days. The trip there went well, and I checked out the construction work already underway. It looked like nothing would be done before I left, but it was good to see the work starting. I spent the night and then focused on building more structures for them in the morning.

After looking everything over, I built two more apartment

blocks. They still had decent legacy food production, so more housing seemed key. That used up most of their excess water, but it used up all their material units, so I was done for the day. I had also taken all their collected settlement tokens, so that was a nice bump to my total. I knew I would need them when I got back and started integrating the buildings waiting for me.

With the construction complete, Donna and one of the guards from O'Donnell's team got in the car with me to head back home by way of the base, where we would pick up three people who had made it through the medical pods.

"I bet you're glad to be going home," I said to Donna as we started heading north. "Alex has been asking me when his mom could come home every time I'm back in town."

"It wasn't too bad because I could talk to them," she answered. "It made it feel like a business trip in some ways. Also, Karen was great to work with. I think they're set up to survive and save most of the people there. It gave me good practice for when you leave, too."

We kept talking plans until we made it to the base, where I recycled more pods, and we picked up the people to take back. Once we picked them up, the conversation turned to answering their questions for the rest of the trip to Augusta.

28

Once Augusta's new residents were dropped off, it was time to pick up Bryan. The research into the custom house building efficiency had reached level ten, and I was excited to share it with him, even if it would cost another 132 tokens for upgrades here and 770 out in Bangor.

Once he was in the car, I read off the new effect for the houses in addition to the 10% reduction in power and water usage.

> **Improved Building Efficiency.** The selected blueprint will require 1% less electricity and water due to improved design. Cost 50 research tokens for Level 1
>
> - Large Custom House. Level 10. First added effect: each large custom house has window gardens that feed two people per year.

"That's a tremendous boost," Bryan said. "It will help here, but they have been building even faster in Bangor, so it's going to make their lives easier as well. Let's stop at the first house you upgrade so I can see what it looks like."

We stopped at the next house, explained what the upgrade would do, and said we wanted to watch how it manifested. The upgrade caused mini-greenhouses to form in the windows. The windows that got the most sun were now bay windows with glass roofs, extra insulation, and the same high-tech grow lights as the greenhouses.

"We'll have to get a few people running the greenhouses to make up a plan for what to grow in all these planters," Bryan said as we looked at them.

There was general excitement among the residents about having some food production in the house and more plants to look at. We realized we needed to tell everyone what was happening to the houses because it was a significant change. We didn't want to surprise people. With 66 houses to upgrade, it took several hours to finish. We also had to integrate three more houses and three more dorms.

"I'm going to have to save some resources to build apartment blocks here," I said when we were done. "I don't think there's going to be enough houses and dorms built by the time I leave to get us to 20%. The food production is taking off, though. The greenhouses tomorrow will vault it over 5,000 people at full rations thanks to these house upgrades."

By the time we made it back to the portal space for a late dinner, everyone knew about the housing upgrades and was making bets on what would be researched next. A few people also asked when Augusta should start adding to the research. I explained that the big drain on the pods now was my attempt to save up tokens for the next mission, and they could use some of those pods for research if they wanted after I left.

"When you focus on it, you can research quickly. Thanks to your population, you have far more pods than Klawock. The system seems to count the population of Bangor and Augusta together to determine the pod limit, so you can have up to 600 of them, nearly 200 more to go," Vlad said. "If you can focus most of your pods on research, that's a lot of advancements you can earn quickly."

"And the bonuses you get every ten levels in a specific research are usually tied to what you need in some way, but they're somewhat random as well. Why would a 10% reduction in water and power equal growing food?" I said.

"Well, it makes sense, really. With 18 people in the house, a 10% reduction in food is the same as food for two people rounded up," Bryan said. "I think it makes perfect sense."

I had not thought of it that way, but I had to agree that when you looked at it like that, it made sense. The other thing I noted was that the bonuses from the different research efforts were applied separately. The custom houses used 25 power units each day at the base level. The 20% bonus from insulation research brought that cost down to 20 units per day. Then the 10% reduction from the new research took that to 18 units a day. If it had been a flat 30% reduction, that would have taken it to 17.5 units a day. I complained about it to Vlad when I figured it out, even though it was a minor difference.

"That's by design," he answered. "Leveling up the same research becomes prohibitively expensive, so it's worth more. You can't find ten research tracks that lower energy costs and combine them all at level ten to drive energy costs to zero.

Instead, doing that will cut it down to approximately 35% of normal."

I had been thinking how nice it would be to get around the increasing cost of the research system that way, so I could not even complain about what Vlad was saying.

The following day, I stayed home because there was no time to make it to Portland and back before heading to Bangor unless I wanted to do that trip in a single day. I was not willing to follow up 16 hours of travel with an eight-hour trip to Bangor. I would have considered it if I were sleeping in the nano car with a driver, but both cars were being used for the newest evacuation.

Instead, I spent half the day helping move supplies for the construction teams and the other half testing people for the builder class and planning long-term strategy with Erin and the council. One of those strategic points was who would do the building. The plan was for Sean to fill in at the portal until a builder from Augusta was found, which was scheduled for after I left. Then Sean could return to Bangor, where he could help them and be responsible for integration there. They would also need one of the builders to travel to Portland regularly until they had found and created one of their own. They would build their own class pod so they could scan local people there and be on their own cost track.

I did not find any builder matches during this round of testing, but I found another enforcer match. With classes still being unlocked, there would be a lot of testing and re-testing, but Vlad said there was no way around it. The class pod could not retroactively say someone qualified for a class. I took a break from testing in the afternoon to integrate the next four greenhouses.

"Just shy of 5,200 people fed once everything is fully producing," I said when those were up and running. "You all will be helping feed people for a while in the future as you keep building those. No one else is close to you with food production yet, so other settlements may depend on you."

It had been a long day, and after dinner, I took a much needed break and played some board games with people. One of the gamers pulled out the Frostpunk board game with a grin, and I had to turn that one down. It was too on-the-nose and way too long to play. Instead, we enjoyed some Pandemic and managed to contain all the viruses just in time. I had not realized how much I needed to relax like that, and decided that for the next mission, I needed to make friends earlier. Waiting until days before I planned to leave to enjoy a good game and make friends was not a good plan to stay sane.

The following morning, I looked at the massive number of resources I had collected for this last trip to Bangor. Over 5,000 settlement tokens and over 3,000 material units gave me a lot to work with. By the time I finished my collection rounds, the free room in my sled was loaded with supplies for Bangor, mainly food and the letters I was delivering. Space was limited, though, because I was taking back the four residents who were not matches for the builder class.

"You need to stay here to use the portals after I leave and until at least one builder for Augusta is created," I had told Sean the night before when he asked why he had to stay in Augusta. "You'll be able to head back home in a few days."

The people in Bangor generally knew when to expect me, but I did not bring the spare communication device this time. It was being used for evacuation runs, and Donna also wanted it closer in case they needed to go to Portland before I got back. As I traveled this time, I was sorry we still had not figured out the resources needed to get the train running, but I knew they were still discussing it. It had just moved way down the list when we all realized how much work it would take to get the resources in place.

I was met by the now usual scout, who I gave a ride into town while he peppered the four people I had brought back with questions. This time, before I could head out to integrate buildings and construct new ones, Dominic asked me to build a large crafting bay in the spot they had saved right by the building they used for a headquarters. I assumed there was an ulterior motive and almost said no from the way he was acting, but Vlad glared. It would actually be useful, so I added it as requested.

They had already heard about the upgrades to the custom houses from research. However, they were still excited to have all the old houses upgraded, so as soon as I built the bay, Dominic and I started on a circuit to upgrade the houses and integrate the ten greenhouses, eight houses, and two dorms they had built. That was over 2,000 settlement tokens in a large purchase, but it made a massive difference.

"That's truly impressive," I told everyone when we made it back to the meeting room. "At quadruple occupancy, you now just need 18 of your 10,298 people in one of the greenhouses or barns. Even better, with enough food to feed over 4,500 people, you can feed almost everyone on half rations just from production. With what I supply this time and what Augusta can ship up, you should be fine there. I'm just going to build some more water and power for you before I go tomorrow. The pace you've been building at is faster than I expected by far."

"Unfortunately, our speed is going way down after this," Dominic said. "We've used up almost every scrap of easily available construction material, so even scavenging, we'll slow down by half over the next round or two of construction."

"As Devin said, it's all bonus now. Each new house lets us spread out, and just a few more food-producing buildings, and we will start increasing the food everyone gets," one of the council members who was big into tracking status said.

"Yeah, and we're stabilized," Andy said. "We already had everyone stashed in nanostructures. The buildings integrated this time just let us spread out a bit. Our use of legacy heating supplies is effectively zero, and no one is in danger of freezing. The little bit of power to heat legacy buildings is the last of our old food production, and that will be moved into farms and greenhouses soon."

I had noticed the 2% legacy food production. Food for 21 people was not much, but as long as they had the resources, there was no reason to stop.

The conversation carried on, but there was not much to discuss now that everyone was communicating through the devices. It was becoming painfully obvious they were stalling, so I told them I was going to build some more windmills and water towers tonight instead of waiting until morning.

"It's nice of you to play along," Dominic said as we headed back out. "If I were you, I would have called them out on it, but they're all looking forward to this."

"I was tempted to find an excuse to head back to Augusta

tonight just to see their faces," I laughed. "I know it's not just for me, though. You all need an excuse to celebrate, and I needed to build this stuff anyway. I may as well give them time to get their surprise ready. I think three more water towers and seven more windmills should do it for now. I want to make sure you are set up to succeed, but also I need to build some stuff back home so I can move on to the next mission."

"Yeah, we should be good now, so this just gets us ready for the next round of integration or the next cold snap. Now that no one is too worried about starving or freezing, most people have mellowed out despite the crowding."

I took my time setting all the pods after the construction was done. Ten of the new ones were set to maintenance, while the rest were assigned to token production to build up my stock before I left. It was well after dark when we made our way back to the meeting room, which had mostly cleared out. Andy was waiting there to take me to a late dinner in the crafting bay, and from the look on his face, he thought I was still clueless, so I played along with their plan.

They did not turn off the lights and yell "surprise," which was smart. If I had not known what was going on, I might have reacted badly. Still, everyone in the building cheered as I came in. I did not act surprised, but I did smile and give a little half-wave that felt dumb as soon as I did it. I had spent limited time with others here beyond the leaders and Dominic, so I didn't know many people personally, and I felt a bit out-of-place even though I was trying to be a good sport.

"So not as fooled by our plan as I thought," Andy said quietly when he saw my reaction.

"No, but this is important for everyone. It's as much your cities' celebration as mine," I answered quietly before letting him lead me around.

People wanted to introduce themselves and say hi or thank you. I talked briefly with everyone I could and heard some of their stories. Many people asked me to pass on messages wherever I went next. Andy reminded them I was carrying a whole stack of mail for various cities in case I went to any of them, along with digital notes and lists of survivors. So far, there had been no connection between these survivors and anyone back home, but the cities were a long way apart. If I went somewhere closer, anything was possible.

"Thanks for making this as easy as it could be to help you," I said as things were wrapping up, and I was told it was time for a speech. "I know you've heard of the problems we've had with other cities, but you all pulled together and got stuff done with no drama. Keep building and get to a place where you can help other people around you. There are still many people out there who need help, and Augusta can't save them all. You all will have to help, too. Don't forget to research when you can. I'll need all you can do. Everyone has seen how much the Klawock research has helped us here, and your research will help them along with wherever I end up next. Most of all, thank you to Dominic, the builders who came here from Augusta to help, and all the teams of workers. I know the custom buildings that have been integrated have been the primary source for your food and housing, but I can't do math on the fly, so I'll let Vlad do that."

"Make the AI do the math," he complained, which got a laugh from the crowd. "Okay, here we go. Of your food production, 2,530 people are fed by integrated buildings, and 1,989 by the stuff Devin built. On the housing front, 1,590 of the official beds come from your building teams and 980 from Devin's builds."

That drew a sustained round of applause from everyone, and I finished by thanking the people who were giving up massive amounts of their time. "And don't forget the over 1,500 people in rotation to keep those pods active. Their time in the pods enabled them to fix the maintenance issues in your overcrowded buildings and generate the tokens to integrate all those houses. Most of them are either in pods now or recovering from a shift, so thank them for me.

I knew every place had eight people assigned per pod, which meant six had to work a shift each day and two got a day off. It was better than just six people assigned, but it was still grueling.

As things wrapped up, I reminded Alex not to allow people to sleep in the bay. I was not sure I had warned them how it could literally vanish if they did that.

When I woke up the following morning, the bay was still there, so they had listened to me. Also, I had not been warned about its misuse in the middle of the night, which was nice. I wondered if I would get a warning in Augusta if they tried to sleep here. It had been set up as a common area for meals, though, so I headed back there for a light breakfast and final goodbyes before I headed out.

"I feel great about everything that happened there," I said to Vlad on the way home. "12,042 people were living in Bangor when we showed up. It's been 56 days, and the population has just dropped to 10,298. The population should be stable now. It's horrible that anyone died, but I think we saved most of those people."

"Deaths now should be from natural causes mostly," Vlad said. "Until they get their food production up, they will have a slightly higher death rate because of mild malnutrition, but that shouldn't add much to their mortality rates if it does not continue long term."

The stop in Pittsfield on the way back was to get the building supplies that were still staged in the firehouse garage out of the weather. The supply runs had finally picked up all the personal effects left behind. After that, Bryan oversaw the collection of all the important building materials, but the trips to Bangor would continue, so items lower on the priority list were stacked to bring back. It took me 15 minutes to load it on my own, and then I headed the rest of the way back to Augusta.

Once I was home, Bryan had people ready to unload the sled while we drove around to integrate the three new houses and four new greenhouses.

"No new research?" he asked as we made our way to the field where all the new construction was happening.

"They are actually continuing to improve the building efficiency research for custom houses. It looks like they are pushing for level 20 on that, which will help you all out a lot. If I had to guess, though, everyone will stop researching each blueprint at level 20," I said.

"That's a good guess because of the cost," Vlad said. "The research is meant to be a help, not a solution. Levels 21 to 29 are 1,250 tokens each, and level 30 is 50,000 research tokens. Even 100 pods focused just on research will take over a year to get a single research from level 20 to level 30."

"Yeah, for the cost of getting one research from level 20 to level 30, you could instead get over 60 from zero to ten," I added.

"Well, I guess that will guide our plans for researching soon," Bryan said as we moved around to some open space. "But that will be after a focus on settlement tokens to get caught up after you leave and buy me a truck or two, though."

"Well, there will be some more pods to generate them soon. I'm about to add a bunch of new buildings," I said.

First up were three new apartment blocks, then one more windmill and two more water towers. As usual, I had overbuilt power for the cold snap, so now we had some excess until the next one. With the influx of people from the pods and the evacuation of Belgrade, we needed 3379 beds to hit the mission minimum, so we were now just about 200 short.

Belgrade was at the top of my mind as I made my way back to the meeting space in the pod bay. Erin was waiting for me with the update I was waiting for. The town of Belgrade had been evacuated, and she let me know I needed to head out with the next team picking up supplies so I could claim the reward.

"We've got a list of where to go next, but nothing will be done before you leave. We'll wait and see if whoever you leave in charge can get quests for rescuing people," Erin said. "Maybe we can make a new boost for the portal after you take this one."

"I've already said I plan to leave Donna in charge of the nanotechnology. She's the most on top of things, and Vlad has confirmed she can delegate the construction work to a builder for each of the portals," I said. "She should be like me, where you all take care of running the place, and she makes sure all the nanotechnology is organized."

"O'Donnell is still pushing—" she started to say when I cut her off.

"I know O'Donnell wants one of his people in charge, but I'm picking the best person for the job. He and I get along a lot better now, but this has got to be about saving people, not building a power faction for the future. We've got the technology to survive, but you all have to make sure you don't ruin it with infighting."

Once again, we were not in private, so people were listening in. I was sure it would get back to O'Donnell and everyone else over time, but I was not going to pull any punches as I got closer to leaving.

"I'll do the trip to Belgrade in the morning, then I'll head to Portland the day after," I said. "After that, it will just be a day or two here before I leave. Start thinking about any last requests for me now. I don't want to leave anything undone."

Even though it was getting late, I found some people who wanted to play another game. Catan was not usually my favorite game, but it turned out to be fun. I lost, but was a close second, and by the time we were done, it was time for bed.

In the morning, I was already seated in one of the cars heading to Belgrade when O'Donnell knocked on the passenger door.

"Mind if I hitch a ride?" he asked as he got into the car. "I wanted to clear the air before you left."

My backup blanket and clothes are still stored near the portal, right? I asked Vlad silently. I did not actually expect O'Donnell to attack me, but it was better safe than sorry. When Vlad confirmed it, I continued out loud. "Looks like you are already inside, so sure. Everyone will appreciate more hands to load the cars and sleds."

These trips to Belgrade used all available snowmobiles and cars to collect as many building supplies as possible. The cars brought back the smaller stuff that could be put on the seats. They were also where heavier stuff, like gravel and bricks, was brought back, as they almost always had some spare weight capacity.

For the first 30 minutes of the trip, there was uncomfortable small talk. He was clearly waiting to get to the point of his conversation, and part of me wondered if he wanted to make sure I could not turn the car around. I had to stop myself from smiling as I thought of my dad telling us to behave or he would turn the car around, back when we were kids.

Finally, he cleared his throat and got to the reason he had crashed my ride to Belgrade. "Look, I know we have not always gotten along, but I do want what's best for Augusta and the area. We need to have a strong force to be prepared for whatever's happening next."

"We've gotten along fine," I said. "We've got the same goals, we just disagree on how to get there sometimes. At some point, there may be challenges that require more force, but for now, it's all about saving people and growth. There are no external threats other than the weather left. The aliens are too spread out to be a threat here now that we've killed all the ones in the area."

"There could still be more people like the ones we ran into in Portland," he answered.

"And how much of a threat were they, really?" I asked. "I know that group was pretty dumb, but even if they were smarter, they would not have been a threat. Even if someone still had transportation running, it would not be enough to attack neighbors. You need to make sure you integrate people into the team. The only threat is internal, and I don't think you need to set up a police state to fight that. Just take care of people."

"As long as there's no problem between us, I can live with that. What you said last night caused people to question what I'm doing," he said. "I don't want to be fighting Donna when you leave."

"That was all about leaving Donna in a secure place. She's the best choice for the role of the people with classes. She'll work with you all, but no one on the council has qualified for a class. If they had, this might be a different conversation," I said. "She's going to have a hard enough time without someone trying to undermine her. I trust her and want her to be in a strong position."

The rest of the conversation was cordial, but with an underlying tension. O'Donnell wanted to make sure Donna would not be against him on everything, and I wanted to make sure he would not give her a hard time. We didn't solve everything, but nothing was worse by the time we were done. I counted that as a win.

As soon as we got to Belgrade proper, I got the mission completion message. We had to go past the lumber mill to trigger the mission. I hurried through the choices so we could head back. This time, I ignored the suggested reward allocation and picked production, production, and building. The building option was a new one and had to be tied to the new class.

Belgrade Rescue Mission: Allocated Rewards

- Material unit enhancement device level upgrade 15 (75 points) - device may be placed on or removed from a portal by an architect. Adds 30 material units per day to the assigned portal. May be upgraded
- Material unit generation (50 points) - 3,750 material units added to Augusta
- Builder support (13.5 points) - 135 settlement tokens

Once again, we only received half a point per person saved. I learned that putting materials in the second slot just generated material units, but at 75 per point instead of 50 like in the third slot. As for the builder bonus, I was underwhelmed by it. I hoped the mission would lower the cost for the next builder, but maybe we need more points for that, or we should rank it higher on the reward list.

Either way, it was a great bonus overall, and the material units would support one last huge build in Augusta. I was glad I had increased the work unit production in anticipation of this. I was telling O'Donnell what the mission rewards were as we headed back to the lumber mill to help pack up.

"We can keep doing these missions to earn stuff and replace the material unit token you're taking with you, right?" he asked.

"The missions should remain similar, but the nano controller will modify them based on its needs and your needs. They are just a way to encourage behavior that aligns with its goals. Saving humanity and stabilizing the nano concentration on Earth to make long-term survival of your species possible," Vlad said.

"And permeating the planet with nanotechnology so even if the 'good' aliens never return, we attract attention to get help. That will be centuries off, though, right?" I asked.

Further conversation was cut off as we got out to help with the last of the loading before heading back to town. There was a lot left to move, and I knew Bryan would be pestering Donna for a truck within a few minutes of my leaving.

When I got back, people were asking me what I was going to build with all the material units, but I said I was going to wait until I did one large final build. I want to confirm exactly what was needed. We were finally at a point where waiting a few days would not cause any problems.

With no tasks for the rest of the afternoon, I met with all the enforcers and Sean to give them my final bits of advice and let them know I planned to take a nano pistol and an inhibitor with me. Once that meeting was done, Donna and I met. She wanted to talk over how she should handle things, and I gave her some advice but no set instructions.

"You're the one who's here for the rest of her life," I said. "Take my advice and then do what's going to work for you. My perspective differs greatly from yours. Just keep people alive and aiming for the same goal, and you'll be fine."

That conversation carried on to dinner, and then we separated so she could head home and I could eat. I was off to Portland in the morning and wanted to get to bed early. I wanted to be well-rested when I left for my next mission, and that meant getting enough sleep and food over the next few days.

29

The following morning, I got moving right after breakfast. I was taking one of the cars to make the trip more comfortable for me, along with the enforcer and the guard, who were going down to replace two people who were returning from Portland. That would still leave three seats open to pick up cured people from the base on the way back. Before we left, I double-checked that I had the material unit generation device I had taken off our portal the night before. Since it could only be used once each day, I wanted to use two charges on the Portland portal to get a little more built there.

"Man, I wish there were a radio in here, or I guess a music player," Cody said from the middle row of seats. "We've all been looking, and we can recreate a lot of our technology from before if we spend the tokens to buy stuff."

"Trust me, I've looked at those. It's just hard to justify it when there are still people freezing out there. Somehow, people are still uploading media. I've seen movies, music, and books I know become available for purchase," I said.

"Someone purchased devices for legacy media and is uploading content. The nano controller will issue them a credit to use for other items. When this planet becomes part of the larger universe, it will sell them everywhere," Vlad said. "It's taking a longer view of the situation to make a profit in the future."

"I'm pretty sure that violates copyright," I said. "Then again, who is going to sue them for it? I guess it's preserving our cultural past for future generations."

If nothing else, the discussion about the morality and legality of uploading the sum of human entertainment for an AI nano controller to later sell to the universe at a profit took up most of the trip. Vlad was emphatic that his people had already expended a massive amount of resources on Earth to save people, and it was only fair that they recoup some of that cost. I maintained that charging us to save a fraction of us, after they had doomed most of the planet, was questionable at best.

Vlad and I rarely disagreed so vehemently, but neither of us was upset despite the arguments. Our views would not change what was happening, so it was more of an intellectual discussion. That did not stop the argument from continuing until we reached Portland.

Before heading to the main area, I stopped at the group in the park. It was tradition by now. They got half my allotment of ration bars and all the bars from the cache we had picked up, since we had room. We ended up taking two people with us to the main area. They needed treatment in a pod, even after I used some healing charges on them and others.

As we got closer to the headquarters, I saw a message pop up and checked that it was the mission completion, then set it aside to review when I was not driving. There was plenty to see as we pulled up, and I had to circle to get to the entrance to the portal space without going through any of the enclosed walkways. On that circuitous path to the crafting bay, I noticed that some houses and greenhouses were done. They had been working more quickly than expected. Before I worried about those, I wanted to turn over the patients and check in with Karen to see how things were going.

"So, did I finish that damn mission and unite everyone, or are there groups out there I missed?" was the first thing she said to me when I walked in.

"It's done. I already got the notice, but I wanted to wait until I was here and not driving to look at it." I said. "I'll read it over for all of you to hear after we get these two people handed off to the medical team."

Neither of them seemed to be in immediate danger, so I was sure they would wait their turn to use a medical pod, but I was not the doctor, so I wanted to pass them off as soon as possible. Once that was complete, I focused on the mission reward notification.

Mission Rewards: Portland

Portland factions are united. There is a plan in place, and they are working closely with their allies in Augusta.

- Water and power use are reduced by 10% for allied factions in Portland

for 30 days • An architect may place five already unlocked buildings in Portland for no resources • Portals in Augusta and Portland can transmit information between them

"It looks like there is one reward for each of the parameters you satisfied," I said. "I'm going to ignore the resource reduction while building. I want there to be enough water and power even without the discount. That will be a bonus for you. Also, I'm curious how the information transmission will work. While you figure that out, I'll place five greenhouses as the free builds. Those are the most expensive buildings I have unlocked, and that will be an instant boost of over 2,300 food production and 50 beds."

Karen assigned someone to test the portal communication, and then she and her head of construction followed me outside. There was some discussion about where to place the greenhouse complexes, but we found spots for all five.

"You might want to let people know there will be an interruption in power and water as I add and integrate buildings," I said. "I'll address it quickly enough, though."

I built the five greenhouses one after the other. As before, I had to pay ten tokens each for their pods even though the building was free. Then I integrated the custom structures. There were six houses and two greenhouses in that category. After that, I needed four water towers, which took longer to build as I spread them out to handle the snow and connect parts of the city. The four windmills went up at the same time, and the resources were back in balance, even improved compared to before everything was built, thanks to the mission reward.

"Well, that was one heck of a reward," I said as we headed back inside. "That's like two weeks of material unit production saved with those five greenhouses. With how much construction you have lined up, I think the rest of my building tomorrow will be more power, so that's ready to go."

Before we could talk more, one of Karen's people rushed over to brief us on what they had discovered about the information sharing. There was basically a texting and email function between the two portals now. It was not as useful as being able to talk, but sometimes documents were better for passing information. Vlad had more exciting news about it.

"This is a very low-power communication option. If it's being introduced now, I could see it being expanded to connect portals over longer distances."

"I'll have to prepare an update for Klawock in case you can contact them later," I said, getting excited. "Even if it's just email, allowing people to share information and even coordinate research would be a big upgrade."

Once we were done talking about that, I received a request to delay my departure to mid-morning the next day. They wanted to rush to construct a few more buildings before I left. With how much more they needed to build fast, I told them I could stay until ten the next morning, but no later. I wanted to save tokens, but I also wanted them to get stuff built. Motivating them to speed up was worth spending a few more tokens.

With all the important stuff taken care of, I decided to hang out and talk to people. Everyone had the same questions I seemed to answer everywhere I went, but they appreciated hearing it directly from me. There were so many questions about the rest of the world, the aliens, and what would happen in the end. I answered what I could and offered informed speculation where it made sense. By this point, I had practiced answers to most questions, so it was all an easy conversation. Since I was going to get a late start the next day, I stayed up later than normal. I also spent some time drafting a letter to Klawock in case either of the portals here could connect with them. I wanted to spend a few days working on it, so I left nothing out.

"You need to switch to a nano tablet," Vlad said. "For safety's sake, do that and get all your information moved over before you head to the next mission."

"Is that a hint?" I asked, always digging for information.

"It's a hint that your sun is still shooting out strange particles, and even though you have most of the information in hard copy too, it would slow you down to lose all the information in that tablet. Just like your legacy communication seems to be dead now, you could lose the tablet despite your best precautions," he answered.

"I'll look at that when I get back," I said. "Slipping the tablet into a Faraday bag every time I'm not using it is not enough protection for all this data, you're right."

They had offered me one of the rooms in the newly integrated houses, and I had taken it, so I had privacy for the evening. I was also using it to meet with the Augusta team in the morning. Everything seemed to be going well, but I wanted to make sure their story did not change when they had a chance to talk privately.

"So, I'm hearing there are no real issues?" I said, the next morning. "There are some things that annoy you all, but that seems normal. I was most worried that people were being treated fairly."

"They are treated as fairly as can be," Wendy said. "They have so few nano houses that a lot of people want to live in them, and they have to decide who gets them. So far, they are allocating the beds to people working in the food-producing buildings, the pods, and then construction. That seems the fairest."

"There are plenty of complaints from people, but as far as I can tell, it's just people complaining," one of O'Donnell's people said. "I'm glad I just have to guard people and not deal with all the complaints."

By the time we finished talking and eating breakfast, it was time to head out, collect resources, grab the portal token, and get to integrating. I built one more water tower and three more windmills while giving the team as much time as possible to finish the buildings they were working on.

A little after nine thirty, Karen grabbed me to head outside to do some integration. "These are the only ones that will be done this morning, so there's no need to keep you here any longer."

I headed out, integrated one dorm, two houses, and two more greenhouses, and talked with the people working on them about how important their work was. The town depended on the people building stuff.

"I've got some time because this was completed early," I said. "Let's look over the updated town information, and I'll pass on some last-minute advice before I head back home."

Portland Settlement		**Population**	19,011
Food Supply	90 days	**Heat Supply**	34 days
Housing	76,197 people	**Survivable Housing**	1,034 people
Food Production	28%	**Secure Food Production**	15%
Power Production	225- 7,045 units	**Power Draw**	4003.2- 13,158 units
Power Storage	2,762/ 3,410 units	**Indoor Pod Slots**	120/ 173
Water Production	2,475 units	**Water Draw**	2,104 units
Work Units	3,520 units	**Material Units**	27 units
Research Units	0 units		
Production Structures	Processing Portal	Work Pods x 120	Large Windmill x 31
Large Water Tower x 9	Large Barn x 2	Greenhouse Complex x 5	Custom Greenhouse x 4
Enhanced Structures	Large Crafting Bay x 1	Dorm x 5	Apartment Block x 6
Medical Clinic x 4	Medical Pods x 8	Custom House x 8	Custom Dorm x 1
Deferred Maintenance	123 units	**Material Maintenance**	72 units

"I've switched 50 of your pods to maintenance. That needed to be gotten back under control now that so much is getting built. The rest are focused on tokens, but at some point, you'll use up that surplus of work units and need more than four pods working on that, too. From looking at the population history, it's been reasonably stable, other than that tragic apartment fire that killed nearly 1,000 people. Hopefully, that's the last of those," I said. "Really, just keep doing what you're doing. Your smaller portal and larger population mean you need to build a lot of custom stuff. Focus on yourselves and let Augusta take in refugees and bring in people from other towns."

After answering a few more questions, I checked I had the heater I was taking back from here, so I would have two to take on the next mission. With that and the portal boosting device safely in my pocket, we headed north. After talking to Karen, I would drop off my ration allotment for the day to the same group by the park. With the food I had given them and the windmill there, they were at the bottom of the list to be connected to the grid or moved. Karen wanted to keep it that way so they could focus on other areas first.

From there, it was a calm ride to the base. The mood at the base was rough, though. A person who had been cured woke up to discover their whole family was gone. They had seemed to handle the news fine, but had snuck out into the cold the prior night, and by the time they were found, it was too late to save them. There had been challenges with people recovering before that, but the base crew was struggling to handle losing someone after so many successes.

I tried to boost morale by focusing on all the people we had saved. There were just 28 pods still occupied, so they were nearing the end of the healing process. They planned to monitor people's recovery even more closely. Unfortunately, walking outside without Arctic gear was a quick way to end it, making it tough to protect people. It was almost impossible to keep people from making that choice without locking them up.

We ended up spending longer there than planned, but I did not want to leave a group of depressed people working there. That could prove problematic for the people who were being cured every day. They did not need to wake up to that.

Adding three people to the car for the rest of the ride back meant another round of questions, but this time I let the others answer and just jumped in if needed. I was glad to see they had most of the answers down and were saying the right things.

"Okay, you all are free to follow these two inside and get your housing and work assignments," I said when we pulled up to Augusta. "I'm going to find Bryan and integrate some more buildings. Probably the spots where you'll be living or working."

Bryan had clearly been waiting for us to pull up as he was getting into the front seat next to me before everyone had finished unloading the car.

"I wanted to make sure you did not get out of this thing before we drove to the other park to integrate the housing," he said. "I've been in the cold far too much today, and I wanted to be comfortable."

I just laughed at that and drove us to the area with the three houses and two dorms ready for integration.

"If everything goes to plan, you'll be making these trips with Donna or Sean after this," I said as I integrated the last one. "I'll do one larger round of building tomorrow, and then I'll be out of here. I'm excited to see where I go next. Going from Klawock to here meant saving almost ten times as many people. If I make that size jump again, it will be to somewhere with 400,000-plus people. I'm hoping it's not quite that many. Even with higher perks, that device to boost material units, and the research, I'm not sure I could handle that many people."

Once we were back in the meeting room, I updated everyone on my plans. I had been looking at different options, but now that I was back, there was no reason to wait.

"I've decided to trigger the end of the mission here as soon as I finish building in the morning," I said. "There's no reason for me to linger here, and if I leave then, I can start a new portal before midnight tomorrow. That means I can use the portal twice, one after the other. If it works like last time, I'll be leaving 12 hours after triggering the end of the mission. So likely around nine tomorrow evening."

"I thought we had one more day than that," Erin said. They all knew my departure was coming, but having the date and time set was hitting everyone hard. "Are you sure you need to move that quickly?"

"Another day here is not going to do anything for you, but it could save people wherever I'm sent. I'm all packed, and I'll have that letter for Klawock ready by morning," I said. "The sooner I'm gone, the sooner you can start making more builders. For now, though, I'll go around with Donna and Sean in the morning to set up the pods the way they want them and talk them through it. Once the building and integration are complete, I'll trigger the end of the mission. I plan to start my construction process with food production. I think I can get that to 40% coverage to improve the mission's rewards. I might even push it to 50% to see if I get a bonus there."

Everyone wanted more housing, but with the demand for food as legacy supplies went offline, they needed more food production. It was even more important given the ramp-up time for growing or raising food and the likely demands from

Portland.

Once people started repeating their comments, I told them I wanted to relax before whatever I ended up doing the next night. I found another game to play until it was time to get some sleep.

The following morning, I had an entire entourage, including Donna and Sean. I started by collecting resources and confirming pod assignments while people fed the portal. I had not put the token back on the portal, so the material units took a hit, but I had been saving them up. The loss of 85 material units would not have a major impact. I was saving that for where I was going. I had 6,257 material units and 14,880 work units, plus all the settlement tokens I could need.

"Okay, first up, we're building seven greenhouse complexes," I said as I focused and watched those form around us. I had to move around a few times to find space for all of them. Building those costs 3,150 material units and 10,500 work units, but they added enough housing in the greenhouse basements to bring the housing up to 20%.

"The mission now shows food as sufficient and housing as marginal," Vlad said. "It looks like there was no bonus for getting food production to 50%, and there's no chance you'll get it to 60% any time soon. Also, there's a severe water shortage and a power deficit. You need to fix those next."

"I warned people we'd have some brief outages as I built stuff," I said. "Now I'll fix the grid, but this will take some traveling."

Donna, Sean, and five other people crammed into the car as I went around to place six new water towers, while the rest headed back inside to where it was warm. Now that we were up to 32 water towers, the snow on the ground was under control in most areas with frequent traffic.

The greenhouses were also power hogs, and I needed to add 13 new windmills to get the power grid back under control. All that was enough to get water to sufficient levels and power to marginal levels in the Augusta mission. Because the peak power demands were so high, I was not sure it was possible to increase the power rating past marginal with the resources left.

"Okay, you two. I have just over 900 material units and almost 2,800 work units left. What do you want as my final builds?" I asked Donna and Sean. “I know the two of you have memorized the build cost list, but ask me if you need a reminder.

“Nope, we had talked about this already. With all the new buildings Bryan’s team is working on, we want two more water towers and six more windmills,” Donna said after a brief pause.

We circled once more as I built those, then headed back to the portal area. “That’s just 7 material units left. Nice work using them all,” I said. “We’ve got all the pods set the way you want them. With the new ones, there are 14 focusing on work units, 20 on maintenance, and 190 on settlement tokens. Since I'm taking all the tokens I’ve collected, you’ll need to rebuild your supply. Also, I’ll be taking all the ones that are collected here and in Bangor until I leave.”

The portal bay was crowded. They all wanted to see what was going to happen when I finished the mission, even though I had warned them it was pretty boring last time. Since there was a crowd expecting excitement, I played it up.

“With food production at 8,701 and official beds at 3,400, that’s enough built out against your population of 16,924 to complete the mission with marginal successes or better. Even more notable, between stabilizing the population here and saving people. Augusta has grown noticeably over the last few days for the first time since I got here. Now, make a little room so I can trigger the mission completion,” I said, moving to my packed supplies. “Last time I had 12 hours to get ready, but just in case it happens right away, I want to be near my stuff.”

I got into position, thanked everyone for all the help in case I vanished right away, and triggered the mission's end. A completion message popped up, and I started to read it. I was sure my face was giving away my surprise as I read.

“Oh, that’s not what I expected,” I said as soon as I finished reading over the message.

30

"Give me a minute to read over this again while I project it for everyone else to see," I said when people reacted to my surprise at the mission's completion message. "We've got 12 hours, but this just got far more complicated."

You did not expect this, did you? I asked Vlad, as I transferred the message to my tablet, to project.

No, I'm not sure what's going on. Also, if you had a nano tablet, you wouldn't need to retype messages like that, he answered.

I need to consider what equipment to buy after seeing this, and a nano tablet is on the list, I said before, triggering the projection.

Augusta Settlement Mission: Update

Earth's rapid cooling has been progressing since the solar incursion. Secure this community to survive up to 200 years in this altered environment while defending against criminal incursions from off-world. Beware: The global temperature is expected to continue decreasing at a more gradual rate before stabilizing. The larger population at this location will require prompt, decisive action to address their issues. You may migrate to the next mission at any time, but the success of the prior mission will determine the starting resources for the next. You have limited time to save outposts of humanity and survive as a species until remediation of your star is possible.

- Food supply sufficient
- Water supply sufficient
- Power supply marginal
- Housing supply marginal

The suggested time at this location was exceeded. Marginal success was upgraded to sufficient based on additional cities and towns saved. This mission will be completed, and the Architect will be sent to their new mission in 12 hours. Performance rewards will be awarded along with starting supplies and processing portal boosts in the next mission location. Designate no more than 16 cubic feet of supplies to take with the Architect to the next location before the timer expires.

WARNING – The Scaled Syndicate is attempting a unified takeover

of a location that will be the site of the next mission. Architect Devin Martin will be deployed as the next available architect. Prepare for conflict upon insertion into the mission location. One additional person and eight additional cubic feet of materials will be transmitted with the Architect. Performance rewards will be further tailored to this mission.

"Okay, we're on a timeline," I said as everyone read over the message. "Can I get all the enforcers who are currently here? I"ll also need O'Donnell, and then whoever he thinks will be helpful in planning for this. Oh, and get any enforcers in Portland and the base on the communication device. If one of them really wants to come with me, they could make it back here in time if they leave right away."

There was a scramble of people as we took over the table in the middle of the room, and people were called in. I held off on answering any questions until everyone was there. We did not have time to be unorganized, and I did not want to repeat myself in the 12 hours we had.

While we waited for the 15 minutes it took to set up the meeting, all of us who were already there took notes and organized our thoughts. My notes were mainly scrolling through what I could buy with settlement tokens and writing down what I might want.

"It looks like everyone is here," Donna finally said to Vlad and me. "Why don't the two of you start by adding anything we should know or any guesses, so we can start planning?"

"Well, I guess the first thing is that whoever comes with us will probably be stuck wherever we go. I would not count on coming back here, and they might not even get to continue with me. Last time the transfer was just for me, and if there's no emergency, it might be just for me next time." I said. "It also seems pretty clear that this will be dropping us into a fight. I'd guess that wherever we're sent must have a human population that is either doing so well that the aliens are attacking, or the humans attacked them and were not able to take them out like we were, leading to a prolonged fight."

"The part about them unifying might mean that more groups like the one where Devin started are losing and grouping up,"

Vlad said. "As far as we know, we killed all the aliens here, but some got away the first time Devin and I fought them. That may have happened with other architects, and there could be a bunch of criminals in one location. That could lead them to trying to take over a large settlement to harvest humans for resources, like they were doing here."

"So dangerous and likely no way home," I said. "The thing is, if the mission is worded like this, it's a risk for everyone, even the people here, if not taken care of. I don't want to pressure people, but I would really like someone to come with me. This also means I'm going to take more equipment with me."

That caught O'Donnell's attention, but he could not argue that there was a real reason for them to keep the nano inhibitors. I wanted to take all six of those and two of the pistols. I tried to take all three pistols, but he talked me down to just two. I was also planning to spend some credits on protective outfits for myself and whoever was coming with me, and to take the spare communication unit and buy another one.

"If humans are hanging on with no nanotechnology, you should pack some ammunition too," O'Donnell said. "We don't have much of anything left that will fire, but we have a lot of ammunition, and your travel restriction is space, not weight."

While all this was happening, the enforcers were talking. I was not part of the conversation, but I was listening in, and a consensus seemed to be forming. Finally, Donna raised her hand and cleared her throat to interrupt O'Donnell and me.

"I think it's pretty clear that Tom's the best fit for the trip," she said, giving me a slightly apologetic look. He was the one we were watching because he seemed too into fighting. "He's the only one with no close ties here. We're all mostly okay with the risk, but not with being stuck someplace new."

"Yeah, I'm good at fighting, and I'm not really tied here," Tom said. "Plus, you'll need someone to show the newbies the ropes. I'm glad you saved all these spheres for this mission."

While Tom had been too into the fighting for Donna and my tastes, the mission update made it sound like that might be a plus where I was going next. I was also glad to have someone who wanted to go, not someone who was pressured to go.

"Sounds like a plan, Tom. Thanks to a few more golem kills

out at the base, I've got 184 spheres now. Why don't you and Donna pack up the eight cubic feet of space you want to bring? If you have any free space, we can use it. I am going to free up room, too, and look at what I can buy for us. I am planning on those high-tech suits that will keep us a little warmer when we have access to power and provide some protection, so I'll be getting those for us," I said. "Donna, you can collect the weapons for me to take, too, right?"

She said she would take care of it. Some of them had to be brought back in from the base and Portland. While she was doing that, I started stripping things out of my boxes. I got my new tablet for 50 tokens, and the two new outfits for 250 tokens each. I also got the second communication device so Tom and I could each appear with one. The rest of the items on my purchase list could wait until we saw what we were facing. I had the list ready and could place the portal and buy other stuff quickly if needed.

I really wished I had some way to fit a vehicle into what we were traveling with, but there was nothing I could buy or take that would be worth the space it would take up. I was wrapping up making room for the ammunition that O'Donnell was bringing in, along with some clubs that we had made for fighting golems, when Erin pulled me aside.

"You probably know this, but we were planning a going-away thing for you tonight. No one expected to be planning to send you and Tom into war. I think we'll make it a lot more low-key and shorter if that's okay?"

"Of course, that's fine. I'm not sure what we're getting into, but I want to plan for as many scenarios as possible. It sounds like Tom and I might not have much time to think when we appear. I'm going to have to read and understand the rewards from this mission, the details of the next mission, and build a base right after I appear. Possibly while being attacked. I can't spend much time at a party when I could be planning."

"Okay, we'll keep it short and right before you leave, so it does not drag on," she said as she hurried off with two other council members to make some changes to their plans.

When Tom got back, we checked what he was bringing and filled in the space we had to bring supplies with more ammunition and weapons. After that, we laid out what we would be wearing. The new suits would be under a layer of warm clothes. We also each had pistols with five 100-shot clips and nano inhibitors with spare clips. The other four nano inhibitors were split between our supplies in case we got separated.

After that, it was time to review what we might face and how to respond. We also looked over the blueprints that might be useful. There were the defensive walls and towers I had looked at way back, that could be bought. They would be useful if I needed a secure location quickly. We sketched out some designs, and I saved them all on my tablet.

We kept snacking and talking until around five that afternoon, until I called for a break. “Look, Tom and I should go get changed, take what might be the last shower for a while, and get into our new outfits. Then we can come back here for a final planning session and send off. It’s just four hours to go.”

I was worn out from all the talk, as important as it was, and took a long shower before heading back. The new suit felt strange, but I could tell the difference outside, even without an outer layer. It was a good thing we were wearing stuff over it to start the mission, as it looked alien. Tom had made it back before me, and the comments about the suits had died down. They looked vaguely like skintight, high-tech wetsuits, so I had expected people to give me a hard time.

The time away had given people more ideas about what we might face, so we walked through a few more scenarios until it was an hour before the mission timer ran out. I had decided not to make a big speech this time. Instead, I wanted to talk to everyone who helped save Augusta.

I went around talking to the people I worked with a lot, as well as the people who made all our plans succeed. There were people from the construction, greenhouse, pod teams, and more. I couldn't speak with everyone, but I spoke with enough people so that my thanks would reach everyone. I knew whatever I said would make its way to everyone who could not be at the gathering. I also shamelessly used Vlad’s ability to remember names to have him feed them to me through our messaging, so it seemed like I knew everyone.

Tom was talking to a few people and still exchanging pointers. As our time was winding down, I spoke with all the enforcers, then said goodbye to Donna. I was not sure I could have kept everything running without her.

"You've saved a ton of people. Keep doing what you're doing and saving as many other people as possible. You've been a hero for this community, and I believe in what you can do after I'm gone," I said. It was great to watch Alex grin as I complimented his mom, and I saw him mouth "hero," to her with a proud smile.

By then, time was running out, so Tom and I headed to our supplies, put on our outerwear, and made sure our weapons were easy to reach. We had debated having them drawn, but if we showed up on the human side of an active fight, having a weapon out was a good way to get shot.

"Thanks for trusting me and helping me get all this built. If I can come back to check in, I will, and if not, I'll send messages through the portal when I find one linked to yours," I said to the group. Then I stopped talking and triggered the mission's end a few minutes early, so we did not drag out our departure.

I had warned Tom I would be doing that, and he was ready as the same blue glow from the last transport covered everything. As my view of Augusta faded away, I saw the whole room waving goodbye.

Epilogue – 24 Days Earlier – Central Alien Base

"Damn it, that Devin and his pet AI messed up another of our plans," the alien that had just appeared in a shower of light said. "At least he's dead. I saw his head blown off before I escaped from Maine."

"Did anyone realize any of you survived the assault there, Skarn?" the alien, clearly in charge, asked as he waved off the guard who had rushed into the teleport room with him when it was activated.

"No, we suppressed the AI before we killed the architect. None of the people left would have known what to look for, so I'm sure I escaped without being seen. The nano controller that those holier-than-thou bounty hunters left had to have sent that architect after me, though," Skarn said. "If it's getting enough power to target us, that would be a problem."

"It was likely a random placement. There is no sign the nano controller is advancing yet, and we have not seen other targeted deployments against us," Sstaz said.

"How else would he have shown up in Maine after killing most of my team in Alaska?" Skarn asked. "You send me to Maine, and he shows up right after. That seems suspicious. At least Draxil managed to kill him before the other humans swarmed him."

"It was just luck of the draw. One more dead architect is good regardless, and with the information your team reported back to us from harvesting the humans, we've accelerated the process here," Sstaz said. "All our forces are using this location as a fallback base of operations. If our people are facing a well-armed architect, they can just pull out."

"All these humans are well armed," Skarn said. "Devin's first team wiped out most of us in Alaska, and after his attack in Maine, I'm the only one left."

"You said Stasl was still alive in Alaska when you left," Sstaz said.

"Just because he went on a scouting run against orders. He was too hotheaded to survive, and without our supplies, he would have to attack them at some point," Skarn said. "If we have not heard from him, he's dead."

"At least the nearby settlement here is leaderless since we killed their architect. We're letting them focus on surviving so we can harvest their people. We will need them as we build more pods or replace the drones we have. The fools think they are actually holding us at bay," Sstaz said.

"Then once we have consolidated power and resources here, we can teleport out and wipe out those communities one by one," Skarn said. "I'm never going to underestimate primitives again. We may have killed Devin, but I want to be the one to wipe out that entire community he was protecting in Alaska."

"All the humans who survive will be dead or used up in our resource pods. Now that we know how many resources are here despite the bounty hunters messing up their sun, we're summoning the rest of the Syndicate. In 119 more days, the signaling device will be complete, and this world will be swarmed and drained by our forces," Sstaz said. "Even if those bounty hunters survive and report what happened, it will be too late. This world will be ours."

The End

Devin's Sheet

Devin Martin		**Age**	33
Class	Architect	**Sub-Class**	N/A
Perks	AI Assistant	Second Chance L4	Boosted Materials L20
Boosted Vigor L10	Boosted Stamina L22	System Integration L10	Boosted Mind L10
Medical Effect L10	Commanding Presence L5	Extended Range L10	Incapacitate Criminal L10
Nano Inhibition L1			
Debuffs			
Physical Score	8 (+32)	**Mental Score**	11(+10)
Leadership Score	7 (+5)	**Offense Score**	4 (+1)
Settlement Tokens	6,564	**Personal Tokens**	3
Spheres	184	**Nano Matrix**	0
Sub-Class Unlocks	Soldier	Builder	

AI Assistant: Vlad
Second Chance: You will recover from a fatal injury. In the case of an injury, you will return to the center of your city. In the case of an attack, you can end your current mission, and you will appear in the next mission settlement instead. Perk is usable four times per refresh period. Perk refreshes every 30 days. Level 4
Boosted Materials: Passively generate 100 material units daily. Level 20
Boosted Vigor: Enough food during a mission can speed recovery and save lives. With this perk, your physical rating will increase by ten points, and you will earn rations for 50 people each day. Level 10
Boosted Stamina: More energy allows you to help more people. With this perk, your physical rating will increase by 22 points, and processing portal capacity will increase by 110. Level 22
System Integration: Access settlement systems at range. Nano Communication unlocked. Range 250 feet. Level 10
Boosted Mind: Your decisions and information recall will guide cities. Better decisions will save lives. With this perk, your mental rating will increase by ten points, and five Settlement Tokens will be generated daily. Level 10
Medical Effect: Provide one hour of healing each day to yourself or a target at the current strength of your nearest settlement's medical pods. Ten uses daily. Level 10

Commanding Presence: Speed is of the essence when rescuing a city. This perk will give your words additional weight and increase the chance that people will listen to and trust you. Leadership unlocked. Level 5
Extended Range: Sometimes, building farther away will save more people. With this perk, you can build items 10 miles from the processing portal per level. Generated resources will not be combined with the primary settlement's resources unless connected by buildings. Range 100 miles. Level 10
Incapacitate Criminal: The targeted criminal in view will be restrained for five minutes. Usable ten times per day. Level 10
Nano Inhibition: Expel a targeted nano. Offense unlocked. Usable once per day. Level 1

Augusta's Sheet

Augusta Settlement		**Population**	16,924
Food Supply	182 days	**Heat Supply**	21 days
Housing	18,547 people	**Survivable Housing**	3,400 people
Food Production	1%	**Secure Food Production**	51%
Power Production	850- 20,870 units	**Power Draw**	14,220- 57,405 units
Power Storage	9,872/ 10,010 units	**Indoor Pod Slots**	324/ 471
Water Production	9,350 units	**Water Draw**	8237.5 units
Work Units	2120 units	**Material Units**	7 units
Research Units	0 units		
Production Structures	Processing Portal	Work Pods x 324	Large Windmill x 91
Large Water Tower x 34	Large Barn x 6	Class Console	Custom Greenhouse x 51
Greenhouse Complex x 10			
Enhanced Structures	Large Crafting Bay x 1	Dorm x 3	Apartment Block x 14
Medical Clinic x 7	Medical Pods x 14	Custom House x 75	Custom Farmhouse x 2
Custom Dorm x 9			
Deferred Maintenance	32 units	**Material Maintenance**	17 units

Research Sheets

Research Options

- Blueprints (Tier 0-1 Options 12,800/25,000 for Tier 3)
  - Improved resource utilization. The selected blueprint will require 1% fewer material units to build. Cost 50 research tokens for Level 1 (1,900 points)
  - Improved work utilization. The selected blueprint will require 1% fewer work units to build. Cost 50 research tokens for Level 1
  - Improved insulation: The selected blueprint will require 1% less electricity due to superior insulation. Cost 50 research tokens for Level 1 (8,200 points)
  - Customization. The selected blueprint allows minor layout customization at Level 10. Cost 50 research tokens for Level 1
  - Improved Building efficiency. The selected blueprint will require 1% less electricity and water due to improved design. Cost 50 research tokens for Level 1 (2,700 points)
- Production (Tier 0-1 Options 3,800/5,000 for Tier 2)
  - Improved resource generation. The selected blueprint will produce 1% more of the selected resource (1% more than the maximum amount for variable resource generation). Cost 50 research tokens for Level 1 (3,800 points)
  - Improved resource storage. The selected blueprint will store 1% more of the selected resource. Cost 50 research tokens for Level 1
  - Reduced variability. The selected blueprint will automatically produce 1% of capacity, regardless of conditions. Cost 50 research tokens for Level 1
  - Improved range. The selected blueprint will connect to structures up to 100 feet beyond the nearest node. Cost 50 research tokens for Level 1
- Comfort (Tier 0-1 Options 950/5,000 for Tier 2)
  - Medical Pod Improvement. Medical pods will be 1% more effective. Cost 50 research tokens for Level 1 (950 points)
  - Dwellings will maintain 1 degree more heat without power. Cost 50 research tokens for Level 1
  - Rest Improvement: Properly populated beds provide 1% more rest when used. Cost 50 research tokens for Level 1
  - Light Improvement: All buildings' lights will more closely mimic natural light by 1%. Cost 50 research tokens for Level 1
- Processing Portal ((Tier 1 Options 950/5,000 for Tier 2)
  - Increased Processing. The processing portal will have 1 additional processing unit. Cost 50 research tokens for Level 1 (950 points)

◦ Increased Efficiency. The processing portal will be 0.1% more efficient. Cost 50 research tokens for Level 1

Purchased Research

- Improved resource utilization. The selected blueprint will require 1% fewer material units to build. Cost 50 research tokens for Level 1
  - Apartment Block Blueprint Level 10. First added effect: each apartment block has a two-unit basement level, expanding its capacity by ten people
  - Greenhouse Complex Blueprint Level 10. First added effect: each greenhouse complex uses 10% less water
- Improved insulation: The selected blueprint will require 1% less electricity due to superior insulation. Cost 50 research tokens for Level 1
  - Greenhouse Complex. Level 10. First added effect: each greenhouse includes a basement to house ten workers.
  - Large Custom House. Level 20. First added effect: each large custom house's base and maximum supported temperature is increased by ten degrees. Second added effect: each large custom house's base and maximum supported temperatures are increased by ten degrees.
- Improved Building efficiency. The selected blueprint will require 1% less electricity and water due to improved design. Cost 50 research tokens for Level 1
  - Large Custom House. Level 17. First added effect: each large custom house has window gardens that feed two people per year.
- Improved resource generation. The selected blueprint will produce 1% more of the selected resource (1% more than the maximum amount for variable resource generation)
  - Large Windmill Blueprint Level 10. First added effect: each windmill has a battery with half its production capacity.
  - Large Water Tower Blueprint. Level 10. First added effect: each water tower has a small hydropower effect, adding 25 units of power production.
  - Custom Greenhouse. Level 10. First added effect: each custom greenhouse supports enough small herbivores to feed an extra five people per year.
  - Greenhouse Complex. Level 10. First added effect: each greenhouse complex supports enough small herbivores to feed an extra 20 people per year.
- Medical Pod Improvement. Medical pods will be 1% more effective. Level 10. First added effect: treatment options will be shown, and any number can be selected.
- Increased Processing. The processing portal will have 1 additional

processing unit. Cost 50 research tokens for Level 1

- Processing Portal. Level 10. First added effect: 10 settlement tokens each day may be converted to material units at a rate of one to five

Acknowledgments

Thanks to Jonathan for all your help and feedback on the story.

Finally, thank you to WDP Author Support Services for being part of my beta team and for editing, proofreading, and formatting.

Other Series

If you enjoyed this, check out my complete five-book series *At the End of the World* on Amazon.

When the System arrives on Earth, a group of five friends must rebuild humanity while rescuing their friends and family members. This series includes some city and kingdom building but focuses more on LitRPG elements, such as leveling, fighting monsters, and dungeon exploration. All five books are available on Amazon and Audible.

Thanks for Reading

If you would like updates on the next book in the series and my writing, please follow me here:

https://justinmarksauthor.com/
https://facebook.com/justinmarksauthor
https://www.instagram.com/writerinak/

If you are looking for some more LitRPG books to read, here are some other groups to check out:

https://www.facebook.com/groups/LitRPG.books
https://www.facebook.com/groups/litrpgforum
https://www.facebook.com/groups/LitRPGsociety
https://www.facebook.com/groups/LitRPGReleases
https://www.facebook.com/groups/LitRPGRebels
https://www.facebook.com/groups/faeblesmagazine
https://www.reddit.com/r/litrpg/

Made in the USA
Coppell, TX
22 June 2026

83183026R00229